DEATH
IN THE
MOORAGH

DEATH
IN THE
MOORAGH

JUDITH C DAVIS

The Book Guild Ltd

First published in Great Britain in 2022 by
The Book Guild Ltd
Unit E2 Airfield Business Park,
Harrison Road, Market Harborough,
Leicestershire. LE16 7UL
Tel: 0116 2792299
www.bookguild.co.uk
Email: info@bookguild.co.uk
Twitter: @bookguild

Typeset in 11pt Minion Pro

Printed on FSC accredited paper
Printed and bound in Great Britain by 4edge Limited

ISBN 978 1914471 896

British Library Cataloguing in Publication Data.

Quocunque Jeceris Stabit –

'whichever way you throw me I will stand.'

(Manx Motto)

On the evening of 27th May 1941 the Princess Josephine Charlotte, a steamer of 1,140 tons, brought the first 823 male aliens to Ramsey. The youngest were schoolboys in shorts; only a few were near the age limit of sixty. Most were in the twenty-five to forty age groups. All carried gas masks which had not yet been issued on the island. This was the first consignment of the eventual 40,000 internees on the Isle of Man. Accompanied by armed guards they were walked to the Mooragh Promenade, where a block of boarding houses had been converted to a barbed wire-surrounded internment camp.

Island of Barbed Wire by C Chappell (1984)

ONE

At the same time as Peter Quilliam was inspecting the grubby gas cooker in his newly leased flat in Parliament Street, Ramsey, Fenella Kelly was wielding a gleaming palette knife in a cramped attic fronting the sea. Both were absorbed, both grim-faced, both had reached crossroads in their lives.

Fenella's strong fingers pressed gouache onto the canvas, scraping chrome white into impressionistic clouds. The sky came delicately to life as she layered paint over paint. The wildness of the waves were now matched in texture, and when her well-laden knife accentuated yellow ochre sand amongst the stippled grey shingle, the composition at once became intriguingly realistic. So much, indeed, as she stood back, pushing a straggle of dark hair behind her ear, she could almost smell the tangy seaweed from the tide line.

She smiled disbelievingly. Out of the chaos in her head a painting had emerged that she could be proud of, at last. Gouache was not her usual medium. She didn't know why she had opted to use it. One might have thought, when so much change was in the offing, that she would stick to what she knew best, serene watercolours. But serenity was far from her prime emotion. She felt at the end of her tether.

Reaching for a rag she slid it slowly down the wide knife blade. That was the trouble with enforced change. It made you question everything. And sometimes, it made you realise that what you already had was worth holding on to, at any cost.

The hundred-year-old cream and brown-painted tram rattled over the tracks into Ramsey station and came to a noisy halt. People spewed from it, laughing and jostling. The old man, waiting till the rest had descended, alighted slowly, his stepping down from the enclosed carriage a considered business. He would have preferred to travel in the open car, but the wind had been cold and his blood thinner than the last time he had visited. As he stood, uncertainly taking his bearings, people crowded round him, late summer trippers eager to stretch their legs after the long ride from Douglas. He wished he felt as carefree as they, their goal a wander through the narrow streets of the town before enjoying the scenic amenities of the Mooragh Park, with its lake, putting green and other satisfactory tourist attractions.

He had not come to Ramsey on a holiday jaunt. Once he had vowed he would never set foot on the island again, this patch of land a mere twelve miles by thirty, tidily set in the midst of the Irish Sea with little to commend it but kippers and TT races, and frequently confused with the Isle of Wight. Yet he had been drawn inexorably back. His burden had to be shed; and where better to shed it than here, where the whole sorry business began?

As he stepped carefully across the road, towards the ornate doorway of a branch of the Isle of Man Bank, he felt an anticipatory excitement grip him. This surprised him, helped his hot feet across the road, made him feel almost young again. It was good that he had some positive feelings towards the matter, and why not? He was about to lay the past to rest. It was the right thing to do.

Yet as the shadows of the bank enclosed him, a harbourside breeze snaked through the doors from the hot street. In an instant he was swept into the past, experiencing a throat-tightening recollection of scents so vivid he felt dizzy.

"Watch yourself, fella." A stolid countryman put out a hand to support him.

He gave a nod of thanks before shuffling towards the counter. The countryman watched, curiously. The pain in the sad man's eyes put him in mind of a dog he'd once put down. He'd had no choice; the animal had been old and ill, yet its frailty had not lessened the reproach in its eyes as he raised the gun barrel.

A stooped woman, in dipping pleated skirt and synthetic blouse, was waiting at a booth. As the old man's eyes swept over her she turned abruptly away, as though she'd seen a ghost.

Charles Peake batted a large palm at a bothersome fly. He was parked, his car window open, on the seaside of the Mooragh Promenade, a wide boulevard at the edge of the sand and shingle beach and wide concrete promenade. As Charlie gazed across the central strip of neatly mown grass he kept biting at an irritating hangnail, which had been paining him for the past hour.

"If that was all," he muttered, glaring at the five-storey property known nowadays as Bayview, though he still thought of it by its Manx name, Rearyt ny Marrey, which meant the same, near enough. The name had been changed after the war, though the building had not received similar modernisation. Now nearing the end of a century of life, Bayview looked down at heel compared to the adjoining new apartment blocks. Even the flower-filled troughs framing the front door had a faded, summer's-end look about them.

"Why won't the bitch sell?" This question was one he'd asked himself too often. If only he knew the answer. He had the cash; Fenella needed it. His money was as good as the next man's, surely? Better, in fact. Now that he was a town commissioner he would have thought that even Fenella Kelly might reckon he was worth a jot of respect.

His left eye twitched. The trouble was, and Charlie knew it, deep down, Fenella still regarded him as the grubby urchin he'd been thirty years before, when they'd been in the same class at Albert Road School. He had been grubby, much of the time, he supposed, though that had hardly been his fault, while she'd always been turned out as if newly pressed, and stayed so throughout the rough and tumble of a long school day. She'd been a strikingly good-looking child, full of confidence, striding ahead of him each day over the swing bridge in her navy pleated skirt and white blouse. He'd longed to walk with her; they both lived across the river, but the way Fenella behaved the swing bridge might have been her private property.

The afternoon sun dazzled. Prickles of sweat formed on Charlie's forehead behind his expensive sunglasses. Ruefully he rubbed his head. One particular day, one particular memory still riled, even after all this time. It had been his last day at Albert Road. After the summer his class was moving to the Grammar. There was no segregation in the Manx school system even then; everyone went to Ramsey Grammar School. Full of pre-holiday high spirits Charlie had waylaid Fenella as she strode across the bridge that day. He'd felt reckless. The prospect of the long summer holiday allied with the stirrings of puberty made him fearless. "Gi'es a kiss, 'Nella Kelly," he'd pleaded.

His entreaty brought an immediate reaction. Fenella had rounded on him, her expression wilting his confidence as swift as fire on gorse. "Kiss you, Charles Peake? A common toad like you! No thanks!" She'd towered above him; he could still remember her expression and the fear that convulsed him from her hot breath. "D'you know, Charles, rather than kiss you, I'd sooner jump in that dirty river!" A final glare, a shriek of laughter and she'd sped away, brown legs flying.

Charlie wiped his forehead and checked his face in the mirror. "That was bloody years ago. Why does it still bother me?

The tic started in his eye again. He'd been cocky in them days, he supposed, though with his home life he'd had to be. Now he had his own building firm and had recently been elected to the Ramsey Commissioners. He might stand for the House of Keys yet. If he got in with that lot Fenella Kelly would have to take notice. One of the oldest parliaments in the world, Tynwald was, with it twenty-four members, equivalent to MPs in England. Besides, he was making his mark in Ramsey, bringing about changes no one could ignore.

"Certainly not Fenella Kelly," he said through gritted teeth, while noting the departure of a garishly painted Mini darting away from Bayview and turning towards the town.

"There goes her bloody stuck-up son an' all. What is it about her family? What have they got that I haven't? An' why do I care? Why I do I waste my valuable time, eh?" Charlie turned on his ignition and smirked as the engine purred into life. He still got a buzz at that throaty roar. No more clapped-out rust buckets for him. His steel-grey BMW had class. He grinned into the rear-view mirror as he drove off. He could afford the best. He was raking it in. Fenella might still have her stuck-up ways, but she was skint, and running out of time. He'd get Bayview yet. He'd see it a heap of rubble before Christmas, one way or another.

No traffic sound penetrated into the kitchen of Bayview, which was hot from newly baked scones cooling on a rack, while faint seagull cries wafted through the propped-open back door, and occasional shrieks and cries of laughter heard from holidaymakers fooling about on the wide expanse of the Mooragh Lake, a five-acre expanse of water, lawns and tropical planting to the rear of the tall promenade houses.

"Seems a funny idea," Marjorie Quayle said, her hands deep in potato-dirty water. "Going out together, but not really committed, if you see what I mean."

"They're young, who's to say they're wrong? I'm no expert on relationships."

5

"No, I didn't mean that, love. I only meant—"

Fenella leaned over her mother's shoulder and inspected the number of potatoes Marjorie had peeled. "That should be enough, thanks. No, I know what you mean, Mum, but it's the way young people do things today. Tom's really keen on Emily and maybe it will work out. They're only young. Even with things the way they are, I could hardly refuse to have her to stay. After all, it's only for a week or so."

"It's a shame," Marjorie said tautly. "You'd think the bank might give you more leeway."

Fenella shrugged as she sliced an onion into neat quarters. "I've had a good run on my overdraft. They can't fund me forever." She placed the onion with others in a bowl pulled a large head of broccoli towards her and began cutting it into neat florets.

"And you won't take Charlie Peake's offer?"

"Over my dead body," Fenella said, chopping the broccoli stem viciously.

Marjorie placed the potatoes, one by one, into a catering-size pan. "You're a stubborn woman."

Fenella continued chopping briskly. "I get it from my mother," she replied.

The front door slammed. Fenella hurriedly scooped the broccoli into a saucepan. "Don't speak about it while Emily's here, will you? Or mention it to Gran."

Marjorie tutted. "As if I would."

Tom burst into the kitchen. "Here she is, ye females one and all. Hey, where's Great-Gran? I thought my entire harem would be here to greet Emily." He ushered a slight, dark-haired girl before him.

Fenella winced. "Tom, don't talk rubbish." She wiped her hands on the tea towel at her waist. "Lovely to meet you, Emily. I hope you've had a good journey. Welcome to the Isle of Man."

Emily Stock smiled and shook hands shyly. From Tom's

6

description she had imagined his mum to be a homely, seaside landlady type of person, who dabbled in watercolour painting in her spare time. This woman was no dabbler, Emily decided, as she felt the firm handshake, and was glad she wasn't staying long. Fenella looked a woman who'd expect others to match her own high standards; Emily doubted she'd come up to scratch.

"It's good of you to have me to stay, Mrs Kelly." She smiled.

"And this is Gran, Em." Tom pushed Marjorie forward. "The best gran in the world, most likely."

"Tom, love, don't exaggerate. Hello, Emily. It is nice to meet you. We've heard a lot about you from Tom."

Emily cast Tom an anxious look.

"Don't worry, all good things." Marjorie smiled. "We're almost finished the dinner preparations and then we'll have tea. Tom, put that kettle on. It's filled ready, and the tea things are set out in the lounge." Marjorie leaned forward and clasped Emily's arm briefly. "I thought we'd have afternoon tea in style. We usually eat in here," she gestured around the cluttered kitchen, "but today we'll play at being guests."

Emily smiled. Tom's gran was nice.

"It won't be for much longer," Tom said meaningfully.

Fenella frowned. "Tom."

Emily caught the glance the three of them exchanged. There was a sudden awkward silence.

"Tea would be lovely," Emily said quickly. "I'm parched. Tom, could you just show me where I can – you know – freshen up."

Tom turned the gas on under the kettle. "Sure. Come this way, madam. We'll take your bags up."

"Room six," Fenella said as they made their way out.

"I know, Mum. I did help Gran make up the bed this morning," Tom shouted as he closed the door.

Fenella lifted her eyebrows at Marjorie. "He's trying to impress her that he's housetrained," she whispered. "It must be the first bed he's made, save his own, since he came back from college."

Marjorie chuckled. "Emily seems nice. Nicer than some he's brought back."

Fenella grinned. "Do you remember Tom's first girlfriend? That glum child who could hardly string two words together?"

"I don't think Tom was friendly with her for her conversational abilities."

"Mother." Fenella winced. "You rarely take people at face value, do you?"

Marjorie, filling the potato pan with water, shrugged. "It saves a lot of heartache if you have no illusions, dear."

Fenella swept broccoli debris into the bin. "P'raps that's my trouble," she said. "I have too many."

As they were about to sit down to tea the doorbell rang.

"Ignore it, Mum," Tom said. "It's probably kids larking about again."

"Indeed I will not. If it's someone on the door then I'm having them. I may be closing soon but till then I can do with all the cash I can get." Fenella breezed out of the dining room. Emily gazed uncertainly at Tom, who made no attempt to explain.

"Yes, milk, please." Marjorie was pouring. After serving them Marjorie filled an extra-large teacup and placed it and a saucer on a tray.

"This is for Tom's great-gran," she said. "She has a nap in the afternoon."

"I'd take it, Gran, only I can't take my eyes off Em, can I, Em?"

Emily laughed. "Belt up, Tom; honestly, I'd forgotten what a fool you were."

Marjorie smiled. "You let him be a fool as long as possible, love. Men grow up all too soon." She picked up the tray and added in a soft voice, as she walked towards the door, "And then they are no fun at all."

Once the door was closed Tom sidled close to Emily and put

his arms around her neck, his fingers fondling her breast through her T-shirt. "Oh, Em, I have missed you. Two weeks has seemed like an eternity." He kissed her ear moistly. "My lover, my ickle pussle-wussle."

Emily wriggled out from his grip. "Tom, don't be a moron. I'm tired. I've been travelling an age. I could do with a shower and a good lie-down."

"So could I," Tom said, his eyes gleaming.

"Well, hard luck, caveman, it's that time of the month, so you'll not be getting your oats for a few days."

"Bugger," Tom said.

"'Nuff of that swearing in the lounge," Fenella said, marching in and closing the door firmly. "There, that's another few quid in the kitty."

Emily swallowed a mouthful of scone. "You must let me pay for my accommodation, Mrs Kelly. I'm getting paid to work on this dig, you know."

Tom laughed. "What are they paying? About a fiver a day?"

"No, Tom. It's a reasonable amount, and certainly enough to cover board and lodging. Please, Mrs Kelly. I don't want to sponge on you."

Fenella reached for a sandwich and bit into it. Her dark eyebrows rose and fell as she considered. When she had digested her mouthful she smiled at Emily.

"A few pounds to cover the cost of your food and laundry, while you're here. Thank you, Emily. I appreciate it."

Tom glanced at his mother, frowning. Before he could interject any sort of comment, Emily nodded firmly.

"Good, there, that's settled." Emily reached for a sandwich and grinned at Tom. She felt easier now, especially since she had seen a fleeting approval in Fenella's eyes.

"So, Emily, when do you start this archaeological dig, at Billown, isn't it?"

"Monday week. I have ten days to please myself."

"And me." Tom grinned.

"But I need to do some background reading about the island. Is there a library in Ramsey?"

"Em!" Tom wailed. "Ten days' holiday, you said. Must we go hunting round libraries? I'll be starting my term soon. I want to show you places."

Fenella reached for jam to spread on a scone. "Sounds as if Emily is going to be a good influence on you, Thomas Kelly."

Tom groaned. "Why do I always get women who are a good influence? Why can't I just, for once, get one who is a bad influence?"

Fenella and Emily exchanged wry smiles.

As they were clearing the table Percy Corlett popped his head around the door, a smile on his good-natured face. "Norah not up yet?" He bent to slip off his bicycle clips.

Marjorie replied. "She'll be down soon. Do you want her?"

Percy grinned, slipping the clips in his jacket pocket. "Aye, I've fetched her a…" he shrugged, "something she was wanting."

Emily looked puzzled. Fenella nodded. "This is Emily, Percy, Tom's friend."

"Oh, yes, hello. I'm Perce. I lodge here." He smiled broadly and Emily could not help smiling back. Percy's gentle smile was infectious.

"Nice to meet you." Emily smiled.

"We'll let her know, Perce. She'll be down soon, I'm sure." Marjorie was collecting the cake stands.

"Good-o – I'll go and freshen up. Had a good ride today – as far as Bride Church. Lovely run. Ta-ra." With another beam Percy darted out.

The family smiled at one another. "Percy's a long-term lodger," Fenella told Emily. "There's one more, Eloise, but she's quite a private lady. Percy's different."

Tom reached for Emily's hand. "Come on, let's get you

unpacked." He grinned. The pair hurried out and bounded up the stairs, Emily looking round curiously. She'd heard so much about Bayview that she'd felt she knew it, now it was real and... well, not quite what she'd imagined. It was clear, by the condition of the décor and the stair carpet, that Bayview had seen better days. Emily recalled Tom telling her that this was the last building on the promenade to accommodate visitors. Its companion properties were either converted or had been demolished and new apartment blocks built in their stead.

"Your chamber, my lady," Tom said, holding a door wide for her to pass through.

"What a view! Oh, Tom, what a wonderful place to stay. You'd think you would be full." She gazed around the lofty room, pleasantly decorated in a modern sprigged wallpaper, with contrasting bedspread and full-length curtains either side of the bay window, in which sea was framed. The yellow of the sandy beach across the road stretched away into a misty blueness above sand hills at the northern end, while the rocky outcrop of Maughold Head protruded into the sea at the south, beyond the pier and the town.

Tom threw himself on the bed. "Yeah, but holidaymaker's expectations have changed since this place was built. This promenade was planned at the height of a late nineteenth-century tourist boom on the island. The First World War put an end to that."

"What a shame."

"Things picked up after the forties' war but once continental travel came in... well. And now the cost of getting here puts people off."

"I can understand that. I couldn't believe the price of my airfare."

"Yes, well, enough of that." He grinned. "Come here and let me say hello to you properly."

Emily sat on the edge of a chair. "Not just for a minute. I want a word." She bit her lip. "About us."

Tom bounced upright. "What? Don't tell me you don't love me anymore. You can't have come all this way just to tell me—"

Emily held up her hand. "No, I haven't. At least." She got up to come over to the bed and then stopped. "Wait, what's that weird noise?"

"I can't hear anything. Honestly, Em, for heaven's sake, what's eating you?" Tom jerked upright. "God, I heard it then too. It's coming from the next room."

A wail sounded through the wall, and Emily reached for Tom's hand. "Cripes, do you think someone's doing away with one of your boarders?"

"Bloody hell. A case of dead and breakfast. I don't think Mum could stand it. Wait here." Tom hurried out of the room, Emily followed nervously, tiptoeing after him. Tom pressed his ear to the door of the adjoining room.

"Perhaps whoever it is was having a nightmare," Emily hissed.

"I reckon you're right." Tom nodded. "I can't hear anything now."

Emily reached out. "Tom," she said, "come back into our room. There, he's moving about. He's OK."

Tom's face was inches from hers. He could smell her scent, a warm spiciness that always sent his heart racing.

Thrusting to the back of his mind a slight unease, Tom went willingly back into the bedroom.

"Now," she said, closing the door, "what was that about welcoming me properly?"

Tom grinned and forgot everything but the matter in hand.

In the next room the old man perched on the edge of the bed, drenched in sweat. Desperately, he wished he had not come. How could he have thought he could relinquish the pain of the past so easily? He had fallen asleep in a pleasant room in a pleasant building, yet his dreams had been of a remembered hell, of bare boards, the guttural shouts of prisoners and the head-pounding tramp of the guards. Marching, marching, they had always been marching. Such noise; there had always been noise. Such smells too, the grim stench of too many men herded together, deprived of freedom and, for most of them, any sense of self-respect.

He knew he had woken with a yelp, and in his sleep he had shouted out, filled with a terror he thought he had long forgotten.

Why had he come?

He stumbled towards the washbasin and splashed his face. His grim eyes staring back at him answered his question. He was here for a purpose. He'd had to come, and he had to stay.

Peter Quilliam set down a bag of cleaning materials and ran hot water into the sink. He disliked housework, but he wasn't cooking anything in that gas cooker till he'd scrubbed at least one layer of grease from it. To think that he'd signed a lease saying that he would keep everything in good order and as clean as when he moved in, and when he got the key he realised that there had been only a cursory clean-up since the last tenant. He would have complained but he knew the agent was away. He probably planned the break deliberately, he reflected as he pulled the plug out of the sink and an unpleasant stench made him wince. Just as well he'd got bleach too. He reached for a pack of rubber gloves, cursing at the polythene wrapping and feeling a sissy as he pulled them on, but cleaning someone else's grime bare-knuckled was not his cup of tea.

He cautiously poured bleach and ran water. Through the window he caught sight of the courthouse and police-station roof. Was he mad to have got a flat so near work? It had seemed a good idea to save on petrol and time, but now he wasn't so sure. Not in coming back to the island. He'd had more than enough of across. Rising crime and constant overtime had disillusioned him to such an extent it was either come back or start afresh – but at what? His skills were solely in policing. He didn't want to work in a stuffy office and what else was there for a man of his age? Retrain as a schoolteacher? Like hell.

At least here he'd have a position in the community here, inspector in charge of Ramsey – God, when he was a cadet he'd never dreamed he'd get this far. Besides, and here fantasy took over, this was the town where Fenella Kelly lived. He'd always had a 'thing' about Fenella – even when she was married. Or especially when she was married. That's how he'd got to know her, through Brian and motorcycles. By the time she was widowed… God, that was tragic, but by then he was married to Susan and Fen had baby Tom. "Ouch!" His thumb poked through the rubber glove on one of the oven rings. He retracted it and continued working a wire pad between the dirty burners. So, yeah, it might be like imagining pigs flying, but… "Oh God, why am I here, doing this?" He pulled the gloves off and threw them down. His thoughts went back to his interview and the police headquarters in Douglas. "Most of the men I worked with seem to have left or retired. Even the civilian staff are all different. Will I fit in?"

He grimaced and sat back on his heels. Housework had always irked him. He swiftly wiped over the cooker top and wrung out the cloth. "Concentrate on the positives," he told himself sternly. "Ramsey is a small town with a mainly law-abiding population. It'll be a great place to work – I can visit the old folk regularly, which will be a weight off my mind, and I daresay they'll be glad to see me, as long as I don't outstay my welcome." He grinned. His parents, who lived in the south of the island and were retired, seemed to have a busier life now than when they'd been working.

On this positive note Peter put his cleaning things away and switched on the kettle. *Thank God for coffee.*

TWO

Norah Tooms blinked awake. She had been having a wonderful dream, in which she was young, maybe seventeen, and about to fall into the arms of a hunky, sexy man – not a boy, mind, a real he-man. Her dream-self had been thrillingly eager to partake in this clinch. Clearly her dream-self was still able to tackle anything.

"If only," Norah muttered, trying to stir her bones into a sitting position. Her eighty-four-year-old muscles responded after a few goes, but then she felt dizzy. What a blinking palaver it was being old – much harder than being young, that was for sure. She repeated the word in her head – young – aye, if only she could forget all her aches and pains, just drift back into that lovely dream, crammed with warm lust and desire.

Talking of *warm* – had she gone again, while sleeping? Oh, heck – from the dampness between her legs she suspected she had. Just as well she was wearing her nappy pants.

Norah sighed and wondered how long it would be before Marjorie showed up. "Come on, Marje, your old mum's gasping." She listened hopefully, but all she could hear was the clock ticking and faraway a muted babble of chatter. "That'll be Percy's telly," she decided.

Percy Corlett was one of two non-family residents at Bayview; the other – fussy, prissy Eloise Green – had no television. She made out that she didn't approve of it, yet she was quick to pester Percy if there was something special that she wanted to watch.

"A pesterer by nature is Eloise," Norah mused. "Never been married, never worked her frustrations out like a proper woman, that's her trouble." Norah's eyes twitched. She knew enough about frustration, the amount she'd had over the years, none better.

She sighed, gazing at her skinny limbs stretched beneath the counterpane and at her witch's hands, spotted and bony. What a sight she'd become, yet still alive. God! Why? Though her hands were strong still, that was a positive, and having a wheelchair wasn't all bad, though it was a pity about her legs. Her pins used to be one of her chief glories.

"Knocked 'em dead, I did, dancin' Saturday nights at the Talk of the Town ballroom." She grinned in retrospect and hurriedly reached for her teeth. Grinning was more satisfying with her teeth in place. As her hand fumbled into the water glass for her dripping dentures she heaved one of her regular 'God help me' sighs. "For by my time of life I need to hang on to all the satisfaction I can get." She chewed a few times to settle the dentures and then leaned forward, grinning, so she could see herself in the dressing-table mirror.

She was never sure whether this was a good idea or not. Once she'd viewed the leering old crone that she was now, it was tricky to imagine herself any different. If she hadn't been able to see what she looked like she might have convinced herself that she was still young and pretty. Like when Walter had married her, all those years ago. Long before the bags under her eyes and her droopy jowls appeared.

"I bet all old fogies say that," she muttered, looking thoughtfully down. Did she feel warmer and wetter? Was she going yet again? She shrugged. "Mebbe."

She glared at the clock. "Come on, Marje, for heaven's sake. What's going on? Where's my tea?"

She thought, momentarily, of trying to get out of bed unaided. Then she decided against it. She could manage, just about, but later she'd feel bloody awful, and what was the point of that? If she felt bloody awful then she'd have no appetite for her evening dinner, and if there was one thing she still relished, it was food.

She shifted and felt the rustle of her nappy pants. This sound made her grin. Some old biddies hated wearing the things. She didn't care. She reckoned there were far worse indignities in growing old than the wearing of incontinence pants. In fact, being able to spend a penny whenever she wanted gave her a sort of confidence. Not so long ago she'd hardly dared go far from a lavatory, living in fear of an embarrassing and unstoppable wee… She'd always had a weakness in that direction; childbearing had done for her bladder, no doubt. Anyhow, lined plastic pants were nothing to be ashamed of. According to a hospital notice she'd read recently, more than seventy per cent of women had weak bladders. It was a wonder that there weren't more accidents outdoors or women squatting in gutters. Not that she hadn't done that a few times, and might again, for as fast as new loos were put up they got vandalised and shut.

No, the incontinence pants were all right. Co-ol, as Tom might say. She had no embarrassment on that score, though she reckoned she ponged a bit, first thing, judging by Marjorie's face when she came to get her up. That was unfortunate, but now that her legs were so weak and she had to practically live in the dratted wheelchair, getting about under her own steam was tricky. Even going to the loo was a chore. She could just about cope when it came to number twos, and that was after being helped on to the seat.

Norah grimaced at her reflection. A right old fool she looked, with her fuzzy white hair and creased face. Her eyes were still with it, though, and she knew what was going on, most of the time. That was the worst thing about being old: the frustration of the whole bloody business. If she'd gone doolally, like that lot at the day-care place Marje took her to once recently – if you didn't know whether you were happy or sad, would a body be better off, or worse? Norah's eyes narrowed. *Gawd, I'd be better off dead.*

A grudging tear crept out of her left eye, which was watery at the best of times. She sniffed and rubbed it swiftly away.

"It's a bugger, getting old," she muttered, just as Marjorie opened the door and entered with a steaming cup of tea.

"What's that, Mum?" she said, laying the cup and saucer on the bedside locker.

"Nothin'," Norah muttered, gasping as Marjorie took hold of her and hauled her upright. "Steady on, I'll come apart at the seams if you wrench me like that."

"Hush, now, Mother, you know I have to lift you firmly or I'll do my back in, and then where will you be?"

"In a home, where you want to put me," Norah snapped. "What's this, no biscuits?"

"Mum, yesterday you said you didn't want a biscuit with your afternoon tea. You said it put you off your dinner."

"Yesterday was yesterday, today's today. Has she come?"

"Who? Oh, Tom's girlfriend Emily? Yes, she's here." Marjorie plumped up the pillows behind her mother. Her nose wrinkled.

Norah glared. "I know. I can't help it, can I? Is there much mess?"

Marjorie grinned. "Not more than I've had to cope with before. Yes, she seems a nice girl, bright and intelligent, I should say. Looks bookish."

"Won't suit Tom for long then. All he's after is sex."

"Mother, for goodness' sake."

"What's wrong with that? It's normal, isn't it?"

Marjorie flung back the bedclothes. "Come on out. I can do you now and then you'll be ready for the evening."

Norah looked at her thin, frail legs. "Many a man they've wrapped themselves round."

Marjorie smiled. "You'll never change, will you?"

"Not till I'm bloody well dead," Norah barked. "No, leave me be, I want me tea first. Go away. I'm not dead yet."

Tom and Emily kissed unself-consciously, the beach shingle shifting under their feet, while a lone dog walker smiled to himself as he walked his terrier past the young couple.

From a window Fenella saw them too and felt a spasm of envy as she laid baskets of bread on each of the blue-clothed dining tables.

The hum of the lift descending into the hall sounded as she finished her task. She carried the tray from the room as Marjorie reversed Norah's wheelchair through the narrow opening of the lift, then swung it towards the lounge.

"No, I want to go to the kitchen. Keep an eye on Nella. No, leave me be. I can do it on my own." Norah's bony hand slapped Marjorie away. "You get on with your own business, Marje. I'm all right now." Norah wheeled herself swiftly along the corridor.

Marjorie raised her eyes heavenwards and was about to make a remark when she became aware of a dark figure between the grandfather clock and the foot of the stairs. In his charcoal suit and sober tie the elderly man looked unusually formal for a holidaymaker. He smiled nervously when he saw he'd been noticed, though he made no movement to step out of the clock's shadow.

Fenella intervened swiftly. "Good evening, Mr Stevens. Dinner will be served shortly." She tucked her tray beneath her arm and made a graceful introductory gesture. "This is my mother, Marjorie Quayle. Mr Stevens has come to stay for a few days, Mother. Apparently he knew Ramsey in his youth."

Marjorie smiled. "Oh, that's nice, and is this your first visit to the island since?"

This innocuous question appeared to fluster Mr Stevens. "Arm, no, yes, many years ago. I was but a child. Er, Mrs Kelly, the lounge? Is it this way?"

"Yes, just along here." Fenella walked ahead of him and threw open the glazed double doors. "There are plenty of magazines and books for you to browse through. And of course there is the television."

The man tightened his pale lips. "No, not television. Thank you, Mrs Kelly, so kind." He nodded politely.

Fenella came out from the lounge and mouthed a word to Marjorie. She didn't understand and shook her head. Fenella walked towards the kitchen, then stopped. Norah's wheelchair was drawn close beneath the stairway.

"Gran, I thought you were going into the kitchen. Why're you skulking there, practically in the hall cupboard?"

"Who's that bloke?" she snapped.

"What? Oh, Mr Stevens? He came on the door this afternoon. He wanted a few days half board. Why?"

"He's not an Eyetie, is he?"

Marjorie gripped the handles of the wheelchair. "For heaven's sake, Mother, keep your voice down. No, he isn't an Italian. He's English."

"Where's he from? Fenella, where's he from?"

Fenella held open the kitchen door and Marjorie steered Norah through. Fenella moved a stool away from the kitchen table and they tucked Norah's chair close underneath. Norah's bony elbows were flapping impatiently by now. "Well?"

"His name's George Stevens and he is from Wakefield, according to what he wrote in the register."

"Is that an Eyetie hang-out?"

Marjorie flushed. "Mother! No, it is not. Honestly, stop over-reacting. Calm down. Would you like a sherry before you eat?"

"Yes, I would, but that doesn't mean I won't keep my eye on him. There's something about him I don't like. I reckon he could be an Eyetie in disguise."

Marjorie and Fenella exchanged exasperated glances.

When Norah was finally settled with a large glass of sherry and her current library book the two women got on with the routine tasks of plating meals into the warming oven and filling serving dishes.

"She's not getting any better, is she?" Marjorie whispered, as she poured gravy from a pan into sauce boats.

"She'll not change," Fenella murmured, glancing towards Norah. "I wish, erm..." She nodded at Marjorie. "It's OK, she's not listening. She's reading. Thank God for Agatha Christie novels. What would we do without them?"

"I suppose the new guest isn't Italian?"

Fenella grimaced. "I doubt it – don't tell me you're seeing a swarthy Italian lurking under the guise of every innocent tourist now?"

"No," Marjorie said, "but I haven't got a reason to, have I?"

Fenella carefully lifted out a tray of roast potatoes. "I've never understood exactly why Gran's so set against Italians. They weren't the only nationality interned here, were they?"

"No, but..." A dribble of gravy splashed onto Marjorie's hand. "Ouch! Let's concentrate on what we're doing, shall we?"

Charlie Peake drummed his fingers on the desktop, the phone clamped to his ear. "Fifty grand, that's my final offer."

"Mr Peake, we have to find somewhere else to live. What's fifty thousand going to buy us?"

"'Nice studio flat in my new block on Gansey Prom. Exclusive of ground rent and service charges, of course."

"I've got three kids and an old granny, Mr Peake. I doubt we'll fit in a studio flat, will we?"

Charlie picked at a pimple on his neck. "Suit yourself. The offer goes down another grand next week. I can't waste time. Time's money, Mr Thomas."

Charlie slammed the receiver down and grinned. He gave the pimple another pick, which drew blood, though he didn't notice, then peeled a strip of gum from the packet by the telephone. "Bloodsucker," he said aloud. "He thinks I'll make myself destitute just to suit him." Charlie popped the piece of gum in his mouth at the same time as he ejected a tasteless piece, spitting it neatly into the waste bin.

The ping of it landing made Helen Brew wince. She had never realised just what a rude man Charlie Peake was, until she had come to work for him.

"You'll get on well with Charlie Peake," her mother had said. "He's going places, is Charlie."

Helen thought she knew where Charlie Peake was going, or at least where he would end up if he didn't watch his step, whether he was a member of the town commission or not. He'd end up at Victoria Road in Douglas. Or maybe even further afield, for they only kept short-term prisoners in the Manx gaol.

"Er, Helen, I meant to ask, there hasn't been a message from Fenella Kelly, has there?" Charlie asked, in a voice that, for him, was almost diffident. When Helen answered promptly in the negative Charlie swore under his breath, bit one of his already well-chewed fingernails and scowled out of the window. Helen was glad she couldn't read his thoughts.

He swung round. "Have you done them letters?"

"Yes, Mr Peake." Helen got up and walked swiftly across to his desk. She'd learned early on in their relationship that it was better to hang over him than let him hang over her. Luckily Charlie had his finger in so many pies he didn't spend much time in the office, otherwise she would have chucked the job long ago. What made her stay was the fact that there weren't many clerical jobs in Ramsey and Charlie did pay over the going rate. Helen reckoned that once she was married she would tell Charlie to stuff himself, even if she had to take a job in a shop or in the local factory. Even now Juan kept on at her to leave, but they needed all their savings for the wedding.

"Fine, fine." Charlie signed with a flourish.

Helen smiled, her cool, professional smile. She knew she always had to hold back with Charlie. He was one of those self-centred men that lived under the delusion that most women fancied him. Helen made sure he didn't get that impression from her. She kept her distance as the florid signature was repeated, over and over. Helen bit her lip as the treacherous thought passed through her mind that it was the only piece of script that Charlie had practised enough to be any good at. His usual scrawl was on a par with a backward child's first attempt at joined up writing.

"That's all for now, Mr Peake." Helen carried the signed sheets back to her own desk and began to fold them and put them in their envelopes.

"I'll be off then, Helen, love. I've got a meeting at the town hall tonight."

"I see," Helen said coolly, licking stamps with an abstracted air.

Charlie absorbed the sight of the small pink tongue projecting between Helen's even white teeth. "M'm, yes, well, cheerio. I daresay I'll pop in some time tomorrer, er tomorrow."

"Goodnight." Helen smiled brightly, pretending not to have noticed Charlie's slip into local dialect. *If only*, she thought, *he wouldn't try so hard to be something he wasn't, he mightn't seem such a pillock.*

Charlie slammed the door of the portakabin, which trembled as he made his way down the flimsy steps.

Helen listened to the roar of his car as it accelerated away, and then she gave a relieved sigh and allowed her shoulders to slump. Sometimes she wondered whether it might be easier to find another job right now. She was not getting married for six months. Could she stand Charlie Peake for another six months?

The evening meal at Bayview passed as most did, in a quietly organised manner, with Fenella and Marjorie working together in a harmonious partnership. Fenella presided over the kitchen while

Marjorie waited on effortlessly, having done so, on and off, from childhood. It was only after her marriage to Donald Quayle that she escaped from the family obligation, common in boarding-house families, of having to work in the family business each summer season. In her early teens Marjorie had perfected her waiting skills, dealing kindly with unexpected testiness from the guests yet all the while gently hustling them good-humouredly through each course, until the post-meal coffee stage was reached. If a group of guests were left to maintain their own pace then the evening would slip by and it could be ten o'clock before the washing-up was finished and the tables laid for breakfast.

Although a different approach was needed a similar attitude had worked for Marjorie in her subsequent civil-service career. She had always worked swiftly and methodically, and because of this she had progressed briskly through the ranks and had recently retired from her senior position with a more generous pension than she had ever expected – if only she had a clue as to what to do with it…

Marjorie hastily brought her thoughts back to the present. Two families had finished their soup first course in double-quick time. She smiled as she hurried across to their tables. "Goodness, you must all have been hungry. Have you had a good day?"

The matriarch of one family, who'd been a regular guest at Bayview for many years, eagerly replied, "Oh, Marjorie, we've had a lovely day. We went on the electric railway – right to the top of Snaefell Mountain and there was a wonderful view. It's given us raging appetites." A chorus of similar remarks broke out, and as Marjorie cleared the plates she found herself beaming. It was easy when guests were happy and had enjoyed themselves. But that didn't mean she wouldn't love knowing she never had to do this again. She'd given enough of her life to Bayview, and the sooner Fenella got herself sorted and moved out the better. Then perhaps she would be able to think straight as to how to organise her retirement, both financially and actively. With a loaded tray she hurried back to the kitchen.

Once the main courses and vegetable dishes were distributed Fenella and Marjorie had a breather while keeping a weather eye open for any tantrums from Norah, who now, under protest, ate in the kitchen, a protective apron laid over her clothes and a napkin tucked into her collar. "Why can't I eat with the blooming' guests again?" she said as usual as they tucked in her napkin. As neither woman answered she gave a sniff and then a sigh, as Fenella reached to adjust the apron, which was already slipping

"Leave it, Nell, I can do it. Leave me."

Fenella moved away and Norah picked up her spoon and fork. Immediately her apron slid to the floor.

Marjorie grabbed it. Norah flipped her hand away. "I'm not a babby, leave me be."

The two women exchanged glances. It was a shame that Norah could not be trusted in the dining room any longer, but she had disgraced herself enough times in front of the guests for it to be easier and better for her to be fed out of sight. While they had got used to her splattering and masticating greedily with her mouth half open, she would be an affront to the more sensitive eaters, who, after all, were paying to stay at Bayview.

Marjorie often felt infuriated by Norah's behavior. It was horrible, as if she wanted to put her daughter and granddaughter to as much trouble as possible.

"For goodness' sake, Mother, watch what you're doing," Marjorie cried, wiping a scrap of half-chewed meat off her own spotless, waiting-on apron.

Norah wrinkled her rheumy eyes and grinned. She dug her spoon in the mush on her plate. She might be ancient, but she could still enjoy a hefty plateful of food.

"How're they doing?" Fenella asked, laying out pudding bowls on a tray.

"They won't be ready yet, love. Table two and three are swift eaters, but the rest are slow, Mr Stevens especially. Tom and Emily are finished, but they're deep in conversation so won't be bothered by waiting. Percy and Eloise are slower than ever." Marjorie sighed. "I wish they'd get something done about their dentures. They're almost as bad as Mum." Marjorie cast a swift glance at her mother and then looked away. Was this really the spry woman who used to take a pride in serving everything daintily and 'just so'?

Fenella's eyes met hers. "Never mind, Mum," she whispered. "We won't be doing this for much longer. There'll just be you and me soon, once Tom goes."

Marjorie cast an anxious look at Norah, but Norah wasn't listening. She was intent on trawling for errant peas with her fork.

"I'd better peep, the families might be getting impatient." Marjorie walked briskly to the dining room and checked on the guests. She had timed it well. Knives and forks were in place on many plates. Efficiently she toured the tables, scraping scraps as she stacked the crockery, smears of gravy sticking to her fingers, yet smiling and calm. "Yes, wasn't it tender. A lovely piece of meat." As she worked her smile never faltered. "Did you enjoy it? Yes, oh, that is good. Well done, nice clean plates, not much washing-up needed on these."

The usual utterances, the unconscious pleasantries which the guests expected were uttered without a thought, and Marjorie smiled throughout.

Until she reached George Stevens' table. "Oh dear, have you lost your appetite, sir?"

The old man nodded, gesturing for her to take his plate away. He glanced at Marjorie's face and his insides twisted. He looked away.

In the kitchen Fenella glanced at the old-fashioned wall clock which hung above the cooker. Only pudding course to go and another day's catering would be behind her. Another day nearer to leaving Bayview. She felt a pang, and yet as she pulled a freshly made apple and blackberry tart from the oven she could not help feeling that what was about to happen was right. She had to leave sometime.

As she pressed her knife into the crumbly pastry and rich blackberry and apple juices bubbled out she sniffed with pleasure. Cooking might be a chore, but the end product was almost always rewarding. Moreover, she enjoyed catering, almost more than her painting, for catering was measurable; one followed a recipe and the end result was predictable. Her art output was erratic, both in quality and result.

With practised skill Fenella divided the pie into eight substantial pieces. She hoped that those with false teeth would not find it a trial – but how can you make blackberry and apple pie without using real, sometimes gritty fruit?

Before she lifted the sections into separate dishes she realised that the vivid colours and the coarse sugar-strewn top made the homemade tart an attractive composition artistically. Maybe she should turn to culinary subjects for a change. Such works of art would suit the modern sort of kitchens folk were getting fitted nowadays. Maybe still-life works were a way ahead?

As she lifted out the second pie – not quite so attractive as the first, as juice had erupted from the centre – her thoughts turned away from both food and the imminent foreclosure. No, what was more bothersome at present was the awareness that Peter Quilliam was not only back on the island but was about to become constabulary inspector for Ramsey. How was she going to face him? After their last disastrous encounter she had been relieved when he transferred to a mainland force. She'd never thought he'd return.

If only they'd kept in touch. If only she'd written. She'd meant to. She'd written the letter in her head often. But it had never got put down on paper. Nor had he written to her, but writing apologetic letters wasn't a male habit, was it? Fenella sighed abstractedly and licked a smear of blackberry juice from her finger. Hurriedly she rinsed her hands under the tap. She was fastidious about hygiene.

Determinedly she began to slice the second pie. Maybe he would have forgotten her by now. He'd been away in total, what? More than ten years? Fenella glanced at Norah, who was still cheerfully munching, her eyes fixed on her large print book. Fenella heard her own insides rumble. She must eat soon. Being hungry always made her gloomy. But she couldn't, yet. She'd have a meal later, when she had the place to herself. Then, with luck she might snatch an hour or so before Norah needed putting to bed. She brightened at the thought of the nearly complete gouache. That was a bonus, wherever it had come from. Fenella grinned ruefully. She had an inkling that the inspiration to paint it had come because of Peter being on her mind. A weird association concerning him and the area she'd chosen to paint, as once, long ago, he'd been amongst a group of friends she walked with around Maughold Head, as far as St Catherine's Well, where they'd all made a wish. Goodness, she had almost forgotten that detail. She smiled. What on earth must she have wished for all those years ago; it was even before she'd met Brian. Her face fell. *Dear Brian... so long ago...*

Anyway, no matter what had happened between them Peter was an old friend, and she hadn't many of those. If they could get on chatting terms it would be nice. Most of her teenage associates had long since dispersed – either left the island or they were worlds apart, with large families and some even with grandchildren. As Fenella frowned, aware that it was probably her fault that her former friends had dropped her, for she had more or less dropped them. It hadn't been her intention to ignore them, but after all, what did she have in common with most of those she'd gone to school with? She hadn't lived a conventional life and she'd never had much interest in socialising for the sake of it. She'd been too busy most of the time just coping.

Fenella lined up more bowls and lifted pieces of pie into each. At times she couldn't believe she'd been here at Bayview for fifteen years. And mostly she'd run it on her own, or with a couple of seasonal helpers. It was good having Marjorie to give her a hand again; she was so competent.

Fenella wondered exactly how Marjorie felt, being back at Bayview. She knew she'd been relieved when Fenella took over the reins from Norah. She remembered Marjorie saying at the time, "You've done me such a favour, love. I don't want to leave my job after all those years I felt I was tied to Bayview."

Fenella had been puzzled by that – fancy wanting to be shut in an office all day rather than having the space and time to do as one wanted when visitor numbers were down or through the long winter season. To Fenella, looking after seasonal visitors was her ideal life. It was what she had done just after she and Brian were married, though their guest house in Douglas was tiny compared to Bayview but had the advantage of being close to where Tom had gone to school when he was little. Of course, if Brian had lived… well…

Fenella sighed, whisking extra milk into a large jug of custard. She'd used the usual quantities, but the consistency seemed too thick. She didn't want any complaints from the diners. Her mind slid back. What on earth must it have been like for Mum and Gran when war was declared? In those days the entire island population relied on fishing, farming and tourism for survival, and with the men about to be called up or already gone to the forces, it must have been a dreadful time.

It seemed unreal to her now that the house she knew as home was once part of an internment camp. The decision to make the island a haven for aliens was made by the British Government, and though it was to bring welcome income and jobs for the many families, having to move from homes and businesses with only a week or so of notice must have been grim.

Mum and Gran rarely mentioned that period of the island's history. No wonder they both tended to be stubborn and self-willed. It was maybe such traits that had helped them survive.

Fenella paused, gazing into space: she often wished that she knew more of the war years; it would have been interesting for Tom to know more as well, yet the war years were inevitably skirted round, if for some reason those times were mentioned. That was probably when her grandad Walter was killed. She knew that must have been hard, for both Norah and Marjorie.

Marjorie pushed open the door, her arms full of plates. "Most are ready for pudding, Fenella, but Mrs Bates doesn't want dessert. Goodness, you look peculiar. What's up?"

"Thinking about what it must have been like here in wartime."

Marjorie frowned. "Why on earth?"

"I don't know – I suppose it has something to do with apple and blackberry pies."

Marjorie smiled. "Does it?"

"Of course. When we went blackberry picking you always said that they reminded you of wartime and getting things off rations."

Marjory's face relaxed. "Thank goodness I don't have that same association now – in fact I rarely think about the war."

"Good." Fenella lifted six dishes onto a tray and handed it to Marjorie. "I'll fetch a tray in in too. Give you a hand."

"Thanks." Marjorie looked pleased. Truth be told her legs were aching, a thing she'd noted recently when she was standing for a while. Once she could have waited on for hours and never felt it. Another sign of age, she sighed as she walked to the dining room. Immediately she saw that Mr Stevens had pushed his plate to one side, though he'd barely picked at anything. She laid her tray on a side table, removed his plate and took up two bowls of the fragrant dessert. "Would you like a pudding, Mr Stevens? It is delicious blackberry and apple pie. Our Tom got the berries only yesterday." She laid a portion before the old man and turned to hand the other to Emily, who smiled yet barely glanced at her, so riveted was she by Tom's conversation.

Marjorie felt her hackles rise. It was not that she begrudged the young pair their happiness, or their youth, but what she did begrudge was their future options. When had she had the mass of opportunities that lay before them? With a set smile she served the remaining bowls, while briefly thinking back to those war years Fenella had mentioned. It was true: fruit bushes, heavily laden with luscious blackberries, were inextricably connected with hot summer days soon after her dear daddy Walter had died, when she used to follow Norah through the fields with her berry basket... Marjorie felt bile rising in her throat. *No, don't go there, you silly woman. So long ago. Another life.*

One of the guests smiled at her as she passed and she involuntarily lightened her features. What was the point of recalling that sad time? Yet her father's death had been a tragedy; the fact of it, not even on a battlefield, so that the name of Walter Tooms did not appear on any memorial. Hit by a bomb aimed at Liverpool docks while returning from a weekend's furlough on the island. He and two others from his regiment – she'd never known their names. So much was hidden from a child in those days.

"Are you all right, Marjorie? You look sad."

Marjorie came to, with a laugh. "I'm sorry, Mrs Bates, I was daydreaming. I must be hungry."

"Oh dear, will you have your meal shortly?"

"Yes, I'll be eating soon."

Mrs Bates smiled. "Well, the pudding looked lovely, but we've been snacking all day."

Marjorie picked up some dinner plates and hurriedly returned to the kitchen, feeling resentful for letting her feelings show. It was unprofessional. She burst into the kitchen in time to catch Norah's bowl as it slid to the edge of the table.

"Mother, look out!" She caught the dish and pushed it close to her mother's chin once more.

Norah looked dazed. "Sorry, love, I was reading an exciting bit, I forgot m' dish." She smiled gummily and Marjorie saw that her mother had removed her teeth.

Before she could comment Norah held out a sticky hand. "Don't fret, Marje, I've got 'em." She opened her fingers to reveal her dentures clutched in a paper napkin. "I couldn't enjoy the blackberries with m'teeth in."

Marjorie laughed. Sometimes she had to laugh at her old mother; it was the only thing to do. Norah returned to her book, which was spattered with custard and blackberry spots. With a cloth Marjorie wiped it resignedly. "You'll be getting what-for from the librarians," she said as she finished. Norah shrugged.

Marjorie helped herself to a portion of soup and took a few mouthfuls. The soup must instill enough energy in her to serve the teas and coffees and help Fenella clear up. She gazed at Norah and felt a hopeless mix of irritation and affection. The old lady should be in a care home, really; her incontinence was tiring and... No, there was no point in going over it again and at least there was one big positive on the horizon. The imminent foreclosure of Fenella's mortgage was, to Marjorie, a blessing; Bayview was way past its prime. It had no en-suite rooms; the central heating was limited to the first floor and was erratic. The roof was dodgy; there was damp in several bedrooms. The fact that Charlie Peake had made a good offer for the place, or at least the site, which Fenella had refused, might well be her daughter's business, but she could not fight a foreclosure. It was that thought boosted Marjorie's spirits each day. Soon enough she could say goodbye to Bayview, forever.

In the dining room George Stevens pushed his spoon into the rich custard. It was hearty, strong and sweet. It reminded him of childhood desserts long ago. The blackberry juice lay thick, like blood. He felt his insides quake. He could not stomach this richness. He lay down the spoon and dabbed at his mouth with his napkin.

Marjorie's face still disturbed him, as it had when he arrived. It reminded him, and he didn't want reminders. He wanted to pay his dues and forget...

With difficulty he got up from the table and moved towards the door.

"See you in the morning," one of the other diners called, smiling.

"Er, yes, good night," he said gravely, and shuffled into the hall. He should not have come. He could have conducted the necessary business by post and telephone. Why had he decided to put himself through this ordeal? Why voluntarily face this well of memories that threatened at every turn, every floorboard creak and window in this wretched building? He had known it might be bad. He had never suspected it could be like this, after so long. He was too old. He should not have come.

With a trembling hand the old man reached the foot of the stairs. As he reached for the banister rail he comforted himself with the realisation that the sooner he acted, the sooner it would all be over, forever.

THREE

"We're off," Tom said, next morning, lifting his rucksack from the kitchen table. Marjorie's arms were deep in washing-up water. "Sorry, love, what did you say?"

Tom and Fenella exchanged a smile. Marjorie had been immersed in a washing-up daydream again.

"I said we are leaving now, Gran. Remember, I said I'd take Emily to show her the school at Peel and then we'll climb the hill, to Corrin's Folly." Tom cast a hopeful glance out of the window. "As long as the weather holds."

"You'll be at it in the heather, I bet," Norah cried, shaking her spoon. "Watch out for prickles on your bum, lad."

"I will, Great-Gran," Tom said. "Oh no, look at you. You've got porridge in your hair. Shall I wipe her, Mum?"

Fenella finished drying a plate. "No, you get off, love. I'll see to her."

"Cheers, then." Tom smiled self-consciously, pushing Emily before him out of the kitchen. Fenella picked up a cloth to wipe Norah then changed her mind and threw it down. She hurried after the young couple who were already at the front door. "Have a good day," she said, following them down the steps to the pavement. "And take care, Tom, in that rattletrap."

Tom looked affronted as he unlocked his old but shining Mini. "I'll have you know this mini could take us anywhere."

"H'm."

"Oh, get in, Em, I want a quick word with Mum." As Emily got into the car Tom hurried close to Fenella. After glancing at the open door, as if to ensure they weren't being overheard, he spoke. "You know the new guest. George Stevens?"

"Yes?" Fenella frowned.

"He is Italian. He was jabbering away like nobody's business last night, and later on. We couldn't help hearing. At one time I thought of getting up and asking if he was OK. It was a bit scary."

Fenella chewed her lip. "You're sure?"

"Mother, I spent a month in Turin. I know what Italian sounds like."

"Right." Fenella gave a tight smile. "Thanks for telling me." She sighed. "Anyway, take care. See you later."

Fenella turned back to the house with mixed feelings. It was lovely in the sunshine. The hall was chilly. It would have been nice to sit on the steps, maybe, rather than cope with the usual chores. She pushed the front door shut and felt a sudden shiver. If George Stevens was Italian he shouldn't be staying at Bayview. If she'd had the least suspicion she would have refused him a room. How old was he? Seventy-plus. M'mm… might he have come with an ulterior motive? It had been known – at other places, though not at Bayview, and surely not after all this time?

Fenella rubbed idly at a smudge on the newel post. Was she over-reacting? So what if he was Italian? She could hardly ask him to leave, and he would be gone in a couple of days. He'd said he was here on a matter of business.

Fenella squinted into the hall mirror and winced, and not just at the dust. *I look my age, all right, and more.* With a sigh she rubbed some colour into her cheeks, still conscious of an odd unease. What sort of business could bring an elderly Italian to this out-of-the-way little town? It was a bit fishy.

She scowled at her reflection. *Dear God, I'm getting as neurotic as Norah.* The man could be here for any of a dozen reasons. As long as Norah didn't discover his nationality, things would be fine; nor Marjorie, for that matter. She'd been touchy enough lately. Though at least she would consider the man's presence merely unfortunate, whereas Norah... "So I must keep it from Gran."

"Keep what from me?"

Startled, Fenella swung round. Norah was close behind her, having wheeled herself silently from the kitchen. Her face was clean, her hair brushed. Marjorie had clearly been at work and Norah now looked like any other pleasant old lady, rather than a messy octogenarian, albeit one with glaring, suspicious eyes.

Fenella flushed. "You and your wheelchair, you do creep about."

"It's modern technology, Fenella. I'm not against it, even at my age. Anyway, what was it you were to keep from me?"

"Nothing, Gran, come on, let's get back in the kitchen. You can help me shell the peas."

"Bugger the peas. What was it?" With a sideways movement Norah blocked Fenella from moving. "Was it something to do with that fella who came yesterday?"

"No, of course not, Gran. It's just... um... it's the bank, they let me know, a week or so ago... erm, but I didn't want to worry you. They'll be evicting us at the end of the month – unless we come up on the lottery."

Norah flinched. "Oh." She looked doubtfully at Fenella. "Do you do the lottery?"

Fenella shook her head.

Norah grunted. "Thought not." Her bony shoulders hunched as she gripped the wheels of her chair. "I'll go into the lounge," she muttered. "Skeet from the window, while I still can."

Fenella watched her grandmother wheel herself away, the creak of the wheels as the old lady negotiated the turn into the lounge adding to Fenella's feelings of guilt. Her grandmother was still strong in many ways. Yet Fenella knew that even if the bank relented, the old lady still must be moved to a care home. Though Percy, Norah's friend and long-time lodger, was a godsend, coping during the day with the old lady's whims and running errands, her incontinence and lack of mobility was getting too much to cope with. As well there seemed to be a mounting tension between Marjorie and Norah of late which boded ill. Fenella dreaded a bust-up between them. The last time they'd had a big row they hadn't exchanged a civil word for about a month. Not that they were ever close, and though Fenella had got used to humouring them both in different ways, the constant friction between her mother and grandmother was wearing.

If only Norah would stop goading her mother. Fenella hoped she'd never get to that stage with Tom. Why would any parent delight in doing that to their child?

Fenella flicked her tea towel across a film of dust and automatically straightened the tourist leaflets. Of course Norah must feel wretched facing the final move from the house in which she'd lived practically all her life.

Fenella suddenly came to, realising that this train of thought had all started with George Stevens and the fact that he might be Italian. Did the fact of his nationality actually matter? Did anything matter at this stage? The process of eviction was well underway. Why was she worrying about revisiting Italians or Peter Quilliam when much bigger things were at stake? What was she going to do when she was turned out into the streets? *She* couldn't go into a care home, and she didn't own a nice little flat like Mum. She'd need to get a job, and fast – though what sort exactly, she hadn't a clue. She was no youngster and she hadn't any worthwhile qualifications suited to today's job market. Though she'd been in the tourist trade for twenty-odd years, tourism was only a small part of the island's economy nowadays; the financial sector was what drove the place. Filthy lucre, the accumulation of cash, for no good reason but to have more than the next man, or woman, more was the pity.

Charlie Peake's face leapt into her mind. Accepting Charlie's offer would be a straightforward way out of her difficulties. He'd said that if she sold to him he'd give her the pick of his 'luxury apartments' when they were built, at a special discount price.

"Wouldn't that make Charlie smile?" Fenella growled. "Me accepting his handouts. Pfff!" Fenella strode briskly back to the kitchen. She was well aware that her dislike of Charlie was irrational, but that was beside the point. "Sell to Charlie Peake?" She spat, flicking at a filmy cobweb she must have missed in her last dusting. "I'd rather knock the place down."

"Fenella, you're talking to yourself again," Marjorie commented as she lifted a tray of crockery for the dining room. "You're not old enough to do that, dear. It's the prerogative of the elderly." She lowered her voice. "Besides, there are guests upstairs. You don't want them thinking we're all mad."

"Honestly, Mother! Yes, OK, I might have been talking to myself, but you didn't need to listen. Now, shall I do the food shopping or will you?"

Marjorie heaved a sigh, passed her and went through to the dining room. She deposited the tray on a table and followed Fenella back to the kitchen, carefully closing the door. "I think you should go, dear, a walk might calm you down."

"Hmph," Fenella muttered, marching into the pantry. Marjorie took the hint and returned to the dining room. A few moments later she heard the back door slam.

Marjorie picked up a cloth to buff the chrome teapots. "For heaven's sake, let her meet Peter while she's shopping," she murmured to herself. "She's been stewing over meeting the man for weeks. Perhaps once she's seen him she'll be fit to live with."

"What's that?" Norah demanded. "What are you saying?"

"Oh," Marjorie swung round, her heart thumping, "I was just saying to myself that if you continue to creep up behind people like you've been doing lately you'll give someone a heart attack."

"Humph!" Norah grinned. "You're too soft, Marje. You always were. I live here, don't I? I can't help it if you didn't know I was across the hall."

Marjorie took a deep breath, glancing at a calendar produced by a local petroleum firm standing on the sideboard. Another ten days or so and this would all change – how marvellous.

"Mother, you're quite right," she said peaceably. "What about a cup of coffee in a few minutes when I've finished in here? I thought I'd make one."

Norah grinned. "With a choccy biccie?"

"If you've left any in the tin, yes."

George Stevens picked his way carefully along the river path. The walkway, a narrow concrete strip beside the sand flats, was strewn with tide-borne litter. The tide was out and the inner harbour was scattered with dormant yachts and dinghies, their hulls catching the morning sun.

Ultimately George had slept better than he had expected. The bed had been soft and comfortable. He had been disturbed by one brief, unpleasant dream, but then sheer tiredness had overwhelmed his bad memories and on waking he almost felt as though he were reliving a holiday in some long-forgotten place, a place of pleasant reminiscences, as well as otherwise.

In truth he had to admit that his time in Ramsey had not been all hardship. Considered objectively, for most of his stay he had been well treated. There were those who were treated badly, but they mostly deserved it, refusing to conform, resenting the indignity of incarceration. Older men, usually men who had already made a position for themselves in life, who had been torn away from family and livelihood to be stranded here.

He had been but a boy. A foolish boy, he knew now, a callow, arrogant youth who thought only of his own plight and despised the locals, even those who offered friendship.

He was back within his memories when he stumbled over a metal boat tether set in the concrete path. This stumble brought on the familiar tightening in his chest and a feeling of momentary breathlessness. It was his nerves; they were jangled, which was only to be expected. He paused a moment, breathed carefully and deeply, determined not to allow neither his increasing infirmities nor a welter of memories engulf his bright morning mood. Yet even as he stood there in the sunshine, it was not easy to stay calm, for since he had returned, thoughts of the past came flooding at every juncture, just as the tide was creeping, slowly but inevitably, over the mud of the harbour beside him. He comforted himself with the knowledge that he would be here only a little while longer. Soon, he would be gone and so, hopefully, would his burden, borne for too many years. He stepped out again, eager to press on. Yes, through most of his life he had this awareness in the innermost recess of his mind, so many years, in which he had worked hard and accumulated wealth enough to make other men envious. Sometimes, as he had received yet another boost to his income, he had wondered at his good fortune. It was almost as though he had sacrificed the usual sources of human happiness in return for wealth. He had been a heedless youth, and for the rest of his life he had paid the price.

He wished this fact was an exaggeration. It was not, and now, in old age, he felt bitter against himself and wished he had acted with honour.

He continued slowly on his way, blinking at the brightness of the sun, pausing every so often to look about him, at the rise of the town above the Mooragh Park, at the peak of Snaefell in the far distance, the only mountain on the Isle of Man, and at the hills just beyond the town, North Barrule and the spruce-clad slopes of Sky Hill.

So had he looked each day, those fateful days, full of romance in his thoughts, imagining himself a martyr to his race. He recalled a book of local history someone had found, a book retelling the great battle of Sky Hill in 1079, when the Manx Celts had been vanquished by the armies of Godred Croven, who was soon after crowned the first Norse King of Mann. How his soul had yearned to conquer in a similar battle over the lackadaisical locals.

"Foolish, foolish youth," he muttered, and continued on his way, stepping more determinedly now towards the swing bridge across the river, which led to the main thoroughfare of the town.

Fenella saw him, walking ahead. She swiftly took a side exit from the river path and hurried along the road lying parallel. She walked briskly, determined to stride off her negative mood. She was crossing the swing bridge while George Stevens was still sauntering beside the river with its flotsam of beached craft. Fenella glanced back just once before she turned into Parliament Street. She saw that he had reached the bridge and was standing looking upriver, his hands on the painted rail, his mackintosh flapping about his ankles, his hat pulled down against the breeze wafting from the sea. Even at a distance the man looked out of place and Fenella couldn't help wondering again why he was visiting Ramsey.

She turned away. It was none of her business. Even if he was Italian, so what? Plenty of Italians visited Ramsey nowadays. Heavens, there was an Italian restaurant in St Paul's Square, popular with locals and tourists alike. Once it would have been shunned.

Fenella crossed the street to the fishmonger's shop, the evening meal now occupying her thoughts. Queen scallops in a light cheese sauce were a popular dish, served with mashed potatoes, garden peas and grilled courgettes. Fenella had always fed her clientele well. No doubt in the future she would miss the creative enjoyment of cooking interesting meals on a large scale.

As she stepped up into the brightly tiled, well-stocked fish shop she'd completely forgotten the fact that she was meant to be keeping a lookout for Peter Quilliam. To discover him standing beside the counter and gazing at her as she entered momentarily took her breath away.

"Morning, Fenella. It's been a long time. How are you doing?"

This familiar local greeting swept away her shock. His handshake was firm, his expression friendly and open. She smiled back. "Peter, hello. Yes, it has been a long time. Good to see you back. What are you doing here?"

"Buying fish, would you believe?" Peter's humorous grey eyes rested on hers.

Fenella felt herself flush. "Yes, of course." She grinned.

"You're looking well," Peter said, his stare unnervingly direct.

"So are you. It's good to see you. It's been a long time." Fenella realised she was repeating herself. Hadn't she said it was good to see him already? But it was. Oh, how good?

"I'm stationed in Ramsey. Did you know?"

"Er, yes, I did hear. This Ramsey posting's a step up, is it?"

Peter smiled wryly. "A move sideways, more like. When I notified the powers that be that I wanted to transfer back I don't think they knew what to do with me."

"Mrs Kelly, are you next?" The young fishmonger, smart in white cap and apron, stood before her.

"Queenies, please, two pounds."

Another assistant came forward and Peter moved towards him and the artfully arranged stock of cod, haddock, herring and the rest on the white-tiled slab.

"Kippers, two pairs, please. For my supper."

As he paid Fenella gave him a swift sideways look, her heart thumping. He looked well. Not much older. Still handsome, still…

"Anything else, Mrs Kelly?"

"No, thank you. Keep me some cod fillets for Friday, would you? Erm, eight or ten fillets. It depends."

"Of course." The fishmonger looked sympathetic. He knew the situation at Bayview. In Ramsey, as in most of the Isle of Man, a person's financial standing, especially if it was problematic, was usually common knowledge.

"Thanks, Mrs Kelly. G'morning."

Fenella looked towards Peter to bid him goodbye but saw that he was engaged in conversation with an erect soldierly man.

"Colonel Baggot." Fenella's heart sank. "He won't get away from him in a hurry."

She turned into the newsagents. The local paper, the Isle of Man Examiner, was on sale. She bought it and an English daily. As she walked out of the shop Peter almost collided with her.

"Careful!" His arms shot out but didn't quite touch. He grinned cheerfully, hefting his bag of kippers beneath one arm.

"How did you get away from the colonel so soon? I thought you'd be stuck with him for the morning."

"Oh, luckily there was some mix-up over his order. Hake instead of halibut or something." Peter's eyes crinkled at the corners in the way she remembered, only there were more creases now and he was beginning to look like his dad. "Besides, I wanted to catch you up. We must meet, Fenella, talk over old times, now that I'm stationed back here. And, well, I wanted to say how sorry I was to hear about your, um… cash problems."

"Charles Peake makes sure everyone knows that I'm cutting off my nose to spite my face, doesn't he?"

"Well, I didn't hear it from Charlie, but I know he has been putting that about. But we all know Charlie. He's always been the same. Not that I believed the talk. You've kept Bayview on its feet for years. It's maybe time you got out, Fenella. Give you a chance to do your own thing." His eyes flashed a look. "Devote more time to your painting," he said quickly. "I heard about your exhibition a while ago."

"Yes, that went well, though it took a lot of work. Yes, we should meet again, soon, but... I must get on. I've got... things to do." Fenella turned and walked away hurriedly, her eyes filling with stupid tears. Sympathy from Peter she could not take. Just his voice was so, so... Inarticulate feelings gripped her as she hurried, head down, along the narrow pavement. She must get hold of herself. God, she hadn't seen him for, what – it was probably more than five or even six years. Yet that awful date seemed like yesterday. If only things had been different. If only that stupid quarrel hadn't happened, if only he had written, or she'd kept in touch with Susan. But now it was just hopeless. He was bound to be with someone else and she was... what? Just the same as she'd been when he went away the first time. She'd heard people talk. She knew what they thought of her. *That odd Fenella Kelly who can't keep a feller and who lives with her mother and her crazy grandmother.* Usually she didn't care what people thought. She liked living her own life. She liked being different. Too many people clung to the treadmill of conformity. She'd always wanted something more.

And hadn't she just got it? Celibacy, loneliness, poverty and shortly homelessness too. So much for being different? Hadn't she done well?

A grin crossed Fenella's face. *Come off it, you twerp. You're not that badly off, and thank God, you've got through the first meeting. Now if you keep your wits about you he and you can settle down to being amicable old friends.*

Yes, that's all you expect and that will be very nice.

By this time Fenella was standing in the greengrocers. Unwittingly her gaze fell on a tray of luscious-looking nectarines, each one reminding her vividly of pinkly blushing buttocks. Not that they looked like Peter's buttocks. His had been pale, and a little soft, delightfully soft.

Fenella gripped her purse and gazed determinedly at the items on her shopping list. "Yes, broccoli, and two pounds of peas, please. Yes, that's fine. Thank you."

God, that was years ago. Before Peter was married, even. Decidedly unsettled, she paid and stepped outside, only to walk almost into the arms of Charlie Peake.

She should have known he was about. She had noted, with peripheral vision, the sleek lines of his car parked outside the estate agent as she'd hurried from the fish shop.

Charlie greeted her in his customary manner. "Morning, Mrs Kelly, as sexy as ever, I'm delighted to say."

You really are creepy, Charlie, with your fleshy lips and thick, pocked skin, Fenella thought as usual in return. "Morning, Mr Peake."

"No news from you yet, my dear. I had hoped…" Charlie let his words fade away while he continued to smile ingratiatingly.

"The bank will be foreclosing at the end of the month, Mr Peake. I daresay you will be able to snap Bayview up at the public auction which will then be held."

"But why, Fenella?" Charlie lifted his hands in mock exasperation. Fenella ground her teeth. Charlie's gold-buttoned blazer was done up too tightly over his swelling paunch. She felt like poking him in his portly middle. No matter what he'd achieved Fenella knew she would always think of Charlie as the cocky schoolboy he'd been, too thick to take O levels and too lazy to do a proper job when he left school. His father had supported him in the small but relatively honest building firm he owned. Only when the old man died had Charlie discovered what minimal talent he had, of building shoddy houses for an astronomical profit and ploughing a little of that profit back into buying up old property to refurbish. Lately Charlie's property speculations had become minimally more respectable, with the building of the new promenade apartment blocks, but in Fenella's eyes nothing would ever make Charles Peake worthy of respect.

"I can't stop, Mr Peake. Some of us have a business to run."

It was a stupid thing to say; she could almost see the reply forming in Charlie's brain, and of course, on cue, it came.

"Not for much longer. Why don't you just give in, Fenella? Why keep fighting?" Charlie laid a detaining hand on her arm, his fingers pressing slightly harder than was necessary.

Fenella angrily pulled her arm away. Before she could think of a suitable retort, a calm voice intervened. "Now then, Charlie, I see your car's parked without displaying a disc." Peter Quilliam raised a warning eyebrow. "You'd better watch out. The traffic warden's on her way."

"Bloody parking laws. Can't stop in your own town now without a petty bureaucrat jumping down your throat." Charlie stamped off, flinging a backward glance towards Fenella. "See you soon, Mrs Kelly."

Fenella turned away from him, flushing. She looked up gratefully at Peter. "Thanks," she said, and for a second or two their eyes locked. It was an unnerving moment, and Peter was the first to turn away. "Don't mention it, Fenella," he said, stepping out of the path of an oncoming twin buggy driven by a determined young mum who gave him an appraising glance. Word had got around about the dishy police inspector relocated to the town. Besides sizing him up, it was as well to get to know his face. Talk had it that he was to live locally and would be out and about in the pubs keeping an eye on folk. Some of Ramsey's less law-abiding inhabitants weren't too pleased by this increased police presence. The young mum grinned at Peter as he leapt out of the way. *He's a looker all right*, she thought. It was a pity she was shacked up with good-for-nothing Jason and three kids.

Fenella, meanwhile, had slipped away, hurrying down Collins Lane, a slit of an alley leading to the quay.

Peter looked after her, sighed and retraced his steps towards the apartment he'd recently rented, overlooking the courthouse and Ramsey Police Station.

Once there he put the fish in the fridge, which stood beside the ancient but now scrubbed clean gas cooker. He removed his jacket and threw himself onto the long, comfortable settee. He gazed at the ceiling, the cracks in the crazed plaster confusingly reminding him of Fenella's face and all the play of expressions that had crossed it in their few moments together. She was as lovely as ever and more than likely as unattainable.

Why, oh why, had he applied for this transfer? He must have been out of his crazy mind.

FOUR

Charlie Peake accelerated furiously away. The bitch, the stuck-up bitch. He could not believe she was so pig-headed. He'd never understand her. Why didn't she just give in? God, he was doing her a favour, wasn't he?

At Parliament Square he swung the car hard left, raced past the cars arrayed on the forecourt of Ramsey Motors and screeched into Albert Road. He braked sharply into the small, public car park alongside the formidable bulk of the Wesleyan Methodist Church and slammed to a halt, barely aware of a burgundy and cream electric tramcar drawing into the station adjoining, to the delight of sightseers and camera-clicking transport enthusiasts.

Charlie crossed Waterloo Road in four long strides, his neck muscles aching with tension and all because of damned Fenella Kelly. He was doing himself no good getting like this. He needed to relax. He might visit the new health therapist who'd set up on the quay later. He'd heard she was a stunner. She'd not look down her nose at him. Yeah, that was a good idea. Forget Fenella Kelly. The way she'd sneered, humph...

He stopped short at the bank entrance. What the hell was he so het up about? Fenella Kelly was no one, less than no one. A two-pot artist who turned out expensive landscapes for dimwit tourists. She'd always been toffee-nosed, caring more for fulfilment and that sort of garbage rather than cash, more fool her.

"Charlie, how goes it? Still raking it in?"

Willie Kaneen under-manager, and friend of sorts, was loitering in the lofty bank porch.

"I'm fine, Willie, thanks for asking. Just calling to check my investments in the FT." Charlie laughed boisterously, pushing the swing door of the bank before him. Willie followed hard on his heels.

Charlie's eyes swept the interior, spotting his favourite cashier, Evie Cannon, at her counter booth. He'd been eyeing Evie for some time, and judging by the way she always made sure he knew she knew he was eyeing her he felt heartened and hopeful. She caught his eye even as he thought this and gave him an alluring smile. Charlie nodded politely before turning back to Willie. Charlie was no fool and he was aware than any liaison with Evie would have to be conducted with care. Evie no doubt felt the same.

As if in confirmation, senior cashier Sheila Quaggin paused in passing Evie and murmured something which made her blush. Yet as Sheila hurried away Evie wriggled her nose derisively, before giving Charlie a swift, wicked wink.

Charlie stifled a chuckle and was about to wink back when Willie Kaneen took hold of his arm. "A word in your ear, Charlie," he breathed. "I've heard a more than substantial rumour that I feel you should be aware of." Willie gripped his arm and shuffled him towards the nearby door, on which 'WK Kaneen, Assistant Manager' was inscribed on a substantial gilded plaque. "You've time for a… coffee?"

Charlie's business antennae twitched. Willie was privy to a variety of information that sometimes turned out worth knowing. "I dare say I have," Charlie puffed, and followed Willie into his office.

It wasn't till they were seated with coffee before them, Charlie's well sugared and with an extra carton of cream substitute, that Willie said more. "Now, Charlie, this is strictly off the record. I'm not talking as your bank manager but as a friend."

Charlie stirred his coffee. "Talk on, Willie," he said. He liked Willie's cheek. He wasn't manager, nor would he ever be, in Charlie's opinion. The man was too much of a bootlicker.

Charlie gulped hastily at his drink which momentarily took his breath away, it was so hot. Willie shot him a sad look while making a slow performance of ripping the top off his cream container and slowly draining it into the strong brew.

Charles felt uneasy. He had a horrible feeling that whatever Will was about to reveal had something to do with Bayview. He could feel it in his bones.

Willie gave a short preparatory sigh. "Bayview, Charlie." He spoke the word portentously.

Charlie hissed, "What about Bayview, for Christ's sake?" He might have known. Even at this late stage the bitch was going to wriggle out of his clutches, damn her.

"Negotiations have been mooted, peculiar negotiations. I can't go into details." Willie demurred, waving one of his soft pink hands while the other held tight to his coffee cup. He took a sip. "You know the bank is due to foreclose imminently on Mrs Kelly?"

"Yes, yes, everyone knows that."

"And I know that you have made Mrs Kelly a generous offer for her property."

"Come to the point, Willie. Who else is in the deal?"

Willie gave an unamused titter. "Here my professional integrity comes into play."

Charlie knew the formula. He couldn't be told plainly, but he could make educated guesses.

"Someone local?"

"No."

"Someone from across."

Willie nodded.

"Links with the town?" It was common enough, a Manx person returning home wanting to invest.

"No, well, not really. Not a recent link. In fact, not a link that most people would wish to admit."

Charlie stared. "Come on, give us a clue, for God's sake. Why would anyone in their right mind want to make an offer for Bayview? Who is it, one of Marjorie Quayle's long-lost lovers?"

Charlie's sneer of disbelief was wiped away by the peculiar expression on Willie's face.

"I couldn't say that. In fact, I can't say more, Charlie, it wouldn't be ethical. But you're on the right lines. That's all I can say, but if things proceed as this, er, client wishes, there will probably be no need for Fenella, or her family, to leave Bayview – certainly for the foreseeable future."

Charlie Peake was not often lost for words. He gaped, unable to comprehend this outrageous revelation.

He picked up his coffee cup with a clatter, drained it and slammed it down. His left eye twitched.

"Do you mean to say that my plan for the Mooragh Promenade, to provide a continuous row of luxury apartments, are going to be foiled by some upstart speculator who has come here to indulge a whim over something that happened years ago?"

Willie rose, shrugged and smiled. "I thought you'd like to know the way things are, Charles," he said coolly. He didn't want Charlie Peake thinking he could let off steam in his office. What he'd done was a favour. Charlie had done him a favour once or twice. Now they were even.

"Right, yes, thanks, Willie." Charlie held out his hand and Willie grasped the proffered fingers.

Charlie's grasp was brutal. Willie did not flinch, but as he showed him out he wondered had he made a mistake, what with 'client confidentiality' and all the other new rules and regulations being brought in from head office. Willie shrugged. Charlie deserved to know; what he did with the information was up to him.

Norah was staring out of the lounge window when George Stevens returned from his trip to the town centre. From her window seat she observed his slow approach. She hadn't been looking out for him; there were more interesting folk to stare at. A coach must have dropped its passengers in the Market Square, and couples and groups were strolling by way of the promenade towards the Mooragh Park. She'd noticed the old man because of his dour attire. His long mackintosh and broad-brimmed hat looked out of place against the summer scene. "He looks like a man from another time." Norah decided, her arthritic fingers rumpling at her crimplene skirt. "Like Humphrey Bogart," she mused, "up to no good, prob'ly."

Yet as he neared, Norah saw that the old man looked nothing like Humphrey Bogart. He hadn't Bogart's assured short-legged gait. Nor was there anything about him that would attract Lauren Bacall – far from it.

"He's a plain old geezer," Norah tittered as he glanced up briefly, though not particularly in her direction. Yet as his gaze lifted towards the roofline of the houses, something about his stance and his eyes made Norah gasp and lift her fist to her chest in panic.

"No!" For a fraction of a second she was taken right back. She peered closer through the salt-smeared glass. No, it couldn't be. My God, she'd nearly wet herself then, all right. But look at him. It couldn't be... this feller was ancient, more than ancient, past it.

Nevertheless, Norah's heart thumped uncontrollably fast. She swept her gaze quickly beyond the dark-suited man and focused on a young couple strolling hand in hand with a pigtailed child between them.

The mother's breasts were jigging beneath under her thin T-shirt; her partner's face was turned, smilingly, towards her. They looked vibrant, full of life, the little girl beaming and giggling as they swung her off her pretty sandal-clad feet. The sight of this cheerful trio brought a nostalgic tear to Norah's eye and a smile to her lips.

"There's bonny now," she muttered, thrusting her jaw up in a grin. "An' look at the biceps on him. He looks as if he could give her what she wants." Norah gazed longingly at this little family. Only after they'd passed did she glance briefly back at George Stevens, who was almost outside Bayview. "Looks knackered, he does. Silly old begger."

She forcibly thrust any suspicion about him to the furthermost recesses of her mind. Over the years she had perfected a determined mind over matter policy when it came to recalling her past. "Practice makes perfect," she muttered. "Thank the Lord m'mind's still working proper. The day I wake up and don't know m'self, or what to think, that'll be the time to do m'self in."

How exactly, she wasn't sure, but she reckoned she had enough inner resources to think of some way – or Percy would, bless him.

Occasionally Norah had tried to review her past, telling herself that by facing the memories fully she might rid herself of the pain, which still gnawed deep inside her. But she'd never accomplished this challenge – and she doubted that she ever would.

"I'm a ninny, I suppose," she muttered crossly. "And no use to no one."

"No, you're not, you old so-and-so," Marjorie had entered on her soft-soled slippers. "Here's your coffee. Nice and milky as you like it, and a Wagon Wheel, to keep your strength up."

Norah gripped Marjorie's hand as she put the coffee down.

"You remember good times, don't you, Marje? We had good times, didn't we?"

"Mum, we had marvellous times, you and me and Dad, and afterwards." Marjorie's honest open countenance looked briefly troubled, but she sped on. "After the war was wonderful. Do you remember that large family, the Banks? They came summer after summer, through the fifties, all five children, mother, father and grandma. They were a lovely lot. And there were dozens more families just like them." She picked up the Wagon Wheel and handed it to Norah, opening the wrapper for her. "There were the Miller boys, do you remember them? So nice-looking, and one of them fell for that little girl Maria Dainty who was staying here with her mum. They sent us a piece of their wedding cake when they got married. Do you remember?"

Norah beamed. "Aye, you're right. There must be lots of folk glad they stayed at Bayview."

"We prided ourselves on being a real family boarding house." Marjorie chuckled. "It used to be on our brochure, didn't it? 'The holiday home from home for all the family.'" She smiled. "I found some of those brochures the other day. I was sorting out some stuff in the attic. I thought I should, seeing as we won't be here much… longer…" Marjorie broke off. "Drat, Fenella told me not to talk about you having to leave."

"It doesn't matter. I know it's coming. I'd like to see one of them brochures, Marje."

The front door closed with a thud.

"Is that Percy? He said he'd get me a mag."

Marjorie walked to the door and looked into the hall. "No, it was Mr Stevens. Mum, why is Percy getting you a magazine? Why couldn't Eloise get it for you?"

Norah plucked at her skirt fretfully, one hand to her mouth.

"Mum, are you listening? Why didn't you ask Eloise to get the magazine?"

"Are you sure that feller isn't an Eyetie, Marje? I reckon he could be, y'know." She raised a bony fist angrily. "If he is a wop our Fenella will have to tell him to hop it. I'm not having him at Bayview."

"Mother, hush. You're not allowed to use terms like that nowadays. Now drink your coffee while it's hot and eat your biscuit. Look, I'll break it in half for you." The heavy front door banged again. "There now, perhaps this is Percy with your mag."

Percy, slim, white-haired and dapper, with energy belying his eighty years, hurried into the lounge, a little out of breath. As usual he was dressed in sports jacket, collar and tie. Cycle clips clipped his cavalry twill trousers. Though a cycling enthusiast all his life Percy had never let his cycling affect his apparel. He was always well turned out.

"Glorious day, Norah. Got what you wanted. Forgot what I wanted, in fact." Percy smiled a crumpled, apologetic smile. "I made a list," he shrugged, "but I must have lost it between my pocket and the town." He reached inside his jacket as if to fish out the magazine.

Norah flapped her hands. "You go off, Marje. Me and Percy have got some talking to do."

Marjorie did as she was bidden, thankful that Norah was content, though she did wonder what magazine Norah had got Percy to buy. She took fancies to read some appalling rubbish.

The kitchen was quiet and tidy. Fenella was upstairs to her attic studio. Marjorie sat at the kitchen table and glanced idly through the local paper. There were all the usual articles about drunkenness and vandalism. Even on the Isle of Man the ways of the outside world were creeping in. Drug offences, violence. It wasn't the place it had been.

"But where is?" Marjorie sighed, opening the paper wide to inspect the births and deaths column, though it was on the latter that she always concentrated. Didn't everyone, as they got older, if only to console themselves that they had outlived their contemporaries?

Suddenly, Marjorie straightened. A small paragraph at the foot of a page caught her attention. She read it intently, and then reread it.

"No," she said, "I don't approve of that at all."

She reached into a nearby drawer for a pair of scissors.

She cut out the small news item and carefully ripped it into tiny pieces, dropping them in the bin. She bit her lip. Now the paper looked odd. But still, looking odd was better than anyone being upset, even after all this time.

Upstairs George Stevens hung his coat on the hanger behind his bedroom door. He had already placed his hat on the chair by the wardrobe.

He lowered himself into the cushioned Lloyd loom chair near the window and kicked off his black leather shoes. Leaning back he let his eyes close. He felt unutterably weary now that things had been set in train. Why? Why wasn't he feeling the relief he had expected?

He put his finger into the knot of his tie and eased it. Always fussy about his appearance, he did not consider taking it off. He sighed heavily; the morning's exertions had taken their toll. He had intended to stay out for lunch and then to make a tour of the town in an effort to make his peace with those places he could still recall.

But the infirmities of his years had made this plan impossible. After the bank visit he'd felt exhausted, mentally and physically, and confusingly puzzled.

Puzzled by how little the town resembled the place of his memories. Of course the colour of those memories had been heightened by the passions of youth. He knew he had been a volatile young man, driven by his selfish emotions. The past, with himself in the central starring role, stood in his mind like a starkly colourful drama. The brutal vividness of that time, short though it had been, compared to the rest of his life, had impacted on his psyche. This small town, with its brilliant appeal, its glittering waters, both lake and sea, beneath skies of almost Mediterranean blue, swiftly changing to dramatic slate greys as clouds raced across the hills, had been unforgettable. He remembered evenings when those hills had been stained by powerful sunsets: town and sea dyed the colour of blood, a melodramatic reminder of the blood being shed by his countrymen all across Europe.

A light dew filmed George's forehead. With a trembling hand he wiped it away. He had come not to dwell upon the past, and his shabby part in it, but to amend those memories and overlay them with generous reparation.

George closed his eyes. It was the only way to find peace. He had been right to come. The person he had been, that boy, would not have been able to understand his viewpoint. In his youth he had been motivated only by ego. Though the same flesh as then, over the intervening years all the cells in his body had divided, altered and been replaced many millions of times. Outwardly, he was the man he had been. Inwardly, in his heart, he was another, quite different being.

But could there be forgiveness at this late stage? That was his fear. He moved uneasily against the worn rattan of the chair. Would he find peace, save in death?

This gloomy question, combined with a nagging ache of indigestion, urged him to slowly stand and shuffle to the tea tray. He filled the kettle at the sink. As he waited for it to boil he swallowed a small pink pill from the box he always carried in his waistcoat pocket.

Shakily he emptied a sachet of coffee into a cup. When it was cool enough to drink he found he could not abide the taste. The flavour subtly reminded him of a poorer, ersatz brand. How many cups had he drunk of that unwholesome brew? After a few mouthfuls he tipped the coffee away and quenched his thirst with the sweet-tasting water from the tap.

"Free as the sweet mountain air," George murmured, a line of the Manx National Anthem rising from some hidden recess of sixty years before.

George collapsed on the edge of the bed, his head in his hands, and wept.

FIVE

Upstairs, in the sunny lightness of the spacious attic room, Fenella sat before her easel and stared at the composition before her.

It had taken two hours to get the bones of the picture sketched and colour washed. The pretty beach of Cornaa, a few miles south from Ramsey, was a familiar subject and Fenella had painted it many times. Cornaa Beach, viewed from various aspects, was one of her regular offerings for the tourist market. She attempted to produce one a month, but the gouache of Maughold Head had put her behind. Her eyes slid to this unexpected creation propped nearby her easel. It was strange, but just glancing at that canvas made her smile. It had that touch, of something, often sought after but impossible to define, that lifted it from a mere representation into, maybe not a work of art but utterly saleable nevertheless, and it would fit well into an exhibition if ever she managed to organise another. Whereas this... she cast a critical eye at the somewhat lacklustre composition before her.

"It's not exactly flat, just boring." She frowned, wondering if it was worth finishing. She sighed. Not to finish it would be silly, especially as she had a contract with the art shop in town. If her pictures stopped appearing locally any cachet she had as an artist would slip away.

So, she lifted her paintbrush again – then, with a shake of her head, laid it down. She reached for a rag to wipe her brush, feeling an unnerving sensation of desolation. What if she was losing her touch? What if that remarkable gouache was a final hurrah?

Her throat tightened; she felt near to tears. She had drawn and painted ever since she could remember. At sixteen she had taken an art foundation course at the Isle of Man College and later she had completed a Fine Art Diploma by part-time study. Yet she'd never intended to stay on the island. Life and serendipity, however, in the handsome form of Brian Kelly, had altered her life plans. Soon after Fenella's eighteenth birthday Brian had picked her up, literally, from the heaving floor of an Isle of Man Steam Packet vessel tossing its way down the Mersey in the teeth of a force eight gale, a not-uncommon occurrence on the Liverpool to Douglas sailing. Fenella had gone away for the weekend to see the fine Pre-Raphaelite collection in the Walker Art Gallery. Trying to sleep on deck when all the lounge berths were occupied, she had rolled off of one of the uncomfortable slatted benches and Brian had scooped her up. They spent the rest of that nightmare journey getting acquainted.

Brian was a qualified electrician and keen amateur motorcycle racer. He'd raced on circuits on the island and in Northern Ireland. Fenella had never been interested in the local motorcycle racing, even though the world-famous Tourist Trophy races and the Manx Grand Prix festival were held each year. These events punctuated the beginning and end of the tourist season. Locals grew accustomed to the influx of bikers and their machines while a proportion of residents ignored them, other than complaining good-naturedly about the crowds, the frequent accidents and the road closures. TT fortnight in June was still the busiest period for hoteliers on the island. From childhood Fenella had been pressed into service waiting on and washing up in school holidays. In her teens she had become aware of the attraction of men in black leather, but until that night at sea she'd never been bowled over by any would-be Agostini or Mike Hailwood.

After this sea crossing, however, Fenella set foot on Douglas quay feeling as though she'd undergone a transformation. The Pre-Raphaelites brothers, with all their luminously detailed glory, seemed outmoded and pale compared to the virile attraction of Brian Kelly. During the tempestuous sea crossing she and Brian had become lovers in spirit, and it was mere days before they became lovers in reality. Fenella's plans for extending her education were cancelled. Marjorie, already widowed, tried to make her daughter change her mind, pointing out that she was too young to settle down, but Fenella was adamant. She saw no reason why she couldn't continue her artistic career and be married to Brian Kelly. After meeting Brian and seeing him and Fenella together, however, Marjorie welcomed Brian into the family and started making wedding plans. Norah viewed Fenella's romance with greedy envy. Fenella and Brian married at the end of August and they settled into a small apartment in Douglas. Fenella found a job with a local design firm.

Tom was born in March the following year. Fenella and Brian had already started to house-hunt. They planned to rent a small guesthouse in Douglas, and with the income from that, Fenella's painting and Brian's electrical work they looked forward to a comfortable future. In the meanwhile, Brian prepared to enter the Manx Grand Prix races that September, for which he'd only recently qualified. It was to be, he hoped, the start of a successful racing career.

By the first week of September they'd signed the lease on their new home and hired a van for the removal of their small amount of furniture; Tom was thriving and everything in their lives was wonderful, tinged with promise for the future and a passionate delight in the present.

On the second lap of his first practice session, Brian Kelly was killed outright when he crashed his motorcycle at Braddan Bridge. He had recently celebrated his twenty-fourth birthday.

Only the resilience of youth kept Fenella going through that dark time, and the cheerful unconcern of Tom, who, at six months, was utterly dependent. He was a happy baby, good to sleep and feed, and a creature of routine. Tom's routine kept his young mother busy each day, though the nights were always hard.

Fenella came to the present with a jolt. What had prompted all those memories. She didn't often dwell on the past. Tom did not resemble his dad and the memories of her young husband had receded to a dream-like blur. She'd had brief affairs over the years, and lurking in the background there had always been Peter, until he too married and left the island. Since his divorce she'd rarely seen him. Fenella rinsed her knife and brushes vigorously and dried them. Now he was back, but what was the point of thinking about him? There were plenty of other matters to worry over.

She placed the brushes, bristles upright, in their jar. There'd always been a spark between him and her, but it had been of the juvenile 'crush' variety which she should have grown out of years ago. True, Peter was probably the oldest friend she still had. He and Susan had helped her a lot through those first sad days of widowhood and she'd missed them when they moved across and had practically lost touch by the time they divorced. There were two children of the marriage; she'd met them a couple of times, a girl and boy, both resembling Susan more than Peter, when they'd visited.

She never dreamed that Peter would return to the island police force, or that he might be stationed so close. It felt slightly like stepping back in time. It would be odd, for sure, and a tad awkward till they both became used to seeing one another. She still could not bring herself to go over that disastrous date without squirming. It had been like a teenage faux pas, only they were both well past teen years.

It was too late for any romance between them. She valued her own company too highly to tolerate the intrusion of any man into her life. She'd made that decision years ago. As this realisation hit her anew she caught sight of her wistful reflection in the bay window glass. Swiftly she moved away. No, it was much too late.

She reached to throw a piece of polythene over her palette. "If only I could just paint, with no guests to worry about, or family worries or money or time restraints..." She glanced at her watch and gasped. She ran from the room and descended swiftly down the several flights of stairs. The treads creaked, with age and underlying rot. Dust motes surged and hung in the still air as the sun streamed into the old building.

George Stevens, lying on his bed, heard the creaking of the stairs. He listened as they faded and far off a door slammed. He'd intended to go out again – but not just yet. He needed to conserve his strength. Besides, the room was soothing. The dull green of the curtains framing the blue-green sea and the view of the sand hills made for a calming outlook. He remembered those hills, sharply etched and golden, which had greeted his young eyes each dawn. Played upon by a thousand varieties of light and shadow, influenced constantly by the seasons and the time of day. The present view of the promenade, wide and free, set with convenient squat shelters at intervals and with modern cars parked along its length, offered a constant invitation to stroll and enjoy the freedom of the open air.

His memory had filed away a very different land– and seascape. A bitter wind had frequently swept clouds of gritty sand through the barbed wire onto the cordoned-off pavements. This whirling irritation had continued regularly across the pavements up the step and even into the hallway, so that his and many other booted feet had made a constant grating sound on the bare floorboards. Even in the bedrooms the floors had been gritty. Georgio shivered and swung his legs onto the worn carpet.

The bleak fact of being held captive had never been the worse aspect. Yes, being trammelled meant discomfort and boredom, but had he been a patient young man his stay might not have been so irksome. If he had been less self-centred, willing to acknowledge that there were hundreds, no, thousands of men and women much worse off than himself and moreover he was only one of many in similar circumstances. If only he had, at that young age, learned a little of the wisdom that had come to him in succeeding years.

"But then," he whispered, "I would not be here. It is too late, George, to repine; you are a foolish old man." He often talked severely to himself. He had got into the habit when here before. He stood, stretched within the limitations of his rheumatic limbs and surveyed his reflection in a mirror.

He viewed a being whom he hardly recognised, for in some ways he still felt like that trapped boy he'd once been. His development had somehow stilled at that period of his life. Yes, his outer carapace had aged, yet the core of him had stilled, as if set in aspic. Yes, he looked old, albeit well-to-do, in his well-cut suit. "A prosperous man, I am." He nodded, and tried to smile. "Tch!" Seriousness suited him. "Mutton acting as lamb is not good." He nodded vehemently. Another habit, ach – he was an old fool. *What must people think of me?*

"Age has crept up on me and soon enough…?" He closed his eyed briefly, realising as he did so that his rest had done him good. He blinked his eyes open and stretched his lips in a stiff, smile. "So, now I go out." He reached for his silver-backed hairbrushes and smoothed his hair; luxuriant enough still, he noted with satisfaction. Again memory intervened. He vividly remembered his hair when he was young. Deeply burnished, lifting from his forehead like a bird's wing. An Adonis, his mother had called him, standing with her hands clasped, gazing adoringly.

"Mama, Mama, if you could see me now."

He lifted his hat and adjusted it carefully. He pulled on his long coat and fastened it securely. He picked up his room key and slipped quietly from the room.

Norah was resting. She had been dozing, in a far distant place, where the high days of summer hung over a land of long grass and heady scents, of honeysuckle, barley, gorse flowers and new-mown hay.

And another scent, the scent of a man, near her, musky, exciting, disturbing, his hands reaching around her and his touch light upon her body. His lips, searching, seeking, finding, making her moan, as the spiralling of pleasure swept through her, a sensation which she remembered with agonising clarity, though the achievement of it had eluded her for years, even in her dreams.

And then she blinked open her crusty eyes and the familiar contours of her room settled around her. Reality plucked away the dream haze in which she was still young, supple and beautiful. Instead she was bitterly aware that she was a withered old woman, with sticky eyes and a raging thirst.

"Bloody Norah," she said. This used to be a phrase on a telly show. She couldn't recall which and it didn't really matter. "Bloody Norah doubled," she muttered, attempting to reach her library book. It was a new Jackie Collins, full of raunchy young bloods and sexy women. She had an Agatha Christie novel on the go too, but that was for when she was feeling intelligent.

She didn't feel intelligent today. Today she was feeling bloody awful.

"Where's my tea, Marje?" she croaked irritably.

She stared at the words dancing on the page. They didn't make much sense. Nor did life, really, when you got to her age. What bloomin' good were you at eighty-four?

"It's all right for some. They keep on their pins into their nineties. But what if you can't?"

It was unfair, bloody unfair; look at Percy. Like a bloody ballet dancer on his dainty size sixes, and he was near her age, eighty-three next June.

"Mm, he's a good 'un, is Percy. A good friend."

Norah put her book down. It was no good. Marjorie would have to clean her eyes with that boracic stuff. Even large print was beyond her. She would have to wait to find out later whether the well-hung Italian had it off with the busty opera singer.

Not that Norah liked reading about Italians. She had almost given up on the book when she'd come to the character of Guido, and she'd told Marjorie off good and proper for choosing such an unsuitable story for her. Not that Marje took much notice. Norah's rheumy eyes looked inward. "It all happened a long time ago, o'course." Her fingers grasped at the candlewick. "But that's the bloody trouble. I can't forget it, that's the worst of it," she gasped, her heart pounding. Old age was bad enough if you were easy in your mind. "If you aren't," Norah sniffed, "it's a bloomin' bugger."

Marjorie put her head around the door. "Oh, you are awake then, Mum. I'll fetch your tea." She came over to the bed. "Shall I plump you up before I get it?"

"Yes."

Marjorie did the necessary and smoothed the covers.

"Why were you swearing?" she asked mildly. "You always seem to be swearing when I come in."

"Mind your own business and get me some of that boracic stuff for my eyes. I can't see a bloody thing."

Marjorie sighed. "I'll bring it up with the tea."

Norah didn't feel bad about biting Marjorie's head off. She was used to it. "She's a good woman, poor sod," Norah admitted when her daughter was out of hearing. "I don't know how I produced her, really. She must take after Walter. She isn't the least like me."

A sudden draught blew the door further open. Norah glared. She didn't want any Tom, Dick or Harry seeing her in this state. Even as she thought this she heard slow footsteps coming down the short flight of stairs near her landing. They got nearer, then paused infinitesimally, while Norah pressed herself back into her pillow and determinedly shut her eyes. The footsteps moved slowly past, onto the top of the stairs, and receded as the person descended.

Percy Corlett cycled dreamily along the road towards the promenade. His mind was far away from the squeaking movement of the wheels turning beneath him. He pushed down rhythmically and the tarmac sped past. Soon he was passing the perimeter wall of the park, the name 'Mooragh' painted in large black letters, renewed each summer by the commissioners' workmen. *Funny name*, he thought idly, glancing over the wall, *it meant miry place, or some such, in Manx, I think*. It was certainly watery, with its huge lake and central island. At this time of day the park was quiet, the lake empty of rowers, just one small boy with a yacht on a string running along one of the waterside paths. Percy smiled. It was a long time since he'd sailed a yacht like that; when he was a small boy he'd often walked to the Mooragh Park with his parents to sail the brig his father had made him.

His fingers pressed on his bicycle brakes at this memory. Gracious, that was before the war and even before he'd become conscious of being different from most boys. He didn't want marriage, he didn't want to leave the island, as so many of his contemporaries did, and he didn't even want a great deal of money, which was just as well because though he'd never been penniless he'd never experienced great wealth. Despite these limitations Percy felt he'd had a happy life, and how many folks could say that, at his age?

He might have been happier, had things gone differently, of course. It was what happened in wartime that had barred his chances. But he'd achieved a compromise. He'd stayed true and he'd lived comfortably enough in this lovely, God-blessed place. He was a fortunate man, and he knew it.

Percy tried never to think of the 'if only's that sometimes reared at the back of his quiet mind. He comforted himself by the acknowledgement that 'if only's had two sides to them, and the achievement of one side might have brought less than perfect happiness. Percy was not habitually a deep thinker, but the sunshine and the quiet, rhythmic turning of his bicycle wheels frequently encouraged contemplation. That was another reason for being glad he lived in this quiet town on this quiet isle. If he lived in a city and began to ruminate while cycling he'd have been run down long ago.

Percy was still deep in meditation when a car pulled up right ahead of him. It came seemingly out of nowhere, jarringly braking with a squeal of tyres and near-knocking him off his bike. Percy's heart thudded as he braked sharply, having to pull his handlebars to one side so his wrists hurt as he juddered to a stop.

Percy's heart was thumping uncomfortably and he felt a touch breathless as he set his feet on the tarmac. He had discovered many years before that motorists were selfish and that the way in which they often ignored the presence of cyclists was aggravating and sometimes downright dangerous. He was about to veer around the shining bumpers of the car that had almost caused him to have an accident when the driver's door opened.

"Percy Corlett, isn't it?"

Percy paused and set both feet on the ground. "It is," he said noncommittally. He knew Charles Peake by sight. Who didn't? But he didn't think he'd spoken to the man in his life.

"You lodge at Bayview?"

"I do."

Charlie emerged more fully, easing himself out of the car and standing close in a confrontational manner. The man's blazer, with its shining gold buttons and glinting badge on his lapel, caught the sun and dazzled Percy. "You'll be leaving soon then?"

"Maybe."

"Come off it, Fenella Kelly's reached the end of the bank's tether. She'd get a good price from me for that property. Perhaps I could do you a favour if you'd remind her of that. I can't wait forever."

Percy raised his eyebrows. "What sort of favour could you do me?"

"Where are you going to live if you get evicted from Bayview?"

Percy shrugged.

"There's lots of council housing in Ramsey. I could put in a good word for you."

Percy continued to stare, with his mild brown eyes. "Could you?"

Charlie shrugged his shoulders importantly.

Percy was put in mind of a brash cockerel.

"I'm the town commissioner, you know," Charlie said, suddenly wishing he hadn't confronted Percy. The man was gawping as though he was simple. No wonder he'd never got anywhere in life.

Percy smiled, a brief sidelong uplift of his soft lips. He shifted his grip on the handlebars. "Aye, well," he said, raising his foot to the pedal, "they'll elect anyone nowadays." He wheeled off slowly, leaving Charlie grinding his teeth with fury.

Tom, turning into North Shore Road, noticed Percy in the distance, riding away from Charlie Peake.

"Uh-oh," he murmured. "What's Charlie been up to?"

"Who?" Emily yawned. It had been a long day and they'd walked miles.

"Charles Peake, local property speculator and builder. He's made Mum several offers for Bayview, but she's determined not to sell to him."

"But I thought you said the bank was foreclosing. Surely if someone wants to buy the place she should be glad of it?"

Tom decelerated as they approached the stop sign at the promenade junction. He waited as a car sped past and then drove the few hundred yards to his usual parking space.

"I agree, but Mum will never sell to Charlie Peake. At least not before hell freezes over."

"Why?"

Tom turned off the ignition, checked the handbrake and put the car into gear. He leaned across and stroked Emily's cheek with his hand. "My love, my love, you will never understand my mother's tortuous mind, so don't bother your pretty head."

Emily glared. "OK, it's none of my business anyway." She tapped him on the nose, which, she noted, had caught the sun. "But less of the patronising tone, thanks, Mr Kelly, I'm not one of your pupils, you know."

"Oh, wow, sorry, Em, I didn't mean to sound high-handed or secretive, honestly. To be utterly truthful," he broke off and looked round to make sure there was no one about, "I haven't the faintest idea why Mum detests Charlie Peake so much."

"But then, your perception rating is not that high, is it, Thomas?" Emily grinned.

"Cheeky toad. You wait till I get you inside."

As they unloaded their jackets and rucksacks Percy wheeled up alongside. "Had a good day out?" He smiled enquiringly.

"Yes, it was great, wasn't it, Em? Hey, Percy, what did Charlie want? I saw he'd pulled up right in front of you. He's not been coming the heavy, has he?"

Percy shook his head. "Just a matter of bribery, lad, but nothing I couldn't handle."

"Bribery! You're not serious."

"I shouldn't mention it to your mother, if I were you. I daresay Charlie's getting desperate. And I don't suppose he means any harm."

"Yeah, it must be frustrating for him, but..." Tom's voice tailed off. "Well, Mum knows her own mind. Come on, Em. Are you coming in, Percy?"

"No, no... There's time enough for another amble along the prom. It's a lovely afternoon. See you... anon."

Tom and Emily watched Percy ride slowly away. Tom took her hand as they climbed the shallow steps.

"He seems a nice old guy."

"He is." Tom smiled. "I'll miss Percy. He's been at Bayview for most of my life. With not knowing my dad it was nice to have a bloke about the place." He grinned. "Even a bloke like Percy."

"Why do you say, 'even a bloke like Percy'?"

Tom shrugged his shoulders. "No reason, really – just that Percy's unique, and, well, that's it, really."

Emily tutted. "It strikes me that there are all sorts of secrets in your life, Tom Kelly, and when I met you I thought you were the most uncomplicated guy ever."

Tom put his arm around Emily. "One day, I will tell you all. I promise." He kissed her ear. "Come on, let's go and say hello to Mum."

Impulsively Emily pulled Tom to her as they entered the hall and kissed him passionately. "Thanks for an ace day out, lover."

George Stevens saw them as they embraced in the doorway. It made him falter as he descended the last few stairs. He gripped the banister rail tightly.

They broke away from their embrace, beaming at one another. Tom, blond and tall; Emily, with her olive complexion and short-cropped hair and soulful eyes reminding George of a dark Madonna, though her lips were fuller and more sensual than any painted statue. Tom nodded politely and guided Emily towards the kitchen, where savoury smells were wafting from, though the evening meal was still an hour hence.

George pursed his lips. He attempted to call Tom back, but his throat dried. He took a breath, slowly. He knew he would not be able to digest a morsel if he didn't get this weight off his chest. He had prevaricated all afternoon, reminding himself that Mrs Kelly would hear soon enough, by official means. But she should be told; it was mere courtesy. Surely, after all these years, he could afford a courteous gesture?

The young couple were still stowing their coats and bags. George summoned his strength. "Ah, a moment, young Mr Kelly? Please?"

Tom turned. "Yes?"

George rubbed his palms together. "Erm, your mother, Mrs Kelly? May I beg a few moments of her time?"

Tom hesitated. "Of course. I'll see how she's fixed." He smiled and pushed Emily before him into the kitchen.

George heard a muttered exchange. He turned away and stepped a few steps towards the glazed door. Now that the moment had come his heart was pounding with such intensity he felt nauseous. He hoped he had enough nerve for this. His hands were clammy, his throat tight, as if his collar was throttling him.

He clenched his fists until the arthritic joints protested. This had to be done. He had to make his peace. So many years... how could he draw back now?

Fenella emerged from the kitchen, her forehead furrowed. She was wearing a spattered apron. George's eyes fastened on the marks. Were they blood?

"Mr Stevens, this is not really convenient. I am in the middle of preparing the meal..." She broke off. "Oh dear, you are very pale. Are you ill? Come into the office and sit for a moment."

George was aware of a buzzing in his ears. Beyond it he could hear sirens, and the surly tones of the guards. He felt himself slipping, his eyes rising to the ornate cornice bisecting the ceiling. He had gazed at the cornice that day too, when the guards had held his arms on either side. They had thrust him into the commander's office, this very same poky room, where he had been reprimanded.

Fenella pushed him into a chair and laid a cool hand upon his forehead. "Put your head between your knees."

He struggled to fend her thoughtful hands away. "No, no. I will be fine, now I sit. Thank you." He had not let a woman touch him for many years. At least the embarrassment caused by her nearness made his blood surge and immediately he felt more in control.

"No, there. I am recovered." He took out a handkerchief and mopped his forehead. The scents and sounds were fading. The quiet reality of the present reassured him.

He forced a smile. "It is but a moment I will keep you, Mrs Kelly." He looked guardedly at her, at her eyes that reminded him suddenly, so he had to look elsewhere, along a shelf of tourist guides and a fat yellow AA book.

"In my business life I have long been concerned with property," he began, his voice uncertain but growing stronger as he went over the words he had practised so long. "I heard… about your… problem."

Fenella frowned, opened her mouth to speak – but the old man lifted a hand. "No, please, hear me out. I have not much to say, Mrs Kelly, and it may seem to you an odd business, but I have a debt to pay. It is a very old debt, of honour." His eyes flickered to hers and she saw something in them that made her feel uneasy.

"I have a proposition to put to you, which is as much for my own benefit, believe me, as yours."

Fenella smiled patiently, though she felt irritation rising as fast as she knew the pans might be boiling over in the kitchen. She hoped Tom or Marjorie were watching them.

"It is a simple plan." George raised his eyes again and attempted a weak smile. "I wish to purchase Bayview, outright, but I do not wish to live here, nor do I wish to do anything with the building or the site."

"What?" Fenella exclaimed. "Whatever has Bayview got to do with you? Is this some sort of a joke?"

He held his hand in a gesture of peace. "It is no joke."

"Then why?"

The soulful, bloodshot eyes surveyed her once more. "My reasons are not so easily explained." He could not meet her eyes. He gazed at his shoes.

Fenella wiped her hands down her apron, her heart thumping. How and why should this stranger be interested in her home?

What cheek. It must be a joke. It had to be. Perhaps Charles Peake had set him up? Yes, that might be what was going on.

"You've been sent by Charlie, haven't you?"

"Beg pardon. I do not understand. This Charlie, I'm sorry. I do not know the name."

Fenella stared. The old man's eyes gazed solemnly back at her. "I assure you, Mrs Kelly, this is a sincere offer. I have been at your Isle of Man bank earlier and have signed the necessary paperwork."

Fenella found herself trembling. She had been prepared to leave Bayview without a backward glance – well, yes, a backward glance and some regret – but... She had forced herself to think that having to sell up might be the very best thing for her. Yet now, if what the little man was offering was true? *Goodness, I can stay, I can live here forever.*

As the old man continued to murmur about arrangements of which she could not make much sense Fenella's head whirled. Deep inside she realised how much she loved Bayview, no matter how decayed and tatty it was, no matter how it wasn't a business-like or sensible place to live; it was what she knew and it was something permanent to hold on to.

She took a sharp breath. "Mr Stevens, wait. I've taken in what you have said so far, though I can't imagine why you're saying it. If you want me to consider this matter seriously you must convince me why I should believe you."

George Stevens could not face her steady gaze. He focused on his pale, liver-spotted hands. He pressed them together, hard... This was the ultimate hurdle. To convince her without admitting... to admit... was impossible. With caution, this would be as far as he needed to go. He could leave in the morning, his duty done.

He cleared his throat. His voice sounded hoarse as he began. "I first came to the Isle of Man many, many years ago, when I was a young man..."

Fenella interjected. "You still look pale. Would you like a drink of water?"

"No, my dear, not now. Please, listen to me. Please."

Fascinated, Fenella listened to a short, rambling explanation, yet when it seemed he'd finished she felt little clearer in understanding than she had before.

SIX

The potatoes were boiled to a mush. Fenella swept them off the cooker and used an unsteady hand to drain them. "Mother, didn't you think to watch these? They'll have to be mashed they're so soft…"

Marjorie had been standing in the yard, fingering the herbs growing in a tub near the door. She turned apologetically. "Sorry, love. I lost track of time. Tom and Emily had been telling me of their day out and I tried to remember how long it was since I'd walked up Peel Hill." She slipped past Fenella, opened the fridge and lifted out margarine. "Here, I'll mash them if you like. What did Mr Stevens want? He had a cheek asking to see you now. He might have guessed you'd be busy."

Fenella cast a look towards Norah. Though she appeared to be reading, was she actually listening?

Marjorie immediately understood. "She's engrossed," she murmured.

Fenella looked dubious. She shook salt and pepper into the pan of drained potatoes and picked up the masher. "No, I'll tell you later."

"You're not listening, are you, Mother?" Marjorie said quietly.

Norah immediately raised her head. "Yes, so if you're thinking of talking about me, don't."

Marjorie tried to smile but felt her chest tighten. She reached for her clean apron and tied it on wearily. God, how glad she'd be to give up these pinnies. Flimsy, embroidered shackles was how she saw them nowadays. Fit for a youngster, maybe, but not for a mature woman in her retirement years. Her childhood summers had passed in a blur, with only brief glimpses of beaches through endless sessions of waiting on and drying dishes. Even when she'd met Donald their dates had been dictated by kitchen duties. Now she was meant to be retired, this was meant to be a rewarding time for all the years she'd worked. So far being retired made her feel more weary than when she'd been commuting to Douglas. It was only the knowledge that soon things would change that kept her going. God knows, she loved her daughter, and Norah, giving the old lady as much attention as possible now that she was in a wheelchair, but enough was enough. Marjorie was counting the days to her freedom.

"Cheer up," Fenella whispered as she replaced the lid on the mashed potato pan. Then in a bolder tone she continued, "Mum, could you give me a hand in the pantry? The boxes are in such a muddle I don't know if I can reach the custard powder." Fenella led the way into the long, cool side room and began to shift boxes and packages. After casting a quick glance at Norah, Marjorie trailed in. "You'd better shut the door," Fenella whispered.

Marjorie shrugged but did so. "Nell, you look odd. You're not ill, are you?"

"No." Fenella pulled Marjorie close. "George Stevens, you know Norah thinks he's Italian – well, she's right, he is, and Stevens is not his name, or rather, it wasn't his name when he was interned here."

Marjorie's mouth fell open. "What?"

"I know, it's weird, isn't it? Anyway, something happened when he was here – he wouldn't give me any details." Fenella gulped, emotion making her throat dry. "Mum. He's going to pay off my mortgage."

Marjorie's mouth fell open. Her heart bumped oddly. "What! Say that again – do you mean he wants to take the place over?"

Without giving Fenella a chance to reply she hurried on. "No, he must be joking, look at him, he's as old as Mother. Oh, Fenella, you didn't believe him?" Marjorie's jaw stiffened. She folded her arms and glared. "What a bloody cheek – why are you taking this so calmly?" Marjorie tried to reverse and knocked a box of gravy mix onto the floor. She kicked at it crossly.

"Mum? Hush, and calm down. It's not a joke. Listen to me. He was serious. Apparently he's into property. He owns other houses over here and that is how he heard about my overdrawn mortgage—"

Marjorie interrupted crossly. "You can't honestly believe this ridiculous proposition. He's having you on, I tell you—"

"Mum, calm down, no, listen. He'd been looking to invest in Manx property, because of his time here. He wants to pay the mortgage off, well, buy it, but…" She turned away. "Gran's getting cross." She moved to pass Marjorie. "We'll discuss it later." As she swung the pantry door open she turned, smiling delightedly. "If he pays our debt, we'll be able to stay here. You, me, Gran – all of us. Isn't that fantastic?" She stepped into the kitchen. "OK Gran? Sorry we shut you out there."

Marjorie stamped after her and banged the pantry door shut. She felt breathless, her heart pattering uncomfortably. "You are having me on, aren't you, Fenella?"

"No, Mum," Fenella cried. "I didn't believe him at first, of course I didn't, but he showed me a document that had already been drawn up at the bank. Apparently I'll hear officially tomorrow, but he wanted to tell me first, in person. He's leaving tomorrow." She ran her fingers through her hair. "I still can't take it in. It's incredible—"

"There's smoke coming from that pan behind you," Norah croaked. "I don't know what you two were gassing about in there but I bet it were nothin' to do with custard."

Fenella grimaced and whipped the smoking pan off the cooker. "Thanks, Gran – oh dear, the carrots have caught."

Marjorie's heart pounded. She stared around the kitchen, her head in a whirl.

Norah narrowed her eyes. "What were you talkin' about? When you're going to chuck me into a home, I suppose?"

Fenella was saved from replying as she dunked the smoking pan under the cold tap. The consequent smell and steam put paid to conversation for a few moments. Mechanically Marjorie threw open a window and the back door. Dazedly she strode outside, pacing to the wall of the adjoining house, trying to distance herself from the shock that was coursing through her.

"Phew, what a stink," Norah moaned as Fenella whirled a tea cloth, attempting to waft the scent out of the kitchen. She screwed up her nose and dropped her library book. "I'll shove off to the lounge," she muttered. "I can't stand this fug." She turned her chair fast and in doing so knocked the table leg. Which in turn rocked a stack of plates waiting to be put into the warming oven.

Instead of pausing Norah repeated the manoeuvre, so that her wheelchair hit the table leg yet again, the plates crashing to the floor with a smash that sounded throughout the entire house.

"Oh, glory." Norah sniggered.

Marjorie stepped back into the kitchen. "Mother, look what you've done, and deliberately too, you horrid woman. No, don't pretend it was an accident. You delight in causing us as much trouble as you can, don't you?" Marjorie gripped the wheelchair handles and crashed the wheelchair through the open kitchen door. She raced it along the hall, flung open the double doors to the lounge and wheeled Norah inside, crashing her chair into a bookcase in the process. "Stay here," she roared, "and mind your own business for once."

Marjorie's hands were shaking – her body felt weighted and a pounding in her chest alarmed yet fuelled the immense rage within her. She did not notice, nor care, whether there was anyone in the lounge. She merely slammed the glazed doors, retraced her steps along the corridor and bounded two steps at a time up the first short flight of stairs. She erupted into a tiny room that had long been her particular refuge at Bayview. In the old days it had been a linen room. She tore off her apron, plucked her coat from its hook and at the same time she kicked off her soft shoes and donned outdoor sandals. She barely breathed, so intent was she to flee. She had finally reached breaking point. It had only been the thought of finishing with this place in the very near future that had kept her going. Now, with Fenella's news, she knew that for her the end had come. She stepped briskly downstairs, gripping the bannister tightly, and marched to the kitchen.

"Mother, could you—"

"No, Fenella, I could not." She reached for her handbag. "I will not lift another finger in this house. I am now going back to my flat, in which I have spent far too little time since my retirement. I'm sorry to let you down, Fen-ella." Her breath was by now coming in gasps. "Yes... I'm... sorry..." She spread her hands wide and Fenella realised that her mother was shuddering with furious pent-up emotion.

Fenella reached towards her. Marjorie backed away. "No, don't touch me! I've got all I need. I'm leaving. I'll be, erm... No... Fen-ella, I can't..." She swallowed. "Sorry..." Tears erupted down her cheeks. "Your news. I... no..." She stepped swiftly into the yard.

Fenella flung down the saucepan she'd been gripping. "Mum, wait. I'll get you a brandy or something. I'm sorry. I thought you'd be pleased. It's been so awful, knowing we'd be thrown out. It was your home too—"

Marjorie struggled for speech. "Stop it, stop it, I hate this place, Fenella. Have you never realised that fact?" Marjorie drew herself up and fastened the buttons on her jacket. "No, stay back. I'm going home and likely as not I'll have a brandy there. You can visit me... later, if you like. I daresay I may feel more myself... by then." She took a ragged breath. "I'd like to know more about this George Stevens and who the hell he thinks he is." She cast Fenella a bleak glance. "But whatever." She shrugged. "This place is nothing to do with me anymore. This is my last moment in Bayview, forever."

Deliberately Marjorie wiped her feet on the worn coir mat before stepping out onto the concrete of the yard.

"Mother," Fenella entreated, "don't go like this, please. I'm sorry if I upset you, telling you so abruptly, for God's sake. If you don't want to stay here you don't have to. I never said that. I thought you'd be pleased."

"Well, I'm not," Marjorie shouted, and slammed the yard door so hard that it vibrated for several moments after she'd disappeared.

The sound of giggles from an upper floor made Fenella look up. Two youngsters were leaning out, listening.

Fenella glared and stamped back indoors. She gave one look at the mess of smashed crockery, sniffed the scent of burned carrots and swore loudly, just as Emily and Tom came walking in, exuding happiness.

"Good," she said tartly. "You're waiting on, tonight, Tom, and you can give me a hand here, Emily. We've got a bit of an emergency."

Tom and Emily exchanged glances and knew better than to object.

Norah had not been unduly upset by Marjorie's outburst. She had long thought that her daughter was too amenable. "It'll do her good, to blow off steam," she muttered as she wheeled herself towards the coffee table set in the bay window. With an eager claw she poked about in the pile of glossy brochures and magazines piled on the small table. "Bloomin' rubbish," she muttered, her hands sliding through the pile and carelessly tossing many of them onto the floor. Finally, she pounced on a copy of Hello.

"I'll bet Fenella doesn't know this is here," she chortled, "else she'd chuck it." Greedily Norah drew it onto her lap and began to riffle through the bright pages. As she was inspecting the grossly ostentatious interior of a minor celebrity's home the door burst open and a couple of children ran in.

As Norah looked up, unbothered by their shrieking entrance but always agog for new experiences, she suddenly realised that she was not the only occupant of the lounge. In the corner, almost hidden by the wing of an armchair, a dark-suited figure was slumped behind a newspaper. Norah's face, primed in a grin for the two youngsters, froze. Dread gripped her. It was that grim-looking bloke she had seen from the window. What had Fenella said his name was? George Stevens?

The children, a boy and girl, were racing round the coffee table, giggling. The man lowered his paper to glare at them.

God! George Stevens? Rubbish, utter rubbish. Christ, she couldn't think how she hadn't known him right away. Strip away the jewels and the creases and his was the face that had haunted her... for decades...

As the children continued to scream and chase one another Norah's and his eyes locked, in what might have been, in ordinary circumstances, a complicit glance between two elderly people at the unthinking behaviour of the young.

Norah felt nausea gather in her throat. She was satisfied to know that her suspicions had been well founded, but this brought scant comfort. She threw the magazine down and wheeled herself to the door. "Open it," she rasped at one of the children, almost tripping the other one in her desperation to get away. The girl backed off but the boy darted forward. "All right, Granny." He giggled, pulling the door wide.

Norah felt panic in the back of her throat. The kitchen was the nearest retreat, but Fenella and Marjorie would be there, and Marje was already in a stew. Besides, though Marje might understand, Fenella wouldn't. She couldn't. She didn't know, did she?

The lift hummed down and slid open. The parents of the youngsters stepped out, looking cross. "Where the blazes have those rips got to now?" the father growled. "I'll give them what for."

"They're in the lounge," Norah snapped, "making a bloody nuisance of themselves." She slipped past the couple, entered the lift and operated the buttons with a bony finger. The doors slid shut, just as she saw George Stevens pass towards the stairs.

Norah's heart hammered. She clutched her chest. She wondered if she might have a heart attack. That would serve them right. She'd said she suspected him, but no one had listened. As the lift passed the first floor she held her breath, terrified that it might stop. He might have been waiting for just such an opportunity to get her. But the lift didn't stop and at the second floor the doors opened to an empty landing. Norah negotiated the awkward turn in the corridor and paused outside room number thirteen. She lifted her fist and banged on it.

"Quick, Percy, let me in."

Percy Corlett, surprised but unflustered, opened the door, a towel in his hands. "Hello, Norah. Come in, what's up?"

"I need help, Percy, I need help."

Percy stood back as Norah wheeled herself into his room.

George Stevens fastened his overcoat and checked his wallet with trembling fingers. He would go out to eat. He had seen an Italian restaurant in St Paul's Square on his morning walk. It would be pleasant to have pasta and wine for supper. He had done his duty. He could now think of his own future. His new, tremulous optimism accompanied him down the stairs and through the front door. As luck would have it, no one saw him leave. It might have been good manners to tell Mrs Kelly that he would not be in for the evening meal, but he evaded that politeness without a touch of conscience. He had put himself out enough for Mrs Kelly and her family.

The encounter in the lounge had been unfortunate.

George stumbled as he stepped off the pavement. He righted himself and thrust his hands in his pockets. He felt uncommonly cold, though it was a mild evening and the air was sweet with wafted honey scents from the heather-clad hills.

George pursed his lips. He didn't care for these rich scents; he would have been happier walking through the less cheerful streets at home. He was not attuned to such bright surroundings. The brilliance of the light haunted him; it swept him back. The sooner he returned home the better.

George's pace increased as his heartbeat slowed. Soon he would leave this right, tight little island, where the past mocked him from every direction. M'm… all at once he felt hungry, properly hungry, for the first time in days. The relief inside him distanced all the negative thoughts that had plagued him for so long. How good it was to be done with… the matter. Sweet Mary, that confrontation in the lounge had been horrifying: the recognition; those bloodshot eyes, mirroring the shock in his own. More than fifty years. How she had changed. He could not have believed it. In his mind she had always looked the same.

A car whizzed past, narrowly missing him. He stepped back, smiling apologetically as the driver sounded his horn. The river was full, the water dancing beneath the evening sun. Boats bobbed, their rigging chattering. His footsteps rang as he crossed the bridge. Smoke rose lazily from chimneys. There was a haze over the water in the harbour and a family of swans sailing serenely had a filmy impressionist look about them.

Soon it would be autumn. George shivered. He would not like to be here then. He had had enough of this place. Tomorrow he would leave. Carefully he looked both ways as he crossed the road to the square. He passed pubs, noisy with evening drinkers. An elderly lady out walking a small dog looked suspiciously at him as he passed. Her face was not unlike Norah's.

George smiled bitterly, making fists of his pocketed hands. She was old, and he was old. All old people bear a certain resemblance.

The restaurant lay ahead. George's nose twitched, already smelling Parmesan, garlic and rich tomato sauce, though when he stepped inside the smells faded.

That was the trouble with old age: imagination and the past played tricks. What was real and what was not often merged; sometimes it became difficult to separate the two.

He was directed to a window table. He refused. He did not want to look out. He wanted to forget Ramsey Town. Now, as far as he was concerned, Ramsey lay faraway in his past.

The waiter approached. George held out his hand for the menu.

An hour and a half later Tom and Emily hurried out of the front door, Emily shrugging herself into her jacket. "Well, what was all that about?"

"I've no idea. I'm sorry I had to put you through that, Em, but I couldn't get out of helping Mum in the circs."

Emily snuggled close. "It wasn't your fault. If it was anyone's it was your gran's. Why was she so furious?"

"I don't know. Well, I know what Mum said but it didn't make sense and I'm not about to have it out with her. Not in the mood she's in."

Emily shivered. "No, she looked livid. Shocked too, I felt sorry for her, but…" She squeezed Tom's arm. "I'm glad we've come out. Where are we going?"

Tom shrugged. "Haven't a clue. The pub, I suppose. It's a bit chilly for a paddle."

Emily grinned up at him. "Poor Tom. You're not very good at waiting at tables, are you?"

"I'm hopeless. I don't know how Gran and Mum cope. I'm always fingers and thumbs and never know what to say, either when I dump a plate or when I collect it." He glanced at Emily and heaved a breath. "Thank God I didn't go in for catering, eh?"

They giggled and hurried along the road, a chill wind blowing from the hills. Emily put her hand into Tom's. "Your mum looked really upset. What will she do?"

"God knows. In my entire life I've never known Gran walk out. Apparently she doesn't want anything more to do with Bayview, period."

Emily grimaced. "Whew! Do you think she meant it?"

"Who'd know? Hell, there's Great-Gran and Percy. We'll go this way. I've had enough of my family for today." He put his arm round Emily's warm body. "We'll go to the Bridge Inn. Gran won't go there – it's usually stuffed with young people. Gran doesn't like young people."

Emily smiled. "She likes you. She positively dotes on you. I can tell."

"That's because I'm different."

"You are." Emily squeezed his arm. "You're unique, and I'm very fond of you."

Tom dropped a kiss on Emily's head and hugged her close. He didn't see the rueful expression rise to Emily's eyes, as if she was already regretting her impetuous declaration.

Meanwhile Norah and Percy had reached the swing bridge. "Where are we going?" Percy asked.

"Try the Trafalgar," Norah snapped. "I want to get drunk."

Percy smiled tolerantly. "You'll fall out of your chair if you do."

"Don't care!" Norah rasped, and stuck her tongue out at him.

Percy laughed. "I can manage a couple of pints, but that's all. It's not pension day, y'know."

Norah stuck her hand in her pocket and pulled out a bundle of notes. "I've raided my piggy bank," she leered.

Fenella stood before the attic window, gazing at the promenade and the rise of the sand cliffs beyond. After the kitchen had been tidied she'd trudged upstairs with the intention of converting her tumultuous emotions into something memorable. Yet all her resolve had weakened once she gazed at a blank canvas. Yet earlier, as she'd carved roast pork she had already had an idea in mind a dramatic composition of vying elements. She'd been on a high for a while – the incredible fact that she was suddenly free from debt, or soon would be, had felt exciting. Though by the time she was doling out the last portion of pudding, apple crumble that evening, she was already feeling anti-climactic. If Marjorie had been serious then change was imminent. So she was virtually back to square one, as well as being estranged from Marjorie.

By the time the dining room was cleared and Tom and Emily left, her optimism had virtually evaporated.

She plumped onto a stool to stare from one of the wide-paned windows. Firstly Gran had to be moved to a nursing home, pronto. Much as she loved Norah, Fenella knew that coping single-handedly with her incontinence and her moods on her own was not possible.

So, with Norah and Marjorie gone, what then? Did she want to rattle about in Bayview on her own? Tom would be at his flat for nine months of his year. She leaned her head against the window jamb, staring at the sea, which was restless that evening, chivvied by a brisk breeze. She'd felt calm earlier, in those first few moments when George Stevens had dropped his bombshell. All the burden of anxiety had tumbled away and she'd felt an amazing lightness of spirits at the prospect of life continuing smoothly, the way it had done for years, only better, because she'd not have to worry about the mortgage.

Sighing now, she smiled sadly, and running her fingers down the flaking paint of the window frame just emphasised that realisation. The house was long past its best. She might love this eyrie, with its sloping ceiling and salt-stained dormer, probably because she'd done some of her best work here. But the truth was that Bayview needed to be either totally refurbished or demolished.

Yes, she had to face it. Unless she wanted to end up like Miss Havisham, she needed to change her life. No matter how many tourist pictures she might produce they would not be enough to fund restoration and food.

A film of perspiration erupted under her cotton shirt. She'd regarded George Stevens' offer as an escape route, but Mum hadn't. Mum had been outraged. Furious, devastated, there was no word too strong, and that was awful. Was this partly her fault? Had she unwittingly been making her mother's life a misery since she'd retired? Poor Mum. Why had she not spoken out earlier? Why had she bottled all that frustration up?

Fenella flushed; she knew well enough why. Marjorie was too polite for her own good and she was used to being leaned upon.

"Drat. Drat. Drat!" Fenella banged her fist on the windowsill. How could she have been so self-absorbed? Why had she not realised sooner that Marjorie hated her duties at Bayview?

Fenella heard the roar of a car outside. Peering down she saw Charlie Peake's sleek grey Jaguar cruising past. She stiffened and quickly moved from the window. "No matter what might happen now, Charlie, Bayview will never be yours," she whispered. And then she felt guilty. Why did she like him so deeply? She turned, surveyed the unfinished composition that she'd had such hopes for. Now all enthusiasm was dead. Bare-footed she padded to the door, put her feet into the mules that she'd kicked off earlier and crept downstairs.

Charles drove thoughtfully along the length of the Mooragh promenade, accelerated up the steep hill beside the Grand Island Hotel, thought briefly, as he paused at the stop sign, of dropping in for a drink, but instead turned left and took the road back to the town centre.

He had fretted most of the day as to what could be done re Bayview. He knew he had to act clever and quickly or he'd lose the property, and even the possibility of such an outcome made his blood boil. Cudgelling over the whole matter since the morning had brought on a bout of acid indigestion, to which Charlie was prone when he got tense and which was sometimes tricky to cure. A brisk tour of his garden after his evening meal hadn't worked at all, like it usually did. His abdomen felt rigid and painful. Rather than try a spot of calm meditation, which his last-but-one therapist recommended, Charlie decided he needed a more prosaic and manly remedy. It was all very well counting breaths in and out, but how many would it take to help his mood and his guts? *Sod that for a game of soldiers*, he thought, changing gear and racing the red light at the foot of Bowring Road. What he needed was a few relaxing pints of Okell's best bitter, and with luck, while he was knocking them back he might hear some gossip about this Bayview business. Then he'd be killing two birds at a bargain price. Charlie beamed, cut across the bonnet of a Volvo at the harbour roundabout and headed along the quay to his favourite hostelry.

Charlie drove fast, blatantly ignoring the thirty-mile-an-hour restriction. He'd like to see the local plod with nerve enough to book him for speeding. Then he had to stamp on his brakes as a woman with a dog stepped onto the pedestrian crossing near the swing bridge, and to crown this hold-up he had to wait while Tom Kelly and his skinny girlfriend crossed as well. He glared after them as they slipped into a side street, long enough for the motorist behind to hoot. Charlie gave a two-fingered acknowledgement and raced towards St Paul's Square.

Though there were several pubs in this picturesque area Charlie had a particular destination in mind and didn't slow till he could see a familiar car parked outside the Viking Hotel. He turned abruptly and drove back to the swing bridge, turning onto it heedlessly, causing a group of children to leap to the safety of the pavement. He crossed the bridge at double the statutory speed and headed for a gap in the parked cars along River Road. Aye, there was one just where he wanted. Pleased, he eased himself out of his seat, clicked on the car alarm and strode breezily back the way he'd come. Strangely his indigestion had lessened already. Within moments he was striding into the Viking Hotel as though he owned the place. The landlord, looking up, muttered to the barmaid under his breath. She grimaced and slipped into the other bar.

"Evening, Charlie," the landlord greeted him. "Your usual?" he asked, reaching for a spirit glass. A customer leaning against the bar quietly sipping his pint almost choked as Charlie clapped him on the shoulder.

"There you are, Willie," he cried. "I reckon we'll settle at a table shall we, to discuss our business, eh? Yes, that's fine, Ted – oh, and a pint. And a chaser for Willie here. You could do with a chaser, couldn't you, Willie?"

Under the window, draining his half-pint glass, Peter Quilliam, newly off duty, watched a grimace cross Will Kaneen's features as he obediently nodded. Peter cast an amused glance at the two men and nodded at the landlord for another half pint.

Casually he watched as Charlie and Will Kaneen settled in a dim corner. Willie continued to look anxious, while Charlie chatted cheerily. Charlie was at his most expansive, beaming and calling the landlord to fill Willie's glass less than five minutes later, though the man had barely sipped his first tot. Charles had swigged his in double-quick time.

Peter smiled, recalling Charlie Peake's unique talent for getting up people's noses while never seeming aware of the fact. He took a pull at his local beer; it was good to be back on the island, enjoying some time off, and at the same watching Charles and Willie planning some undoubtedly dodgy deal. This was also markedly better than sitting in his dismal flat watching a dreary TV soap. Whatever the two chums were discussing Charlie was clearly putting pressure on Will Kaneen. The man was sweating and shifting restlessly like an anxious child. Idly Peter was not overly interested in what they might be discussing. Charles's dealing didn't usually merit official attention; he was much too canny for that.

Peter began to feel drowsy. A match was playing on the large screen. Idly he watched, because it was there, and because he was enjoying his beer. After a while, he considered another drink, consulted his insides and decided that a takeout Chinese supper would benefit him more and possibly give him the required energy to catch up on his pile of ironing.

The town clock was striking the half hour as he left, nodding farewell to the landlord and noting in passing that Will Kaneen now looked drained, while Charlie Peake looked elated. There was little space on their table for another glass.

Unaware that he had verified an early-evening alibi for the men, Peter strolled towards St Paul's Square and the alley that would lead him swiftly to his chosen takeaway. He was feeling almost cheerful. If he'd been across on the city streets across at this time he'd be on the lookout for trouble. Here there was no trouble – life was slower, simpler. He was, for the moment, content.

Fifty minutes later Charles emerged unsteadily from the pub. He gripped a nearby lamppost then inhaled deeply and smiled, a full, fatuous grin. He felt on top of the world. Willie had told him all he needed and a little more besides, and then had weaved his way home.

Charles had thoroughly enjoyed his evening. He'd exchanged pleasantries with a few punters; he'd ignored some who needed ignoring. That was the one of the good things about living where you'd grown up. There was always someone to natter to, usually someone to impress. Just a pity there hadn't been any women about.

Without too much hesitation Charlie ambled across the quay and focused his steps towards the swing bridge. The tide was high, water was lapping beneath the roadway, sucking and slapping, river and seawater combining. Charlie hiccupped, belched and proceeded unsteadily. He generally parked on the far side of the bridge, reckoning it was safer than the quay. He didn't want his car vomited on, or worse. Even Ramsey had a few vandals and he had no intention of making his pride and joy a target.

"The problems of prominence," Charlie mouthed to himself, though the words didn't come out easily at all. He sniffed energetically. The night air would soon freshen him up. He prided himself on always taking the air last thing; it was something someone had once told him was beneficial. "Helps a person sleep." He chuckled, though the observation wasn't really comical. That made him frown, then smile. What he did like, last thing, was to plan for the morrow. After chatting to Willie, well... He smiled toothily, pulled out a cigarette and lit it, tossing the wrapper heedlessly into the glittering river while smugly reflecting on Willie's fascinating disclosure. Charlie had always known there was some ancient festering secret concerned with Fenella's family. He recalled his mum twittering about it. What Willie had revealed was more than juicy; it had been downright spicy. More than enough to shame Fenella Kelly if it got about. Not that it would from him. Not now. Not when his plans came to fray-oo-shun... Was that what he was trying to say...? No, it wasn't. Why was his tongue so un-con-roll-able?

He fumbled for his car keys, realising it might be sensible to get home. His hand deep in his pocket, he saw a hunched figure ambling ahead of him. Blearily Charlie peered again until recognition dawned. When it did he smiled. Tossing away his cigarette he pocketed his car keys and turned to follow the now-shadowy figure. He tried to hurry but found that hurrying was beyond his sluggish limbs. *My gum all*, he thought anxiously. *Mebbe I took more than w's wise.* Doggedly he pursued his quarry, while trusting that the night air might sober him up. He had sense enough to be grateful he had not got into his car. He might have got copped. That'd be bad. Now, by following this old man he might… well, he din't know yet, but what a chance? "Jus' wait, Fenella," he slurred. "I'll get yer house yet."

SEVEN

Bertram Bryant rose regularly at six am. After a mug of peppermint tea and feeding Bessie her customary half tin of Pal he would don his jacket and cap, clip on Bessie's lead and they would leave the house. Bertram had walked Bessie at the same time each day for ten years. The dog was now his only companion. Mildred Bryant had died the previous autumn, and though Bertram missed her company, he was not sorry to be alone. His life had been devoted to Mildred's every whim and occasionally he had resented this obligation – for she had rarely been grateful.

Whereas Bessie needed nothing more than a couple of walks and a couple of easy meals each day and was constantly loving. He and Bessie had the ideal relationship. She listened to each word he said and never answered back.

"You're a good lass, Bess," Bertram declared, smiling at the little dog as he pulled the freshly painted gate shut behind them. As they crossed the road, Bessie pulled on her lead. She still yearned to walk in Mooragh Park, so close and previously so convenient. Ramsey town commissioners had recently decided to exclude dogs from this large public amenity, whether on a lead or not, so Bessie had to be walked and sometimes let off her lead on a stretch of grass beside the rugby field, just across the road from the sea. Though each morning Bertram did his brief recce of the park and its splendid lake as they walked beside the perimeter hedge. He enjoyed the daily differences in the water surface. On calm days there would be reflections of trees, bushes and of the substantial houses on the hillside opposite, and when the weather was stormy the lake would be alive with jostling waves that jogged the pleasure boats at their moorings.

It was glassy-calm that day, the entire mirror-like surface reflecting all that was around and above it. Bertram paused, smiling at the reflections presented, of palm trees on the central island, of various shrubs beside the café and the rowing boats and canoes jigging gently at their moorings. He sniffed the cool morning scents and beamed.

"It's grand being alive, isn't it, Bessie?" he said, and his gaze rose to the rise of hills above Ramsey and the masts on Snaefell Mountain and beyond.

As his eyes swept back across the view a peripheral flash of something out of place in the tranquil scene made him jolt to a sudden halt, involuntarily jerking Bessie so that the plump old dog sat down with a jolt. Reproachfully she whined, turning big eyes in unspoken hurt.

"Sorry, old girl," Bertram muttered, trying to reconcile what he was seeing with any likely explanation.

It was no good. He couldn't. "That doesn't look right, Bessie, something's amiss. That fella's lying uncommon still." He pulled the dog's lead gently. "Come along, old girl, I reckon we'd better investigate, and you're coming too. Ramsey town commissioners can go hang for once."

Bertram and Bessie hurried to the nearest entrance, a yellow-painted gate that opened with a squeak of unoiled hinges. Bertram had to step carefully as he pulled Bessie through the gateway and hurried down the short, steep path. His eyes kept flickering to the figure he'd spotted, lying near the lake. The man, if a man it was, was slumped askew, his head almost submerged, or... "Oh dear, I don't like this at all," Bertram gasped, the thump of his heart sounding in his ears. As he got closer, the figure's stillness, and the fact that the head and shoulders of the person were not visible, told Bertram that what he was approaching could only be a corpse.

Yet he approached warily, unwilling to make a fuss should someone, for whatever reason, be merely taking an early-morning wash, or a drink of the clear, lapping water.

Yet his hammering heart told him that this person had drunk his last, and probably some time ago. The water was lapping at the person's neck and judging from the puffy blur, which was all Bertram could make out of the face through the green-tinged water, and the glistening dew on the man's dark overcoat, Bertram reckoned he had been lying dead for some considerable time.

Bertram stared around desperately, hoping that some other early riser might be in sight. But there was no one, either in the park or on the road.

"We'll have to go home and ring the police, Bessie," he said briskly. "Come along, old girl. I can't lift the poor fellow out of the water on my own, and I doubt it's worth trying. It'll not make a difference." Bertram retraced his steps, casting anxious glances back every now and then, in case, by some chance, he had been dreaming. But he hadn't. His thumping heart told him that.

He hurried to his bungalow and fumbled in his pocket for his keys. Bessie looked distressed. "Poor lamb," Bertram soothed. "You'll have to go in the garden, don't go messing on my rose bed, there's a girl." Bessie, released from her lead, obediently trotted off to the farthest corner of the garden. Bertram let himself into the house, gathered breath into his lungs, which made him cough a little but calmed him enough to lift the telephone receiver and speak into it.

"Police, please, and hurry." Bertram looked at his watch. It was still only six twenty-five.

Marjorie opened her eyes as the police siren sounded somewhere nearby. She had been dreaming. She, Donald and baby Fenella had been about to set sail for Australia, and a new life.

Reality flooded into her mind along with the bright morning sunlight dappling through the curtains onto her narrow bed. Dismay flooded her. Donald was long gone, bless his heart, Fenella was a grown woman and she was a grandmother who had yesterday walked out on her responsibilities.

She sighed but resolutely glanced at the clock and closed her eyes once more, willing herself to sleep again; it was too early to start to worry. Besides, hadn't she decided last night that from now on she was to think of herself first and plan out what *she* wanted to do next? It had seemed an easy decision to make with a couple of brandies inside her. Now, in the bold lemon light of early morning she knew it might not be an easy resolution to keep.

She snuggled into the smooth sheets bought from Looney's shop in the town and tried to think selfish, pleasant thoughts. Didn't she deserve a lie-in? Wasn't that the least she could give herself at the beginning of her new life? Especially after what had happened last night, before the brandies had numbed her…

Fenella heard the sirens too, though she was already awake. She padded to her bedroom window which overlooked a lane, though between the houses beyond she could see tiny glimpses of the park. She saw the edge of a brightly painted vehicle – a police car.

"More vandalism, I expect." She sighed, recalling some shrieks from that direction the previous evening. With her dressing gown securely belted she stole downstairs; the old house, with its familiar morning creaks, greeted her every step. In the kitchen she filled the kettle, switched it on and unbolted the back door, just in case. She didn't think Marjorie would come, but if she did, she wanted it to be easy. She hoped her mum was regretting her outburst. It was just not like her to take on so.

As Fenella brewed tea and started to collect breakfast cutlery she tried to feel cheerful about the day ahead, though she did not dwell on what the old man had revealed the previous evening. Had it maybe been a ruse? Her insides twisted. But what if it were true? She shook herself into brisk concentration. She had ten guests, eight adults and two children checking out after breakfast that day, so there would be plenty to keep her busy. Several guest rooms would have to be cleaned and prepared for the new arrivals due later.

Fenella perched on a stool and sipped a cup of hot strong tea – a good morning cuppa – and though she tried to stay upbeat she felt bad. She hated rows, hated that her mother was unhappy – and realised too that she felt tired. One good thing was that the summer season was almost over.

"And I'm glad," she murmured.

The kitchen door swung open. "'Allo, 'allo, talking to yourself?" Tom, tousled and bleary, stepped inside and pulled the door shut. "Morning, Mum," he croaked. "I heard you come down. What's all the palaver at the park? It must be something serious, or they wouldn't have used the siren."

Fenella shrugged but said nothing.

Tom patted her hand. "Don't worry, Mum, it'll work out. Gran will come round and Great-Gran will—"

"No, Tom. Don't even attempt to gloss things over. Norah needs to go into a home and that's that. Mum has done more than enough for us here and she deserves some time for herself." Fenella traced the pattern on her mug with a finger. "It's time for a change for me too."

Tom stared. "But… you said this guy wants to buy the place, so that you, Gran and Great-Gran can carry on here. Isn't that what you've always wanted? You've been dead set against moving. This is our home and where you paint."

Fenella shrugged. "M'm. Now that I may not have to leave it's just struck me that I'd be mad to stay on. God, Tom, it's time I got a life. Taking in visitors is not much of an existence, is it? It would be different if we were really busy but those days are long past. The Isle of Man might still be lovely, but guesthouses are not a tourist's first choice any longer, certainly not if they're like this place, old-fashioned and run-down. It's finance and business, as well as the TT races, of course, that fund the island, not kipper-loving visitors who want to stay in quaint, out-of-the-way places."

"Is that a good thing? I couldn't believe how busy it was at lunchtime when I was in M&S in Douglas recently. Full of guys and girls in suits, all talking jargon."

"There you are. So who am I to fight the tide?"

Tom scratched his stubbly chin. "I mean – well, when I'm gone?"

"I meant to ask, is Emily staying here as originally planned while she's on the dig or staying at your flat?" Fenella enquired with a subdued grin.

Tom shrugged. "I think maybe she'd like to stay with me at Peel. You don't mind, do you?"

"Course not. It's natural and I'm happy for you both."

"Nothing's settled, Mum. After she goes back, well, who can say?" He looked glum. "She's got things to achieve, apparently. I'm not sure where, or if, I fit in."

"That's natural. You've got a career to concentrate on too, don't forget."

"I know," Tom sighed. "I think Emily's great, Mum, and I'd like to, you know, but once she's away?" He heaved a sigh.

Fenella got up and, after a glance at the clock, refilled the kettle. "I'm glad you're being sensible." She took down a tray. "If I give you this for Norah can you take it up while I shower and dress?" She laid a plate and cup and saucer on the tray.

"OK," Tom said, grimacing.

"It's all right. I'll clean her up. I wouldn't expect you to do that."

"Thanks." He squirmed. "I couldn't. I don't know how Gran's

stuck to it for so long. It makes me glad I didn't go in for geriatric nursing like Great-Gran wanted me to, do you remember?"

Fenella chuckled. "Of course I remember. It was when you'd got your GCSEs, wasn't it? She was having you on, you know. She used to go into fits behind your back."

"Did she? The wily so-and-so. I'd got a starred pass in biology and chemistry, and she got all that bumph from the local day centre about geriatric care. They were on a recruitment drive or something."

"She's a case," Fenella agreed wryly, filling a teapot and setting it on the tray. She added a piece of bread and butter and a couple of biscuits. "There you are, get her roused and tell her I'll be up soon."

Tom picked up the tray. "Wilco."

"And do your dressing gown up, or Norah will be making comments about your body."

"What's wrong with my body?"

"Nothing when you're your age. When you're her age the sight of all that youthful flesh rankles."

"I suppose it must," Tom said, hastily knotting his belt. "It can't be much fun, being old. At least you don't have to worry about that, Mum." He eased the tray around the door.

"Thanks," Fenella said dryly, trying to take the comment as a compliment. "Off you go and let me gather my thoughts before the guests appear, sniffing for bacon and eggs."

"Right! Hey, listen," Tom cried, as another police siren sounded. "Once I've roused Gran I'm going to see what's going on."

"If you must." Fenella yawned.

Peter Quilliam looked down at the body, feeling the usual mix of dread, excitement and revulsion that being a suspicious death evoked. Though he'd seen his fair share of corpses in his years of service there was still a pang, and this one was tinged with outrage. He hadn't returned to the Manx force for this. Dead 'uns might be part of the daily routine 'across' but here – it wasn't right. He pushed this and other unprofessional thoughts to the back of his mind. "How long since, Derek?"

The police surgeon looked up grimly. "About eight hours ago? Drowned, I'd surmise, but I can't state that categorically. See here? This contusion looks recent." He sat back on his heels. "Could be his heart just gave up. He's in poor shape. So, a possible natural demise due to a fracas."

Peter frowned. "He's lying at an odd angle. If he'd collapsed he'd have stuck his hands out, wouldn't he? Do you reckon he's been, um, maybe, arranged?"

The police surgeon raised his eyebrows. "You're the detective, Pete. I'll not try to tell you your job."

"Sorry, Derek. Go on."

"There's not a lot more to say. Rigor has worn off, so that gives death at, m'mm, eleven-ish last night, though it was mild, so maybe later."

Peter surveyed the elderly man's attire. "Looks uncommonly formal. I wonder who he is? Not local?"

"M'mm, I agree. Certainly I've never seen him about, and notwithstanding his immersion his facial skin is sallow. I would say he's not been subject to the bracing Manx air for long. Yes, a city type, I'd guess. His clothes are good quality. Hands clean, nails carefully trimmed." Derek jumped nimbly to his feet. "I'll do the necessary, once your blokes have got photos and so on. The PM will provide more substantial information. OK?"

"Yes, thanks, Derek." Peter turned away and spoke to the young officer who had been first on the scene. He gestured for him to accompany him as he approached the elderly man who was standing uneasily some distance away, a terrier close by his side, as if guarding him. Peter smiled as he neared. "Good morning, Mr Bryant, isn't it? I believe you found the body?"

"Aye, I did. Me and Bessie."

Peter smiled at Bessie, who wagged her stump of a tail. "I think you can get off home now, sir. Thank you for contacting us. An officer will call later today to take a statement."

Bertram frowned. "I might not be in later. I go out with Bessie regular, through the day."

"Um," Peter glanced at the young officer, "why don't you go with Mr Bryant, Davis? Take a statement now, while things are fresh in his mind. All right?"

PC Davis nodded and touched his helmet respectfully. "Yes, sir. Come along, Mr Bryant, you live across the road, don't you?"

Peter watched the pair walk off, Davis's head nodding at Bertram's side as the old man talked, confiding that he'd never found a body before and was quite shook up. Peter heard Davis reply that a cup of tea would be just the ticket and would set them both up. Peter smiled. The young constable was clearly at ease in his job and had a natural rapport, which was heartening to observe. *A young officer worth watching*, he thought approvingly, before turning back to the sad remains with reluctance. Sudden death was always shocking, no matter how many corpses one had viewed. The CID photographer completed his work and the body was declared ready to move.

Detective Sergeant Dave Colvin held up a plastic bag. "I've emptied his pockets, Peter. There's not much, save for cash. Whoever did for him, if it was deliberate, then robbery wasn't the reason." He held out an evidence bag holding a wallet packed with credit cards and a well-filled notecase. "There's also a pen, handkerchief and gold fob watch."

"Yes, but who was he?"

Dave held the bag closer so that Peter could read through the polythene. "Curiously he has business cards in two names. Georgio Stephani on some and George Stevens on others."

"Unusual." Peter gazed towards the figure as it was hoisted expertly onto a stretcher and carried swiftly towards the mortuary van. "We'll get back and run some checks on both identities. I don't think there's much more we can do here. The SOCO boys will be busy for a while." Peter had a word with the scenes of crime officer, whose men had rigged tape and posts around where the body had been found, before he and Dave hurried back to their car.

As they drove away they passed Tom Kelly crossing the road to the park. Peter raised a hand in greeting and at the same time gave a gusty sigh.

Dave glanced sideways. "What's up? Who've you seen?"

"Nothing and no one." Peter's tone was brusque. "I'm hungry, that's all – missed my breakfast, didn't I? Now, let's dwell on the matter in hand. If we can get this sudden death sorted it will mean that Douglas won't send down a posse of high-powered detectives who'll push us around."

Dave looked uneasy. "They'll come whether we do or not, won't they?"

"Probably, even so. It's not that I've any relish for solving a sudden death, but it'd be good if we could deal with it ASAP."

"Suits me, guv." Dave grinned. "What do we do first?"

"We get some food inside us," Peter said feelingly. "Let's stop at the bakery for some pasties."

"Good plan." Dave smiled and drove just above the speed limit towards the early-opening confectionary shop in St Paul's Square. The church clock struck eight as they parked.

Tom slammed through the backyard gate, walked in four strides to the kitchen and threw open the door. "Guess what's up, Mum? One of your guests has got himself knocked off!"

Fenella was frying eggs. Emily was cutting crusts off bread to be toasted. They gaped.

"Old Daddy Bryant found him, you know, the bloke from the first bungalow," Tom jerked his head, "across from the Mooragh?"

"Yes, heavens, Tom, this is dreadful. Who is it?" Fenella laid the spatula on the edge of the pan while the eggs hissed and sizzled.

Tom frowned. "You're not going to like this, Mum. I was talking to one of the scenes of crime officers. Barry – er, I dunno, Barry someone, I was at school with him. He wasn't meant to let on, really, but it'll be all over town soon enough, and they needed to know where he came from, so when I said he was staying here they were dead grateful." Tom almost giggled at his pun then went hurriedly on. "They thanked me for telling them and one of them got on to Peter Quilliam. So you'll hear from him next, I suppose."

"But who's dead?"

"Yes, Tom, who?" Emily said, waving a bread knife threateningly.

"George Stevens." Tom shrugged. "I thought you'd have guessed by the way I was building up to it."

Fenella gasped.

"Sorry, Mum. Heaven knows where this leaves you but I bet there'll be no transaction going through now."

Tom giggled. "God, this is exciting. I expect we'll have the press and Border TV and all sorts pestering us." His eyes gleamed as though the prospect pleased him.

"Tom!" Fenella and Emily both exclaimed.

Fenella glanced at the frying pan and saw that two of the eggs were more than well done. She hastily lifted them out, grabbing a tea towel to wipe her hands. She turned the gas down and slid the pan off the cooker. "Now, calm down and tell us slowly. How did the poor man die? Do you think I should go over? Did he fall in the lake? Tch! How tragic. He looked ill last night, but—"

"I don't know," Tom said. "No, don't go over – his body's just been taken off and I think they're treating his death as suspicious. Apparently he was lying half off the path with his head in the water, so they don't think it was accidental."

"Good God," Fenella paled. "How dreadful." She groped her way to a chair.

Emily glared at Tom. "Cool it, Tom. Why don't you make it even more graphic? Can't you see your mum's shocked, even if you aren't? Make her a cup of tea or something."

Tom looked guilty. "Sorry, Mum, do you want tea?"

Fenella opened her mouth, then glanced at the clock and jumped up. "Yes, but we must get on. The guests will be coming down."

"One of them won't," Tom remarked brightly, earning himself another glare from Emily. "Well, it's true. He's dead, and I suppose someone had better go up to his room and look for details of his next of kin."

Fenella pushed the tray of eggs into the warming oven. "No, leave things exactly as they are. If the police are involved we mustn't interfere with anything." She sat at the table, running her hands through her hair. "I can't believe it. The poor devil, he can't have returned last night. I didn't realise. I locked the door at eleven as usual and never suspected he wasn't in." She sighed despairingly. "I might have known what he offered was too good to be true. Still, we're no worse off than we were before, whereas he... Poor old fellow... Thanks, Tom." She took a filled mug from him and shakily sipped it, her eyes blurring with sudden tears. Quickly she wiped them away and swung round to look again at the clock.

Tom followed her glance. "Mum, forget the guests for once. There's only ten, um, no, nine now, oh, and Percy and Eloise."

Fenella gulped at the hot tea; she could hear footsteps already on the stairs. "There, guests are coming down. If the police are on their way then we must get everyone fed, and then whatever happens that's done. Thank God it's the end of the week and this lot are going home today."

"Will they be allowed to go?" Emily asked curiously. "Won't everyone who has been in contact with Mr Stevens be under suspicion, you know, like in TV crime shows?"

Fenella looked startled. "Surely not? It won't be murder. Things like that don't happen in the Isle of Man."

Emily shrugged. "Don't they?"

The doorbell rang stridently. Tom leapt up.

"No, I'll go," Fenella said, pushing past. "Ring the gong for the meal, please, Tom. All the cereals and stuff are out. Then would you and Emily plate up the eggs and bacon, and make toast? I daresay I may be a few moments. I'll take whoever it is into the lounge." Fenella took one last gulp of tea, smoothed her hair with her fingers and hurried to the front door.

Peter Quilliam and Dave Colvin stood on the doorstep.

They looked uncommonly solemn. Fenella felt a jab of fear beneath her ribs. This was a reliving of an old nightmare. The uniforms, the solemnity, the tension in the pit of her stomach; it had been more than twenty years since similar men in uniform had called to tell her of Brian's death. Some experiences are never forgotten.

EIGHT

Norah yawned as Fenella stripped her of her nightdress. "Christ," she said. "What a night. I had an ache in my guts for blooming hours, and my dreams were 'orrible…" She shuddered. "Wakin' up's the devil, Nell, when you're old. You'll find that out, one day."

Fenella smiled. "Thanks, Gran."

"I'm right, y'know. It's when you feel your age. Lying helpless, like." She gazed up at Fenella, feeling the strength in her arms as they gently moved and washed her. Though this wasn't the first time Fenella had done this morning task, it felt awkward for both of them.

Norah tried to think of something funny to say, though it was hard, as her granddaughter's efficient hands touched parts of her that no one, save herself or perhaps a lover, should touch. There she was, thinking of the past again. She'd been determined she wouldn't; what was the point?

"I feel like a babby," she muttered. "I wish you didn't have to do this, Nell."

Fenella smiled but continued in silence. "Comfy now?" she said at last, putting the towel on the rail and stooping to pick up the stained sheets.

"I'll do," Norah said shortly. "Is Marje doin' breakfast?"

Fenella straightened, clutching the sheets. "She's not coming, Gran. I told you last night, don't you remember? She said she'll not come here again."

Norah glared. "I thought you were joking. Where does that leave me in the scheme of things?"

"I don't know." Fenella bit her lip. "I phoned her late last night but she wouldn't discuss anything, save that she wasn't changing her mind."

Norah blinked fretfully. "So when do I go to jail?"

"Gran, for heaven's sake. Don't be like that. It's not that we don't care for you any less, but we just can't… manage… the way things are." She heaved a sigh and perched at the foot of the bed. "I have something else to tell you, Gran. I don't want you to get upset, but something dreadful has happened, and you'll have to know, because, well… two police officers are downstairs."

Norah was trying to fasten her cardigan buttons. She froze, her fingers unable to find the right holes. It was maddening.

Fenella dropped the sheets and leaned to help. Deftly she slipped the chunky buttons into place. "You know that elderly gent we had staying – Mr Stevens?"

Norah looked down at her woolly. "I don't know how you did that so fast, Nell. I'm all thumbs lately."

"Gran, are you listening?"

"Yes, that old geezer, I remember 'im all right."

"Well, he's been found dead, by the park lake."

Norah's eyes widened. "Christ, he'd looked on his last legs, but I didn't think he was that far gone."

"It's possible he drowned."

Norah sighed shakily. "Oh, crumbs, well, I doubt he'll be a great loss, so if that's all the news… Can I have m' breakfast now?"

Fenella gathered the sheets again. She wondered whether Norah had actually taken in what she'd said. Sometimes – often, in fact – lately the old lady deliberately didn't listen and then she complained later that they were keeping things from her. Judging by the stubborn look on Norah's face she decided not to bother asking. "Yes, Gran, of course you can have your breakfast. Do you want me to help you down?"

"No, just get me into my chair, Nell. I daresay the police fellas'll be wantin' you."

Fenella heaved Norah into her wheelchair, then threw open the bedroom window before dumping the dirty sheets into a linen basket in an unoccupied bedroom.

Once Fenella had hurried downstairs Norah wheeled herself to her dressing table, tidied her hair, dashed a smear of her favourite mauve lipstick on her thin lips, before steering herself adroitly out of her room and along the corridor to the lift.

Wheeling herself inside, she jabbed the descend button. As the lift travelled she gazed fixedly at the veneered wall while her crabbed hands flexed uneasily. So, he was dead? Well, good riddance. She'd not cry over him. He didn't deserve anyone's tears.

As Fenella reached the ground floor she heard the lift descend and expected Norah to be on her way down, but the mechanism paused on the floor above.

She frowned, then, shrugging, she hurried to the kitchen. Emily's dark head was bent over the sink, her arms deep in sudsy water.

"Emily, love, you don't have to do the dishes. You're meant to be on holiday."

"I don't mind," Emily replied cheerfully, "though washing up isn't one of my favourite occupations. How you cope with it every day I can't think."

Fenella plucked at a tea cloth. "I focus my mind on other things, usually whatever daub I'll be working on later when my chores are done."

Emily began to work more quickly. Fenella's drying was brisk. "The police are still waiting, you know."

Fenella shrugged. "I know."

"They're talking to the guests at present. Tom's there too." She raised her head. "Oh, it sounds as if they're finished. There's a stampede for the stairs."

Fenella nodded, polished a final plate and threw down the tea towel. "I don't suppose being questioned by the police will have been an aid to their digestion. Thank heavens they'll be allowed to leave later. I told Peter – um, Inspector Quilliam – about them all being at Douglas Carnival last night. I was dreading him saying they'd have to stay." She lifted the piled plates into a cupboard. "I don't expect this experience will enhance my reputation."

"It's hardly your fault. It's not as if the man died here, is it? Tom and I saw him last night, wandering across the bridge, I remember remarking to Tom that I thought he looked poorly, or as if he'd had too much to drink."

"Did you? Did you tell Pete – the police?"

"M'm, Tom did."

"I see." Fenella clattered cutlery into a drawer. "It's ironic, isn't it, yesterday evening Mr Stevens tells me he is in the process of buying this house, solving all my financial problems at a stroke, and a few hours later he has a stroke himself, or I presume he did, and that's that."

Emily wiped around the sink. "Did he say why he wanted it? Bayview, I mean?"

Fenella shrugged. "He didn't clarify much. He rambled on about having stayed here when he was young and ever since feeling an obligation, and he looked so frail I didn't press him to explain. I wonder if he was ill?"

"I expect so," Emily said comfortingly. "Now… um, Fenella? Excuse my asking, but you look a bit… er… peaky. Have you eaten anything this morning?"

Fenella smiled wanly. "I feel peaky, and no, I haven't had breakfast. I felt queasy when I found what had happened and now I feel just odd… shocked, I suppose." She began to stack cups noisily on their shelf so ineptly that Emily wouldn't have been surprised had they smashed.

"Perhaps you should have something? Tom and I can finish and clear the dining room. We've got nothing planned for today."

Fenella's shoulders slumped. Sympathy was hard to take. "No, I'll be fine." She flashed a smile. "You're very kind, Emily – oh, here's Tom, good."

Tom looked unhappy. Peter Quilliam and Dave Colvin were on his heels.

"Mum, they still want to speak to you."

"Of course." Fenella heard herself inviting the two officers to have coffee and moved briskly to make it when they politely accepted, though her heart was hammering, and not just with nerves. She knew she looked a mess. She hadn't had time to think of make-up and suspected that she had not even brushed her hair properly, having pulled it carelessly into a scrunchie. Only by the careful intake of deep breaths and forcing herself to act casually did she accomplish the making of strong coffee, by which time she did feel a little more in control. Soon they were sitting around the scrubbed kitchen table with steaming cups before them and some shortbread biscuits that Fenella had found in the snack cupboard.

Fenella was puzzled as to why Norah still wasn't down. Her cereal pack, bowl and plate were still on the table. Usually the old lady was eager for any meal.

She served the coffee and sat, feeling awkward. Tom and Emily diplomatically stepped into the yard with their drinks.

"I think we've got most of the information we need, Fenella," Peter said, formally glancing through his notes. "No, thanks, no sugar. I daresay the old fellow's death will turn out to be natural causes, but we have to follow procedure."

"Of course," Fenella murmured, the words echoing in her mind; they had said similar words when Brian died... but of course, his death had not been natural... such an awful time. She had been so young, Tom just a mite in her arms. Hurriedly she brought herself back to the present.

"Now, you said the deceased intended to leave today. Had he booked in for just the two nights then?"

"Not exactly, he came on the door – you know, called on spec – and asked if he could stay for two or three days. I assumed he was here on business; he certainly didn't give the impression of being a tourist." Fenella kept her eyes on her coffee cup. It was the only way she could stop herself from meeting Peter's gaze. It was the uniform, so close, it had brought it all back... poor Brian... She blinked and tried to look more alert.

"And last evening he told you that he would be leaving today?" Fenella nodded.

"He didn't have contact with any other guests while he was here? Didn't know anyone, from his past, for instance? You said he mentioned he had been here a long while ago?"

Tom poked his head in from the doorway to the yard. "He must have been here during the war, or just before, mustn't he, Mum? We worked that out last night, after he told Mum he wanted to buy Bayview."

"What?"

Fenella blushed crimson. "Yes, sorry, I should have said, as soon as you called, but I was still, m'm, shocked. What he said then, now seems unreal." She shrugged. "Perhaps he was having me on. I couldn't really believe it. Now it's just as well I didn't."

"Let me get this straight. This man, known to you as George Stevens, but otherwise Georgio Stephani, offered to buy Bayview?"

Fenella's mouth fell open. "Georgio Stephani? He was Italian, then? Goodness, Gran was right to suspect him."

"Sorry? Suspect him of what?"

Fenella looked embarrassed. "Oh, Gran's been prejudiced against Italians for eons. Her dislike stems from the war years, I've never been told why she was so prejudiced."

Dave Colvin banged his fist on the table. "Of course, this house was part of the internment camp, wasn't it? When was that, 1940, '41? Certainly soon after the start of the war."

Emily had been listening. She pushed past Tom. "Was it really? You never said, Tom."

He shrugged. "I didn't think. I've known it forever, but it was a heck of a long time ago – no one thinks about those times now."

Emily looked shocked. "Whew."

Fenella looked up. "It was spring 1940 when the war commission announced that the island would be used for an internment centre. I suppose it was ideal. Natural sea defences and all that. All the boarding house keepers were given only a week or so to vacate their homes. My grandfather had enlisted by then and so Gran and Mum found temporary lodgings in Waterloo Road." Fenella blinked. "They were still there when Grandad came on his last leave."

Peter took a sharp breath.

Fenella glanced at him. "I suppose you know about that, Peter."

He nodded. "Three Manx soldiers were killed in the Liverpool dock bombings of 1941 returning from leave on the island. It was tragic."

"Oh, that's sad," Emily murmured.

Fenella sighed. "Gran had lost a baby to pneumonia in the thirties, apparently, when Mum was three or four." Fenella gulped at her coffee. "So when Grandad died too, she was hit hard."

"Poor thing," Emily murmured.

"Yes, Norah can be tricky, but I always try to allow for what she's gone through."

The two men looked grave. Both knew about Brian and were probably thinking that Fenella hadn't had it easy either.

"Anyway, eventually they moved in with an aunt in Lezayre where they stayed till the end of the war. They didn't return here for almost five years, by which time Mum was going on fifteen."

Emily nudged Tom. "Why didn't you tell me any of this?"

Tom frowned. "Sorry. But Mum, Norah's aversion to Italians can't have started here. Fraternisation wasn't allowed, and this block was enclosed by masses of posts and barbed wire. I saw photos at that museum exhibition a while ago."

"You never said you'd been to that."

Tom shrugged, and Dave Colvin spoke: "Non-fraternisation was the rule, but a lot went on. My Aunt Maisie's a fund of knowledge about the time. Like the fact that groups of internees were taken to the cinema regularly, so some fraternisation rules were ignored."

Peter glanced at Dave in surprise.

"And there was land work," Emily put in. "Internees were used for agricultural labour all over England, so I suppose they would be used here? I learned that from World War II social history, there was a shortage of able men."

Peter sighed. "It looks as though we'll need to speak to Norah, Fenella. Just in case she'd known this chap Stephani before."

"Must you? She's not too clear in her thoughts at the best of times. If this business turns out to be something to do with some dark secret she's bottled up for years it might not do her any good."

"Come on, Mum, she isn't that loopy." Tom grinned.

Fenella gave him a glare. "Tom, you don't know the half of it, and nor do I. Mother's never let on about whatever happened to Norah after Walter was killed, but it must have been dire, for I know Gran spent a certain amount of time in a mental ward at Ballamona Hospital. I've never been told exactly why." She shrugged awkwardly. "Raking up those times could harm her, Peter. Surely the old man died of natural causes? I mean, last night I was concerned with how unwell he seemed when he was talking to me."

Peter remained impassive. "Sorry, Fenella, I must insist."

Fenella got up. "Right," she said tersely. "I'll fetch her." She got up and left the kitchen, closing the door with unnecessary firmness.

Tom collected the cups. "She's upset," he muttered apologetically. "It's all been a bit of a shock. Come on, Em," he said, stacking the cups in the dishwasher. "We'll scoot. I'm sure Great-Gran won't want us here."

"You look real peaceful," Norah murmured, smoothing Percy's sparse hair over his cold forehead.

When she'd knocked and there was no reply she had thought that he had gone for breakfast or was still asleep. She'd shouted through the door and then opened it, like she always did. Seeing him lying in bed she'd wheeled herself inside, still talking.

"The police are here, Percy. That bastard's dead. I thought I was still dreamin' when Fenella told me."

Percy didn't respond, but then Percy had always been a champion sleeper. She'd gone close, wheeling herself with care across Percy's rag rug. He'd had that rug for as long as he'd been in the house. His mother had made it when Percy was a small boy. Norah had known Percy all his life. He'd been a lean, good-looking lad, who used to carry her books and walk her home from school. She'd thought, as a child, that she might marry Percy. Then, when she was fifteen she'd met Walter Tooms at the Palace Ballroom in Douglas. Walter had swept her off her feet. *And onto me back*, she gleefully remembered. Percy had had no chance after that.

Yet despite her marriage Percy had remained a dependable friend, especially after Walter died, when others shunned her for, to her mind, no good reason. Percy hadn't gone to the war. He'd had a reserved occupation and delicate health. His delicacy had preserved him to a ripe old age.

Until now.

"It's a bloody shock, Percy," Norah said, gripping his cold hand. "I've relied on you to act as m'legs. Gawd, what am I goin' to do now?"

Norah's mind roved over all the things Percy had done for her, all the messages he'd run, all the gossip he'd fetched along with her favourite mags and the illicit sweeties that Marjorie didn't like her eating, cause they loosened her bowels. Percy had always been a quiet authority on local gossip too, usually in the know as to who'd died and who'd been rushed into hospital. Such skeet, as they called it locally, provided the savour to old age. "Christ, Percy, I'll have to rely on Eloise for the gossip. What a prospect."

Norah felt more resentment than grief as she tried to take in all the ways Percy's death would affect her. She felt suddenly depressed and deprived. "You might have had the decency to wait until I'd popped off, you silly old bugger," she muttered, dropping his hand and pulling her cardigan tight around her thin frame. She'd gone chilly, in need of a hot drink and another cardie, maybe. This was tragic. No one else would feel it as much as she would. Why could he not have hung on, at least till she'd gone into a dratted home? She'd needed to talk to him, today especially, not just about what had happened but about the dead fella. Who was she going to confide in now?

A stomach rumble reminded Norah that she had not yet had her breakfast. She gave a final pat to Percy's hand, turned and wheeled herself to the door. She looked back, once, gazing around his room, neatly stacked with the memorabilia of a lifetime, and felt angry and hungrier than ever. She knew it was pointless berating Percy, but he was an inconsiderate sod all the same. Who could she moan to now? She slammed Percy's door and headed towards the lift, nearly colliding with Eloise Green stepping out of her room.

"Morning, Norah, have you heard? What a dreadful thing. Poor man."

"Humph." Norah snorted, wheeling herself into the lift. "He hated you. You needn't cry crocodile tears." She pressed the button and the lift doors whirred shut.

Eloise stared after her. "But I didn't know Mr Stevens," she protested. "I didn't exchange a word with him, save for good evening." But the lift had already descended. "How blunt Norah is becoming." She shook her head. "This place is not so… nice as it was." She sighed. "And Percy didn't show for breakfast. I hope he's not ill."

Eloise glanced at the dainty diamante watch she always wore, a present from Hubert many years before. She was due to help at a Red Cross coffee morning later than morning, but she had a little time to spare. She would check on Percy, see if had he any errands for her in the town. It would be a nice excuse; that charming nature programme would be on the BBC that evening. If Percy was agreeable she would watch it with him.

"I'm glad you're down," Fenella said as Norah wheeled herself out of the lift. "I was coming to fetch you. The police want a word. They're in the dining room. I'll take these into the kitchen if you want me to stay with you." She was carrying a loaded tray. Norah opened her mouth to reply when from upstairs there came the sound of a shriek and then a pounding of footsteps along the landing.

"What now, for heaven's sake? That sounds like Eloise. Has the dratted woman seen a mouse again?"

Norah grinned as Fenella stared upwards, while Peter Quilliam and Dave Colvin burst from the kitchen. "No," Norah beamed, "I reckon she's found Percy – he's dead."

Fenella was not usually given to nerves, but this was too much. Her grip on the tray loosened and she swayed. Luckily Dave played rugby and was good on his feet. He lunged and caught the tray just before it fell to the floor. Only one cup tumbled, unbroken, to the carpet.

"Christ," Norah said, "well caught, Copper. Now, I'm off for my breakfast." With a grin she turned her wheelchair and headed for the kitchen. "Them fellas can come in while I eat, and no, I don't want you with me, Nell."

Peter's eyes met Fenella's. "I see what you mean about your gran, Fenella." As Dave hurtled into the kitchen with the tray Peter pushed past them both and raced upstairs. Dave was soon on his heels. Their progress was abruptly halted on the landing by a departing family – mother, father and two children – laden with cases, bags and assorted toys, and all standing rigid as Eloise Green indulged in hysterics beside them.

"Sorry, excuse me. For goodness' sake…" Arms wide, Peter enfolded Eloise Green in a swift bear hug. "Come along now, missus. It can't be that bad!"

Eloise sobbed into his jacket. "He's dead. Dear Percy is dead. Aaaahh!" Abruptly she went limp. Peter handed her to Fenella, who had followed the men. She bundled Eloise onto a convenient chair as Tom reached the landing. "Get Eloise some water!" she snapped. "Room thirteen at the end of the corridor!"

After all the fuss the reality of Percy's condition was utterly peaceful. The old man had clearly died in his sleep. His clothes were neatly folded. His book, a half-read Patrick O'Brian, was laid squarely on his bedside table, a woven bookmark marking a page.

Peter felt for a pulse, laid his head near enough to check that the old man had breathed his last and stood with a sigh. "He's gone all right."

Fenella's breath would not come for a moment. "No! Oh, he was a dear, dear old man," she gasped finally. "Such a good friend to Gran, and more like family…" she gasped again. "He's been with us so long."

Dave patted her shoulder. Peter stood quietly while Fenella caught her breath. She found a tissue in her apron pocket and blew her nose while tears coursed down her cheeks.

"I'm so sorry, Fen," Peter said sombrely, and then, unwittingly, he sniffed and studied the room. Not seeing anything out of place, he made a mental note. "Poor you," he said, ushering Fenella into the corridor. "What a thing to happen, on top of the other business. Would you like us to contact the necessary people?"

"Please," Fenella whispered, and found to her horror that her tears were now gushing. "Hell," she sniffed, "I need to sort the bill for the Burridges, too. Oh, crumbs." She wiped her cheeks with her wrist.

Peter gazed at her blankly.

"The family who're downstairs. They're about to leave."

"Of course." He could hear them now, on the ground floor, their grumbles percolating upwards. "Off you go. We'll have a look round if that's all right."

Fenella was at the top of the stairs, blowing her nose furiously before the significance of Peter's words registered. She glanced towards Percy's room, but the door was closed and the two men were inside. A look around for what?

Tom had taken Eloise Green into the lounge. Emily fetched her a tot of brandy and a small coffee, and she was sitting on one of the high-backed armchairs, sipping both alternately, a faint colour returning to her pale, powdered cheeks.

"I shouldn't be taking this," she said tremulously to Tom. "I've always been teetotal. I promised Daddy. And I'm due to help at a coffee morning later. Do you think they would understand if I cancelled?"

"Of course they would, Miss Green," Tom said kindly. "Why don't you have a lie-down? I'll let them know what's happened if you like."

Eloise smiled wanly. "You are a good boy, Tom. I know Percy thought so too." Her watery eyes filled again and Tom looked helplessly at Emily.

"Shall we give her more brandy?" he mouthed.

Emily shook her head. "Shall I help you upstairs, Miss Green?"

Eloise looked blank for a moment, then she straightened her thin shoulders, smoothed her tweed skirt, laid down the glass and cup, and began to ease herself from the chair. "Thank you, dear, but no. I must go out. I gave my word. It won't do to mope, and Percy never let anyone down. I'm sure your grandmother can vouch for that, though at the time no one would have blamed him if he had."

Tom looked blank. "Sorry?"

Eloise stood shakily. "Yes, I feel better." She pulled her cardigan sleeves straight and dabbed at her nose with a tiny hanky. "I'll fetch my coat and be on my way." She turned graciously. "Good morning."

"Good morning," Emily said politely. Tom smiled and put the stopper on the brandy bottle.

When she had left Tom and Emily stared at one another. "What did you think of that?" He grinned.

Emily laughed. "I hope I'm as game in my old age."

Tom exhaled gustily. "What a start to the day! For heaven's sake. Two deaths already. What will the rest of this blessed day bring? Do you think I'd better hang on to this brandy, just in case?"

Emily looked at Tom, who, for all his six foot of height, looked as though much of his macho stuffing had been knocked out of him. She felt a welling of tenderness towards him and put her arms around him, pulling him close. "I'm still here," she whispered. "How about a kiss, lover?"

Tom looked into her eyes. "Oh, Emmy," he said, "I thought you'd never ask. I feel in need of some warm human contact. How about going to bed?"

At that moment the door opened. "Is your mother about?" a hectoring voice enquired. "We'd like to settle our bill and get out of this ruddy madhouse."

Tom turned, his 'always be polite to the guests' face on. "Of course. I'll fetch her." To Emily he whispered, "Later?"

And he was elated by her beaming nod of agreement.

NINE

"I hate bananas. You're only trying to make me go," Norah snapped as Fenella chopped slices of the fruit onto her cereal.

"Keeping regular is important at your age," Fenella said, equally curtly. Peter and Dave were still waiting to speak to the old lady.

"Didn't do Percy any good, did it? Bloomin' bananas." Norah crashed her spoon into the cereal, splashing milk on the table and herself. "Now look what you've done," she cried, before Fenella could. "Didn't get bananas in the war, we didn't," she muttered, wiping her fingers on her skirt. "*He* never had bananas."

"Who?" Fenella murmured, abstractedly dabbing at milk with a tea towel. A plan had slid unbidden into her mind. Would it be craven if she off-loaded today's new guests? She didn't feel up to playing the jolly landlady today – or ever again. The shock of Percy's death was awful, much worse than that of the old man.

"That geezer. The dead one, I mean!" Norah shouted, digging into her cereal and spooning too much towards her mouth. "Force," she mumbled, dribbling.

"What?" Fenella glanced at her watch. Her new guests would be travelling on the afternoon sailing from Heysham. If she got onto Millie Blackwell maybe Trevor might collect them in his minibus from the Sea Terminal. They probably would be glad of the business and it would be nice for the travellers, not having to catch on a service bus to Ramsey.

"Are you listening, girl? Force, that was the cereal they made us eat in wartime. Made of cardboard, or floor sweepings stuck together with whale oil."

"Was it?" Fenella said distractedly. "I need to make a call, Gran. I won't be long. Shall I put your toast in?"

Norah glared. "Where's me boiled egg?"

"Gran, when you got up you said you didn't want an egg."

"Put the toast in then. You don't want me to starve, do you? Look what happened to Percy. He never ate enough, the fool."

Fenella tightened her lips, pressed bread into the toaster and hurried from the kitchen. It took but a moment to get through to Millie. She lowered her voice. Peter and Dave were still waiting in the lounge.

"Of course we'll take them, Fenella," Millie Blackwell agreed promptly after Fenella had explained the circumstances. "Sounds as if you could do with a break, girl. Poor old Percy. Yes, me and Trev will cope. Getting in at five thirty, you said. Six adults and two kiddies. Right?"

Fenella put the phone down, feeling a sense of relief. She needed some time… Poor Percy, he'd had no family. She, Marjorie, Norah and Tom had been his family for the past thirty years. Fenella felt her throat tightening and wiped away a tear. She paused, took a breath then pushed open the door to the lounge.

Both men turned to look at her, Peter's face so full of sympathy that Fenella's eyes prickled. "Gran's about ready. You'll maybe get some sense out of her now. I'm sorry you had to wait, but she's… difficult at the best of times, and, well… Percy was her closest friend." Fenella's mouth dried. The knowledge that Percy had suddenly changed from being a cheerful old man to a chilly corpse was shocking. Yesterday he had been his pleasant, gentle self…

just like Mr Stevens. Her face froze. It was no good. She could not speak.

"Thanks, Fenella." Peter smiled gravely as he and Dave passed her and headed to the kitchen. Fenella closed the kitchen door firmly after them. She didn't want to know what Norah might say. The fact that she would no doubt repeat whatever the men asked her and gabble about it later anyhow meant that she would eventually know all.

Fenella clenched her arms around herself. She hurried desperately to the front door and wrenched it open. She needed to see the sea, look upon something eternal, something unchanging. Her heart was pattering horribly yet she felt so cold. She supposed she was feeling delayed shock.

The sight of the surging and receding waves brought scant comfort, even as she inhaled and exhaled as they swept in and out. Death had stamped its impress on her twice that day. She knew she would never forget this awful, hollow feeling. Death was inevitable and shocking, a dark stranger who had barged into her easy, commonplace life.

A neighbour strolled past, carrying a heavy shopping bag. "Morning, Mrs Kelly," she called, with a pleasant smile.

Jolted, Fenella managed a wan greeting in return and hurriedly backed into the house once more. With a police car only a few yards distant she was surprised the woman had not stopped to gossip. Fenella leaned against the closed door. As she slipped into her small office she had to pull out another tissue. When she felt composed enough she dialled Marjorie's number. It rang a few times before Marjorie said, "Hello?"

Fenella's mouth was dry. "Mum? Hi. I-I'm afraid I've got some bad news. Perhaps you'd better sit down."

Marjorie replaced the receiver shakily. Sometimes she didn't replace it correctly and incoming calls couldn't get through. She'd never had the same trouble with her old phone, but this new one was flimsy. "Two deaths – only an undertaker would cheer," she muttered bleakly. Then, as a tremor of shock ran through her, she shuddered. "Poor Percy. I'll miss him."

She moved to the window. She forgot that she'd been loading the washing machine when the phone rang. She fumbled for a hanky. Percy had been at Bayview so long it was hard to think of the place without him. She stood for a few moments, reminiscing. How odd; the evening before she had riven all contact with Bayview, and now fate had taken a further hand to change things even more. She smiled grimly, aware that she'd felt pleased with herself, every time she wakened in the night, for being strong enough, finally, to make the break. What a shock though for Norah – poor Mum.

Marjorie's lips tightened. Yesterday she had walked out on her mother; today Percy had, in effect, done the same. Though she'd often joshed Norah about Percy Marjorie knew that the two old people had been closer than many who were married. Without Percy's assistance Norah would be utterly lost.

Marjorie moved to the window and gazed thoughtfully out. For the first time she noted that the leaves on the trees in the park had coloured to an autumnal hue already. Poor old Percy; an end to all his summers too. A shudder ran through her – a funeral to organise. Another duty to be got through. Marjorie disliked funerals.

She sighed and pulled her shoulders back. There was no point in following that line of thought. She'd done with mourning for times gone. It was her future that must take precedence. *I want to enjoy what's left of my life; that's what's important.*

First, it was essential to keep positive. Let's face it, the consequences from Fenella's other bombshell, the death of the old Italian, drat him, might disrupt her plans.

Stern-faced she marched to fill her kettle; she needed a strong cup of coffee. She lifted a mug down, spooned grains inside and stood, erect. It was only when she reached for the sugar pot that she noticed her fingers were trembling. "God help me," she whispered. "It might have happened fifty years ago, but I bet that man's death will still cause a stink."

Moments later Marjorie sipped the strong brew. A glance at the clock told her the day was half gone already.

"I'm going out," she said, leaving her mug on the coffee table and hurrying into her bedroom. "If I stay in I'll mope, and there's been too much of that over the years. I'll get the bus to Douglas. Treat myself to lunch, maybe. To hell with Norah, Fenella and all the rest of them. I've got back my freedom and I'm not giving it up now, no matter who's died."

Peter Quilliam slammed the car door, determined not to look back at Fenella standing to see them off. God, she still moved his guts like no woman he'd ever known. If only he'd got in years ago, when he'd had the chance, and he'd had the chance, before she'd met Brian. But as she had, he'd taken up with Susan. Sue was fun, easy to please – it was only later they found that neither were really suited to one another. If only he'd stayed on the island. He should have persuaded Susan to go across on her own. God, just being near Fenella revived desires he'd long thought had died in his twenties.

Dave Colvin, wisely staying silent, accelerated away, though casting Peter swift, curious looks. He'd never seen the man so ill at ease as in Bayview. It wasn't as if the old lady had been any trouble, after all their long wait. In fact, she'd seemed uncommonly helpful.

As they turned from the promenade and headed towards the town Peter heaved a great sigh, causing his seat to creak ominously. He knew he'd put on weight since returning. Another sign of age and sloth. He shifted again, wrestling himself into a more comfortable position as thoughts flew through his head that he was actually thoroughly fed up of police cars – another treacherous realisation that didn't bode well for his career, or his health.

"That went OK," Dave remarked as they drove along the quay. "Mrs Tooms seemed a game old biddy. Not that she told us much that we didn't already know."

Peter grunted. "If any of what she said was true. There was a sly look in her eye I didn't take to."

"Was there? I didn't notice."

Peter shrugged. "Perhaps I was looking for things that weren't there. She must have been shocked. Having just found your best friend dead in bed must have been upsetting. Still, if I'm that bright at her age I'll be doing all right."

"It's sad about old Percy. He was one of the town characters, but with a small 'c', if you know what I mean." Dave grinned. "He and his Raleigh bike will be missed." He chuckled. "Norah knew how to ramble, though, didn't she?" He negotiated a roundabout and passed Shoprite, the main supermarket in the town. Dave was not prepared to remind Peter of the near-knuckle remarks Norah had made regarding Fenella – remarks that were tasteless in the circumstances.

As they neared the police station he said, "Percy's room – God, it was apple-pie tidy, wasn't it? Not a thing out of place. Bit different to our house."

Peter nodded. "I doubt my home will be like that at his age – should I live so long."

Dave glanced at him. "What's up with you today? You're not set on popping your clogs anytime soon, are you?"

Peter's expression made him wish he'd not spoken. "I still can't place that smell…" Peter murmured. "It seemed out of place."

"Perhaps they'd been to a smoky pub?"

"Hmmph, maybe?"

"Was he, you know, that way?"

"No! Percy wasn't gay. He was old-fashioned, yes, and I suppose he'd been restrictively brought up by his mother."

As Dave pulled the car adroitly into the courthouse yard and parked Peter murmured, "He'd have been called up, though?"

"I'm not certain but I think he was in a reserved occupation."

Peter undid his seatbelt. "Anyhow, Percy is not our worry. We need to focus on George Stevens, alias Georgio Stephani." He climbed from the car and headed for the rear entrance. "I'll notify next of kin and have a chat. If you will ring the bank about this mortgage business. It seems a most unlikely transaction. It was common knowledge that Charles Peake was slavering to get hold of the place."

"And she was stubbornly refusing his offer. Which is also weird," Dave muttered. "What grudge does she have against the man?"

"He and she were in the same class in junior school, I believe, and I think that's when the enmity began."

"Cripes." Dave grinned. "Of course, we Manx are keen on our grudges, aren't we?"

"Yes," Peter said slowly. "I'd not thought of that." He narrowed his eyes. "You mentioned your Aunt Maisie a while back. Is she still compos mentis?"

"Very much so."

"And she lives locally?"

Dave looked wary. "She does."

"How old must she be now?"

"Knocking on eighty-five, but my God, she's all there. She can still rattle off who's related to who, not just in Ramsey either, more like half the island."

"Good." Peter nodded. "This afternoon I think we'll call on Auntie Maisie, if she's at home."

"She will be." Dave grimaced. "She lunches out three days a week but not Wednesdays. She and Sarah, that's her friend who lives in the next flat, they hold a sort of open-house 'cooish.'"

Peter grinned. He was Manxman enough not to need a translation that a 'cooish' was a meeting to turn over the latest gossip.

"Good." He beamed. "We'll offer her some gen and see what she can offer us in return."

Dave gaped. He'd worked hard to get promoted, to learn modern, up-to-date methods of detection. Visiting old and often curmudgeonly relations to gossip hadn't figured in any of the police manuals he'd read.

"Right. Shall I ring to let her know we're coming?"

"Do." Peter nodded. "It's better if we're expected. By lunchtime the news will have spread about our shy Italian and his demise in the Mooragh Park, and about Percy's sudden end. I'll be interested to know what the gossips dredge up."

Emily stretched out on the bed, panting. Tom slumped at her side, breathing heavily, a proprietorial hand laid on one of her soft breasts.

"I liked that." Emily grinned and ruffled his hair, shifting his hand.

"Gerroff. Good, I mean, I'm glad that you liked it." Tom propped himself on one elbow. "You were meant to like it, my darling."

"For pity's sake, don't call me 'darling' in that sick voice. You sound like my dad."

Tom rolled away from her after giving her nipple a quick kiss. "Sorry, Emily. I am allowed to call you Emily, aren't I?"

Emily sat up, leaned towards him and put her hands firmly on his chest, pressing him down. "You can call me anything real, Tom, but I hate the words 'darling' and 'sweetheart'. My dad tossed them about like candy and yet there was no love in the words. He would sneer and call my mum 'sweetheart'. I hated it."

Tom gazed up at her leaning over him, so utterly gorgeous and desirable, so warm and so alive. He shivered. Impulsively Emily lowered herself and hugged him. Her nakedness was a comfort and Tom clasped her, relishing her warmth. "I'm sorry, Tom, for being a nag, when you're upset."

He hugged her again. "And I'm sorry too, for being not what you want."

Emily continued to cuddle close, and he loved her for it, but she didn't refute his remark, and that hurt, almost as much as the sick feeling inside him every time he thought of old Percy, dying alone in his room.

Emily sat up. "Shall we go for a walk? Or is there anything we should do, around the house? Your mum went to see your gran about the funeral, didn't she?"

"M'm, and we can't go out, because of Great-Gran. Luckily she's asleep."

"You're quite a family, aren't you?"

Tom put his arms behind his head. "Not for much longer. Great-Gran will be put into a home. Mum will move out. Gran will stay in her flat, which she loves, and I will move to Peel." His eyes looked questioningly at Emily.

"And I'll go back to college," she whispered, her face coming down to his, while fingers wandered down his chest and further. "And there'll be a whole ocean between us." Her eyes locked with his and she moved even closer so that he could smell her warm, sweet breath. "Well, if we can't go out to get some exercise," she said softly, "we'll just have to stay here and get some more, won't we?"

"Ouch," Tom yelped. "Yes, OK you can do that. Oh, yes, yes, please do…"

Emily giggled. "Sex is such fun, isn't it?"

Tom wriggled from under her, grabbed her shoulders and threw himself on top of her. "I'm glad you approve of something, Emily Stock, would-be archaeologist. Here, what do you think of this!"

As the car drew up outside the sheltered housing complex of Cooil ny Marrey Peter looked up at the rows of windows. "I'll probably end up somewhere like this soon enough."

"Cripes, Peter, you're still youngish."

"Sure. I'm forty-six years young, divorced, homeless, apart from a shack of a cottage I never get a chance to do up. If I retire after my thirty years I'll probably become an advocates messenger, only fit for chatting up young typists and moaning about how the police force isn't what it was in my day."

Dave Colvin laughed. "Go on like that and you're sure to get on with Aunt Maisie. You've got her to a 'T'. She's never happier than when she's rambling about the recently dear departed, and when one of her friends dies she hacks another notch on her walking stick."

Peter chuckled. "I know the feeling. Oh well, let's get this over with. I thought it a good idea earlier. Now I'm feeling doubtful."

The two men marched along a well-polished floor of the long corridor, following the painted arrows. They stopped at flat twenty-two and Dave rang the gleaming doorbell.

It swung open smartly. A smiling upright lady with a round pink face and the unmistakable manner of a retired teacher beamed.

"Young David," she exclaimed, opening the door wide. "Come in, do. I'm Sarah Craine, by the way," she added for the benefit of Peter.

As Peter stepped past her he felt as though he'd been transported to an old folks' home he had visited regularly as a lad. A scent of camphor, lavender and the fusty smell of old people in a heated environment settled, like a blanket. He almost expected his Aunt Kate to shuffle from towards him, proffering a paper dry cheek to be kissed. Instead Sarah ushered them towards a cheerful elderly lady seated in a capacious Parker Knoll chair, where she was, in semi-royal fashion, giving audience to a couple ensconced on a low floral upholstered settee before her.

"Well, there you are, David, I was thinking you weren't coming. You'll know Mr and Mrs Brew, David?" Not giving him time to answer, she smiled. "And this must be Inspector Quilliam?"

"How do you do, ma'am?" Peter nodded, removing his hat.

The old lady beamed. "Sarah, isn't he the spitting image of his grandfather, Harold Quilliam? Now, sit down, the two of you, and we'll get acquainted. No, you're not going, William. Oh, well, if you must."

William and Cissie Brew had half raised themselves at the arrival of the uniformed pair. Now they hurriedly sidled out. Maisie did not wait until they were out of earshot before commenting, "Cissie's always been nervy; she gets upset at uniforms, I believe, and William's maul at present." She lowered her voice dramatically. "Most of his insides have been cut out; his heart's not too good either. They gave him a by-pass, but it doesn't seem to have done him much good." She heaved a knowing sigh and leaned forward, then patted a vacant chair next to her and beamed. "Sit here, Inspector Quilliam. Tell me what you're wantin'. David, put the kettle on, there's a lad. You'll have a cup of tea in your hand? Good." She settled in her seat while Sarah disappeared into the tiny adjoining kitchen, followed a moment later by Dave.

Maisie beamed. "Now, they're telling me that the man found dead in the Mooragh was interned here, and that Percy Corlett's passed away, poor soul. Is that the way of it?"

Peter smothered a grin. "Mr Corlett died – of natural causes, we believe – at home at Bayview, but we've not confirmed that the deceased gentleman found in the Mooragh was an internee, Mrs Colvin."

Maisie waved a plump hand. "No, but he was – I didn't see him, but Bertha Quaggin did, David'll know all about Bertha."

"Oh, yes?"

Maisie hurried on. "Bertha was in the bank when the old fella came in and was took bad, by the heat, they said. The manager took him into his office." The old lady twisted in her chair. "Sarah, what are you doing out there with David? Come and sit down."

David, grinning, emerged and did as he was told.

Maisie leaned forwards. "David. I wanted to know how your father's doin'? I heard of his... trouble." She turned back to Peter. "As I was saying, Inspector, that man was an internee here, right enough. Bertha would know – she'd never forget a face."

Peter was politely sceptical. "It was fifty years ago, Mrs Colvin."

Maisie looked at him sharply. "The eyes don't change, Inspector. Bertha was one body who had reg'lar contact. She recognised him all right. Aye, it was a while ago, but he was a rum one, memorable, like, and then, well, there was some... trouble. Hushed up, o' course, but it made him stand out, like."

"I see. I'd like to talk to Bertha Quaggin."

"Aye. Not that she'll tell you much. She's close, is Bertha. Always was, that's how she got to work as liaison secretary for the council. Good at the shorthand and typing, was Bertha, and as smart as they come, though you'd maybe not believe it now."

Sarah entered with a laden tray. "Bertha rambles," she said sharply.

"Yes, but if you can get catch her in the right mood, she'll tell you a lot."

Peter accepted a cup of scalding tea, sipping it doubtfully, trying to not dwell on the negative effects of tannin. After all, these two eighty-four-year-olds looked fit as fleas. Perhaps they knew something that dietary experts didn't.

"What was it like here in wartime? Did the locals resent the internees?"

Maisie sipped her tea and looked at Sarah. "What would you say, Sarah? Did we resent them? It was impossible to ignore them when they were marching about on exercises. I remember that, but most of the time they were kept out of our way. The promenade was well guarded."

Sarah laid her cup and saucer carefully on a side table. "It wasn't easy seeing them about when our men had all gone to war. At the outset the locals were pleased that they were to come here. Lots of

Manx folk were near on the breadline without the summer visitors. The Lord alone knows what would have happened if the internees and military hadn't settled themselves here. There wasn't much else to make an income from in those days."

"Not like now," Peter said encouragingly. Maisie opened her mouth to continue but Sarah broke in, wagging her finger to emphasise her point. "No, none of these finance places messing up the towns and filling the young ones' heads with nonsense and ideas of big money. Do you know, a slip of a girl can be earning ten thousand pounds a year in her first job in Douglas nowadays? Do you wonder that crime is getting worse? Thirty shillings a week I got in my first job, and I felt it was a king's ransom."

Peter smiled politely. "So the townsfolk were happy enough to move out for the internees?"

"They were doing their duty and getting a payment, which helped. They were allowed to move out their personal belongings and their... beds." A sudden maidenly modesty affected Maisie and she gave a shrug. "But when the internees were settled, it wasn't quite like we were led to believe. Most locals kept well away from them."

"Why?"

Sarah flicked off one of the bars of the substantial electric fire. Peter was relieved; his trouser leg already felt scorching.

"Some were nothing more than brutes," she snapped. "Ill-mannered, ungrateful savages. They didn't realise that the locals were having a hard time, bedded with relatives or anyone who'd put them up, while these strangers, enemies in all but name, enjoyed three square meals and all found in *their* homes."

"Some of the men spat when we passed," Sarah added, her face showing disgust. "After a while most folk gave the camps a wide berth."

"And the girls that fraternised weren't thought much of," Maisie said meaningfully as she and Sarah exchanged a look.

Peter didn't comment. "What nationalities were held here?"

"Mostly Italians and a few low-risk Germans. The Germans were usually better-behaved. Most had left Germany long before the war started. They had a reason to be grateful. The Italians weren't so content – most were bitter about being brought here."

"You can understand why," Dave murmured. "If they were British-born they were probably no more sympathetic to the enemy than, say, the Scots or the Irish."

Maisie looked scathingly at her nephew. "You wouldn't have said that openly in those days, my lad. We kept our opinions to ourselves."

Peter was jotting down notes. "To get down to basics, what was so different about this particular man, Georgio Stephani, that made him memorable?"

Maisie and Sarah exchanged glances. Maisie sighed. "We aren't the ones to tell you that, Inspector Quilliam."

"Do you mean that Bertha might?"

Maisie nodded to Sarah to fill her teacup. "No," she said, "I mean you should go to the horse's mouth, if Norah Tooms is up to it."

Peter stared. "Fenella's grandmother?"

"You're well in with the family," Maisie said crisply. "I heard you were seen chatting to Fenella in Parliament Street."

Peter flushed. "Well, yes, I've known Fenella since I was a lad."

Maisie spooned sugar into her tea. "Aye, well, if Norah won't tell you, the other's gone who might have done."

"You mean Percy? Would he have known?"

Maisie nodded curtly. "Percy Corlett should have married Norah Tooms. He was always slow on the uptake where it mattered, more fool him, but then, that's men all over." She gave Peter a look, which was unambiguously direct. Peter breathed heavily but forced a polite smile and got to his feet. "Well, I think that's all for now, ladies. Thank you for your help."

"Any time, young man. Sarah, give him Bertha's address. He'll need to see her. Come again, won't you, and tell your father I'm sorry to hear about his trouble, David, but it's his own fault. I told him years ago he should give up farming."

Sarah scribbled down an address, gave it to Peter with a quiet smile and showed them to the door.

Both men hurried along the stuffy corridor. "Phew," Peter gasped, once they'd got outside, into the fresh air. "Are all your relations like that?"

"No," Dave sighed. "Most of them are worse."

TEN

Fenella ran up the stairs to her mother's flat. She knocked and rang the bell.

"Mum, it's me, Fenella. Let me in."

She rang again and then reluctantly decided that Marjorie was not at home. This was odd. Her car was outside. As she ran downstairs the door to the ground-floor flat opened. Ben Cowin stood grinning at her. She felt irritated.

"Hi, Fenella. Your mum's gone out. She's gone to Douglas on the bus."

Fenella frowned. "Has she? That's unlike her – especially when..." She broke off, aware that Ben was not a known gossip.

"I heard about ol' Percy earlier. It's a sad do, isn't it?" Ben shuffled his slippers and said awkwardly, "I'm right sorry for y's all."

Fenella smiled. "That's kind of you, Ben. Thanks, I'll call on Mum later. It was nothing that can't wait. Cheerio." She turned and hurried out of the front door, her heart bumping. She hoped Marjorie was not so distraught she'd felt she had to get away. She dithered on the pavement for a moment then resignedly turned back towards Bayview. There was no point in going elsewhere. She had plenty to do, after all – planning her move? Maybe she could sell some furniture to raise some cash? She retraced her steps listlessly. It was a lovely day, sunny and with only a slight breeze: the sort of day that would have suited Percy. She dabbed her eyes with a tissue hurriedly pulled from her pocket. *Oh, Percy, why did you have to go so suddenly? What will Gran do without you?* She thought of Percy's many possessions. They'd all have to be gone through, and what of his trusty bike? Oh dear. The poor old chap, going so suddenly; it seemed like a bad dream. Percy had been part of Bayview for so long it would not be the same without him, trotting about, always looking smart and always smiling. She sniffed and blinked hard. As for the other old man's sudden demise – well, that was extraordinary. His entire visit had been so unbelievable – like something out of a TV drama.

A car was parked outside Bayview. Fenella's insides tightened. She knew the owner by sight; he was a local reporter. She marched past the vehicle and skipped swiftly up the steps to Bayview. Only as he jumped out did she turn and say frostily, "I have no comments to make and wish you to leave."

The man had been smiling. His smile faded, but by then Fenella had unlocked the door and had slipped inside.

It was four o'clock before she rang and found her mother in.

"Mum, are you all right? I was worried about you."

"I'm fine," Marjorie sighed.

"I was surprised when Ben said you'd gone to Douglas."

"M'm, I didn't, actually. By the time the bus had reached Laxey village I knew I didn't feel up to trawling through shops so I got off. Had a walk in Laxey Glen, quite enjoyed it too. The quiet, the tall trees and the memories of happy times we'd had there."

"Oh, Mum… well, I'm glad you're OK."

Marjorie sighed. "It was so sad… about Percy…" Her voice trailed off.

"I'll come round, shall I?" Fenella said softly.

"That would be nice. Oh, but can you? With Norah…?"

"Yes, Tom and Emily are here. She'll be fine."

"Good," Marjorie sighed. "Yes, good, she needs looking after…"

"I'll be with you soon. Put the kettle on." Fenella slammed the phone down. *Poor Mum, she sounded low. Hardly to be wondered at, what with the row last night and then…* Fenella hurried to the stairs. "Tom?"

"What?" He stepped out of the lounge, grinning.

She smiled. "Sorry, love, I didn't know where you were. I'm off to see Mum. Organise some food for you and Emily, will you, and keep an eye on Gran, please."

Tom saluted. "Wilco, ma'am!"

"Daft boy," Fenella said affectionately, pulling down a jacket.

Within ten minutes she was climbing the stairs to Marjorie's flat.

"Thanks for coming." Marjorie smiled wanly as she opened the door.

"It's no trouble. Oh, you look whacked, Mum. No, you sit down, I'll make coffee, OK?"

Marjorie nodded, sinking into her favourite chair wearily. Fenella's insides quaked. *Poor Mum.* She hurried into the kitchen. "Hey, you've been making scones."

"I felt at a loose end early this morning."

"M'm, lovely, we'll maybe have one later."

Fenella soon emerged moments later with mugs of coffee. "I'm so relieved I off-loaded my guests," she said as she laid the drinks on a small table. "I don't think I'd have coped with any catering this evening. I'm feeling a bit pooped myself."

"Oh, was it Millie Blackwell you got onto?"

"Yes, and she was really pleased. I don't think they can have had a good season. So my loss was of some benefit after all." Fenella beamed. Marjorie gazed wonderingly at her, aware yet again of Fenella's strength of character in times of emergency. When

Donald had been killed it had been the then-teenage Fenella who'd swung into action and helped guide Marjorie though that sad and difficult time. When Fenella's young husband, Brian, died racing it had been Fenella's gritty resilience that carried the three of them – she, Fenella and baby Tom – through that tragedy.

"You're tough, girl," Marjorie said enviously, sipping her coffee.

Fenella shrugged; she didn't feel tough. In fact, deep down she felt strangely fragile. It was actually this fragility that generated some unprompted inner urge to get everything sorted, and fast, so that life could return to an equable normality. Not that original normality was ever fully achievable, but some driven instinct forced her on.

Fenella, gazing from the window, realised she was focusing on the far side of the Mooragh Lake, where two dark-clad figures were standing. One was Peter. Even at this distance there was no mistaking his stature. She was still staring when Marjorie returned with two buttered scones on pretty plates. "It seemed silly not to partake. I suddenly feel hungry. Oh, love, come away from the window. Are the police still there?"

"M'm." Fenella swivelled round and pulled the coffee table towards her. "I feel as though we're part of a detective story. It's very strange." She eyed the scones hungrily. "They look tasty." She gazed at Marjorie. "I still can't believe what's happened in the past twenty-four hours. Percy dying, and that old man, it seems unbelievable."

"It does," Marjorie muttered.

"He did look ill last night, Mum, when he talked to me. He must have had a heart condition, I suppose."

"Would you like jam?" Marjorie asked.

Fenella stared. "What? Oh, no, thanks." She lifted one of the scones and bit into it. "Oh, Mum, this is divine. I totally forgot about breakfast." She picked some crumbs from her lap. "Gran will be jealous if I tell her. You still make nicer scones than me, even after all my years of catering."

Marjorie smiled. "You can take her some," she murmured, "though she will no doubt say they're not raised enough or are not sweet enough, or find some other defect." She sighed. "Mum likes to carp."

"M'm… She's jealous. Oh, this is gorgeous, honestly." She reached for her mug. "It's been such an odd day. I made Eloise a sandwich for a snack lunch. She'd been helping at a coffee morning and returned exhausted. She shouldn't have gone, she was awfully upset earlier, but I daresay it kept her from moping. She was fond of Percy."

Marjorie stirred sugar into her coffee. "We'll have to arrange his… um, service." Marjorie clamped her lips as though she could not bring herself to say the word funeral.

Fenella patted her hand. "It's all right, Mum. I contacted Kinvig's, earlier. They were very kind. Of course there will have to be an inquest."

"Not for Percy, surely?"

"For both men," Fenella murmured. "It's usual."

Marjorie's shoulders slumped. She sipped, took a breath. "Things are going to come out, Fenella," she said tremulously. "Th-things you should have known, long ago."

"Mother, don't. What's past is past. I don't need to know anything; nor does anyone. What's the point?"

Marjorie shook her head. "I wish I could agree, but… it's because of what happened years ago that I'm afraid…" She lay down her cup. "No, I'm not afraid, I'm just…" Tears erupted suddenly and poured down Marjorie's cheeks. "I'm scared, Fenella, really scared… I can't… you see, I can't help thinking… oh God, oh God." As if a dam had burst Marjorie began to sob with a violence that shocked Fenella. She put her arms around her, though Marjorie tried to wriggle away. Marjorie's head drooped. Saliva, tears and scone crumbs fell onto her lap. "Oh, Nell, Nell, Nell, what have I done? What have I done?"

Fenella gasped. "Mum! For God's sake? What *have* you done?"

Charles Peake grunted. It was not a pleasant sound. "No, it's not convenient. I'm going to play golf."

The voice on the other end of the phone jabbered on.

Charlie's sallow skin flushed; the tips of his ears reddened. Anyone face to face would have known to back off. But the speaker on the phone could not see the effect his words were having and so they kept on nagging, over and over …

"For Christ's sake, shut up, you bloody fool." He slammed the phone down with such violence that the receiver cracked. Grabbing up his golf club cap, his clubs already in the car, he slammed out of the house.

Betty Knowles, slightly deaf and profoundly unimpressed by anything her employer ever did, tutted as she descended the stairs, duster in hand. She stood by the cracked phone and raised her eyebrows.

"Well," she sighed, "I'll pretend I haven't seen it. Let him sort it with Manx Telecom himself."

She shuffled to the kitchen, dusting the hall table and a mirror as she passed. It was time she left; she'd done enough. Her weekly pay lay on the table.

"Thank goodness that call didn't come before he'd left my money," she muttered, removing her apron and placing it in a drawer. She paused beside the washing machine, still in mid-cycle. She watched as she fastened her anorak and pulled on her cycle clips. Fancy him doing a wash? He usually left things for her to sort out. Charlie wasn't good with machines. He'd put a jersey through on hot wash once. He'd gone mad when it came out half its size. It had been a posh jersey from the Laxey Wool Mill.

"Serve him right for having more money than brains," she huffed as she let herself out, taking a last look at the washing machine, still not onto the rinse cycle.

"I wonder what he's put in it. I cleared that laundry basket yesterday." She pulled the door to, threw her leg over her bike saddle and cycled down the crunching gravel of the drive. "Perhaps he had an accident on his way home from the pub," she mused as she paused at the gate to look both ways. He'd looked well over the eight when she'd seen him crossing the swing bridge.

She cycled to the main road and slowed as a police car passed in the other direction. She was unaware that one of the occupants craned his neck and said something about her to his colleague.

Peter stared at the still water of the lake, untrammelled by any pleasure craft. The boat house had been closed for the time being. It was a lovely day and the sensational news that a body had been found in the park early that morning had brought people from all parts of the island to gawp. Luckily the park was large and there was space enough for the crowds to amble along the far lakeside without interfering with the cordoned-off area. Nevertheless, Peter was not happy with the holiday atmosphere that the pleasant weather had created. A couple of coach operators had even chosen to fetch groups of sightseers, adding considerably to the congestion at the parking area between the rugby pitch and the promenade.

"Keep them away." Peter was terse with the young constable who'd approached for instructions. "We'll close the entire park if we have to, and tell those kids across there to get off that hedge."

It wasn't just young kids that were clambering about on the fence and hedges: adults, mostly with cameras, were fighting for a view of the cordoned-off area, though there was by now nothing to see. "Not that there seems much point in our being here," Peter sighed after having spoken to the scenes of crime officer in charge of the few men still present. "No traces of anything untoward save a bag of litter and some dog mess."

"Dogs aren't allowed in the park, are they?" Dave Colvin, hands in pockets, was staring at the messy pile of bits and pieces being scooped from the lake bottom.

"No, but dogs can't read. I've seen them myself, wandering through here, early in the morning," Peter quipped sardonically.

Dave grinned. "Perhaps we should put out a call for all dogs with information to call into the station."

Peter nodded. "You're right. Let's go. We're wasting time. We may as well see if there's been any response to our Wakefield number."

They had only just driven away, watched eagerly by the onlookers, when one of the men in waders lifted his head and shouted, "Here's a find, Sarge, what about this?"

And he held a tiny object above his head.

Norah woke up and flapped her hand towards her book. She found it, fumbled for her glasses and had propped them on her hook nose before she remembered.

Then she dropped the book and stared at the ceiling, each crack in the plaster magnified by her smudgy spectacle lenses.

Percy was dead. Her dear friend, her oldest friend, was gone for good. She'd never see his comfortable, familiar face again. What did the goings-on of storybook characters matter? What did anything matter? Life was sliding past and slipping out of reach so fast, and no one cared. Marjorie had gone and left her for good. Yes, after all this time she'd dumped her old mum and left her. It made a body think, didn't it? Fenella would be there to call on, o'course, but a granddaughter wasn't the same as a daughter, was it?

Norah crimped her lips. She'd done a lot for Marje. She'd made Bayview over to her, all those years before. If Marje had subsequently handed it, lock stock and barrel, to Fenella that was her business and was beside the point. No, she'd provided her daughter with a job for life, which she'd turned down. She'd preferred to get a dithering civil service job! Civil service, huh – over-paid fat arses, they were. Look at the trouble she had that time with her income tax? Had any of the stuck-up government bodies given her a hand?

No, they had not. She had not deliberately withheld any income, either. She'd just got mixed up with all the forms they sent. It was always the same: without a man around things like that didn't get done... without a man?

Norah swallowed hard and wrinkled her nose so that the specs bounced and the wallpaper blurred.

When she thought back... really dwelled on the issue – that was a new arty-farty expression she'd heard on the radio – she'd actually been without a man for most of her life. Crikey! Odd, that, really, because so had Marje and Fenella. That had been a screaming shame, that had. Fenella's fella, Brian, had been a real cracker. A stunner, especially in his racing leathers, which had left little to anyone's imagination. She'd had a pash herself on Brian Kelly, and when he was killed it hurt, just as it had hurt when Walter died, and when Donald was smashed up by that drunk driver. It justified all her pessimism towards men that got involved in their family. That three men should die was more than bad luck; it was more like a curse. "The Bayview curse," she muttered, clearing her throat. Her mouth hung open. No, Fenella and Brian hadn't lived at Bayview together, so that notion didn't hold water.

"It was bloody tragic, all the same."

She found it hard to recall Walter's face; it was so long ago when they'd had that lovely weekend when he'd got an unexpected leave. They'd sent young Marjorie out to play and spent most of their time in bed. Then he'd barely gone back over on the evening ferry and she was still aching 'down below' from all their lovemaking when she got a telegram. He'd been killed by a bomb, near Lime Street Station. Christ, what a life, dogged by death.

Fifteen years later Donald had kicked the bucket, leaving Marjorie a widow with Fenella to rear. A nice quiet fella, Don had been, though with not much in the way of brains and he'd been doing a friend a favour when he'd gone to fetch some stuff and been killed. Poor Don...

Now Percy had gone as well. Not that Percy had been what Walter had. He'd have liked to think he was. He'd told her he loved her many a time over the years and she believed him. But Percy's love wasn't like what Walter's had been. She hadn't felt like that for any other man, save…

Norah struggled to sit up. Her glasses slid on the coverlet and bounced to the floor. "Hell," she whispered, panic gripping her. She felt dizzy, she was alone and no one loved her anymore and if she dropped dead right that minute no one would care.

Besides, he was dead too. "Georgio." Norah's cracked voice uttered the name she'd suppressed for years. Once she'd sworn she'd never say it again, ever. He didn't deserve it. After what he'd done he deserved to be damned in hell. Wasn't that what the papists believed? She didn't. She'd been to a sensible Wesleyan Sunday school when she was a lass, and later, well, later, no one would want her in their church and she didn't care.

It had been a shock, seeing Georgio, changed from a handsome boy to an ugly old man; she had never thought of him as getting old. She'd always seen him as he'd been that… day. Except that she had tried for years not to think of him. For nigh on fifty years she pushed any thought of him away, though she had never forgotten… or forgiven…

"Bastard…" Norah wailed, and slow tears slithered down her crepey cheeks. She sobbed and wiped her face on the bed sheet.

"I'm not cryin' for him," she shouted to her reflection, which was gawping at her, that old harridan's face which she could never get used to and which was looking worse than ever. "'M cryin' for Percy, the old fart…" Her chin crumpled and she began to howl. "Who'll love me now, eh, who?"

The door opened. Emily peeped shyly in. "Are you all right, Norah?" She faltered. "I heard, um…" She looked away from Norah's stricken face as she hurried in. "I've brought you a cup of tea? Tom's cutting sandwiches. He's going to come and get you up in a moment. Are you all right?"

Norah hastily blinked back her tears. She was glad it was Emily and not Tom seeing the state she was in. "Aye," she gasped. "Give us a minute, love."

Emily put the cup on the bedside cabinet and handed Norah a box of tissues from her cluttered dressing table.

"Thanks, pet," Norah said gruffly, blowing her nose. "I'm fine, love, give us that tea a bit closer, aye, that's grand."

Emily did so and stood quietly as the old lady drank with great greedy gulps.

"Don't you let young Tom out of your grasp," Norah rasped, her crabbed hand gripping Emily's arm with surprising strength. "Don't waste your chances, girl. Not like me."

Emily was astonished. Norah looked so frail, yet her grip was like a vice. "I won't." She quavered, but she would not let her eyes meet Norah's.

"Mother," Fenella whispered. "What do you mean?"

"I'm telling you, love. You've read it, haven't you?" She held out the flimsy piece of newsprint that she'd cut out from the paper. "All that it says?"

"Yes, but what does it matter? The war was such a time ago. How can it harm anyone now?"

"Oh, it can, Fenella, and I told him so. I told him he'd be stirring up a can of worms if he gets people mulling over the war years and that he should forget the whole idea."

"Mum. You said that to Charlie Peake?"

"Yes, I told him straight. For goodness' sake, I remember Charlie Peake when he was a dirty little urchin trailing you home."

Fenella's lips tightened. "I do too, but that doesn't mean I'd deliberately annoy the man. He can be nasty, Mum."

Marjorie's face reddened. "Fenella, no one could have upset him more than you've done these last few months, refusing to accept his offer for Bayview. What I did was nothing more than give him a piece of my mind. I was feeling upset and I let on about things more than I meant. I'm sorry, Nell, but I let on to him about the offer you'd had."

"You didn't. Mum, how could you?"

"I wanted to shut him up, love. He wouldn't listen to a word I was saying. You know what he's like. He refused to consider not going ahead with this wartime memories project. I pleaded with him. I told him that there were lots of his parents' friends who'd be upset if he went ahead."

"What did he say to that?"

"Laughed in my ear and swore. I thought he was going to ring off, and then he got all oily and started to butter me up. He offered to reconsider the whole venture if you would change your mind over Bayview. I was furious by then, with myself as much as with him. Fancy him, Charlie Peake, dictating to us. I told him straight that we didn't need to accept his measly offer as you'd just got an unconditional offer which you intended to accept."

"Mother, for heaven's sake."

"He got me cross, Nell, as I said. I was upset, not myself."

Fenella put her arm round her mother's shoulders. "Never mind. It doesn't matter, does it? Nothing will come of George Stevens' offer now."

"But that's not the point, Nell. Late last night I was standing here, staring out. I hadn't been able to sleep, though I'd gone to bed early because I felt so wretched. I was having a cup of Horlicks, and I saw Charlie crossing the road, towards the Mooragh, trailing after him."

"What? Trailing after who – you mean Charlie was trailing George Stevens last night?"

"Yes. I saw the old man first and I saw Charlie Peake, following."

"What did you do?"

"I went out. I wanted to have it out with him, with the both of them; I was fed up of bottling everything up."

Fenella stared, horrified. "Oh, Mum."

Peter stared at the post-mortem report before him.

"Daniel's been quick," Dave commented.

"M'm. Here." Peter handed it over and Dave quickly read through the salient points.

"Bruising on the back of the neck, but death occurred due to a coronary... the amount of water in the lungs makes it likely that the heart attack happened before the deceased's immersion... M'm, and so on..."

Dave scanned the rest of the two closely typed sheets and handed them back. He shrugged. "So, what do we deduce from that?"

Peter shrugged. "You tell me. Was it murder or was it death from natural causes?"

"Could he have fallen into that position? As you said, he'd have put his hands out if he was suddenly taken bad. He'd not have landed with his hands tucked beneath him."

"No, that's why I can't take the evidence on face value. For heaven's sake, we've seen enough sudden deaths from natural causes, and if that was a natural cause I'm a Dutchman."

"Unless—"

A knock at the door interrupted Peter's speculations.

"Message from Wakefield, sir. They've been in touch with the next of kin."

"Good. Is someone still on the line?"

"Yes, sir."

"Deal with that, Dave, would you?" Peter picked up the PM report again and began to read through it more carefully.

"Shall I put it through?"

"No, I'll come out. I want to get a coffee from the machine."

Dave Colvin followed the CID officer out. "Ready for the match on Thursday, Ian?"

"Oh, yes, sir. I never thought I'd be picked for the team."

Peter heard the exchange and smiled as his eyes ran swiftly down the sheet of close typing. To be picked for the police football team was no distinction. To gather eleven fit men who could kick straight was about as good as the selection process got.

His eyes focused on a technical point and he read a few words, over and over. "Interesting," he murmured, making a note on his pad.

"There, that's done." Dave came in, carrying a polystyrene cup of coffee. "You're sure you won't have one?"

Peter shook his head. "So who's coming, a son?"

"A nephew, Luigi Stephani. Apparently the deceased was a bachelor."

"I see."

"He's flying from Manchester and will arrive at Ronaldsway at 10.30am."

"Good enough. We'll meet him."

"Will we?"

"I'd like to keep this investigation low-key. If it turns out to be a natural death then the sooner all sensational speculation is quietened down the better. We'll meet him in plain clothes and we can dodge the press."

Dave sipped his coffee. "Blimey, this is worse than usual. I think they've got detergent mixed in it."

Peter grimaced. "Glad I'm not having one, then." He stood and stretched. "Right, it's getting on for five o'clock. Is it time we'd find Bertha Quaggin at home, do you think?"

"Cripes, must we?"

"Every avenue, DS Colvin, every possible lead must be explored. By the way, did you get on to the coroner about Percy Corlett?"

"Yes. He's going to try and fit both inquests in on Thursday."

"Good, the sooner the better." Peter doodled on his pad. "Fenella Kelly should be told, I suppose."

"Why don't you give her a ring, sir?"

Peter noted the 'sir' but didn't comment. "No, you inform her, please, Dave. I'll just slip down to the SOCO room before we go out."

The phone trilled. He snatched up the receiver. "Peter Quilliam, yes? What! Where? You're kidding. Great heavens. Right, bring it round." Peter slammed the phone down. "Damn."

"What's up?"

"That was Kevin Quine. The SOCO team have found a gold lapel pin in the lake, right next to where George Stevens' body was lying."

"A gold lapel pin. Well, that could be anyone's and it might have fallen in any time."

"Yes, but this was a Manx Festival pin – you know, a Chruinnaght pin – and they're not that common."

Dave whistled. "A Chruinnaght pin. No, they're awarded for sponsorship or similar towards the annual Celtic festival, aren't they?"

"Yes," Peter said slowly, "and I was close to one recently. Too close, in fact."

"No?! Who was wearing it?"

"Charlie Peake."

Dave Colvin grinned, displaying his small, white, even teeth, which made his resemblance to a good-natured ferret even more marked. "Oh-hoh!" he said. "Things are looking up."

"They are," Peter said slowly. "Come on, let's go to Bertha's, and after that we'll run Charlie Peake to ground."

Dave swigged the last of his coffee and even its bitterness didn't remove the grin from his face.

"This case is beginning to be interesting." He chortled.

ELEVEN

Next morning Tom came running downstairs as Fenella pushed the front door open. She was panting. She'd been for a run along the promenade. It made a pleasant change from cooking breakfasts.

"Mum, glad you're back. Great-Gran is off colour."

"Oh dear! Is she up?"

"No, she's not likely to be, either. She's not right."

As Fenella pulled off her jacket the doorbell rang.

Tom scowled. "Ignore it. It's the press. They've been pestering since you left."

Fenella sighed. "Should I give them a statement or something?"

"Not now, no. I reckon we should get the doctor, though Emily thinks I'm over-reacting. Come and see her, please."

"Right, I will. Sorry I went out, Tom, but I needed some fresh air."

"Did you see Gran?"

"Her curtains were drawn. I hope she's having a lie-in." Fenella was already halfway up the first flight. "I'll call later." She raced up the second flight and was soon opening Norah's door.

Emily was sitting at her bedside. She jumped up. "She's very hot, Mrs Kelly, and she's rambling. I'm glad you're back." Emily's usual confident front had left her. She looked anxious.

Fenella hurried over. "Thanks for staying with her, Emily."
She leaned close to the old lady, who was twitching, her eyes half
closed, her fingers grasping and ungrasping the bed cover.

"What's all this then, Gran?" She laid a hand onto her forehead.
"Yes, she's running a temperature." Fenella's nose twitched. There
was an acrid smell about the old lady too, different from the usual
urine scents.

"Oh dear, Gran, what's up?" As she leaned closer Norah's eyes
opened wide. "You'll not let them take me, Marje, will ye? I didn't
mean ter do it. What was I to do with the blighter?" She gripped
Fenella's wrist, her eyes unfocused. "I'm cold," she mumbled. "Shall
we go indoors?"

Fenella gently released Norah's clutching fingers and smoothed
the bedding. Tom entered.

"You're right, Tom, about the doctor. Would you give the
surgery a call? The number's on the pad in my office. There should
be a locum on duty." She smiled, as Norah's eyes suddenly slipped
into focus. "There now, Gran. You're not cold. You're in your own
cosy bed. Yes, it's me, Fenella, and Emily. You like Emily, don't you?
Tom's girlfriend, you remember Emily?"

"Is she foreign? I don't want no foreigners near. They're not
to be trusted. That's what I told Marje. I told her straight. Don't
let one of them get you, Marje. They're not all like Georgio, an'
Walter wouldn't like it." She gripped Fenella's sleeve and tried to
pull herself up, her eyes swimming. "Is that you, Nell? I'm sorry.
I've done it again. I didn't mean to go. I thought I was on the
bog."

Fenella gave a shaky laugh. "Oh, Gran, never mind. Emily,
would you leave me while I clean Gran and change her?"

"I'll help, if you need—"

"No, I'll be fine. You and Tom make us all a pot of tea."

Emily slipped out, looking relieved. Fenella pushed up her
sleeves and ran hot water into the hand basin. She soaped a flannel

and put it and the towel ready, then she leaned over Norah once more. "Now, Gran? You're still with me, aren't you?"

Norah looked puzzled. "O'course I am, where else'd I be?"

Fenella chuckled. "That's better. Good. Hup-a-daisy. If we get you up just a bit then I can strip you easier." She eased Norah into a sitting position.

The old lady smiled, then her eyes rolled; her body went slack. "Blim-ey," she said incoherently, "the room's all…" All at once the old lady's full weight lay in Fenella's arms.

She swiftly laid Norah prone. "Oh, Gran, don't do this. Don't you go too, for goodness' sake." Frantically Fenella hunted for a pulse. It was there, thank God, and strong, though incredibly fast. Fenella swiftly stripped Norah and easing the soiled sheets from beneath her. "Just rest, Gran dear, till the doctor comes," she said soothingly, realising that she was talking to calm herself as to Norah. It was instinctive – it would be unbearable if Norah slipped away too. It was too soon. There was so much life still in the old lady.

After some desperate moments Fenella's heart leapt as Norah's eyes flicked open.

"I dunno what you're doin', Nell, but I'm bloomin' tired. I think I'll take a nod."

Fenella heaved a sigh. "Yes, old dear, you do that," she said softly, "and I'll just finish getting you respectable." The task wasn't easy, or pleasant, but it had to be done and she, like Marjorie, had got used to it.

Bertha Quaggin's home was a narrow red-bricked terraced cottage in Shipyard Road. She answered the door promptly to the two police officers, though she seemed displeased by their appearance.

"Oh, it's you, young David. Maisie Colvin said you might call." She looked them over truculently. "I suppose you'd best come in, but I'm not saying anythin' without a solicitor by me."

"Good afternoon, Mrs Quaggin." Peter smiled. "It's just a little information we'd like, if you have the time. There's nothing to be afraid of or to require the presence of a solicitor."

Bertha had been leading the way along a gloomy lobby. She swivelled abruptly. "Who said I was afraid? I wasn't talkin' t' you, mister. It's David who's come to see me, Maisie Colvin said he would call, an' it's David I'll talk to. Who're you, anyways?"

Dave hastily intervened. "This is Inspector Quilliam, Bertha. He's recently been posted to Ramsey. I'm his assisting sergeant."

Bertha's gimlet eyes inspected Peter up and down, then, as if she'd not been much impressed with what she'd seen, she returned her attention to David. "Your mam was right proud of you gettin' your sergeant's stripes, David, lad. Come on. Would you like a cup of tea, David?"

Raising his eyes despairingly David trotted obediently after Bertha into her cluttered sitting room. Peter tried to fade into the background. As the narrow room had a deal of weighty and substantial furniture, this was not an easy task. He subsided on a narrow upright chair beside a looming court cupboard.

"Now, what was you wantin', David, lad?" Bertha eventually asked, after she fetched a tea tray and the formalities had been gone through as to how they liked their tea. Peter, who took neither milk nor sugar and had said so, several times, was clutching a Coronation mug liberally sugared and topped with full-fat milk. This he bravely sipped while Dave proceeded with the interview.

"It's the wartime you're askin' after? Well, now, that's a long time ago, David. Can I recall much about it? Just suppose I can. Will it be worth my while?"

David looked helplessly at Peter, who gave a minute shrug, which David understood only too well. It was of the 'you cope with this, it's beyond me' variety.

Dave smothered a grin, realising by the expression on Peter's face that he was having trouble stomaching Bertha's tea.

"You had a position of responsibility in the administration of the Ramsey internment camp, Bertha? In your position you would have had some contact with the detainees?"

Bertha had put three spoons of sugar in her tea. She stirred this, her spoon ringing around the cup at great speed for some moments until it was doubtful whether any interior pattern on the china might survive. Once the brew was stirred to her liking she took a sip, laid the cup on its saucer, smoothed her skirt, patted her steely hair and ran a finger over her pale lips. David waited anxiously, glancing at Peter. Maybe Bertha was gathering herself for an immense pronouncement.

At last the old lady leaned forward confidentially. "We couldn't get no sugar in them days, David. We had butter and milk aplenty and Father was allus sayin' we were the most fortunate people in the British Isles, what with all the farms about. Only for the lack of sugar it wasn't that bad a time, David, but thank you for askin'."

After this revelation she shut her lips tightly and glared at them, one after another.

David looked taken aback. "Er, I beg your pardon, Bertha? We were asking about your connection with the Mooragh Internment Camp?"

"Oh, aye?" Bertha's eyes narrowed. "Maisie didn't say that's what you was wantin'. If she'd tol' me first, like, then I might have said somethin' about the man in the bank, but seeing as she didn't I don't know as I will. It upset me good and proper, catching sight of the fella, I can tell you that for nothin'."

It was approaching the end of a long day, and Dave Colvin experienced the feeling, which swept over him every now and again, of wishing he had taken up any occupation other than what he had. He sighed dolefully and half closed his eyes. This, amazingly, provoked an immediate response. Bertha brightened; she sat up, suddenly alert. "You're not lookin' good, David. I meant to say when I opened the door, fer your age, you're lookin' awful weary. You need to take care, David. Your pa didn't," she paused dramatically, leaning forward, "an' look at the state of him now."

David sighed. "Aye, well." He cast Peter a look as if to say 'why do we bother?', a look which Bertha's observant eyes didn't miss either.

"There now, you take after your granfer, don't you, the poor soul. It's real odd the way some men change when they're grown an' others look just as they did in their prams." She swung a glare towards Peter. "That dead fella hadn't changed, had he? Aye, he got oul'-lookin' but he still had a cocky strut in his oul'-man stagger and his eyes – well, David, the eyes never change." Bertha took a brisk sip of her tea and nodded with satisfaction. Dave leaned back in his chair and tried to look supremely uninterested. Finally Bertha had got going and he had an inkling that she'd not stop till she'd got what she wanted to say off her chest. He recalled a snippet of advice given on one of his first training courses, about finding a person's trigger to make them open up. Clearly he'd unwittingly pressed Bertha's trigger. Now it was just a case of letting her talk herself out. He wondered, glancing idly at the clock, how long it might take. He'd promised Maxine he'd try and get home before the kids went to bed for once.

"I said to Evie I'd seen him before, and that was when she let slip that he was after Bayview. I've never taken to the place being called that. It makes no sense, changing Manx names, just to make it easier fer them English wans who don't know the Manx. Rearyt ny Marrey was the buildin's name when Norah and Walter Tooms took it on. I don't suppose you'd remember Walter, would you, David? Mind… you always were young fer your age. Your mother used to say she had a terrible time gettin' you out of nappies. I don't suppose you recall that, either?" If this was a question, Bertha didn't wait for a reply. "Our Evie is havin' the same problem with her li'l Jimmy." Bertha took another draught of tea and looked suspiciously at Peter. "Quilliam, you said. Was it you who got divorced some years back?"

Peter barely had time to nod before Bertha continued.

"That's the modern way, I suppose. Even you polis aren't up to much. Six constables was all they had for the whole island in wartime. The others was called up, the whole scutch of them. They brought special constables over, o'course, and they had to draft in the militia when there was riots in the Peel camp, but the polis then were tough men then and no scamp would cross a copper, nor call him names like the young terrors nowadays."

As David and Peter sat, temporarily sedated by Bertha's whining voice and a loudly ticking mantle clock, it was as if they'd once more slipped back in time. As he clutched his Coronation mug Peter hid a smile. This was one of the Manx characters his parents were always saying were dead and gone. Well, this one was alive and kicking, and boy could she talk.

"So, when I saw him, like, I was drawn right back and it took all Evie's remindin' to get me rememb'r'in' what for I'd gone into the bank."

Bertha paused, gulped the remainder of her tea, emptied the dregs in a slop bowl and poured herself another dose. "He was a good-lookin' fella, back then, was that lad; sort o' childish, mebbe, an' I can understand Norah Tooms fallin' for him. She was in a state, after all, an' so might I ha' been." Bertha ladled sugar into her cup and began the stirring ritual.

"Though I wasn't interested in scallywagging. I had a good man over by and I knew he'd come back, an' come back he did. I'd been to a clairvoyant in the glen at Groudle, ye see, at the start of the war, and she tol' my fortune. She was right too." Bertha chinked the spoon into her saucer. "I don't suppose you fellas have time for clairvoyants?"

David opened his mouth to reply, but Bertha rattled on.

"Aye, I had my work, an' plenty of it, with the internees, an' I earned good pay. I put by a good bit, too." Bertha sipped gingerly. "Norah Tooms wasn't the only one slippin' off the path of righteousness, but he was a strange one, that fella. Most of them stuck together. He was a loner and she got stick from the locals. People knew… all those men gone away to the fightin' and gettin' injured." Bertha's watery eyes stared mistily into the fire. "There was a scotch of bad feelin' t'wards women like her. Kep' myself to myself." Bertha looked up, frowning as though they'd spoken. "An' why shouldn't I? You've not come to make trouble, after all these years, have you, David? I don't want no rakin' up of those days. I told Charlie Peake as much when I saw him the other day. Him and the commissioners, tryin' to put on a war exhibition. Who wants to remember them times? It's to make themselves feel good, they're doin' it. No good reason for that. Mostly they didn't live through it."

Peter cleared his throat. David cast him a look. "What happened all those years ago between Norah and Georgio that made him return, Bertha?"

Bertha's mouth tightened. "Aw, well, I'm not tellin' tales, not after all this time." She picked up her cup, drained it and then glanced at the slow-ticking mantel clock. "Well, my laws, look at the time. I've got to meet the li'l fella from his bus. Evie's workin' late." Bertha jumped up, snatched the cups from their hands, glaring at Peter for leaving so much of his drink. "I daresay you've got people to lock up and suchlike things to do anyway." Bertha bore the cups towards her kitchen. "Let yourselves out, David, lad?" she called over her shoulder.

David and Peter rose. "Thanks, Bertha, we will."

"Thank you for your time," Peter said, as she emerged.

"I'll always do my duty to help the polis, Mr Quilliam."

Peter managed to keep a straight face as he and David hurried along the dim hall and let themselves out.

"Well," Dave took a deep breath, "are we further forward?"

"We know your mother had a terrible time getting you out of nappies." Peter shrugged.

"Thanks. Perhaps you'd like me to make a note of it on a statement."

"No, lad. I'll just put it a memo on the station noticeboard."

Dave groaned as he slumped into the car. "I feel as though I'd been battered about the head. I always feel the same after visiting my parents' generation. I never get a word in edgeways."

"Poor you," Peter said unsympathetically.

"Have you no old relations we could question?"

Peter shook his head. "I grew up in Douglas, remember? I'm a southerner and beyond the pale to Ramsey residents."

"How come you know Fenella Kelly?" Dave asked bluntly as he fastened his seatbelt.

"What?" Peter gave him a pained look. "Oh, er, Fenella and me go way back, Dave. You really don't want to know."

"Don't I?" Dave looked hopeful. Peter, his face impassive, nodded curtly to start the car. Dave, hiding a grin, obeyed.

Charlie Peake stared grimly at the empty horizon. The wind, always strong at the Point of Ayre, the most northerly tip of the Isle of Man, buffeted his car, spatters of sand blasting at the immaculate paintwork. Charlie's eyes were screwed up, glaring at the misty haze that was Scotland, a mere fifteen miles away. Charles wished he were there. In fact, he wished he were anywhere but where he was. His insides were queasy with anxiety and the aftereffects of over-indulgence. Foolishly he'd gone to the golf club. He'd imagined that after a few holes he might have worked off his ill temper and tension. But the atmosphere had been unpleasant; there were rumours afoot. He could tell by the way people glanced and looked away as he'd entered the members' bar. He had one drink and left. He'd got himself into a mess all right and this time he wasn't sure that he could bluff his way out of it. He eased his neck, which was rigid. His eye was giving him jip too. That dratted tic had started up again. It wasn't as though he wasn't used to a bit of strife; he usually had some deal on the go which wasn't entirely above board. Such speculations were a necessary spice to a life that rarely came up to expectations. But this was different. This time he'd got himself in a real fix, and he wasn't sure what to do. Besides, the realisation that what he'd done might put his future as a commissioner at risk made him wish to God he had acted differently. Being impulsive had always been his downfall, and this time…

"Bloody hell," Charles murmured, running his stubby fingers through his thinning hair.

He knew he was not as bright as some; occasionally this bothered him. Mostly it didn't. He believed he made up in animal cunning what he lacked in intelligence. It was his lack of forethought that sometimes caught him out. He'd not got mired in anything like this before, though…

Oh, cripes. He put his arms on the steering wheel and lay his head on it. "Blast Fenella Kelly," he groaned, banging his head harder than intended so that the horn sounded. He winced and jerked upright. This unwise movement in turn wrenched his neck. Charles groaned loudly, glared at his reflection in the mirror, then, deciding on a course of action, he leaned forward and switched on the ignition. He reversed, too fast, off the shingle parking area so that the car skidded. He fought with the steering wheel, corrected the steering, rammed the car into forward gear and headed back along the narrow track to the main road as though seven devils were after him, which, in his mind, they were.

The route from the Point of Ayre to Bride village snaked between alluvial sandy hills. In the distance the central spine of the Manx mountain range rose in an undulating purple spine of gentle peaks and troughs, with the highest of these peaks being Snaefell, the only Manx mountain. The sight of those not-too-faraway hills, etched against the afternoon sky, lured Charles Peake.

In his mind he was already up there, intent on a clear, fast run to Douglas and a precautionary visit to his lawyer friend in Athol Street. It would be a sensible move, in the circumstances. Charlie felt a smile burgeoning inside him. A blast over the mountain section of the TT course usually blew any worries away and helped put things into perspective. Yes, he could almost smell the heather-laden breeze and the exhilarating thrill of watching his speedometer rise past a hundred miles an hour on those tricky but splendid bends.

Unhappily, at the precise moment when Charlie was feeling a growing sense of optimism, he was not heeding the much nearer bend that he was fast approaching, while from the opposite direction, also approaching the bend, overlooked by a pair of idyllic thatched cottages, was a substantially laden refuse lorry, which through necessity had to cross the centre white line on the arcing curve.

The impact was inevitable; Charles could neither swerve nor brake as his bonnet caught the full force of the impact. The grinding clash of metal rang loudly in his ears as his car was flung on its side and cannoned sickeningly into the sod hedge. Fastened by his seatbelt Charlie felt a dizzying sensation of noise and breaking glass before breath and consciousness was knocked clear out of him.

The men in the refuse lorry were ashen-faced as the driver juddered the large vehicle to a creaking stop.

The crash alerted an elderly occupant of one of the cottages. "I'll phone fer an ambulance," he shouted from his gate.

One of the refuse crew, a young lad, raced to Charlie's car, took a look inside and immediately wished he hadn't. He did not recognise Charlie Peake, though the driver, who'd by now also jumped out, an older Ramsey resident, had recognised the car even as he'd tried to take avoiding action.

"Bloody hell, Charles," the man said, trembling and backed away, pulling the lad and his mate with him. Charlie Peake was too well wedged in the mess to be extricated and there was no point in putting themselves at risk. The men stood fearfully while steam and fumes rose from the mangled wreckage. An old woman brought out mugs of tea and they sipped them gratefully, leaning against the harebell-dotted hedge until eventually they heard sirens approaching.

TWELVE

George Stevens' nephew, Luigi, was short, stocky, and though he looked Italian, he exuded Yorkshire bonhomie. His guileless smile immediately endeared him to Peter and Dave as they introduced themselves at the airport.

"Good to meet you." Luigi beamed, his dark eyes lively. "I should be sad, in the circumstances, I suppose, but I'm not. You see, Uncle Georgio's been failin' a while."

The officers were relieved. It was often difficult dealing with sudden bereavements if the relation was close.

"Have you lived in England long?" Peter asked as they were walking to the car.

"Since I were born," he answered promptly. "I'm Yorkshire through and through."

"Are you indeed?" Peter smiled.

"When I was nobbut a bambino I was taken to meet my nonna in Tuscany, and we had a few holidays over there, but it were always too hot for me. England's my home." He spread his hands expressively. "Yorkshire's in my blood, tha' knows, and I'm proud of it."

Dave winked at Peter as Luigi settled himself in the back of the unmarked vehicle.

"Trust mi' uncle to be a trouble even at his end. We've a family wedding arranged for this Saturday coming an' it's too late to postpone. I had to call in a few favours to fly over."

"We're very grateful," Peter said, over his shoulder. "And we should not need to keep you here long, sir."

Luigi shrugged and sat up, looking about with interest as Dave started the car and headed for the airport exit.

"Ee, don't get me wrong, I don't object to a change of scene any time and flying today was a right adventure." He gazed around delightedly. "It's right nice, this place, by t'looks of it."

As they joined the main road to Douglas Luigi's head swung from side to side. "It's a bit like the Dales, isn't it? Eh, look at that view. I've never been to the Isle o' Man before."

Peter smiled. Their guest was a pleasant chap, for sure. Cheerfulness seemed to radiate from him. His 'ooh's and 'ah's kept them amused as they drove along the narrow, tree-lined roads. Clearly Luigi was not mourning, which made one wonder why.

"Did your uncle ever talk of his time here?" Peter asked, once the significance of saluting the 'Little People' while passing the Fairy Bridge at Santon had been explained, obeyed and laughed over.

"No, Uncle was not a man to reminisce. He was canny when it came to business, mind. He made a lot of cash with all his properties." Peter glanced at Luigi in the rear-view mirror. He saw the man's face crumple. "Eh, but he was a miserable feller. I don't know why, either. I once asked him. 'Uncle George,' I said – he had a thing about his name, too. He liked allus to be called George. Anyway, I asked him straight, 'Why are you so miserable when you're rich enough to buy and sell folk?'"

"What did he say?" Peter queried interestedly. Dave, glancing into the driving mirror, glimpsed Luigi's rueful expression.

"He told me to mind my own business and be respectful to my elders. Then he muttered something about not looking back."

"Was he married?"

"Naw! Uncle George, marry?" Luigi chuckled. "Who in their right mind would have taken on the old miser?"

Peter smiled. "He would have been good-looking as a young man, though?"

Luigi beamed. "As a young man he was an Adonis. He should have had a good marriage and fathered lots of bambini. They'd have geed him up!" With a grin he reached into a pocket. "I've fetched some photos, I didn't know if you'd need any? These were given me by Mama, his sister. It's good to see that at one time he knew how to smile."

"Thanks, Mr Stephani, they may be useful." Peter reached for the snapshots and looked at them briefly. "Could we make copies?"

"O'course, lad," Luigi said, and leaned back comfortably to enjoy the remainder of the drive.

Peter gazed at the small black and white snapshots of a dark-haired handsome young man, a lad with brooding eyes and an unsettling intensity of gaze. He could imagine the effect such a fellow might have on an ingenuous Manx girl, especially in wartime, when eligible men were thin on the ground. This made it all the more intriguing as to what must have happened between the man and Norah. Something momentous for a careful man like George Stevens to wish to pay reparation so many years later.

As they drew up outside the grim stone mortuary building Luigi shifted uneasily. "Ah'll be glad when this is over," he muttered, rubbing his hands nervously as they ushered him inside and along a cool corridor. Though Luigi could pass easily for a native Italian and his name conjured up visions of a sun-drenched countryside, Peter suspected he would be more at home in a town with a fish and chip shop within hailing distance.

When they emerged, by which time Luigi was looking decidedly pasty, Peter was proved right.

"I could do with a bite to settle m'stomach," he declared fervently. "Do you know of a chippy hereabouts?"

By the time the two officers returned to Ramsey Police Headquarters Charlie Peake's accident was on everyone's lips.

"Head-on impact, they say," the station sergeant said grimly.

"He looked a mess," Colin Davis put in. "I was at the Cottage Hospital when he was stretchered in."

"Isn't he at Nobles?" Peter asked. Most serious cases were taken straight to the main island hospital on the island.

"He is now," the sergeant nodded. "The ambulance went clanging through half an hour ago."

"Shall I find out how he's doing?" Dave Colvin asked, frowning. "If he is a gonner then we can scrub him from our enquiries."

Peter grimaced. "Give the bloke a chance, Dave. Much as I dislike Charlie I wouldn't wish a road death on him. Go on, then, see what the state of play is – I'll be in the office."

Dave Colvin picked up the phone and dialled the hospital number. He asked to be put through to the accident and emergency department.

"Hi, is that you, Maggie?" he asked the bright voice that answered. "Dave Colvin here. I believe Charles Peake's been brought in. Can you give me an update?"

"Sorry, Dave. They're still cleaning him up. He's in a mess, but I believe he's not as bad as was first thought."

"That sounds like Charlie." Dave chuckled. "He's probably only done it for publicity; isn't there a commissioner's election coming up soon?"

"Dave Colvin." Maggie Kerruish sounded shocked. "For goodness' sake!"

"Sorry, Maggie, just a joke. OK, shall I give you a ring in an hour or so?"

"That might be a good idea, Sergeant Colvin. We should have made a more accurate assessment of his injuries by then."

"Oh, right, the doctor's listening, is he?"

"Yes, thank you, sir." The line was cut, abruptly, and Dave

winced. He hoped he'd not got Maggie Kerruish into trouble. She was a distant cousin and a nice girl. She and he had played doctors and nurses as children. It was good that Maggie had achieved her childhood vocation. Dave was glad he hadn't. Being a detective was gory enough at times, but most of the villains he dealt with were unbloodied – well, apart from Saturday nights.

Fenella heard the sirens as an ambulance hurtled down Bowring Road. She'd been stripping a bed in one of the second-floor bedrooms. It was not a job she relished, and that day she wished she could be doing almost anything else, but things had to be done, and now that there seemed little chance of staying on at Bayview, she thought she might as well get stuck into the job of making the place tidy.

Whether the bank would allow her to take any of the bedding with her was another matter. Would they be entitled to repossess everything, even personal possessions, to recoup their mortgage loss? Idly she wondered about the two televisions. Tom would be put out if he had to buy a TV as well as all the other items he needed for his flat.

"Put out." Fenella wrenched a pillowcase off and tossed it on the growing pile. "What an understatement. His home is to be swept from under him, that's the bloody truth of the matter." Fenella felt tears prickling, which was totally ridiculous because hadn't she been preparing for this time for months? She glanced out of the window at the familiar view of the beach and felt a horrid 'pit of the stomach' pang. She would miss that view so much, seeing the sea every day in its every mood.

She straightened. Yes, well, she'd viewed the sea for long enough. It might be nice to have a change.

Taking a sudden impatient glance around the room she knew that she would miss the sight of the sea much more than these high-ceilinged rooms which she'd decorated, scrubbed, vacuumed and dusted for enough years to be glad that such chores were almost at an end. "Perhaps I should have accepted Charlie's offer ages ago," she muttered, hefting a mattress and standing it against the wall, then pulling the valance off and folding it loosely before tossing it with the other dirty linen.

"If only," she sighed, pulling the mattress back and straightening it. "If only the old man hadn't died." She gulped. And what about Percy? If ever a man had deserved to live longer it had been Percy. *Oh God, why is all this happening?*

She gathered the bedding and stuffed them into yet another bin liner. "Do I really want to stay here? After whatever happened in the wartime? How would I feel only being able to stay here because of something awful that went on all those years ago?"

"Grrrr!" She wrenched at the last pillowcase and stood back. "Another room done," she groaned, pulling the bundle to the landing and dropping it over the bannister rail, where it bounced and bumped its way to the ground floor.

Fenella opened the door to the next room, recently occupied by the Burridge children. Immediately she scented dried urine.

"Messy little blighters," she sighed, noticing crayon scribbles on the wall and strips of torn wallpaper. It was just as well the room didn't have to be used again soon.

As she bent once more to remove bedding her thoughts returned yet again to Georgio and his unexpected offer; even if it was null and void it was still a weird happening.

The bank hadn't rung her yet, but it was only a matter of time. The date for repossession was less than a week away. She could not imagine anything stopping it now. "Not even death," she sighed, uncovering a stain on the sheet which had penetrated not only the undersheet but the mattress too.

"Urgh." She growled and wrenched the bedding off. "I shall not, however, be sorry to see the last of incontinent children and old people."

Then she felt horribly mean. Norah could not help her incontinence. And as for old Percy, he'd been such a lovely, gentle man; his presence and his good nature had been inextricably woven into their lives. She was surprised how upset she felt each time she realised she could never see Percy again, cycling around the town, seeming to not have a care in the world.

She paused with a bundle of sheets close to her chest. If she felt bad, how must poor Norah feel? It was no wonder the old dear had become ill. Percy had been her constant support and friend. And Norah could hardly help her incontinence. It happened; maybe it would happen to her, one day. She heaved a sigh; Norah would not be soiling many more sheets at Bayview anyhow. Arrangements had been already made with Barrule Park Nursing Home to admit her into their care.

Fenella trailed wearily to yet another room. Soon another bag was ready to be tossed over the bannister. She gazed down, listening to the quiet murmurs of the house, the creaks she'd lived with for years. The tick-tock of the grandfather clock with its comforting heartbeat. She must certainly take that clock with her or – oh, hell, or could she? A flurry of laughter sounded through one of the open front windows, startling her. Some folk had no worries, lucky things.

Fenella paused. Norah must still be asleep, dosed up by the doctor, who had confirmed that the old lady had nothing more serious than a mild fever and needed rest. Tom and Emily were downstairs playing chess. Eloise Green had gone to a cousin's to stay. Fenella knew she wouldn't have her back. At the funeral she'd have to tell her that she must take her belongings and go. "I might be reduced to staying with a cousin myself soon," she muttered aloud, "if I can find one who'll have me."

The thought was depressing. The busy life of Bayview was over; soon the building would be locked and deserted, and she would be homeless, save for Marjorie's sofa bed. That would be a stopgap, at least, and then what?

This abrupt ending wasn't what she'd planned when she'd taken Bayview on when it was a thriving business. She'd not expected to make a fortune, but never in her worst nightmares had she thought she'd end up turfed out on her ear. Why had it all gone so wrong?

She entered one of the two large front rooms with their lovely sea views. As she bent to strip another bed the ringing of the phone on the ground floor did not register for some moments, so absorbed was she in self-pity, so when she heard Tom shout she felt nothing but weariness. No doubt it was a misguided holidaymaker trying for a booking. She continued to pull off sheets.

Tom's feet, pounding on the stairs, made her look up. She stepped out. "It's not Mum, is it, Tom?"

"No, it's the bank. They want to speak to you."

Fenella's heart bumped. This was it then. She hurried down the creaking stairs, flashing Tom a resigned smile as she lifted the receiver.

"It's Will Kaneen," Tom said abruptly as she was about to speak.

"Huh!" Fenella gripped the phone crossly. *It would be him*, she thought dismally, *a real Job's comforter if ever there was one.*

"Hello, Fenella Kelly speaking," she said brightly, though it cost her and her insides clenched.

"Good morning, Mrs Kelly. I am ringing to inform you that all necessary monies have been deposited against your mortgage. We will, of course, send a confirmatory letter in today's post."

Fenella's head reeled. "I'm sorry?"

"Ah, yes, maybe we should have let you know sooner, but the paperwork took longer to complete than we'd hoped."

"No, erm, what do you mean?" Fenella's confusion made her speak testily, and she knew she sounded rude, but it was not the moment for niceties. "I think you must have got something wrong, Mr Kaneen. Mr Stevens did tell me of his proposed offer, but surely with his death it's void?"

"Goodness, no!" Will Kaneen sounded outraged. "Mr Stephani, er, otherwise, Stevens, paid the debt in full by banker's draft before his death. I understood that he informed you thus?"

"Well, no, er, yes, in a manner of speaking; at the time I wasn't sure whether to take it seriously, and when he was found, um, when he passed away I decided that his intentions had almost certainly died with him."

"Oh no, no." Willie sounded outraged. "When the old gentleman died everything was already in place, Mrs Kelly. Your mortgage has been cleared. Bayview is yours to do with as you please. According to our information, from Mr Stephani, a debt has been exonerated." Willie lowered his voice. "Of course, I don't know any details of the origin of this debt, which occurred, I believe, many years ago, but the transaction is now complete. All deeds and other documents will be ready for collection, at your convenience."

"Oh... um, goodness... thank you, Mr Kaneen, thank you very much. Erm, yes, erm, goodbye."

"Oh, before you go Mrs Kelly? You may not have heard of Mr Peake's accident?"

"No, I hadn't heard. What happened?"

"His car collided with a refuse lorry near the Point of Ayre. It was a serious accident, I believe. I just thought—"

"Um, yes, well, thank you for telling me." Fenella frowned. *Poor Charlie.*

"No problem, my dear. Well, I'm sure you have lots to do. Good morning, Mrs Kelly."

"Thank you. Yes, thank you very much, Mr Kaneen."

By now Tom was standing by Fenella's elbow and Emily was close behind. Both were grinning.

Fenella put the phone down and felt shaky. Abruptly she collapsed on the bottom stair. "Goodness," she said, "I feel dizzy."

"Shall I get you a glass of water?" Emily offered.

"No, thanks, Emily. Just give me a minute. I can't take it all in."

She rubbed her forehead with her palms and took a deep breath. "Is there any booze in, Tom?"

"Mum, it's only half eleven – in the morning!"

Fenella leaned back on the stairs and grinned. Suddenly she shook her head as if to clear it, then thumped her fists into the air. "Yes! We're solvent, Tom. Bayview is utterly ours!"

"What!"

"George Stevens paid off our debts before he died. Isn't that amazing?"

Emily looked doubtful. "He can't have. How did he have time? I thought he died soon after telling you what he was going to do?"

Fenella's face, so pale a moment before, flooded with colour. "He'd already settled everything. It's cut and dried. I can collect the documents from the bank whenever."

Tom's mouth hung open. He gaped at Fenella and then at Emily. "Mum, are you kidding?"

"I'm not. Well, unless Willie Kaneen is kidding, but I don't think so. I doubt if Willie Kaneen has ever kidded anyone about anything in his life."

Tom's face split in a broad grin. "Mum, that's fantastic. The wily old guy. I feel sorry now for being mean about him, whoever he was, and whatever he and Great-Gran got up to. What are you going to do?"

Fenella looked at the pile of bin bags full of dirty linen lying nearby. Her firm intention of dealing with them evaporated. It was not a day for mundane work. It was a day for celebration.

"Do? I'd like us all to go out for a slap-up lunch, but as Gran isn't well enough to leave and Mum's not here, I'm not sure."

The three of them looked blankly at one another. Fenella thought of all the food in the fridge that she had no intention of cooking. Who would want to cook at a time like this?

"I could get us a takeaway – Chinese?" Tom said.

"I'd rather have fish and chips." Fenella grinned. "Let me find my purse. I'll root out a bottle of wine and set the table. We'll have a long, lazy lunch and toast Georgio." Fenella hurried to the kitchen. She handed Tom some notes from her purse.

"Oh, and Willie said that Charlie Peake's had a serious accident. See if you can find out how serious while you're out?"

Tom frowned. "Why? Charlie Peake has always got your goat. Why the concern?"

Fenella shrugged. "I'm feeling generous-hearted – if I can't be today when could I be? Go on, you might hear something while you're at the chip shop."

"OK." Tom leaned towards her and kissed her cheek. "Great news, Mum, I'm so glad. Come on, Em, let's mosey." He grabbed Emily's hand and they ran down the steps and across the road to the car. Fenella saw a pair of reporters watching from the other side of the promenade. One of them got out and tried to speak to Tom before he drove off, but he waved them away.

Fenella felt like rushing over and giving the reporters an exclusive on her good fortune, but common sense prevailed; she put the snib on the door and hurried to the kitchen to put some plates in the oven to warm.

Her heart was still thumping. The cavalry had come to the rescue in the nick of time. Thank heavens for Georgio Stephani, alias George Stevens.

Fenella wondered whether to race upstairs to tell Norah but wisely stopped herself. Gran didn't need to know; besides, she might get angry or upset. Suddenly sober, Fenella did go upstairs, but she climbed the stairs quietly so as not to disturb her grandmother.

Norah was fast asleep, snoring gently and peacefully. Fenella heaved a sigh and blew her grandmother a kiss before hurrying down again, her heart still pounding.

Late that afternoon Peter Quilliam and Dave Colvin arrived at the grey bulk of the Henry Bloom Noble Hospital in Westmoreland

Road, Douglas. They parked and strolled inside, where they enquired at the desk for Charles Peake.

"Mr Peake has recovered consciousness," Staff Nurse Julie Kneen told them, when they'd reached the relevant ward. "You may see him briefly, but I wouldn't be surprised if he doesn't make much sense." She stared as though expecting them to retreat.

"Thank you," Peter said pleasantly, "just a momentary chat will suffice."

"Charlie often doesn't make sense at the best of times," Dave whispered, as they approached the bed. Peter's mouth tightened. He disliked hospitals. They were a reminder of one's mortality.

Julie Kneen drew a curtain to one side.

"Hello, there, Charles," Peter said quietly, as the injured man turned bloodshot eyes towards them. "My, you do look a mess." His head was bandaged, his left arm in plaster. Julie confided quietly that that he had two fractured ribs as well as a broken collarbone.

"I feel awful," Charlie whimpered. "What state's my car in?"

Peter hid a smile. Trust Charles to be more concerned about his vehicle than himself. "I believe it's a write-off."

"Oh," Charlie sighed, pain flickering in his eyes. "Well, it's insured." He heaved a resigned sigh and Peter, who'd never liked the man, felt suddenly sorry for him. Charlie had no family to comfort him or grieve over his accident; indeed, many would cheer, which was a sad reflection on anyone's life.

"We're sorry to bother you at this time," Peter said. "But we need to talk to you about something that was found near to the body of Georgio Stephani in Mooragh Park."

"Oh." Charlie's voice gave nothing away.

"One of our officers found a Chruinnaght lapel pin in the lake close to where the deceased was lying. I have reason to believe it might be yours. Was it?"

Charlie's eyeballs slid towards the ceiling. Peter and Dave exchanged a glance. A moment before Charlie had looked as if he knew what was going on; now he seemed to have lost contact. They wondered whether he was faking. His pallor had faded to an unhealthy grey. A pulse in his neck was racing.

"Charles?" Peter prompted gently. He gave Dave a swift look, as if to say 'I think we've got all we're going to'.

But then Charlie's eyes swivelled back to them and he spoke, slurring his words as if it was an effort to formulate them. "Aye," he said slowly, "it was mine." He swallowed, his prominent Adam's apple bobbling. "But I didn't do the old bloke in." He met Peter's gaze. "He was laid out when I fell over him."

"Laid out?"

Charlie's lips moved, as though shaping the words before they came. At last he produced one husky syllable. "Dead."

"I see. Why didn't you alert anyone? Why didn't you contact the police or call an ambulance? For all you know he might not have been dead. He might have only been concussed; there might have been a chance of reviving him."

Charlie eased his head on the pillow before replying, and as his gaze swivelled there was a glint of the old Charlie cockiness in his eyes. "I'd had a skinful, but I know a dead man when I see one. It brought me up short, I can tell ye'. There was nothing I could do, or anyone else, an' I was in no state to make a good citizen phone call. I'd just been…" He stopped abruptly and pursed his lips. "Give's a drink o' water, would you? I feel groggy."

Peter lifted the man's shoulders and Dave held the plastic cup to Charlie's pale lips.

"Aye, that's better. Oh, I'm buggered. I don't think I can answer any more… questions now…" He glared at them with blurry eyes. "I didn't have nothin' to do with the ol' geezer's death, though I knew who he was and why he'd come."

"Oh, did you, well—"

"I'm sorry, you've had longer than is reasonable already." Julie bustled up behind them. She lifted Charlie's wrist to feel his pulse.

"Oh dear, his heart's racing. He's not fit to talk further, Inspector Quilliam, so I'd be obliged if you'd leave him in peace. He won't be going anywhere for a while, so you can call again, all right?"

Peter and Dave accepted defeat. They nodded farewell to Charlie and strode out to the corridor, ingesting the knowledge that had been given but saying nothing till they'd passed through the exit doors.

The air outside was fresh; there were faint scents of autumn in the breeze blowing across from the bracken-covered hill, where Carnane mast stood sharply etched against the sky.

"Do you believe him?" Dave asked as they fastened their seatbelts.

Peter shrugged. "Probably." He cast a look over his shoulder. "OK, clear." He settled back then took a glance at his watch. "Oh, is it that time already? We may as well head back. Get our paperwork up to date. Have an early night for once."

"You could visit Mrs Kelly and let her know how things are going," Dave said, deadpan.

"Now why should I want to do that?" Peter muttered defensively. Then he thought of Fenella's mane of dark hair and how her head had once, years before, nestled in his shoulder as he embraced her, and he knew that Dave was right. What he wanted more than anything was to let Fenella Kelly know how things were going.

But how were they going? Did he have a murder inquiry on his hands or was this curious crime an accidental death? An old man, feeling himself ready to die, had decided on a whim to return to the Isle of Man prompted by an event that happened long ago. The event, of whatever kind, involved Norah Toms. His intentions had not been equal to his constitution and he had died, more than likely of natural causes. Was this the truth? Or enough of the truth to make no difference?

THIRTEEN

Marjorie gasped. "You mean the mortgage was already paid off before the old man died?"

"Yes!" Fenella's face was pink with excitement. Marjorie turned away, feeling no such emotion. Good God! That crazy old man! No one had ever thrown money in her direction so lavishly. Also, if Bayview were sold now – even at a knock-down price – her daughter would have cash to squander. Swallowing a host of further acidic realisations, Marjorie forced a smile. "That's good, Nell, you must be happy."

"I want you to be happy too, Mum." Fenella laughed. "It relieves the pressure on you as well, don't you see?"

Marjorie reached shakily for her cup of coffee. She'd not wanted this meeting, but Fenella had insisted, persuaded her that they both needed a change of scene and that it would be good to meet in the Grand Island Hotel lounge.

"Neutral ground," Fenella had pointed out. "We'll be able to relax for once." Marjorie had wondered at Fenella's suppressed excitement when she rang. At first Marjorie had panicked, fearing Fenella had been served with an eviction notice or that Norah had taken a turn for the worse.

Now, sitting quietly with the sun streaming onto the white-clothed table, highlighting a centrally placed china vase of fresh flowers, Marjorie felt torn: glad there was no new crises yet still she felt unsettled. Percy was dead, there was a funeral to face, her mother was soon to go into care, and that man… he had left a taint by his extraordinary transaction. Why, after so long, had he done this?

Marjorie's heart raced, then, aware of her daughter's anxiety, she forced herself to relax. Fenella had been right: it was good that she was here, feeling distanced from the location of the hurt at the heart of this matter. This hotel was a place full of good memories and happy times.

Marjorie put out her hand to touch Fenella's. "The coffee is good here too." She smiled. Fenella understood and relaxed into her chair.

Marjorie glanced around. Only two other tables were occupied. Elderly couples were studying a crossword at one, a scatter of tourist brochures nearby. A lone man was hidden behind a *Daily Telegraph* at another. He was local; he'd nodded good morning as they arrived. Subdued music issued from wall speakers; there was not quite overwhelming sound from the nearby kitchens. Marjorie released her pent-up breath. Yes, coming here this morning had been a good idea.

She gazed at Fenella. "So, you will you stay put for a while then?" She reached for a bowl of demerara sugar and spooned a little into her milky coffee. Fenella took hers black. It was one of the differences between them. Sometimes, Marjorie wondered how she and Donald had conceived this attractive, intelligent woman. It was sad that Donald had not lived long enough to know her as an adult.

Fenella frowned. "I'm not sure."

Marjorie's eyes widened. "Now, that I didn't expect." She did not question Fenella's change of heart. If it was because her daughter was working up to asking her to return as a helper she didn't want to know. As she sipped her coffee she smothered a yawn. She'd had a disturbed night. She would have a nap that afternoon.

She had enjoyed her trip on the bus the day before. She had browsed through some expensive sweaters and clothing at the Laxey Woollen Mills and had had bought a few items. Tom and Emily had called to visit during the evening. She'd been polite but annoyed that Fenella had not called again. It was only after Tom explained about Norah being ill that she understood and then her conscience pricked. After they'd gone she had a luxurious soak in the bath and had slept fitfully, falling only into a heavy doze only as the sky was lightening.

Fenella was saying something; Marjorie came too with a start.

"I suppose I'd got so worked up about moving that when I knew I didn't have to I felt a sense of anti-climax when I found I could stay." She sighed, tweaking her coffee spoon. "I'm not taking guests again, that's definite, and I shan't have Eloise as a lodger any longer. I shall probably tell her at the funeral."

Both women fell silent. Percy's funeral was three days hence. Summer apparently was a slow time for deaths and the funeral director had offered an early slot. Fenella had put a notice in the window at the local newsagent, as was the custom in the town. There were no relations to inform, but his many friends would certainly turn up if only for a free tea. "It's good that there's no inquest," Marjorie said. "Tom mentioned it last night."

"Yes, apparently Percy had dropped into the doctor's only last Wednesday." She frowned. "I hadn't known his heart trouble had got worse."

"I wonder how many will come?" Marjorie murmured. "He was a popular character locally."

Fenella chuckled. "I'm pleased he left such detailed instructions for his send-off."

"Yes, the old pet. It makes things so much easier."

Fenella took a breath. "Mum, I didn't meet to discuss Percy's funeral. I've got all that in hand."

There was a long pause. Marjorie knew she was expected to make a response, but she stayed silent, her hands clasped loosely in her lap, her face in determined repose as she looked past Fenella to the view through the window, of fields and a distant rise of hills.

Fenella, used to her mother's usual easy acquiescence, was nonplussed. She gazed, struck by the lines of her mother's profile. Had Marjorie always looked so serene? No, she'd studied Marjorie's face enough times; there seemed a subtle difference about her that day. A steely tautness in her expression, and in the erectness of her posture, as though she was expressing her feelings – not a tension, more a sense of resolution.

Fenella sat back, her artist's eye critical. What had brought about this subtle alteration? Had Marjorie really been so unhappy at Bayview?

Fenella felt a qualm, a sudden tugging at the fabric of her life. Marjorie had always been easy-going, biddable, the perfect, dependable mum. Yet now she looked... Fenella's heart beat faster. Was this change a result of her mother finally rebelling, or had something happened that had brought about this change?

Was it connected to the sudden death of an old man whose puzzling history was linked to their family? Had his death freed Marjorie in some way? Or was the reason more grievous, because Marjorie had been involved – oh God, surely not – because she'd in some way contributed to the old man's death?

Fenella pushed such a ridiculous suspicion determinedly away. Marjorie could not put anyone to death. The very idea was a joke.

Though not a joke to make her smile; instead, to fill the gathering silence she said impulsively, "Mum, I'd like to paint you sometime, looking as you do now. May I?"

Marjorie flushed. "What a nice thing to say. But why?"

"Because you're my mum and I love you," Fenella said, and then flushed. "God, I sound like a character from an American soap. But you know what I mean."

"I do." Marjorie inhaled, then leaned across and patted Fenella's hand. "I know what you mean, love, and thank you, I'd like that, but," and she paused meaningfully, "whatever else you're planning, don't include me in any plans for Bayview, will you?"

Fenella shook her head. "I wouldn't dare." She smiled, stretching her arms above her head. "Oh, it's so good to get away from home. Much as I've loved the place sometimes I have felt hemmed in. Living and working in the same location is not good. It's time I did something else." She shifted in her chair. "What are you doing for lunch? Shall we stay on here? Push the boat out?"

Marjorie frowned. "What about Mother? You can't leave her so long."

Fenella shrugged. "Tom and Emily are with her and prepared to cater to her every whim. She seemed almost recovered this morning. I reckon her symptoms were brought on by her reaction to Percy's death. It must have been an awful blow. She wasn't even bolshie over her breakfast today. Still a tad subdued. It must have been horrid finding him… gone."

Marjorie sighed. "Will she be fit for the funeral?"

"Oh yes, she said, 'I'll see Percy off if I never do another blinking thing.'" Fenella laughed. "Well, that's a paraphrased version."

"Good. I wonder what they'll make of her at the nursing home. Um, you've made all the arrangements?"

Fenella topped up her cup from the coffee pot. "I did. The matron sounds nice – Stella Cannon's her name. I explained how strong-willed Norah can be. Stella seemed pleased rather than taken aback. She admitted that they enjoy having residents with some fight still left in them."

"Oh, she still has fight in her all right." Marjorie pulled out her hanky to dab her eyes. "It will be a relief when she's settled." She sighed. "How odd, Percy gone and Mum moving, all in a week. It doesn't seem possible."

"M'm," Fenella sighed. Marjorie had known him all her life. She must have felt the loss of him tremendously. Poor, dear Percy; it seemed wrong to be lightheartedly referring to him as if his passing had been a trivial event. No, it had hit them all hard. Marjorie sniffed and dabbed her eyes. She looked suddenly doleful and Fenella felt her fists tighten. Was her mum fretting just about Percy, or was it to do with the death of that other old man?

Marjorie stood up abruptly. "I'll fetch a menu," she said, "and I'll pop to the ladies', won't be long."

Fenella watched her mother walk swiftly away.

Tom and Emily were in the lounge, cosied up on a settee they'd drawn near to the window. Tom's arm was lying lightly on Emily's shoulders.

The sea, at which they were both staring, though neither was particularly aware of it, was grey, with a season's-end look about it. White-capped waves were tossing beyond the breakwater and the empty wet sands looked uninviting.

"I've never been this close to the sea for so long before," Emily murmured, her words coming out as a sigh. "Do you think you'll ever move away?"

Tom twisted to look at her. "What d'you mean, will I ever move away? I'm not trapped here, you know. I can leave the island. I was at college, remember?"

"Yes." She stroked his hand. "But in a way, Tom dear, you were never entirely there, like the other guys. I think that's what attracted me to you in the first place. You were different. You had a distant look in your eyes. No, don't mess around, Tom, listen. I always wondered what lay behind this difference. When I found out where you came from I wondered if you were a bit scared, coming to the mainland after living on a small island all your life."

"Oh yeah, I was really scared." Tom's hands began wandering to the edge of Emily's T-shirt.

"No, don't, Tom. I'm comfy. And I mean it. You were different from other guys." She wriggled and half sat up. "You had a sort of look in your eye at times that I could never understand. It wasn't an apprehensive look, just sort of puzzled."

"I'd probably been overdoing the lager the night before."

"Tom, I mean it. Don't make fun."

Tom felt aggrieved but managed to assume a patient expression.

"Sometimes I got a sense from you that no matter how you were enjoying yourself, well, there was something missing, something that you cared desperately about and couldn't have. After a while I decided the reason for this could only come from your upbringing. In everything else you seemed... not ordinary but not extraordinary either."

"Oh, well, thanks very much." Tom sat up and scowled. "I'd no idea I'd come across as a weirdo."

"Tom, grow up. I'm trying to explain something." Emily gave him a consoling hug. "And since I've been here, what I thought's been confirmed. You love your island home. You're relaxed and happy here in a way you never were at college. I think this is the place you're always going to want to be."

Tom opened his mouth, but she put a hand firmly across his lips. Assuming a ripe Yorkshire accent, she growled at him. "Listen here, sonny, as mi gran would have said, 'Tha's got roots, lad, that's why thou're as thou are.'"

"You're too clever by half," Tom grumbled.

Emily picked up one of his hands and stroked it. Tom felt passion rising inside him but subdued it manfully. Though he did wonder if Emily was as astute as she thought; he'd not felt different when he'd lived away. He'd missed the island, but who didn't get homesick when they went to college?

"I think you *need* to live here, Tom. I think you've been

influenced more by your surroundings and upbringing than you realise." She noticed the scepticism in his eyes and smiled. "It's nothing extraordinary, you know. Everyone's influenced by their home area, to a greater or lesser extent. You love the Isle of Man, don't you?"

"I don't know about love, exactly."

"I do. You belong here and know it. You feel for the land and the sea. You love the hills. You were all lit up when we climbed up to, what was it, Corrin's Folly, on Peel Hill and that other hill we nearly passed out on, what was it? North Bar-rule?"

"Yes, Barrule. I was shattered, I don't know about lit up. I'd forgotten it was such a stiff climb."

"Yes, OK. Just imagine, how would you feel if you could never visit such places again?"

A shadow crossed Tom's eyes, but his answer was pat. "There are other hills, in other places. You're trying to ask whether I would ever want to settle anywhere but over here, aren't you?"

Emily nodded. "Not would want to – but could."

Tom thought back to his three years at college. Funny, he hadn't really considered that time since he'd returned and found a job. Now, the sudden sad jolt which ran through him when he thought of that grotty student bed-sit came as a complete surprise. He'd not felt particularly unhappy across. He'd been too busy, for one thing, and for another he'd met Emily, who had made up for so much, and he'd come home for weekends whenever he could…

He sighed. It wasn't as if there was anything wrong with settling down here. There would always be a need for good teachers on the island, and Tom intended to be as good as he could be. "It's history you're taking, isn't it?" he asked ruefully. "Not psychology?"

Emily laughed and cuddled close. "I think the most important thing is knowing yourself, Tom. And so far, you haven't done much growing up in that direction."

Tom growled. "Oh no," he said, hugging her tightly. "I might be a primary-school teacher but my needs are seriously adult, you impertinent undergraduate."

Emily giggled and capitulated. She thought she'd got her message across, or at least part of it. Tom had to realise that for her there were more exciting places to be discovered than a small island in the midst of the Irish Sea. His needs were not enough for her. In the long term, that was. In the short term, however... "Don't you think we should go upstairs? What if someone comes to the door? They might see us."

"No, they won't," Tom said, and rolled her gently onto the floor.

Walking back on the long Mooragh promenade an hour and a half later Fenella felt sated and satisfied with her outing. As for the rest, her mind was still in turmoil. For once the crashing of the sea and the wide expanse of Ramsey Bay stirred no response, artistic or otherwise. She was puzzled and irritated by the way her thoughts alternately soared and nosedived. A proportion of this state of mind had no doubt been induced by an unaccustomed and substantial lunch, which she had enjoyed very much indeed for not having to prepare a jot of it. Yet now, with things sorting themselves in a natural progression, she felt no sense of relief; in fact, as she gazed ahead to the block of high houses at the end of the promenade, she felt a sudden overwhelming sense of desolation at the thought of her future bumbling about in Bayview alone.

For alone she'd be, with Norah in a nursing home, Marjorie in her flat and Tom living and teaching on the other side of the island. Moreover, the entire burden of the shabby old place would be on her shoulders.

This thought was depressing. If she didn't sell up now she'd probably never do so. She'd grow old there, the building crumbling around her, a Manx Miss Havisham because she was too stubborn to change her life. She'd become like Norah, only she wouldn't have a generous-hearted daughter and granddaughter to care if she lived or died. Fenella squinted into the sun, which was already lowering into the west. Gosh, what had she eaten? She was becoming morbid. Not long since she would have welcomed the chance to be on her own. How many times had she longed for her family to be elsewhere so that she could get on with her painting? She had long relished periods of quiet. But loneliness by choice in her upstairs studio for part of the day was one thing. Rattling about on her own twenty-four seven was quite another. Though she'd often despaired of finding any peace with Mum and Gran around, the fact was that one of them, or Tom, had always been near. She'd never lived an entirely solitary life before.

By some obscure thought Charlie Peake's lugubrious face suddenly leapt into her thoughts, as an example of one person she knew who lived a solitary life. Charlie had lived as a bachelor ever since he'd moved out of the cramped terraced house by the shipyard where he'd grown up. The townsfolk often cracked jokes about Charlie's romances, which were frequent but never lasted. It suddenly struck Fenella that in the pubs they probably cracked similar jokes about her. In some respects she was like Charlie. On the outside tough, yet on the inside, well, she bet under his skin Charlie Peake longed for a loving companion, just as she did. It was his ill fortune, like hers, never to have met the right person.

Fenella kicked out gloomily at a pebble thrown onto the prom by the tide. Perhaps she and Charlie should get together. This thought did make her giggle and she immediately felt less glum. No, that was too ridiculous. Poor Charlie; how much dislike had been directed against him over the years, yet as soon as word of his accident got about she and many others had felt sympathy towards him. She'd been surprised by how upset she'd felt when she believed he'd been seriously injured, and how relieved when it turned out he wasn't. When she'd imagined him at death's door, she'd felt irrationally unnerved. Coming so soon after George Stevens' and

Percy's deaths it had seemed hard to bear, as though all the familiar jigsaw pieces of her life were being scattered.

Fenella had always been irritated by Charlie Peake, imagining herself superior, a feeling which now made her feel ashamed. How wretched he must feel now, all crocked up, his beautiful car, his pride and joy, a write-off, and all his doings and personal business the talk not only of the town but of half the island.

Fenella stood at the pavement edge while a car passed. She crossed to the land side of the promenade, where blackberries were flourishing from rampant leggy brambles on the uncultivated grassy slopes of the brooghs.

She picked a few plump berries and nibbled them as she strolled on. The seasons moved remorsefully; the crops were being gathered in for harvest already and soon it would be winter.

"Ph." Fenella spat out a gritty scrap of berry. *I'm greedy*, she thought. *I ate enough at lunch to last till tomorrow.*

It had been good, though, to share a meal with Marjorie and clear the air. As they'd parted Marjorie had looked far more relaxed as they hugged one another. She'd offered Fenella a lift, but full of food as she was, she'd opted to walk back. It was less than a mile along the prom to Bayview.

Yet she'd enjoyed all the extra calories. It was always the same when she was stressed. Other people got jaded by sorrow and lost their appetites. She always got extra hungry as if to supplement her energy levels. She'd need an excess supply this week. Funerals were always sad. A bramble snaking out from the verge threatened to trip her. She hopped over it, the thorny branch laden with trembling berries. *They should be picked*, she thought, *and if they weren't by the roadside I'd come back and pick them myself. Or send Tom.*

Fenella smiled inwardly. Yes, she felt in the mood for jam-making. She'd have lots of time to make it this year. There was nothing more delicious on dark winter days than eating a homemade scone with blackberry jam, a conserve that held a perfect encapsulation of summer scents and taste.

Yes, she'd fit in a blackberry expedition before Tom left. She and Emily could squash into Tom's Mini. They might take a picnic to the Sulby Valley.

And I'll take a jar of fresh-made blackberry jam to Charlie Peake when he gets home. That'll surprise the old so-and-so. Fenella began to hurry, feeling more cheerful yet also guilty at having been out so long. Norah would need a wash and to freshen up. She'd also need to be told about George Stevens' generosity. That might take some tact.

As she hurried past the perimeter hedge of the Mooragh Park Fenella glanced across at the lake. Several row boats were being steered erratically by end-of-season visitors. Children were laughing and shouting in the play area. The school term would soon recommence and the park cafés and boat outlets would close for the winter.

There was still a cordoned-off area at the foot of the lake. A shiver ran through her. When would this horrible business be cleared up? It was awful not knowing what lay behind the old man's death, and his generosity. If only Percy had not died. It would have been so much easier asking Percy about the war rather than Norah, and certainly easier than prising anything out of her mother. That was if she even knew the truth. Marjorie must have been about ten when the internees came to Ramsey. Fenella thought back to Tom at ten, though it was not a fair comparison. In the forties children would have been less informed by their elders; it was still a time when youngsters were more 'seen than heard'.

What could the secret be? What on earth had weighed on that old man's conscience so heavily for all this time?

She could make no sense of it. She tried to think of something else. Her feet, for instance. They were painful. She'd not intended to walk home, or she'd have put something more comfortable on.

What price vanity. The shoes looked good, but *ouch*, she was going to have a couple of blisters by the time she got home.

Still, not too far now. She looked ahead, beyond the nine-hole golf course towards the block where Bayview lay. As she stared a distinctive white car emerged from North Shore Road. Her insides tensed; it was a police car. She willed it to keep moving, but it didn't. It pulled in before Bayview. Her heart thudded. She'd had enough confrontations for today. She didn't want to see Peter now, when she was hot and tired. Even as she thought this a welter of emotions churned, unasked, emotions that she feared to examine. For pity's sake, why couldn't he just do his job and leave her alone?

No, not leave her alone – well, yes, at present leave her alone as far as police work was concerned, but otherwise… oh… drat… She saw him alight. He stood on the pavement and stared towards her. She gave a tentative wave, hoping he'd turn away and let her get close without watching her every step.

To her annoyance her heart was thumping, as if with pleasure. For a few ridiculous moments she wondered what would happen if she ran up to him, threw her arms around him and said, "Let's make a new life together." Then reality kicked in: her feet were sore, she could not run, she was tired and hot, and the last thing she needed was a romantic complication in her life. She had her self-respect to maintain. She wasn't a gullible teenager; she was a grown woman… and he was a… very well-grown man…

Fenella came to a sudden stop. In a split second of inner perception she knew that the last thing she should even consider was to stay on at Bayview. She'd be a fool if she did. It was a time for change, a time to break free. She straightened her shoulders and began to hurry, her hot feet now feeling less painful.

Peter smiled. "You needn't have hurried," he said apologetically. "It's nothing urgent. Sorry if I alarmed you."

"I wasn't alarmed, it's just that, you know." Fenella shrugged, folding her arms and trying to appear nonchalant. "Would you like to come in, or shall we let the neighbours oversee whatever it is you've got to say?"

Peter looked up. Curtains were twitching in several windows in the nearby apartments. He grinned. "Yes, inside might be best."

Fenella ran up the steps and pushed open the front door, holding it wide for him. "I'm home," she shouted as he followed her through. "I left Tom and his girlfriend in charge." She smiled, turning. "I wouldn't like to walk in on them suddenly. I remember what it was like – at their age…"

Peter grinned, pretending not to notice the flush that suddenly suffused Fenella's face. "Me too," he said. "Though teenage years seem an age ago." He looked suddenly wistful. "Another life."

"Yes," Fenella agreed briskly. "We'll sit in the office. Would you like tea? Or coffee?"

"Tea, thanks." As Fenella hurried away Peter settled himself on a wooden stool. The office was a glass and wood-partitioned cubicle that looked as if it had definitely seen better days. Though it was scrupulously tidy, he noted. Simple shelves, neatly arranged ledgers and books. No computer. In this respect, as in others, Bayview was hardly of the twentieth century, let alone almost the twenty-first.

"There." Fenella returned, pushing the door shut behind her and placing a tray on the ledge between them. "I've brought some biscuits, though I don't want any. I've just had a long, lazy lunch with Mum."

"At the Grand Island?" Peter said.

"M'm, you deduce right." Fenella grinned.

"Oh, something to celebrate?"

Fenella poured out the tea. "You could say that. Georgio Stephani paid off my mortgage before he died. I'm solvent." She flashed a rueful smile. "Probably for the first time in years."

Peter's eyes widened. "I see."

"Do you?"

"Well, no, but by all accounts he was an astute businessman. So he had the matter cut and dried before he, um, passed away?"

"It would appear so, according to Willie Kaneen."

"You'll be glad, to be able to stay – here, I mean."

Fenella hesitated. "Well, I've just realised that I don't want to live here any longer. In fact, as I was walking along the prom I decided I must sell up. It's time I did something else with my life."

"Oh." Peter stirred his tea and sipped it thoughtfully.

Fenella cast him a look. She wished he would put into words whatever he was thinking. She'd appreciate his opinion, if nothing else, and some light conversation might dispel the palpable tension between them. Without realising it she reached for a biscuit.

"Whatever happened in the war years must have been something extraordinary, to make any man wish to make reparation after all this time," Peter murmured, picking up his tea.

"Mustn't it?" Fenella swallowed a crumb the wrong way and coughed. She hastily gulped a mouthful of tea. "I haven't a clue about any of it. Mum and Gran rarely mention the war years. It was a difficult time, with Grandad having been being killed and their having to cope on their own." Fenella fastened her gaze on Peter's tie. She feared that if she looked at his face he might sense her anxiety. No, anxiety was maybe too strong a word, yet she had a feeling that Marjorie might be hiding something and she certainly didn't want to let Peter suspect. Then it struck her forcefully that if she didn't try and act naturally then he'd think that she was hiding something. She sighed; her eyes met his. "So what was it you needed to tell me?"

If Peter had noticed her evasiveness he didn't make any comment. Instead he gave a grudging smile. "I called to bring you up to date. We've got a relative of George Stevens over from Wakefield. He's identified the body. The inquest is to be held on Friday, but of course in the circumstances, with Percy's funeral happening, I quite understand that you can't be present. Oh and of course we got the coroner's message that an inquest on Percy is not required. He had visited his doctor only days before his death."

Fenella's eyes misted. "Yes, it was still sad, though."

"Of course."

"It will be an emotional day. Percy was so much part of our household, and he was so good – with Gran."

Peter smiled. There was an awkward silence which at last Peter filled. "Um, we now have a connection between Charlie Peake and the deceased, that night."

"No? Oh dear."

"He's admitted to being in the park at the time."

"Oh." Fenella's insides tightened.

"Was that a surprised oh or an 'I knew that anyway' oh?" Peter said curiously.

Fenella flushed. "It was a non-committal oh," Fenella said, folding her arms. "You surely don't think Charlie did the old man in?"

Peter shrugged. "He was in the park at the right time. He admits as much. He says, and here I'm speaking strictly off the record, that the deceased was already dead."

"Oh, gracious, yet he didn't call the police?"

"No," Peter said gruffly. "We know he's hiding something. We knew how he felt about you and your property. We knew that he knew, goodness, this is sounding complicated. We know, from Willie Kaneen, that Charlie was aware of the negotiations going on over your mortgage."

"Was he?"

"M'm, probably before you did."

Fenella frowned. "Well, that's not right."

"No, and knowing Charlie, and his reputation for being hot-tempered, well, he may have hit the old man harder than he meant and regretted it afterwards."

Fenella lowered her eyes, knowing that she was flushing. Marjorie's words came back to her. "I followed Charlie and the old man in the park…" Could the thing that Charlie hadn't wanted to reveal have something to do with Marjorie?

"Are you all right, Fen? You look pale."

Fenella chuckled nervously. "I'm OK. My, it's a long time since you called me 'Fen.'"

"I know, sorry. Do you mind?"

"No, of course not." She shrugged. "No, but it takes me back…"

Peter grinned wryly. "Me too."

"Your wife – erm, ex-wife, Susan, she's well, is she?"

"Yes. She's got another partner. No marriage this time. He's nice enough."

"Not in the force?"

"Oh no. Susan wouldn't take on another copper."

Fenella shifted and looked at her watch. "Well, I don't want to rush you, but I've got things to do…"

Peter jumped up. "Of course."

They walked to the front door. Fenella held it open. She cleared her throat. "You don't seriously suspect Charles, do you?"

Peter shrugged. "The old guy might have died from natural causes for all we know, just fallen awkwardly. We've traced his movements that night and know he'd imbibed a fair amount of wine. It is an odd thing, the fine line between living and dying. What will kill one man another will shrug off. One thing I've learned in the force is not to be too quick to jump to conclusions."

"Patience is a virtue, they say," Fenella said inconsequentially, and then stammered, "God, did I say that?"

"You did. Similar to what you said to me on our last… erm… encounter."

"M'm." Fenella tried to laugh, but it was hard, with him so close that she could smell the scent of his aftershave. "I've always been pompous."

"Oh, I don't think so. Strong-willed, and very high-minded."

"Yes, well, look where being high-minded has got me."

Peter sighed. They both avoided eye contact and the silence between them lengthened. Fenella felt her clenched palms moistening. Her heart was thumping. Why didn't he go, for heaven's sake? Why was he standing so near when he must realise the effect he had on her?

"I don't suppose you'd… er… come out for a drink with me one evening, would you?" Peter stammered at last.

"Why, you've not got something else to tell me, have you?"

"I don't know, should I have?" Now it was Peter's turn to flush.

"No, of course not."

Fenella found that her mouth had dried. She grinned. "Yes, please. I'd like to. If you're serious."

Peter's eyes suddenly looked full of mischief. "Not as much as I should be, the chief super reckons. He says I haven't the gravitas to make a convincing senior officer."

"You look as if you're working on it," Fenella said, giving a meaningful glance at his middle.

Peter raised his eyes. "It's my home cooking," Peter said. "I make a mean lasagna."

"Goodness, you have progressed. I remember a young police cadet who didn't know one end of a boiled egg from another."

Peter laughed. "OK, let's continue the reminiscences over a drink. Where do you fancy? Local or not?"

"Not," Fenella said firmly. "Everyone will think you're interrogating me."

Peter took an intake of breath. "I'd never do that."

Fenella flushed.

"I'll pick you up – Friday night? After the funeral?"

"That's an Agatha Christie title, you know."

"Is it? Oh dear, would another night be better?"

"No, it would be lovely, something to look forward to."

"Good, erm, eight-ish?"

"Yes, fine. You're sure going out with me is OK? You don't suspect me?"

"Of what?" Peter asked, and raised a finger to lightly touch her shoulder. "No, I don't suspect you of anything illegal, Fenella Kelly."

"Right, good, thanks."

As Peter got into the police car he looked back, his face suddenly anxious. "Unless something else happens, of course, but if so I'll ring to say." He slammed the car door and drove off.

Fenella's elation dwindled. She felt sad and guilty. That poor old man had died possibly because of something concerning her family a long time ago. And in just over forty-eight hours she would be going to Percy's funeral, another unexpected and unwelcome death. It seemed heartless to be arranging a date in the circumstances, even if it was with an old friend. He was still the officer in charge of what might yet be a murder case. She flushed with mortification. What had she been thinking? She should be ashamed.

And yet… Fenella gripped hold of the newel post at the foot of the stairs and put her slim, strong fingers around its narrow neck. "Yes, but this is Peter I'm going to have a drink with," she murmured, her throat tightening at the thought, "and there were times, long ago, when I might have killed someone myself to get close to Peter Quilliam."

Fenella's lips curved in a lascivious smile as her fingers laced themselves tightly around the smooth, hard wood.

Watching from the landing above, Tom drew back, put his finger to his lips and pushed Emily gently back into the bedroom.

FOURTEEN

The weather for Percy's funeral was good: quiet and mild, like the man himself. There was a pale sun, a sky faint with blue patches, wispy clouds and a gentle breeze.

Norah, Marjorie, Fenella and Tom were collected by one of the undertakers' cars at ten o'clock. A gleaming hearse with the coffin already aboard topped by flowers was waiting at the quayside chapel of rest, along with a cluster of locals paying their last respects to a man who'd been well known and liked.

Two sober-suited elderly men and three women, Eloise Green amongst them, climbed into another dark limousine, and at ten fifteen precisely the cortege left for the sixteen-mile drive along the winding mountain road, to the Douglas borough crematorium. In his careful instructions Percy had requested that the funeral party take this route, rather than the coast road. Percy had been a motorcycle enthusiast all his life and the route was part of the world-famous TT circuit. Although he had never ridden the course on a motorbike his trusty cycle had carried him around the thirty-seven and three-quarter-mile course many times. The mountain sector had been his favourite part, especially the stretch known as the Veranda, close below Snaefell summit, a spectacular piece of road curving between high hills and with amazing distant views of land and sea all around. Percy had stipulated that his ashes should eventually be scattered at the Guthrie Memorial, another racing landmark facing Ramsey Bay and the north of the island.

His personal wishes had been found in a folder clearly marked in the top drawer of his dresser. Good-humoured to the last, he hoped his friends would remember him cheerfully, and he requested no formal funeral service save for a reading of Psalm 23, a hymn, 'All Things Bright and Beautiful', and a simple prayer should be said. He wanted no resume of his life, spoken by an unfamiliar cleric who'd not known him from Adam, and he did not want people to feel miserable at his passing. He'd rather they remembered him as he hoped he'd be up till the end: active and useful. He requested a recording of Louis Armstrong's 'When the Saints Go Marchin' In' to be played as his coffin was carried into the crematorium, and the curtain to close on his life to the strains of Johnny Mathis' 'Moon River'. Cassette copies of both recordings had been tucked into a worn cardboard folder along with his will, as Fenella had discovered as she tearfully went through his possessions.

The occasion, as planned, matched Percy's character perfectly. Marjorie remarked as much as they settled themselves in the hushed crematorium. "Never one for fuss, was he?" she murmured, pushing Norah's red deerstalker hat more firmly on her head. The old lady's hair was so thin that the hat sat loosely, but she'd insisted on wearing it.

Norah didn't take kindly to the adjustment. "Let me be," she barked. "I'm miserable enough without you fiddling with mi titfer."

Fenella and Marjorie glanced at one another. "He'll be missed by a lot of people, Gran," Fenella whispered pacifically. "Not just you."

"That's up to them, isn't it?" Norah grumbled, pushing her hat askew again. Marjorie sighed but forbore to interfere. It wasn't a day for fussing about things that were unimportant. It was a day for remembering a lovely man. This fact brought tears to many eyes as the minister read the short psalm and murmured a Celtic prayer, and despite Percy's request for a cheerful service all found the occasion poignantly moving.

By the time the curtain drew across on the coffin Norah was clearly feeling the strain. She'd been argumentative from the moment she'd blinked awake that morning, refusing breakfast but demanding a snack to take with her 'just in case' – and once she'd been persuaded into her best suit and coat she'd refused outright to wear the sober hat Fenella had chosen. The pillar-box red deerstalker with black feather had been a Christmas gift from Percy some years before.

"He liked to see me in it," she'd declared stubbornly, and for the sake of peace Fenella had given in, realising that the old lady's bad temper was understandable and that probably Percy would prefer his best friend to wear red rather than gloomy black. So she gave in and had pushed tissue paper into the hat band in an effort to make it sit squarely. Of course this packing fell out before they'd even left the house. Norah didn't seem bothered; grabbing her hat gave her something to do rather than just look and feel miserable. She stayed stony-faced until the final strains of 'Moon River' faded, by which time she was steering her wheelchair towards the exit and the waiting clergyman. At last Norah offered an opinion: "Percy must a' been jokin' with that music, the silly beggar. Hope you don't get Johnny Mathis to see me off!"

"Mother, shush." Marjorie blushed as the clergyman looked momentarily disconcerted. Then he grinned and warmly shook Norah's gloved hand.

Marjorie smiled gratefully. "Thank you so much, Vicar, Percy would have been pleased that his instructions were followed to the letter."

"So glad, so glad." The cleric looked puzzled that he was being thanked for an occasion that seemed utterly lacking in funeral solemnity, but he was a good, kind man and realistic; Christianity had more or less gone by the board. Humanism seemed the norm of late, even in the Church of England.

With Fenella's help they negotiated Norah's wheelchair through the narrow door and then they were outside gazing across serried ranks of gravestones. Marjorie's heart beat faster; she didn't like cemeteries, but then who did? *It won't be long till I'm under a stone*, she found herself thinking, until a glance at Norah revealed tears coursing down her face. Marjorie swung her mother's chair away from the exiting mourners and pulled out a bundle of tissues. "Here, Mum," she said softly, pushing them into Norah's hand.

Norah grimaced and scrubbed her face. "Ta, now leave me be for a while," she growled, wheeling herself along the gravelled path till she was isolated amidst the memorials.

Marjorie looked around for Fenella and Tom, who were exchanging remarks with the minister. As the pair emerged into the sunlight they were surrounded by people wishing to offer their condolences. She smiled serenely, though her heart thumped. This felt so awkward; none of the family had actually been related to Percy, but it was polite to shake hands, and what else could they do? Fenella's navy winter coat soon felt weighty in the sunshine, but she was glad she had donned it. Most of the mourners had clearly made an effort and dear old Percy had always been nicely turned out.

Eloise, having chatted to a pair of other old ladies, wriggled close to Fenella, her hand outstretched. "Very nice, very sad," she said, her voice trembling, clasping Fenella's hand with fingers as light as a butterfly. Eloise was dressed entirely in funereal black of a quality and cut that was old-fashioned yet eminently suited her.

Fenella smiled. "Thank you so much for coming, Eloise."

Eloise turned and was about to approach Norah, who had wheeled herself nearer, but the old lady suddenly swung her wheelchair in an arc that took her instead close to the display of floral tributes.

Marjorie spotted this manoeuvre and swiftly intervened, holding out her hand to Eloise. "Eloise, dear, good to see you. Mother's upset, as you may imagine," she said soothingly. "Percy would have appreciated your presence, I'm sure."

Eloise smiled gratefully. "Percy was a dear friend."

"And how is your sister?" Marjorie asked, leading the old lady to one side. She had offered to pass on the news that Eloise must leave Bayview. The facts had to be faced and she hoped Eloise did not feel hurt. As it turned out, Eloise had realised that things must change. Her sister had happily offered to accommodate her already.

Fenella left the cluster of mourners and walked with Tom a little way along the gravel drive.

"I don't blame Em for not coming," Tom said, scuffing at the ground with a well-polished black shoe that didn't often see the light of day. "It *was* sad."

"M'm," Fenella said, choking back tears. "Though it was very Percy. He was such a nice old man." She dabbed her eyes and sniffled.

Tom felt awkward and embarrassed. He and his mother were not demonstrative. They'd never been a family for cuddles or kisses, but seeing Fenella was upset, so was he. Impulsively he swung an arm around her shoulders and pulled her towards him in a swift embrace. "He had a good life, Mum, don't cry."

"I'm not," Fenella sniffed, touched by Tom's gesture, though it had made her feel even more tearful.

Tom cleared his throat. "It seems weird. I've never come close to death before, and now there have been two in a week."

Fenella glanced sideways at her tall son. He looked grown up yet immature, though probably no more so than she'd been at his age. He was fortunate that he hadn't experienced any sudden deaths earlier. When his father had been killed he'd been a babe in arms, and never knew his grandfather.

"It must have been awful for you, Mum, when Dad was killed," Tom said as if reading her mind, as they stood next a weathered headstone on which the lettering had long ago faded.

"It was, but I had you to keep me busy." Fenella smiled. "And lots of lovely memories of your father. They stay alive, even when the person's gone."

Tom put his hands in his pockets. "You should get yourself another fella, Mum. You really should."

Fenella laughed. "Oh, yes, men looking for middle-aged women are falling off trees all over the place."

"Someone will be looking, Mum," he said, his face unusually serious. "It's just that, well, you're a bit, er... daunting, at times. Perhaps if you'd, er... easy up a bit?"

Fenella felt suddenly breathless. How dare he tell her to ease up? If only he knew how hard it had been rearing him, running the guesthouse and keeping up with her artistic output. She'd hardly had a moment to herself for years, and she'd fended off a fair few men during those years who had assumed she'd want to jump into bed with them. Though of course the one man she did fancy, when he had made a move, she'd told to go to hell.

She dabbed her eyes with her by now soggy tissue and heaved an uneven breath.

Tom put his hand on her arm. "Sorry. Mum. It's none of my business. You're you and if you want to stay single who am I to object? It's just that I know how good it is to have a... partner." He stopped, embarrassed, and then said in a rush, "I've never felt about anyone like I do about Emily. But I know I'm going to lose her. She's determined to finish her college course and then what? There'll be nothing for her to do over here."

Fenella heard the anguish in Tom's voice and suddenly realised that she wasn't the only one going through a time of change and upheaval. Nor was her tall son any longer a heedless teenage boy, which was how she tended to think of him. He was older than she'd been when she married his father. He was an adult and perfectly entitled to offer her advice. Heavens, she was always trying to advise him.

Abruptly her irritation dropped away.

"It's odd," she grinned, "becoming aware than my little boy is a man." She smiled, pushing her arm through his. "Well, done, love, and I know how you feel about Emily. It's plain to anyone when you're together. But try not to pressure her. You and she are very young. If it's meant to work out in the future, it will."

"Yeah," Tom said doubtfully. "I guess."

Fenella looked back at the cluster of people near the crematorium steps. "I daresay we'd better get back. Mum and Norah are still a bit touchy with one another."

"Oh, for grown-up grandparents," Tom said sotto voce, making Fenella smile as they hurried back.

The sky was very blue behind the crematorium chimney and Fenella felt she could almost see Percy's soul flying heavenwards in the rising white smoke. Such fanciful thoughts were comforting. One needed some comfort at times like this, whether one believed in an afterlife or not. Brian had died when he was twenty-five. If she died when she was Norah's age would Brian recognise her in the afterlife, and would she want him to?

"Mum, you're daydreaming," Tom said, squeezing her arm. "Come on. By the look on some of those old folks faces I reckon Great-Gran is talking scandal again, probably about Percy, and they'll never think well of him again. Let's get her home before she disgraces us all."

Fenella and Tom smilingly broke up the cluster of elderly mourners. Fenella levered the brake off Norah's wheelchair. "We shouldn't stand around, it's breezy, isn't it?" she said pleasantly. "Say cheerio, Gran. We'll see you all back at the Grand Island Hotel, I hope, for a drink and a bite to eat? Do come, for Percy's sake. He loved a bit of a party."

Any elderly folk who'd been insulted suddenly turned cheerful. A chorus of willing agreement broke out.

Fenella hastily steered Norah away. "Say cheerio indeed," Norah snorted, as they headed for the waiting limousine. "I was talkin', Nell, I'm not ready to go back. I don't get many outings, do I? And I'll get none in the future. You needn't look so glum, Marje. You're gettin' me out from under your feet as you've always wanted. Hey, watch it, girl, you'll have me shaken out the way you're bumpin' me on this gravel."

"Sorry, Gran, I can't help it. Besides, what on earth were you saying to those old biddies? Some of them looked shocked. Eloise especially."

Norah wrinkled her nose. "Always was a wimp, was Eloise. Even at school she was a wimp."

"But being unkind isn't like you. They were upset about Percy, as it was."

"So was I," Norah muttered, her lips quivering. "He ought not to have died, the bugger."

Fenella cleared her throat noisily as the young chauffeur approached. "Yes, thank you, if you could help me with the chair." She gave a despairing look at Norah, who cast a truculent look in return, although she meekly allowed the driver to settle her into the limousine.

Tom, Marjorie and Fenella followed. As they set off, Norah declared loudly, in a voice that no amount of throat-clearing could cover up: "My, I wouldn't have minded a stint on this back seat with this young driver fella, a few years ago."

Marjorie flushed, Fenella looked resigned and Tom grinned. "Percy would have been proud of you, Great-Gran. You've certainly made this a day to remember."

Peter Quilliam stepped out of Douglas courthouse and turned down Prospect Hill towards the town centre. The inquest on Georgio Stephani had been brief, and adjourned. Luigi Stephani had attested to the identity of his uncle's body, and as the autopsy investigations were complete, his uncle's remains were officially released to his next of kin's care, for transfer to the mainland. The cause of death was left in abeyance for a further date.

As Peter strolled towards Strand Street, he reflected on the investigation so far. They'd completed the usual house-to-house questioning, they'd taken a fair amount of statements from residents in the vicinity of the park, but there seemed little helpful information and as yet scant motive for harming the old man.

Peter knew that as time passed any motive was unlikely to appear if it hadn't by now. It was quite possible that they would never discover the truth of Georgio Stephani's last moments. Clearly they'd been dramatic, but whether this had been of his own making or because of a confrontation was a matter for conjecture. The unexpected death of a seventy-six-year-old tourist who chose to walk at the edge of a lake in the encroaching dusk after partaking of his supper and two carafes of red wine was neither surprising nor particularly sensational. Not compared to a vicious knife attack in a Douglas night club or a drug-related incident, which were the usual causes of sudden death on the Isle of Man, where crime figures were inexorably rising.

Youngsters had been seen cycling through the park about nine thirty. When tracked down, the teenagers said they'd seen a couple 'snogging' in one of the lakeside shelters. This pair had not come forward, but they might have been tourists who'd already left the island. A lone woman had been seen walking briskly through, possibly with a man, at about ten o'clock. This was vouched for by a resident of one of the houses overlooking the park as she'd closed her sitting-room curtains for the night. A little later another such curtain-puller had seen what he thought was a man pushing a pram, which he'd noticed only because prams and babies were on his mind. He was babysitting his grandchild and he'd only just quelled her screams by putting her pushchair in front of the television.

Peter's recent interview with Chief Superintendent Kinvig at Douglas Police Headquarters had given Peter a certain amount of food for thought, but thankfully his superior had wisely not exerted any great pressure towards further conclusions.

The chief superintendent was a policeman of the old school. He was a sensible man whose talents would be missed on the occasion of his retirement, which was looming.

"The reasons for the victim's visit are fascinating, Peter," had been his opening comment as he'd riffled through the report in front of him, his tanned brow furrowed. "What do you think about the autopsy findings? They're hardly conclusive, are they? The chap was on several medications. He'd over-indulged on red wine, and he was more than likely in an emotional state, having expunged a matter from his conscience that must have weighed on him for nigh on sixty years." The superintendent looked up, his shrewd brown eyes crinkling. "I think I'd have been likely to fall into a lake myself in his shoes. The whys and wherefores of the case are fascinating, however. Why did he come back? Why did he feel he had to buy this place – this Bayview? Good gracious, how much has it cost him, a hundred grand or so?"

"Ninety thousand to clear the outstanding mortgages on the property, and related charges on top, I understand."

"Good gracious. It will be worth more than that, surely?"

"Oh, considerably more, for the site alone."

"I'm taking it for granted you've exonerated the beneficiaries in this case?"

"Yes, sir," Peter answered promptly. Determinedly he did not voice the fact that he would be taking the chief beneficiary out, with possible romantic intent, that very evening. "The debt was certainly related to a wartime incident, though I believe the driving incident has never been made known to the present owner."

"Indeed."

"Yes, sir. Besides, when the old man died Fenella Kelly, the owner, had only just been told, by Stephani himself, that he intended to repay this debt. She had no idea that he had completed the transaction. It would have been foolish for her or one of her family to harm him at such a time."

"M'm, I see, like killing the goose before he's laid the golden egg?" The superintendent nodded sagely. "Family secrets, eh? We Manx are great on secrets." He picked another paper from the file. "Forensic haven't been conclusive, I noticed. What about this lapel pin and Charles Peake? I can think of a few who'd like to stick something on Mr Peake, and not just a Chruinnaght pin!"

Peter shrugged. "He admits to being there. He says he didn't kill the man, and forensic tests have discounted any physical contact with the deceased."

"Oh."

"Mind you, Charlie washed his clothes that night: an unheard-of occurrence, according to Betty Knowles, Charlie's housekeeper. He'd washed them at the wrong setting too. Ruined his jacket apparently."

The superintendent grinned. "Indeed. And what does he say about that?"

"That he'd spilled a bottle of red wine when he got home. That's true enough. The red wine stains are still present, even after his clothing was washed."

"M'm, he should have poured on white wine to remove the stains. Even I know that."

Peter frowned. "Is that so, sir?"

Superintendent Kinvig smiled. "I knocked a bottle of wine over when we had the chief constable to dinner recently, and I thought Sheila had lost her marbles when she poured most of a bottle of a blinking expensive white wine on top of the puddle. It cleared the stain all right, and luckily we had one of those rubber table protector things on under the cloth."

"Really?" Peter's interest was polite. He doubted if he'd ever be invited to dinner with the chief constable, which was fine by him.

"M'm." The superintendent glanced at some notes on a jotter on his desk. "What about these tyre tracks on the verge?"

"There were a number of tracks, they were some distance from the body, but that bank is a favourite cycle way for the local kids. They're not allowed to do it, but they have a route through the bushes along that side of the lake."

"One of them couldn't have knocked the old man over, so that he fell and bumped his head?"

Peter shrugged. "They say not, and of course they were home by nine forty-five. Their parents backed them up on that, and the time of death of the deceased was reckoned to be no sooner than ten o'clock."

"Right." Chief Superintendent Kinvig's eyes scanned another sheet of the neatly typed report. "Ah, here we are, a bit of detail on this mortgage repayment on the Mooragh Promenade property, ahm, Bayview."

"Yes, sir?" Peter wished the chief would keep from mentioning Bayview. It meant his mind would keep focusing on Fenella.

"The whole thing seems quite extraordinary. Could the next of kin tell you anything?"

"Not much. Luigi Stephani – that is, the deceased's nephew – has given me a brief resume of his uncle's character and history, but I'm still in the dark about exactly what happened all those years ago and why the man felt he needed to make amends. I've got Sergeant Colvin at the Manx Museum at the moment, scouring through microfiche copies of the newspapers of the time to see can he find any scandal relating to the people involved, and Bayview in particular."

"Indeed, that should be fascinating. My father was in the Manx force here in the war. He's told me of some of the goings-on in the camps. But it's such a long time ago. One cannot conceive of a man holding a guilty secret for what, almost sixty years and only now thinking of making amends."

"Fifty-five years ago, sir – we know that Georgio was interned here in May 1941 and left the following summer."

"Repatriated, eh, that soon? Why?"

"He had a job arranged, so his nephew understood. Apparently if a man had a legitimate job to go to on the mainland he could apply to be repatriated. Like many of the internees who were shipped here at the beginning of the war Georgio was English-born. He'd been classed C risk at the Enemy Alien Tribunal. That was the grade of those reckoned to be of little risk. We got that information from the war office."

"Indeed, indeed. Good gracious. I bet they don't get many requests about the Enemy Alien Tribunal nowadays." The chief shook his head wonderingly, his balding dome gleaming under the strip lighting. "It must have been an unsettling time for the native population, with the thousands of interned men in the various camps. And women, of course. You know that Port Erin was given over wholly to female internees? My family came from Peel, and of course Peel Camp was where the troublemakers and persistent escapers were held. Nazis and racists mainly, who were intent on escaping if they got half a chance. There was an uprising in Peel, you know. A riot, at one time."

"So I believe, sir."

The phone on the chief superintendent's desk rang. "Sorry, Peter, excuse me. Yes?"

A terse conversation followed, to which Peter tried not to listen. Finally the chief banged the phone down. "Sorry about that. I'm afraid I'll have to cut this short." He smiled with sudden warmth. "Interesting though it's been, Peter, and we must have another talk about whatever else you discover, sometime." He heaved himself upright. "It seems that one of our garrulous MHKs has been making a fuss on Manx Radio about the rising crime on the island, and the chief constable thinks I should make a prompt response." He gathered the papers in front of him, pushed them into the file and handed it to Peter. "Well, Inspector Quilliam, carry on with your investigation and let me know if anything interesting turns up in those old newspapers. I'd like to know what the root of this peculiar case is."

"Of course, sir."

The chief preceded Peter and opened the door. "Best of luck, Inspector Quilliam." He smiled, then added in an aside as he came out into the corridor, "I often wish I was back at the coalface of investigations again, instead of coping with silly politicians with more voice than brains."

"Right." Peter grinned and hurried away towards the station canteen. He just had time for a coffee before heading for the courthouse and the inquest, which was to begin at eleven thirty.

And now, Peter thought, as he walked down the sunshine-splashed hill, amongst workers who were pouring from their offices for lunch, *that's over, and I can concentrate on the business in hand.*

So saying, and with a slightly faster heart rate than usual, Peter pushed through a set of double glass doors and felt in his pocket for his wallet.

Norah stared out of the window as the limousine drove away.

"And good riddance," she said, as it turned at the junction of North Shore Road.

"You weren't very nice to Eloise," Tom said, undoing his tie.

"Well, why should I be?"

Tom pulled his tie off and rolled it up. Emily and Fenella had both gone upstairs to get changed. It was the first time he'd been alone with Norah all day. "Great-Gran, why are you so crotchety all the time? It isn't fair on Mum, or Gran."

Norah glared. "If I'm not sharp I might blub. I'm going to miss old Percy, and what have I got to be cheerful about, Thomas Kelly? I'm going into an old folks' home. What do you think that makes me feel like, eh?" She banged the arms of her wheelchair. "Useless old git, that's what, being pushed out of sight."

Tom knelt beside her. He put his arm around her shoulders. "You're not a useless old git, Great-Gran. An annoying old git, I'll give you that, but no one's pushing you out of sight. We're putting you where you'll get the best care and treatment. You know that."

"Marjorie's given up on me," Norah muttered, "an' I don't blame her."

Tom grinned and gave Norah a smacking kiss on her whiskery, papery cheek. "Well, I haven't. I'll come and take you out at the weekends and I'll race you round the BMX course in your wheelchair."

Norah laughed and Tom grinned, pleased that the sad look had gone from Norah's bloodshot eyes. Then, as her arm shot out and gripped his shoulder, he winced at the strength still in her. "You will come and take me out, Tom, won't you? You won't forget?"

"Great-Gran, I promise. I won't forget." He got up. "Now, what do you want to do tonight? Play cards with Em and me? Go for a ride along the prom? It's fine enough."

Norah leaned back and looked out at the window. "Aye," she muttered, "I'd like that. You and Em take me out. It'll be one of the last times I'll be comin' home here. Besides," she looked up at him speculatively, "I like to see you together." She reached out her hand again and he took it, smiling. "You keep hol' of her, Tom. Don't waste your life like I done."

Tom nodded but said nothing. There was nothing he'd like more than to keep hold of Emily. But would Emily let him?

As Peter Quilliam drove over the harbour swing bridge, at the lawful five miles an hour, he couldn't help thinking of the last time he and Fenella had had a date.

It had been a disastrous evening, entirely misjudged on his part. He'd been on an impromptu visit back to the island to see his parents. After catching up with family news he'd thought to ask Fenella out, for old times' sake, though he'd been more of a mate to Brian than a friend of Fenella's. When Brian was killed racing he'd been devastated. The fact of his death had made him rethink his decision to join the police force, till his father had took him to task and told him not to be stupid. Poor Brian had lost his life doing what he loved – it was Peter's duty to live a full and worthwhile life, for his own, his parents' and for the dead lad's sake. He'd sent Fenella and young Tom a Christmas card for a few years. Then he and Susan had moved across and naturally things changed. Why he'd imagined she'd been awaiting him all the years he'd been away, he had no idea. If he'd been more perceptive things might have gone differently. But he hadn't been perceptive. He'd barely been polite. He'd greeted her effusively, he remembered now, to his shame, chatted her up as if the years between had not ever happened and then had blatantly propositioned her, fool that he had been, boosted by a few unwise pints before he'd met her and stupidly imagining that she was as desperate for company, i.e. sex, as he was.

Peter's face crimsoned. He slowed the car and pulled into the pavement, sweating beneath his shirt. What had been driving him that awful day? That he was feeling pretty low at the time was no excuse. He'd been snowed under by work problems. That was why he'd taken the trip home, using his parents as an excuse for unwarranted leave. It was soon after he and Susan had been divorced, and she had found herself a new man, though their children, young teenagers at the time, had taken against in a big way. They had laid the blame for this on him, accusing him of being the dodgy one in the marriage break-up and not being much of a dad. It had been a trying few months and he thanked God he was now on good terms with both offspring.

He'd been wallowing in self-pity at that time. He should never have contacted Fenella. He'd not really considered how she might be feeling, meeting up after so long. He'd been totally concerned with his own petty needs. God, those memories hurt.

He grinned philosophically and drove off. "Best not look back," he told himself. "Time's passed, we're both a good deal older and hopefully wiser." He glanced in the rear-view mirror. "This is just a catch-up, two old friends who go way back." He almost convinced himself, took a deep breath and gazed at the sea across the road from the stop sign at the promenade junction. All was calm that evening, dainty white-tipped wavelets creeping up the sands, drawn by the moon, propelled by nature and all things wonderful.

"Whew, keep that mindset, lad," he told himself, and drove the last few hundred yards and pulled in outside Bayview. He was a different man now from that last time. Susan was settled happily and his children were grown, forging their own alliances. Peter had dated a few women since then, but his heart had rarely been engaged in those brief affaires. Six months ago he had applied to transfer back to the island. He'd used the excuse that his parents were ailing, though they'd put no pressure on him. He knew that his motivation was not just that. Brian's early death had been tragic. If Fenella had got married or had acquired a partner… at least he'd have known she was content and beyond his reach. But she hadn't. She's stayed single and… she'd always been there, on his mind and on his conscience. He grimaced, still not sure whether he'd done the right thing in coming back. Things were different even here now. He wasn't sure he'd fit in anymore – he wasn't sure he wanted to, at first. Now was he beginning to relax and appreciate the differences here and what a relief it was to be back. He had already perceived how good it was here, where life proceeded at a more civilised pace. A few times lately he'd felt a joyous rush at the sight of the sea, almost whooping with pleasure to know that it was all around him and that he was truly 'back home'.

The posting to Ramsey had been a gamble that he reckoned was worth taking. Early on he'd discovered that Fenella was still single. He'd done his homework on that front all right. Not that it would have put him off entirely if she was happily married. He'd have been glad for her. He'd got used to living alone, and there were other Manx women who might take to him; he had done his best to keep himself 'personable,' as his mum had advised when he got divorced. "Don't let yourself go, lad. Avoid fatty food and flab, use your head and your hands, cook for yourself, eat good food and you'll live a long life." Peter grinned; his parents were sensible, honest folk, now in their early eighties but still active. That's how he'd like to be at their age.

He got out of the car, his mouth dry, feeling like a teenager on his first date rather than a mature middle-aged man. Cripes, his heart was pounding more than it had that afternoon before meeting the superintendent. He raised a hand to ring the doorbell, but before he could press it Fenella had opened the door and stepped out, smiling.

"Hi."

"Hi, yourself. You look nice," he managed to say calmly.

She shrugged. She was wearing a cowl-necked cream sweater and sage-green narrow-legged trousers. She wore a swinging necklace of sage-coloured beads.

"Thanks, I dithered for ages, not having much of a social wardrobe." She squirmed at this admission. Why practically boast it that it was so long since she'd had a date she couldn't remember who it had been with? Peter did not need to know.

He grinned, as if he'd barely heard, guided her with a gentle touch on her arm to the car and as he closed her door smiled tautly. Fenella realised that he was edgy too and that made her relax and flash him a smile. Though as he fastened his seatbelt and she caught a whiff of his potent aftershave her heart thudded and the back of her knees felt like jelly.

"I thought we'd head for Peel? OK?"

"Fine," she agreed, willing herself to keep cool, trying to think of anything other than Peter's long legs and bare chest, a teenage memory from a long, long-ago beach party that had appeared unwarranted.

As he steered the car sedately past the apartment block where Marjorie lived Fenella glanced up and glimpsed her mother sitting by the window. She guessed that Marjorie would be doing her embroidery. She hoped she was feeling relaxed and not worrying over Norah. Norah wasn't worrying about anyone or anything. She'd been sparky and cheerful, looking forward very much to going out with Tom and Emily that evening.

Fenella suddenly said, "I must ask, you're not breaking any rules, are you, going out with me, entertaining a suspect, so to speak?"

"You're not a suspect," Peter assured her as he slowed for a stop sign. His eyes gleamed as he surveyed her. "You're an old friend."

Fenella smiled. "I suppose I am," she said slowly. "We've known each other a long time, haven't we?"

"M'm." Peter nodded, and Fenella knew he was remembering Brian. So was she. *Poor Brian*, she sighed.

As the car turned into Lezayre Road Fenella felt regret sweep through her. How different life would have been if Brian had lived. She'd loved him so much, stayed loyal to his memory for years, breaking relationships before they got too intense, feeling it would be a betrayal if she allowed herself to love someone else. Maybe she'd been unfair to herself as well as to Tom. After a while she'd stopped looking at men in *that* sort of way, and they had politely reciprocated.

Fenella closed her eyes. Her eyelids felt droopy. It had been a long, emotional day. Perhaps it might have been better to put Peter off and have an early night.

She blinked awake. Peter glanced swiftly sideways. The look he gave her was enough to banish any desire for a quiet night on her own. Her throat tightened. He must be as conscious as she of the mounting sexual tension between them. If it got much stronger it would steam the windows. "Peter," she said softly. "It's a long way to Peel."

"True." He grinned and took the next turning off the main road.

FIFTEEN

Charles Peake was fed up; his injuries were healing, but his spirits were at rock bottom. He'd got over the relief at being alive and was counting the cost of his stupidity and regretting every penny.

His car was wrecked; heaven knows how long the insurance would take to fork out, but that was nothing compared to the damage his reputation had suffered. No doubt it was all round Ramsey that he'd been drunk and incapable in the Mooragh Park when that old bloke died, so drunk that he couldn't, or daren't, summon assistance. How folk would chortle. All the know-alls would have been waiting for something like this. How would he hold his head up after this?

Long years it had taken to drag himself to what he thought of as a position of importance in Ramsey. Now it was more than likely he'd have to resign from the town commissioners, and then what? He didn't want to move. He knew Ramsey inside out; he knew every nook and cranny and knew every crook who might do him a favour. Some years ago, doing moderately well, he'd thought to move to the capital town to try his hand, but he'd soon realised that he'd be a kipper out of brine in that set-up. He'd got pally with few Douglas councillors over the years, and talking to them was an eye-opener. Ramsey commissioners were pet goldfish compared to the political sharks in the island's capital. He soon realised that they were in a superior league – one that he couldn't take on – nor ever would now that he'd got himself into such a mess. Gloom enveloped him once more. He eased himself on his pillow. No, he was finished. Abso-bloody-lutely finished. And all because of a few drinks. Well, maybe several more than had been wise, though not more than many a man downed regularly. Worse, he'd been found out because he'd obeyed the law and had not driven home. He sighed deeply; if he had been done for drink driving he would have been less upset. And if he had got done for driving when over the limit there were those who'd regard him as a bit of a lad. Folk were odd like that.

"Visitor for you, Mr Peake."

The nurse's bright voice sliced through his self-pity. Charlie groaned. Who was it now? Not Betty Knowles again, he hoped, moaning about her wages and how the boiler was playing up. What could he do about the ruddy boiler?

A waft of outrageous perfume billowing through the ward made Charlie's sleepy eyes blink open. "Evie!" he gasped.

Evie Cannon beamed. "Hello, Charlie, I thought you might need cheering up. What naughties have you been up to to land you in here then?" Without waiting to be asked Evie plumped herself onto the bedside chair, wriggling provocatively. "You don't mind me comin' to see you, Charles?"

Charlie's heart pounded as he surveyed Evie's tight red leather jacket and short skirt. "By God, Evie, you do a broken man a power of good."

Evie put a firm, nicely manicured hand on Charlie's pyjama-clad arm and leaned towards him, presenting a deep cleavage that momentarily made his throat dry. "You're not broken, Charlie," she murmured, "just a bit dented." She grinned and wriggled again. "Would you like me to hop in beside you? I bet I'd soon set you on your feet again." She chuckled wickedly. "Though it'd be easier doing' it lyin' down."

Julie Corlett, taking a patient's temperature two beds away, suppressed a smile. It looked as though Evie's visit would do more good for Charlie than any medication. Then, as a blast of coarse laughter broke out, she turned a warning look on the pair. Not so much noise, please," she said firmly. "You'll disturb the other patients."

The man whose temperature she was taking gripped her arm. "Eh, don't send her out, love. Just look at her thighs. Wha-hey, what I'd give to have a feel o' them."

Julie smiled as she noted the flicker of life circulating across the ward. It looked as though Evie's appearance was doing all her gentlemen a power of good.

"What's going on?" a colleague asked as she entered, pushing a loaded drugs trolley, aware of the changed atmosphere.

"Mr Peake has a visitor," Julie murmured, "and much as I've never had time for the man it's good to see him smiling. My guess is he'll be out of here in a couple of days," she lowered her voice, "if only to get into her knickers."

"Julie!"

"Well, look for yourself and where her hand is."

"Good heavens. Shall I tell them to cut it out?"

"No, leave them be. I'll be giving him a painkiller in a mo, that'll break it up."

Luigi Stephani held out his hand.

"Cheerio for now, Inspector Quilliam. It's been good to meet you, even in the um, sad, circumstances. Thanks for making things easy, like. It's a grand place, this little island, and I've enjoyed my visit. I'll mebbe come back with the wife one day."

Peter shook Luigi's hand warmly. "Goodbye, Mr Stephani. Thanks for coming. And if you do return, let me know. It would be my pleasure to show you and your wife around."

"That's most civil, lad. I will." Luigi touched his forehead in an old-fashioned gesture. With a final beam the little man hurried through the boarding gate.

"He looks a happy man, getting back to his family in time for the weekend wedding." Dave grinned. "I've never seen a man more delighted than when you said he could go home."

Peter nodded. "I know. The collection of the coffin's sorted at the other end?"

Dave nodded. "All done. The funeral director seemed very on the ball. He's clearly used to these transportations. His men will collect it from the airport. The Stephani family is already known to the firm."

"Good. Let's go. Nice bloke, wasn't he?" Dave remarked as they exited the cool airport and stepped into the sunshine.

"Wasn't he?" Peter agreed. They paused for traffic as they headed to the police vehicle. "Interesting too. Now, bring me up to speed about what you found at the museum."

Dave heaved a sigh. "It was tedious in the extreme, especially as I didn't know exactly what I was looking for. Loads of local goings-on in the internment years, of course, but much nefarious was another matter. I found one tiny bottom of a page item I'd like to follow up. In the spring of 1943 an unnamed woman was arrested on suspicion of deliberate harm. To what or whom it didn't say. I checked the weeks prior and later but there didn't seem a follow-up."

"So we've no indication who it was?"

"No."

They'd reached the car park. Peter slipped into the front passenger seat and fastened his seatbelt. "So, what next?"

"I've left some notes with one of the librarians whom I knew from years ago at school, Sandra Teare, so I asked her could she look through the motley collection of internment period newspapers. She showed me the archive but it was enormous. Otherwise," he sighed, "I'll need to find a local source." Dave winced.

"Aunt Maisie or Bertha Quaggin, you mean?"

Dave grimaced. "Bertha Quaggin has always given me the creeps. I couldn't just have a natter to Norah, could I?"

"I'd rather you didn't," Peter said. "I don't want to upset the old biddy. She's moving into a nursing home any day."

"Oh, I'd forgotten. OK, I'll brave Aunt Maisie, if I don't hear from Sandra in a day or so. Would you like to come?"

Peter grinned. "Do you know, I think I won't," he replied cheerfully.

Dave started the engine, feeling inquisitive and intrigued. He wished he knew what Peter had been up to off duty. There was a suppressed elation about him. Whatever had caused it Dave was pleased. He had looked forward to working with Peter; the man had earned a steely reputation across. Yet so far since he'd arrived he'd been totally unremarkable. He was a competent officer and his experience showed, but there was a lack of energy in him that was a bit off-putting. Now there seemed a glint in his eye that Dave was glad to see. Whatever the man had been up to in his time off had clearly done him good.

They drove through the sprawling village of Ballasalla and headed speedily for Douglas. They could have cut through the centre of the island by way of St John's village and Cronk y voddey or travelled back to Ramsey by way of the mountain road but Peter had intimated that he liked to use the coast roads when he could, as the police car provided a reminder on those lesser-used routes of speed limits and driving with care.

Dave loved driving almost as much as much as he loved his wife and children. He grinned in retrospect. It had been good the previous night, though. His parents had babysat and he and Selina had dined at a local Chinese restaurant. What a joy, no noise, no interruptions or tantrums. It had been a treat. He was a lucky man.

"Hey!" Dave braked abruptly as a motorist took a chance at the Blackboards junction. "Silly fool," he said mildly, aware that the offending motorist had clocked their checkered presence as they screeched to a halt. "You're not worth chasing, you idiot," he muttered as the offending vehicle roared off, "but maybe next time." He took a mental note of its number plate. When he got back he would look it up. They drove off, now beneath a canopy of trees, the shaded road lined either side by wilting wild garlic plants. Halfway along this pretty route both men nodded. "Morning, fairies," they said as they swept past.

"Honestly, anyone listening to us would think we were daft." Peter grinned.

"They can think what they like," Dave said. "I'm Manx and I always greet the li'l people as I pass the Fairy Bridge and that's that."

"I've noticed," Peter said, suppressing a smile. Dave was invariably touchy about his nationality and the island's fast-altering population. Manx-born folk comprised less than half of the island people now. This was a sad situation. Peter had soon learned to avoid such issues.

Dave slowed behind a bus. "So what's next, guv?"

Peter shrugged. "If Charles would cough up some gen it would be good. The hospital report was definite: his fading black eye wasn't a result of his accident; it happened earlier."

"Do you really think he'd come to blows with a doddery old man?"

"I can imagine his fists itching if he saw him after a few drinks."

Dave tutted. "All the same, much as I don't hold Charlie in greet esteem I can't see him as a killer."

"No, but we need to question him again."

Dave glanced at the dashboard clock.

"No, not today. I need to go through the statements again. You've collated them?"

"Yes, oh, and a scrap of new info. I meant to say earlier, but I didn't get a chance, with Luigi present."

Peter sat up. "Oh yes, anything interesting?"

"Only a small detail, but it might mean something. Some of the pleasure craft on the lake were disturbed on the night in question. You know how they're tethered? Well, apparently next day they weren't as they'd been left."

"Could have been kids messing about?"

"Possibly."

"Why didn't this come to light earlier?"

"The regular boat man was sick. He had an asthma attack soon after he reached the park. He rang his son to take over for the day and went home. It was the son who was questioned and he didn't know about the boats having been disturbed."

"Oh."

"It was only later that his dad told him that they'd been messed with overnight."

"Cripes, what does that mean? That Georgio or someone had tried to take one out?

Dave grinned. "I doubt it."

Peter frowned. "Were there pleasure boats on the lake in wartime?"

Dave slowed behind traffic on Richmond Hill. "I have no idea. Don't tell me that I'll need to go back to the museum again? That microfiche does my head in." He changed to third gear as they passed a thirty mile-an-hour sign.

"No, a few enquiries in Ramsey should furnish the answer. Perhaps you can ask Aunt Maisie?"

Dave groaned, "Yes, I suppose."

Tom drew up at a flat-fronted four-storey house on Peel promenade. "That's it," he said, pointing opposite. "Lyndale, top floor."

"Wow," Emily said. "What a view you'll have!" She jumped out of the car and ran across the road to the promenade railings, staring across the crescent bay towards St Patrick's Isle, a rocky five-acre outcrop dominated by the imposing sandstone and slate ruins of the twelfth-century Peel Castle.

Tom laughed as he hurried to join her. "Yeah, isn't it fantastic?" He put his arm around her. "You could see this view every day if you moved in with me and forgot about college," he whispered, kissing her ear.

Emily laughed and pushed him away. "Don't be mean. You've got your qualifications. You can't begrudge me getting mine."

Tom cheerfully relented. "No, of course not." He glanced at his watch. "Let's go, the landlady said eleven o'clock. It's just past. Let's see my new pied-à-terre." He put his arm around her again. "I hope it's as good as I remember, cause the last tenant's stuff was everywhere and it was a bit of a tip."

"M'm," Emily mimicked, "pied-à-terre, eh? Going all upmarket now you're to be a single man about town?"

Tom gaped, then rang the bell. "Flip, Em, that sounds weird, I don't think Peel's got space for men about town. It's a down-to-earth place, you know."

Emily squeezed his arm as the door opened and the proprietor of Castle View Apartments faced them. Mrs Cannon, a wiry, short woman in a jersey and jeans, sized them up with an experienced eye. "Come in, come in, Mr Kelly, eh?"

"That's right." Tom nodded. "Oh, this is my girlfriend, Emily, she's on a dig over here for a couple of weeks, and then she'll be going back to college."

"From across – m'm?" Mrs Cannon gave Emily a doubtful nod. "I'll take you right up. Follow me."

Tom and Emily hurried after Mrs Cannon's energetic legs. A lingering smell of cooking hung in the hall as they climbed the first flight of stairs. But by the time they'd got to the top floor this aroma had been replaced by a fresh air from an open landing window and a hint of bleach.

"There y'are, love – as I said when you looked round last month, sitting room, kitchenette, bedroom, bathroom and bit of landing. Three fifty a month and no pets."

The rooms they inspected were clean, the furnishings minimal, but that suited Tom. The decor was predominantly cream and beige, and some of it freshly painted, and the light flooding in through the two windows overlooking the prom gave the flat a cheerful air.

"Yer meters are on the landing. This here's a fire door and has to be kept shut. There's a ladder out o' that winder. All fire regs up to date." Mrs Cannon sniffed and then frowned. She was wondering if she dared give her Jimmy fish and chips again for dinner. She'd meant to get to the shops but she'd got talking to Mrs Garrett next door about the murder in Ramsey and now it was gone eleven. Jimmy would be home from the builder's yard in half an hour.

"Yes, it's fine. I'll take it, Mrs Cannon." Tom drew out his wallet and cheque book. "I'll be starting at the Clothworkers' School on Monday and this'll be ideal. I'll give you a cheque for the deposit and a month's rent." He scribbled his signature on a cheque he'd already made out.

"Will yer?" Mrs Cannon seemed surprised. "You're a schoolteacher, eh?" She smiled, showing an interesting set of teeth. "I thought you must be one of them finance sector lot." She took the cheque and glanced at it. "Oh, you're from Ramsey What about this murder in the Mooragh then? Know anythin' about it, do ye?"

Tom was taken aback. "M'm… not really, do we, Em…?" His eyes urged Emily to say the right thing.

"No, we don't," she responded. "It's very sad, though."

"It is." Mrs Cannon stared at them both for a moment and then grinned. "Right, I'll get yers a key." She turned towards the stairs. "Knock on me door, will ye, when you're ready, an' I'll have the paperwork done."

Emily nudged Tom as the landlady's footsteps receded. "I think we handled that quite well, and it seems you've done all right coming here. She clearly thinks more of schoolteachers than anyone working in the finance sector."

Tom grinned. "She's Manx, do you blame her?" After another quick look round they clattered down the stairs to fetch the rest of his belongings from the car. This was a noisy process. The stairs were covered with hard-wearing cord matting that did little to deaden any sound. Tom wondered what it would be like when the other tenants were home. It could be filled with noisy TV-enslaved people who didn't sleep till the early hours.

Emily read his expression. "Go on, you don't have to stay here for ever. And the views are fabulous. Think of my grimy room at college."

Tom did and felt suddenly nostalgic for Emily's garret room with its ever-present scents of perfume, candles and sex.

"Sometimes I wish we were back," he said gruffly as they reached the front door.

Emily kissed his cheek. "We can't go back, Tom. We've got to move on. You have your new school to cope with and I've got to put in another term after the dig."

Tom shrugged. "I know, but I'll miss you loads. I've never known anyone like you, Em, and I'm so glad you've come over. You've been a godsend this week. It must have seemed hellish for you, with people dying and funeral teas and stuff." They grabbed the last of the bags and bundles from the back of the Mini.

Her arms full, Emily nudged him fondly. "It's been good, being here, Tom. I wish certain things hadn't happened, but they did, and – well, we coped, didn't we?" They stepped indoors again and Emily pushed the front door shut.

"I know," Tom said. "I still feel guilty about, you know. Should we have said something?"

His question was never answered. Ms Cannon emerged with his keys and lease. The rest of the day passed in a fun blur of unpacking and making the attic rooms into Tom's first grown-up home.

Fenella stared at the canvas before her and tried to stop smiling. Why couldn't painting always be like this? This was fun. This was what being an artist was all about. Purposeful work and, hopefully, an eventual financial reward by a happy purchaser.

It was such a joyous change to feel elated. After the past week of emotional highs and lows she felt she'd reached a plateau of virtual calm, with mostly only good things on the horizon. Not the least of which would be getting Norah off her hands, bless her. Much as she loved her gran it would be a relief not to have the responsibility of her care any longer. This cheerful awareness had suddenly transformed all the messy business that was caused by her incontinence. Fenella flushed. She felt bad about that, but day-to-day coping with such a condition was no fun. Now that both of them knew it was for a limited duration it had seemingly made the chore less onerous, though that fact had to be handled with tact.

"You needn't creep round smilin', Fenella Kelly," Norah had snapped only an hour or so ago, as Fenella had cleared her lunch tray. "I know what you're thinkin' an' you should be ashamed of yourself."

Fenella had bitten her lip. Norah was much too perceptive, yet for once Norah had mistaken her cheerfulness. She hadn't been lighthearted because of her grandmother being soon taken off her hands. She had been reliving the pleasant memories of the previous evening.

She'd managed to laugh, though. "You'd have been burned as a witch in the old days, Gran. Can you really read me so easily?"

"Aye," Norah said, with a knowing leer.

"Well, I'm going upstairs to paint. Will you be all right for an hour or so?"

"Course, I'll be glad of some peace before I get shunted off to bedlam."

"Don't be silly." Fenella gave her a hug before preparing a talking book cassette. She inspected the title on the cover. "I'm sure you listened to this Catherine Cookson story only recently?"

"So?" Norah queried, flapping her away.

Fenella grinned, checked that the player was close enough to the old lady. Norah liked to, as she put it, 'fast forward through the rubbish bits', and also, Fenella was aware, she replayed certain hot bits. Norah liked the passionate passages and who could blame her? Content that all was as it should be she ran swiftly upstairs, knowing that for once she felt truly in a creative mood. Tom and Emily, off to Peel to unload some stuff at Tom's new flat, would not be back till late. She had the makings of ham sandwiches for lunch and a crab salad for the evening meal.

A pang smote her as she reached her easel. Crab salad was one of Marjorie's favourites. It seemed to silly that she would not join them to eat, especially after the sad finality of the recent funeral.

Fenella felt that she should be feeling downcast but somehow, she couldn't. After all, Georgio had accomplished what he'd intended, which must have been a relief after so many years. That in doing so he'd transformed her life was weird considering she'd never even known she existed, nor he her. She frowned. *No, that was not right – he'd known that I existed because he knew about the mortgage, although the debt originally was to Marjorie and Norah. Or was it just to Norah? Oh, but he must have known Marjorie too, mustn't he?* Fenella sighed. It was no use – unless someone revealed some further details she would never know what was behind the old man's gesture.

She was glad he'd made it, though. Smiling, she plucked a brush from the jar in which an assortment was crammed. She flexed the bristles with her fingers and caught a waft of perfume from her wrist. She smiled. Who cared about old secrets? New ones were much better. Last night had been good. Why hadn't she realised earlier how positive life could be if you decided what you wanted and went after it?

She repressed a grin. It had all been entirely proper, which made it more memorable. She'd been home by eleven. Peter had been a perfect gentleman; in fact, it was she who had wanted their swift embrace at the end of the evening to last longer. But he had held back. Oh God, it was lovely… like phantom champagne.

It was good, she decided, this calmness between them, as if they were aware of their good fortune and sensible enough to treasure it. She found her hands moving over her body in recollection of Peter's gentle hands during their one kiss. She quickly picked up her brush and palette. "Transfer the emotion," she told herself briskly. "Don't waste it." She focused on the blank canvas before her. She would colour wash and then sketch in the dramatic landscape of the Point of Ayre, the stark lighthouse against an indigo sea while the land was grey shingle, green furze dotted with gold and highlights of pooled water. It was an invariable good seller if executed with panache.

Only a few moments later, the telephone trilled. Her heart lurched.

"It can't be Peter. He said he'd be tied up today." Fenella grimaced and laid down her brush. She'd been working no time at all. Should she leave the phone to ring?

No, she hurtled down the stairs. Perhaps it was the funeral director. He'd said he'd ring. Dear old Percy; the pang inside her was still raw.

She reached the ground floor, panting. She must get a mobile phone; it was time she embraced progress.

"Fenella, it's me."

Fenella gasped. "Mum, what's up?"

"Nothing, well, no, I'm OK – are we still on for next Monday?"

"Yes, of course. The nursing home would like Norah to be there about teatime, so that works out very well. You are coming for lunch at the Grand Island, aren't you?"

"Yes, of course, Mother will enjoy that."

There was a silence. Fenella waited anxiously.

Marjorie inhaled. "I went to the doctor's today. I've been so anxious. I got myself in a state."

"Oh, Mum."

"There's nothing really wrong with me, of course. It's all very well Dr Swanston saying I mustn't feel guilty for putting myself first, but it's difficult after all these years."

"Did he prescribe anything?"

"He's given me an anti-depressant – not Prozac, I wouldn't have that. And he said I was – we were – doing the right thing with regards to Norah. He reckons she's tough enough to outlive us all." She laughed shakily. "She won't, of course."

"Mum, do you want me to come round?"

"Are you busy?"

"Erm, I was painting."

"Oh, I'm sorry I disturbed you."

"It's fine. It's just that Tom and Emily are out – he's taken his stuff to Peel, remember? Gran's listening to one of her tapes, so I can't come right now."

"I see. Well, never mind. I'll have some lunch and then perhaps a little rest. Um…"

"Mum, is something on your mind?"

"No, no… I daresay I'm just suffering from reaction, you know, after the funeral and… everything?"

"Shall I come this evening?"

"Could you? That would be… m'm, good, yes, please. Sorry again that I disturbed you. I wanted to check. About Monday…"

"Of course. See you later, bye, Mum."

Fenella put the phone down thoughtfully. Something was bothering her mother. Something had plagued her enough to consult her doctor – an unusual action in itself. Whatever could it be?

At the other end of the line Marjorie replaced the receiver and stared unseeingly across the Mooragh Lake which was silver-tinted with the reflection from a lowering sky. She wished Fenella could have come. She needed to talk, and who else was there? With a sigh she headed determinedly towards her neat-as-a-pin kitchen.

"Keep busy," the doctor had said. "Get yourself some new interests. Find a man." Marjorie had felt insulted at first when he said that. He was always blunt, was Dr Swanston. When she'd protested that she was too old for a man, he had looked at her with those bloodhound eyes of his and had said gently, "No one is ever too old, Marjorie. Don't underrate yourself. You're still an attractive woman. Get out and survey the possibilities."

Smothering a weak smile Marjorie reached for a couple of eggs. It was a nice thing to say, even if it wasn't true.

She caught sight of her reflection in the kettle and peered at it. "I suppose I'm not that bad-looking for my age, compared to some. But I'm no spring chicken."

She cracked eggs into a jug, then sighed and reached for butter and the omelette pan, pushing various jostling thoughts to the back of her mind. Secrets as old as the ones she had were surely unimportant. Almost everyone involved was dead.

Fenella laid down her palette at four o'clock, well pleased. She cleaned the camel hairbrushes and then her hands, smiling as she sniffed her wrists after drying them. The fragrance lingered, an intense musky scent that she'd always adored; even diluted by turpentine and soap it remained. Fancy Peter having remembered after all this time?

She left the canvas on the easel. Another few touches and it would be complete. It had a spark all right, she decided, smiling as she looked it over once more before laying a piece of light protective fabric over it.

She clattered down the stairs hungry and happy. Tiptoeing into Norah's room she found her asleep, her mouth open and a thread of spittle reaching to her collar. Fenella gently wiped this away and crept out. She stood by the landing window. For once in her life she felt at a loose end. It was an uncommonly strange sensation. Usually at this time of day she would have been well into dinner preparations for her paying guests. To be freed from all that maybe for good, or until she stepped into some new routine, was like being thrown some amazing gift.

She peered at her reflection in a small, ornately framed mirror hanging on the wall at the top of the stairs and found herself grinning inanely. If only Tom were back she could have gone to Marjorie's flat. How strange that thought seemed. She'd barely stepped out of doors any afternoon at this time of day for many, many summers.

Impulsively she ran downstairs and out through the front door. The sun was shining on the front steps. She sat on the top one and gazed around. *This is the start of the rest of my life*, she thought, and the idea of a new start thrilled her. A new start, and all because of that old man who died. Abruptly she stood up and returned to the house, stepping into the lounge where only days ago the old man had sat, nursing his generous gesture because of something that had happened long ago. Now he was dead, and the nephew who'd visited to identify him was probably back home. All at once she felt guilty for not having spoken to the bereaved visitor. She had even wondered whether the transaction concerning Bayview had been at the expense of his existing family. She'd been relieved when she realised that her debt had apparently been a small affair in comparison to Georgio Stephani's wealth. Fenella shook her head, feeling suddenly aimless. She stood by the window. She wondered how the old man had observed the view now. It had not changed much in the past fifty years. On the far pavement there were still traces of where in the 1940s posts had stood for the high fences of barbed wire. Fenella remembered asking Marjorie once about these filled-in post holes and being brusquely fobbed off. Only later had she learned the truth.

It had been cruel, viewed from today's perspective, being summarily taken from one's home, corralled in some collection centre and then transported across the sea. It must have been frightening to those men and boys, young men like Tom. No wonder there were sometimes problems during their detention.

She really knew very little about the Second World War. Norah had not talked of those times much, nor had Marjorie. Fenella had always assumed that was because of Grandfather Walter's death. Now she suspected there was more to their aversion than just the memory of hard times. Whatever might it be?

A thought struck her. It might be polite to send a note of condolence to Georgio's address in Wakefield. The old man had come to Ramsey on a matter of business and had suddenly – her heart faltered – passed away. Some of his family must surely be mourning him.

She headed purposefully towards her office, sat and reached for a sheet of notepaper. Sunlight was filtering through the glass of the front door. It lay brightly on the chair the old man had sat on when he'd dropped his bombshell. She affixed a Bayview address label at the top of the cream sheet. She picked up her pen and caught a waft of fragrance from her wrist. She smiled; afterwards she would compose another letter. A letter she should have written a long time ago. Her insides tightened. If only she had done so a long time ago, if she had not been so stubborn, then who knows? Maybe the old man might not have died.

Next morning Peter Quilliam and Dave Colvin drove again across the mountainous spine of the island to Nobles Hospital in Douglas.

"It'll be a wasted journey if he's been discharged," Dave said as they drew up at the grey sprawl of hospital buildings. "I meant to check before we left."

Peter shrugged. "I don't think that's likely yet and I don't care. I'd almost forgotten just how good it is to be driven across the mountains. I've missed it while I was away. You know every bend, Dave, don't you?"

Dave's good-natured face beamed. "I felt giving it a bit of welly – I hate crawling round the local streets keeping to the speed limit."

"One would not have suspected as much," Peter said dryly. "Come on, let's find out the worst. If he's discharged we can catch him at home, though I wouldn't feel like grilling him at home. He's not going to be in a fit state yet."

"He's tough is Charlie, you know he is."

Peter grimaced. "Nonetheless, I could have throttled the chief super when he rang first thing suggesting I put pressure on him. I always thought the super was on our side."

"He'll be getting leaned on too. You know what a field day Manx Radio and the press are having, spreading rumours about vandals doing for Stephani and suchlike."

Peter gritted his teeth. "I felt like a rookie, as though I didn't know how to handle a man like Charlie."

"Who else have we got to interrogate?" Dave said, sotto voce, as they entered a dim and antiseptic corridor. "It's still iffy whether the old guy died of natural causes or whether he was clobbered."

"I know."

"But then, define natural?" Dave muttered as they neared the ward they were seeking. They walked in quietly. Charlie's bed was empty. Peter sighed.

Julie Corlett was at the ward desk. She looked up from writing. "Are you looking for Mr Peake, Inspector?"

"If he's still about, yes," Dave replied, grinning. "Morning, Julie."

"Good morning, David. Good morning, Inspector Quilliam. Mr Peake is in the day room, awaiting a doctor's all-clear." She gestured helpfully. "This way."

The officers followed. "He's not alone." She smiled as she pushed open the door to the day room.

Evie Cannon jumped off Charlie's lap.

"Morning, officers." Charlie grinned while Evie straightened her skirt, which, judging by the way it had been rucked, had been in need of adjustment.

Peter's face remained impassive. "We'd like a word, Mr Peake, in private."

Charlie looked stricken. "Evie's drivin' me home. Can she stay?"

"It's up to you, Mr Peake." Dave smiled pleasantly as he took out his notebook.

Charlie licked his lips. "Go out a minute, love. I'll not be long." He watched as Evie tittupped to the door. "Will I?"

Peter ignored the threat in Charlie's tone and closed the door behind Evie. He remained standing by it while Dave perched on one of the high-backed chairs, notebook and pen at the ready.

"We have a few discrepancies to discuss, Mr Peake."

Charlie was very pale. Peter felt uneasy. He hoped this was not going to end in having to put the man away. He'd have sworn that Charlie was not a violent man. Ruthless, perhaps, and always ready to take advantage. Could that be what had happened? Had he taken advantage of an old man?

If the he'd died accidentally, and Charlie had witnessed this, why not admit it? He'd been near, and drunk, that much had been proved. If he'd knocked the old man over in a fit of temper because of the Bayview business, well… Even as he was weighing up the scared face gazing at him Peter was fully aware that his heart was not in this investigation. He'd not have admitted it to a living soul, but quite honestly he didn't care whether Charlie Peake was behind the old man's death or not. All he cared about was that the case had given him an excuse to get close to Fenella. Compared to that nothing mattered. That this was absolutely against all that he stood for as an upholder of the law he knew. He also knew that he was only human and had had just about enough of police life.

Outside the sun broke through the clouds. A swift glance from the window revealed a pretty but distant view of Carnane television mast on the green hill behind the town. One day he'd stride across that hill with Fenella's hand in his. One day…

He forced himself back to the matter in hand.

"Charles," he said, "I'm sorry, but I've been told to charge you if you can't give us the answers we want."

It was clear that Evie Cannon was listening outside, for as he ended his sentence they heard her wail and her footsteps recede. Charlie's features turned ashen, but there was a stubborn thrust to his jaw. "I've told you all I'm goin' to. Any more an' I want my lawyer present, so put that in your notebook, Peter Quilliam, that's all you'll get from me."

Dave and Peter exchanged looks. "As you wish, Mr Peake. We'll see you again soon."

SIXTEEN

Two days later, Fenella was climbing the stairs to wake Norah when the phone rang. She raced to answer it. "Hello, Bayview guesthouse."

"Hi, Fenella."

The voice was unmistakable. "Peter," she gasped. "I didn't expect you to call today. There's nothing wrong, is there?"

"No, I just wanted to... Oh hell, I felt like hearing your voice, that's all."

"I see. That's nice."

"Do you mean it, or are you being polite?"

She laughed. "No. I enjoyed our catch-up. We covered some ground, didn't we?"

"M'm." Peter paused. "I'd like to catch up some more."

Fenella's heart bumped. What did he mean? Sometime a long way ahead, or...? She hesitated, struggling for words. "Um, Gran was chuffed we went out together. Not that it meant anything, of course... but..." Her mouth dried. This was ridiculous. She was behaving like a teenager.

"She's quite a character, your gran, isn't she?"

"M'mm... oh, thanks again for the perfume. It was very kind of you."

"Nonsense, just something I had lying about."

"Gift-wrapped?"

"Well… I wanted to make up, for, you know, that other time. Being with you again… reminded me. Fenella, I am sorry."

"For what?"

"For my utterly awful behaviour that night."

Fenella giggled. "Goodness, Peter. It was years ago."

Peter sighed. "I know, but I couldn't help remembering. I could barely sleep later…" He broke off. "What…? Yes, oh hell, I'm needed apparently. The trouble is, for some reason I can't concentrate… I wish I could see you tonight."

"That would be lovely."

"But I can't. Too much on."

"That's a shame."

"M'mm… we're interviewing Charlie again tomorrow. A reliable witness has said he saw Charlie following Stephani along River Road on the night in question."

"Oh!"

"So he needs to tell us what he was up to."

"Should you be telling me this?"

"Um, no, but—"

Quickly Fenella broke in, "Charlie's always been a blusterer, Peter. You don't really believe that he would harm anyone?"

"I don't know what to think. Well, yes, I do. To hell with detecting and Charlie. You will come out with me again, won't you?"

"More than likely." Fenella smiled.

"I know it's tricky at present, and you'd say, wouldn't you, if you'd rather I kept away for the time being? I don't want us to fall out again."

"Yes, I'd say…" She took a breath. "Erm, as you've asked, might you be free a week on Monday? I might be in dire need of company then."

"Why?"

"Tom will have moved, Mum's already gone and after we treat Gran to lunch at the Grand Island we will take her to the nursing home…" She paused.

"I see, yes, you might need a pick-me-up. Look, I can't promise, it's too far ahead. I'll try to be free."

"Good," Fenella sighed, "that will be lovely." The front door slammed. "Oh, Tom and Emily are back. I must go."

"So must I," Peter said briskly. "See you soon." At his end the phone slammed down. Fenella let out her breath. *Maybe my future won't be entirely bleak.* She smiled.

Tom poked his head in. "Hi, we've had a great day, Mum. Hey, you look bothered. What's up?"

"Nothing." Fenella suppressed her grin. "Make yourselves a coffee. I'm off to rouse Gran."

Tom's keen eyes followed her as she slipped past him and took the stairs two at a time. Emily tugged his arm. "What's up?"

"I reckon my mum's got a fella," he grinned, "just as I'd suggested. Don't let on, will you?"

"As if," Emily replied, snuggling up to him. "Now, what about that hot chocolate you promised, lover boy? I'm exhausted. We walked miles."

"Nonsense, I intended we'd get to loads more places before your dig." He pulled her to him. "We'll have to cram walks into your weekends off, that's all."

Emily wriggled away and headed into the kitchen. She plumped onto a chair. She would be glad to get on the dig. It could hardly be more strenuous than playing tourist with Tom.

"Wakey, wakey, Gran."

Norah stirred crossly. "I wasn't asleep. I just had my eyes closed."

"Good. Shall I sit you up to read or would you prefer to get up and dressed?"

Norah lay on the pillow, looking at her with eager eyes. "Why? Is something going on I should know about?"

Fenella chuckled. "No, Gran, but as it's almost the end of Emily's stay I thought we'd break out some wine and have our meal in the dining room this evening. Get dolled up, as you call it."

Norah threw the covers back. "I'm game for that. Gimme a hand, Nell. Fill the basin and I'll wash."

Norah permitted Fenella to sit her up but then thrust her away. "Now, clear off. If I'm going to this home I'll need to be doin' for myself, won't I?"

Fenella's heart bumped. "Oh, Gran, don't. You know I'd keep you here if I could manage."

Norah gripped her arm. "Aye, well, that's as be. Now push off and get some food ready. I'm starving."

Fenella turned to the door.

"Wait!" Norah flapped her hand. "Fetch me that dress your mum got me at Christmas. I'll have to wear it sometime."

Suppressing a smile Fenella fetched the jersey dress and laid it on the bed. "There, it's really nice, Gran, I don't know why you said you didn't like it." Fenella vividly recollected the moment the garment had been unwrapped on Christmas morning. Norah's reaction had spoiled the entire day. Thank goodness there'd be no more festive days like that.

"I still don't like it." Norah grimaced. "It's a dress for an old lady."

Fenella did not even try to suppress a burst of laughter and Norah let out a yelp too. "The trouble with Marje is she could never see a joke."

"You're wicked, Gran."

Norah shrugged. Fenella left Norah crooning to herself and fumbling into her underclothes.

Downstairs she briskly laid out ingredients for their meal from the fridge and freezer. Homemade leek and potato soup to start and a gooey gateau to finish. Salmon fillets for the main, with broccoli and new potatoes. Unconsciously she noted that there were not many frozen salmon fillets remaining. But then, this really didn't matter now, did it?

She laid one of the large tables in the dining room near a window, putting out cutlery and glassware. It looked all right but a little bleak in the large room. She fetched the vase of fresh flowers from the hallstand table. Yes, that looked nicer. It was a lovely room to dine in, always had been. She stood, gazing out at the sky and the sea, calm that day, with delicate frills on the wavelets surging towards the marram grass that grew prolifically at the top of the beach. It was a lovely view, but it might be refreshing to have a different outlook.

She leaned against the curtains, aware that the faded brocade was well-worn and sun-faded. The curtains should have been renewed years ago. Yet each season she'd get them cleaned and had put off the expense. It didn't matter now she was approaching the end here and it was right. She was smiling as Tom strolled in. "Hi," she said. He'd got changed; he looked smart and young and ready for anything. A tinge of envy ran through her, but she smiled it away.

"Will dinner be long, Mum? I'm starved. Hey, you've laid wine glasses and candles too. What's up?"

"I thought it might be nice." Fenella patted a chair. "Sit for a minute, Tom, I want to tell you – well, I've decided I'll definitely sell."

Tom gaped, then laughed. "Good for you, Mum, it's about time."

"What? I thought you might be upset – you seemed bothered when you thought we could be evicted."

Tom shrugged. "That was then, this is now. No, it's the right decision, Mum. After all, we're all splitting, aren't we? Hey, you're not... Oh, don't, Mum." Tom pulled out a hanky. "Here, use this."

Fenella buried her face in her hands. "No, I've got a tissue." She dabbed at a rush of tears that had welled up unbidden. "Oh, glory, check on Gran for me, would you?" She sniffed and hurried out.

Tom sighed. Women! He'd never understand them. He bounded upstairs, the thought occurring that perhaps he should feel regret at leaving Bayview, but somehow he couldn't feel anything but excitement for the future. He'd look back fondly on the rackety old place, but its day was past.

As he reached the second landing a cheerier thought struck him. His mother would make a tidy profit by selling. Maybe some cash would come his way. A Mini upgrade would be ace.

The family meal that evening was that rare event, an utterly cheerful occasion. Norah was in great form and told a succession of risqué jokes that Tom found hilarious, and while Emily laughed, she was actually slightly embarrassed, though she and Tom contributed cheerfully to the conversation. They gave a detailed description of Tom's flat and his garrulous landlady, which was funny and made Fenella keen to meet the woman, though well pleased that he'd got himself lodgings in what sounded a respectable place.

For once Fenella felt herself at peace. Tom paid enough attention to Emily, stroking her and gazing lustfully while trying to look discreet so Norah was thrilled, though Fenella felt a little sad remembering his babyhood and childhood. Now he was a man and about to fly the nest.

It was late when they eventually left the table. Emily guided Norah into the lounge while Fenella and Tom cleared the plates away, leaving a lot of the debris for the next day. "I'll take that," Tom said, whipping a loaded tray away as Fenella reached for it.

Grateful for his offer, Fenella leaned to blow out the candles.

At the same moment a car executed a swift three-point turn in the road outside, its lights swinging like searchlights across the room. Fenella stood stock still while the light flicked across her and then the vehicle sped away. She was swept back to the reality of those internment days and the fact that searchlights might often have swept this building when Georgio was held here. She felt a sudden sadness for his abrupt demise, which had been sad and wrong. There was still wine in her glass. Thoughtfully she held it up. "To Georgio," she said huskily, and gulped the last sour dregs. "May he rest in peace."

She left her glass on the table and walked slowly into the hall.

Norah and Tom were laughing in the lounge. Fenella frowned. Would she ever find out what had happened here? More importantly, did she really want to know?

She threw her hair back, straightened her shoulders and hurried into the lounge.

"When'll I do my packing? Am I going today?"

"No, Gran, you are going next week. I told you, we'll meet Mum for lunch at the Grand Island and then we'll take you to Barrule Park."

"Bloody nursing home. I'll hate it," Norah said querulously, banging her fist on the table.

Fenella was washing up. Norah had been difficult ever since she got up. Too much alcohol the previous night, Fenella was well aware and felt guilty. She always forgot how much it affected the old lady. Today was going to be a trial, and no mistake. It was a pity. It would have been a good day to get a lot of sorting done.

Fenella removed Norah's plate, tipped the crusts into the bin and dropped it into the washing-up water. Then she turned, dried her hands and sat by Norah.

"Gran, if you could do anything at all today, what would it be?"

Norah looked perplexed and suspicious. "Why?"

"Because you could do with a treat. I know how you feel about next week, but believe me, I bet you'll enjoy it once you've settled in. There'll be plenty of people to gossip with."

"Old people," Norah said truculently.

Fenella couldn't help laughing. "I daresay they'll mostly be old people, yes."

"Laxey," Norah declared, lifting her fist. "I'd like to go to Laxey. See the wheel, have dinner in that fancy café that used to be a nice little cottage. Go along the prom. I've not been to Laxey in an age."

Fenella smiled. "Good. Then that's what we'll do." Fenella took one of her grandmother's liver-spotted hands in hers. "And there's something I must tell you, Gran. I don't want you to get upset about this, but although the mortgage has been paid off I've decided it's time I sold Bayview."

"Have you, indeed." Norah looked taken aback for an instant and then her face split in a grin. "So we're all leaving this place."

"I hoped you wouldn't be upset. It's been your home for such a time."

Norah snatched her hand away and swivelled her wheelchair neatly. "Why should I be? We're all leaving, an' it's the right time, Nell, girl. Things've changed, all roun'. I'd not want to be stayin' here, not now." She wheeled herself swiftly towards the open door. "I'll get ready, then, Nell. Goin' to Laxey today, eh." She half turned in the doorway. "An' perhaps we can choose a place to scatter Percy's ashes on the way back."

Fenella stared after her, listening to the click of her wheels as they rotated along the hall and the whine of the lift as it ascended. Well, that had been an anti-climax. She hadn't broken the news about selling up yesterday in case the old lady got upset.

Upset! Honestly, did anything upset that old so-and-so? She wouldn't want to be staying on here anyhow! Though it had been her home for sixty-five years. Mortgaged up to the hilt in all that time, of course. Yet now, since Georgio had paid off the mortgage, Norah wanted to move.

A cold feeling gripped Fenella as she picked up the tea towel. What made her grandmother so bitter? What had happened all those years ago?

Marjorie walked briskly along the river path towards the swing bridge. It was a pleasant, blustery morning, with the sun about to break through at any moment. She felt better, well rested; the pill from the doctor had helped her sleep and today she was determined to push away all the unsavoury memories that had plagued her since the old man's death. After all, that time was long over, and with luck it would lie forgotten. As long as no one was charged, of course. The old man had tripped, what could be more likely? He'd been noticeably unsteady on his feet.

"Tut." *Stop it. No more thinking about him.*

A man emerged abruptly down the steps from the roadway tugged by a lively black Labrador.

"Good morning, Mrs Quayle," he said, touching his cap. "A nice one it is too."

"Isn't it, Mr Killip? And how's Freddy today?" Marjorie patted Freddy's inquisitive head. "No, don't do that, Freddy, there's a good boy." Freddy was trying to push his head under her skirt.

"Heel, lad," Mr Killip ordered hopefully. "He's so good at dog obedience class, but when I get him home he does exactly as he pleases."

"He's young," Marjorie said. "He'll learn."

"Mr Peake returned home the other night. Have you heard? He was looking poorly, though he's got a new, ah, lady friend, I noticed."

"Has he? Oh, well, I'm pleased he's back home."

"M'mm, he'll be causing ructions within the commissioners again soon enough." Harry Killip laughed and then he had to run as Freddy had pulled the lead from his hand.

Marjorie walked on, and though overhead the sun had come out, she felt as though a black cloud was hanging over her. So Charlie was in circulation again, was he? Was that good news, or bad? *Oh God, please let this matter die the death it should have done long years ago.*

"Is Marje coming?" Norah asked as Fenella got her settled in her shabby old Volvo Estate car.

"I didn't ask her. Would you like her to come?"

Norah nodded. "Aye. Why not?"

Fenella got into the car and slammed the door. Norah had been bright enough leaving the house. Now, after the process of getting her from her wheelchair and into the front seat, the old lady looked tired and every inch her age. Fenella felt guilty for the many rancorous thoughts she had directed towards Norah lately. The indignities of age could not be easy to bear.

"We'll call at the flat. I'm sure she'd like to join us."

"Yes." Norah nodded, her false teeth shifting.

"Her car's there," Fenella said as they turned from the promenade into North Shore Road. Marjorie's dark blue Ford Fiesta was parked in front of the Calor Gas Company building.

Fenella rang the doorbell three times, but there was no reply. She stared up at her windows; she knew that if her mother was listening to the radio she sometimes didn't hear the bell. Eventually she accepted that she must be out.

"She must be shopping," she said as got back in the car. "We'll maybe pass her on the way." Fenella drove smoothly off. "You don't mind if we take a minor detour, Gran? I want to drop a letter at Charlie Peake's."

"What for?" Norah grunted as they turned up Bowring Road.

"Just a matter of business," she replied shortly. "Nothing special…" Her voice died away as she turned the Volvo into the cul de sac where Charles lived. "Oh no, there's a police car at Charlie's house, and another opposite. I wonder what's going on."

By the time Fenella was level with Charlie's front door she could see a sad procession, led by Peter, in which Dave Colvin and two other PCs were escorting Charlie from his house towards the waiting police car. She jammed on her brakes and leapt out, leaving her car, its engine running, angled across the road.

"What on earth's going on?" she shouted, marching towards the group of men.

Peter looked up, startled and then annoyed. "Fen... Mrs Kelly. Mr Peake has agreed to come to the station to help with our enquiries." His face was like stone. "If you'll move your vehicle, please, we can carry out our orders."

"Peter, for God's sake. Charlie couldn't have had anything to do with that old man's death. Don't be ridiculous."

Peter's face flushed crimson. The PCs looked amused then wary. Dave Colvin moved towards Fenella, but she shook him off and pushed in close to Charlie. "I've brought you a letter, Mr Peake. Here, take it with you." She pushed it into his hand. "You'll no doubt be home again soon. The idea of your having anything to do with murder is... just... plain stupid."

Charlie, his face almost as pale as the sling on his arm and the plaster on his foot, looked astonished but grateful. He flapped his good hand. "I keep tellin' them, Fenella. But they won't listen. Ta." He stuffed the letter into his pocket before ducking his head as they bundled him into the waiting car.

Fenella rounded on Peter, her face flaming. "For heaven's sake, Peter. What are you doing this for? He could sue for wrongful arrest, you know."

Peter's face was white, his expression wooden. "I would be obliged if you would move your car, Mrs Kelly, we need to drive Mr Peake to the station." He then spoke in an undertone through gritted teeth. "Fenella, for God's sake, keep out of this. It's nothing to do with you."

Fenella glared. "Oh!" she shouted, slamming into her car and accelerating noisily away, causing Norah's head to rock back into the headrest with the impetus and the car alarm to sound. Not that the old lady cared about the speed or the noise.

By gum, she grinned. "I've never been at an arrest before." She craned her neck to peer over her shoulder. "Old Percy would have liked to see Charlie Peake being manhandled from his own house."

"He wasn't arrested, and he didn't do it, Gran," Fenella seethed. "How can Peter be so stupid?"

"How do y'know he didn't do it?" Norah snapped. "He's a nasty piece of work, is Charlie Peake."

"That's enough, Gran. Let's get out of this dratted town." Fenella struggled to fasten her seatbelt with one hand as she drove. "Narrow minds and bigots, gossips and scandal-mongers, sometimes it all gets a bit much." She accelerated over the bridge and turned onto the quay.

"Look, there's Mum. Shall we stop and pick her up?"

Norah clapped her hand over Fenella's wrist, almost making her swerve. "No," she snapped. "Don't. Let's go to Laxey on our own, Nell."

"But Gran?"

"No," Norah shouted, and Fenella, confused, drove past Marjorie, who, having seen the approach of the Volvo, was standing, smiling, expecting them to stop.

In the rear-view mirror Fenella saw her mother gazing after them. Fenella felt irrationally angry all of a sudden, with Norah, Peter, with her mother and more so with herself. What had she done? What had driven her to react like that? Letting her stupid feelings take over…? And for Charlie Peake? She must be stark-staring mad!

Once out of the town's speed limits she let the car engine have its way. They roared up Slieau Lewaigue Hill as though the black dogs of Peel Castle were after them and raced through Glen Mona and past the Dhoon Glen in record time. Only as they raced around the everlasting bend of the coastal road and could see Laxey village in the valley ahead did she at last calm down, and then, of course, disgust at her behaviour swept through her. Well, she'd messed up her relationship with Peter good and proper – before it had even got going. What an idiot she was.

Yet maybe it was all for the best. She should clear out of Ramsey. Make a fresh start elsewhere. Even go across to live…

"You're doin' more than thirty, Nell," Norah said, in a voice that sounded unusually quivery.

Fenella glanced sideways. She'd been so furious that she'd more or less forgotten that Norah was by her side. Her temper fled; reality clicked in.

"Sorry, Gran, shall we go down to the prom first? I'll push you along beside the beach."

Norah grinned. "Aye, that'll be grand, love. Are you all right now? I've not seen you so riled before."

Fenella turned into the steep incline of Menorca Hill. "Sorry, Gran, yes, I'm fine now," she said blithely. But inside she felt as though her heart was breaking. She'd ruined things between her and Peter before they'd even got started.

SEVENTEEN

As Fenella opened the front door the telephone was buzzing.

"Betcha that's Marje," Norah murmured. "I'm goin' to watch telly." She wheeled herself towards the lounge as Fenella hurried to the telephone.

"Hi, Mum, yes… I'm sorry about this morning. We were on our way to Laxey."

Fenella glanced along the hall; the TV was already blaring. Norah was out of earshot. "Gran was in one of her contrary moods. I called at your flat—"

"Did you?" Marjorie exclaimed, disbelief in her voice.

"Of course! But by the time we saw you Gran said to keep driving and, well, I was in a bit of a mood myself and I did as she asked. As I said, I'm sorry."

"M'm," Marjorie muttered, then added, "Why were you in a mood?"

"Nothing, I felt out of sorts." She wasn't about to admit to shouting at Peter because it had been shameful and she felt furious with herself.

"Oh well, I suppose that's OK," Marjorie sighed, "but…" Her voice changed. "So, what did you do in Laxey, and did Mum enjoy herself?"

"That isn't what you were going to say."

"No, but it's what I am saying. Did you have a good time?"

"Mostly. Gran was grumpy for a while, but she cheered up after a good lunch."

"She would. Where did you take her?"

"The Mine's Tavern, by the tram station. Before that we'd been to the prom, I walked her along the front, which was nice but chilly. She jabbered on about things she remembered and where so-and-so had lived, you know what she's like, and we came home via Hibernia."

"Gracious, why?" Marjorie exclaimed. "The last time I took that track was ages ago, and it was awful then."

"Gran wanted to go that way. She remembered it was a shortcut to the TT course near the Guthrie Memorial."

"Oh… I see," Marjorie said curtly. "Oh, of course, Percy's ashes. You've not got them? I wanted to be with you when they're scattered."

"I know, Mum. No, Gran wanted to choose a spot. Though when we go to scatter them she'll probably have changed her mind."

"Yes, she likes to be contrary," Marjorie murmured. "Oh God, Fenella, sometimes I just wish Mum would go suddenly… like Percy—"

Fenella responded quickly, "That reveals that you're tired and fed up. You're not a vindictive person, Mother, so please don't act as if you are." Fenella knew she sounded terse; she felt on edge. She didn't like to hear her only parent being inconsiderate.

Marjorie laughed shakily. "Am I not? Maybe? I just wish Norah wasn't my mother."

"Well, we can't choose our relations," Fenella declared. "Oh, not that I would want to change you, Mum."

"No? Anyway, on a more positive note, how's Tom? Has he moved out yet?"

"In spirit, yes. He and Emily were up at the crack of dawn cramming his car with stuff. They'll be back later tonight, but that's it. They'll be staying at the flat tomorrow."

"Oh, love, you'll miss them. Well, Tom anyway."

"I will."

"Tell him to pop in before he goes. I've got him a small 'new career' present."

"Oh, that's nice. I meant to get him a card. I'll get one in the morning."

"Yes." Marjorie's voice became more brisk. "Oh well, Vivian Quine's coming round this evening, which will be nice, so I'll say cheerio for now, dear. I'm glad Mum had an outing today. It was a good idea on your part. See you soon." Marjorie put the phone down swiftly, almost cutting Fenella off.

Fenella tutted; she'd meant to tell her mother about Charlie being taken in for questioning. She shrugged. *I don't suppose it matters.*

The interview room was stuffy. Charlie Peake was sweating. He was tired and in pain.

At last Jeremy Dawson walked in.

"Jerry, where the hell have you been all this time?"

"Sorry, Charles. I was on the golf course. Need the exercise, you know." Jeremy patted his well-padded middle. "What have you been up to, old man?"

"Don't give me any of your old-school chat, Jerry. I just want you to get me out. They're holding me on a trumped-up charge and they haven't a leg to stand on."

Jeremy Dawson looked at his client. He didn't think Charlie had knowingly made a pun, and he decided it might be as well not to laugh. Certainly Charlie looked in a far from humorous mood. He looked ill, his complexion faintly green, not unlike the colour of Jeremy's argyle golf socks. The sweat on Charlie's forehead was not, in Jeremy's opinion, the sweat of a guilty man. It was the sweat of a man who'd not long ago been in hospital after a nasty accident.

"I'll settle this, Charles. Keep calm." Jeremy dropped his briefcase on the interview table and marched out, closing the door quietly behind him.

Peter Quilliam and DC Colvin were sitting at a desk in the CID room adjoining. Peter stood up.

"What do you think you're playing at?" Jeremy began to bluster. "My client is clearly a sick man." Jeremy stretched himself to his full height, and though a portly five foot three does not usually command respect Jeremy was used to throwing his weight about in court and had learned how to sound authoritative at close quarters. "We could be talking harassment here, Inspector Quilliam, or unreasonable provocation. We could be talking civil rights and being unfit to plead."

Peter suppressed a grin. "Come off it, Jeremy, you can't have it all ways. We brought Mr Peake in with reasonable evidence. He refuses to clarify a point in his statement and we have a perfect right to hold him."

"I must protest that my client—"

"But…" Peter held up his hand, "if you'll let me finish."

Jeremy closed his mouth but looked truculent.

"I was going to advise your client that he should go home. When he is feeling better we should then like to speak to him again."

Jeremy opened his mouth. "But—"

Peter quickly added, "Or you could have a swift chat with him now and get him to tell us what we want to know."

Jeremy wriggled his glasses on his snub nose. "Ah, well, it is a pity that you brought my client here in the first place, Inspector. You must have been aware of his recent stay in hospital?"

"We were fully aware, Mr Dawson," Peter said stiffly, "but sometimes we have to act under orders that we do not necessarily think in the best interests of anyone, let alone a man recovering from a serious accident."

Jeremy shuffled. "Erm." His nose twitched. "Higher powers, eh? Um. Message understood." He swung round. "Right. May I escort my client home?"

"Of course, Mr Dawson. Take him – with our compliments," Peter added the latter under his breath.

As Jeremy marched out Dave whispered, "We could have taken him home, guv."

Peter gave him a stern look. "Jeremy will need to make this visit viable. He can hardly charge Charlie an arm and a leg for a five-minute chat."

"Of course." Dave nodded lugubriously. "Those poor, hardworking advocates, they have to get by, don't they?"

"And being the chief constable's godson means that Jeremy has to work extra hard to make sure people don't think he's doing well merely through nepotism."

Dave Colvin looked askance at Peter. "You're very acidic, all of a sudden. Would you like an indigestion remedy? I always carry some."

Peter grinned shamefacedly. "No, but thanks. The sort of heartburn I've got won't go away with a tablet."

They nodded politely as Charlie emerged from the interview room, assisted by Jeremy. "I hope you're feeling better soon, Mr Peake," Peter murmured, but Charlie didn't have the energy to retort.

"He isn't well," Peter said glumly. "If we do get done for harassment you can be sure that the chief won't admit getting him in was his idea."

Dave yawned. "So can I go home now? I think the kids should see me before they go to bed. It will be a treat if they recognise me."

Peter grinned. "Go on then, but I bet you'll regret it. Storytime and all that stuff."

"Nah, they don't want stories anymore. They read their books themselves. Cheerio." He banged out and Peter heard the squeak of his boots as he strode along the corridor. Peter sat, twiddling with a biro. He looked at the phone, reached his hand to it and then drew it back.

He got up, switched the lights off and walked out.

"Damn all women," he muttered, after nodding to the duty sergeant before exiting. He walked around the courthouse gardens and crossed the road to his flat. All at once he wished he didn't live so near. Entering the hallway, full of scents from the ground-floor café, now closed, he felt hemmed in, physically and mentally. The linoleum-covered stairs creaked under his boots. It was a relief when he entered his flat to find sunlight still shining through the large sash windows, though. If only… "Oh, damn and blast police work – and women." He walked to his bedroom, tore off his tunic and trousers, remembering this time to close the curtains so as not to allow the people in the flat above the estate agent to glimpse him in his underwear, and headed to the shower. Once refreshed he pulled on T-shirt and jeans, thought about making a snack, decided against it and headed out. He needed to clear his head, get some fresh air into his lungs. He turned towards the harbour and the beach beyond.

He would have preferred a jog on the south beach, but there were always folk sitting about there and kids with buckets and spades, even this late. He headed instead towards the Mooragh Promenade, carefully avoiding being seen from Bayview, just in case. After her unwarranted outburst he'd felt fury and mortification in equal measure. Now that reaction had passed he just felt sad. He should just accept that he and she would never be more than casual friends and get on with his life, try and meet other single women. He was certain that there must be women on the island eager for a new partner, even an ageing copper. He had some good points, after all. He winced; he was damned if he could list many.

Well beyond Bayview he walked onto the beach. Half-heartedly he began to jog just above the tide line. It wasn't easy, on shifting sand and shingle. He knew he was out of condition; that had been another reason to come home. He'd got frustrated across where there was often barely space to move, let alone run through a park, without tripping over bodies, kids with bikes or spent needles. Here there was ample space; the beach stretched for miles. He moved faster, feeling his heart quicken and his spirits rise infinitesimally. Looking ahead he could see as far as the Dog Mills. In that entire vista only two dogs plus owners, and a lone swimmer, disturbed the landscape. He felt a surge of pleasure. Yes, this was doing him good; he should take more exercise, get himself fit again. It was good to be back here, on the 'the land of his birth', as extolled in the stirring Manx National Anthem. This small isle was indeed 'a gem on God's earth' and he had all the pleasure of becoming reacquainted with all five hundred square miles again with a fresh eye. He gulped in longer breaths and lengthened his stride, his heels regularly striking the sometimes firm, sometimes yielding sand. It was hard going, but that was good. He needed to tone his slack body and conquer his still-restless 'newly arrived' feeling. He had lived long enough off-island to value this new contentment.

After a short time his mind moved, as he knew it would, to review the shock of Fenella's attack and, grudgingly, understand her viewpoint. Charlie Peake had not been fit enough to answer questions, he had said as much to his superior when the order was issued, and he vividly recalled the icy silence that had prefaced his superior's tart rejoinder.

"Officer Quilliam, it might be policy on the mainland to ignore an order, but any man in the Manx Force not complying at once will find himself on a charge. Is that understood?"

"Yes, sir." Peter had entirely understood. He had carried out his orders. To be then berated by Fenella – well, it just wasn't his day.

He leapt over a stretch of seaweed and winced as his landing jarred his ankles.

The trouble was, he could understand the episode from her

point of view. She'd been understandably shocked. He knew about her hot temper. Poor old Brian once told him about their many furious rows early in their marriage. Not that he'd moaned about it. In fact, by the gleam in his eye, which Peter never forget, he surmised that Brian enjoyed giving as good as he got, and the necessary making-up. They were both passionate people. Such high emotions weren't to his taste – he could be enthusiastic but getting in a rage was not his way. Susan could vouch for that. It was apathy rather than arguments that had driven them apart.

He paused to catch his breath, hands on hips, gazing with pleasure at the thousands, no, millions of scattered pebbles edging the sands. All shapes and sizes, myriad colours from pitch black to palest pink. He straightened and, feeling his back twinge, decided he'd jogged enough. His heart was banging. He turned and sauntered back, close to the lace-white wave edges, the surging sea taking him back to days long ago, endless hours spent on the Manx beaches, in childhood and in his teenage years. He gazed around pleasurably, his head clearer now and hunger pangs reminding him he'd skimped on lunch. He plodded at a comfortable pace and was pleased that he'd taken this spontaneous exercise.

As he approached the promenade end and neared Bayview he made a diversion towards the promenade wall, stepping up on the sand and marram grass bank that had accumulated over many years. The area was trodden with paths made by dog walkers and picnic parties who enjoyed barbecues there on warm evenings. He walked slowly, enjoying the quiet, with only gulls' cries and the mild bleat of oyster catchers pecking nearby. He kept a weather eye open for dog mess, which was always a hazard, no matter how many bins were placed about the beach and prom. He spotted a recent pile of poo and veered towards the remains of a recent fire. He passed it and had taken a few more careful steps when he paused, looked back and retraced his steps. He inspected the remains, which looked innocent enough. There were the usual half-burned embers, a few scraps of wood and a couple of larger debris. He picked over the remains, lifting a heavier shard, frowning. A memory stirred, provoked an association. He gazed more closely and his heart bumped. He tutted, stepped away, then got down on his haunches so that he could inspect the burned remains more closely, sniffing at them, crumbling the blackened wood between his fingers. He crouched for a moment, staring, thinking, trying not to strain his suspicions, which might lead him to have reached an utterly ridiculous conclusion. Even so, his insides tightened. He stood again, took a breath and kicked the debris, as though kicking his suspicions into touch. Then he hurried off, trampling through the tangles of bramble and marram, stamping over thistles, nettles and thickets of pink Valarian. He did not want to dwell too long on what he'd found, or might have found. He'd come across the remains of a fire, lit probably by kids. It had meant nothing. He looked back only once, but the site of the fire was totally hidden by the vegetation, just another dead fire among a dozen or so others.

He vaulted over the promenade wall, stamped the sand off his trainers and hurried homewards. He had enough to cope with without chasing red herrings – well, dark pink ones actually. It had meant nothing; it was just a coincidence.

He started jogging, crossing the road in half a dozen determined bounds, heading sharp left along North Shore Road, increasing his pace, running fast and hard. Exercise was what he needed, not an unlikely hypothesis. He might be a member of the constabulary, but no man was paid to poke his head into a hornet's nest. His years across had taught him that. Sometimes – most times, in fact – it was better and safer if in doubt to 'do nowt'.

The phone, ringing at ten to eleven, had Fenella racing towards it, her heart racing, hoping against hope that it might be Peter and that he'd forgiven her. "Hello?"

"Fenella, did you know that the police had taken Charles Peake in for questioning regarding that old man's death?"

"What? Well, yes, I knew, but—"

"You should have told me! Vivian knew. I expect everyone around Ramsey knows. Fenella, why didn't you say?"

"Why? What does it matter? Charlie's hardly the murdering type."

"How would you know? What's made you a forensic expert all of a sudden?"

"Mum, calm down. What does it matter? Don't get in a state."

"Don't you tell me not to get in a state. Don't you order me about. I'm your mother, remember?"

"Mum, Mum, calm down. I'm sorry. Go and put the kettle on. I'm coming round."

"There's no need for that," Marjorie snapped.

"Yes, there is. I'm coming. So open the front door." Fenella slammed the phone down. "Damn." She looked into the lounge, where Tom and Emily were slumped before the television. "I'm going to Mum's. I shouldn't be long, but don't wait up. I'll take my key."

Tom grunted. Emily didn't even look round.

She pulled on a jacket and still shivered as she stepped out. Across the promenade the sea roared. High tide was near and clouds of misty spray were sweeping across the road.

She slammed into her car. *What was it I was thinking only last night? That life was going to be more simple now? Huh! That will be the day.*

It took only moments to reach Marjorie's flat. Many of the windows of the apartment block were dark; only Marjorie's and one other still had lights ablaze.

Her mother was waiting on the stairs. "You needn't have come this late," she said curtly.

"Let's go up, Mother," she replied. "We can't talk here."

In an awkward silence they reached the warmth of the cosy flat.

"Tea?" Marjorie asked stiffly.

"No, thanks. I don't want tea. I don't want coffee. I just want you to tell me something – and I want the truth this time, Mum. What connection did Georgio have with Gran, and why are you so upset about Charles Peake possibly being concerned with his death? You didn't kill him yourself, did you?"

This question, uttered in an effort to lighten a tense atmosphere, made Marjorie sit up with a palpable gasp.

Fenella was shocked. "Mum, for goodness' sake, I didn't mean it."

"I know you didn't. I'm so strung up." Marjorie shuddered. "No, of course I didn't… murder him, that is, or kill him by accident, even, which is what I'm sure will turn out to be the case," she looked doubtfully at Fenella, "whoever did it."

"OK."

"About the other matter," Marjorie added hastily. "I'm sorry if you feel in the dark, but I can't tell you about that. That subject, which has been secret for too long, isn't mine to talk about. It's your Gran's."

"What? What do you mean? What sort of secrets can Gran have that I might be shocked at? I know she was clearly a bit of a girl in her day, but there's no real harm in her, is there?"

Marjorie's eyes didn't meet Fenella's frank gaze. "That's a matter of opinion," she said huskily. Then her voice became more brisk. "Anyway, those memories have nothing to do with Charles and his antics. That's what I'm concerned about." Marjorie pulled a cushion from behind her and plumped it fiercely. "Why didn't you let me know he'd been arrested?"

"I didn't know till I saw Peter and some other officers marching him to their police car. I just happened to be passing."

Marjorie looked down. "Oh dear."

"I told Peter he was being foolish." She sighed. "I didn't mean to shout at him, but I did, and that's that."

"Oh, Fenella, you didn't. What a shame."

Fenella frowned. "Why?"

"Vi Quine was telling me." She shrugged. "She saw at the pub in Sulby. She said you both looked… so right together." Marjorie's lips pursed. What Vi had really said was that they looked as if they were ready to tear each other's clothes off, but she didn't expect Fenella would appreciate that description.

"The cheek of the woman."

"Oh, Nell, you know what the island is like. Sneeze in Douglas and it will be known in Ramsey before you get home. We're a small community; people are interested in each other."

"Well, they've no reason to be, and no, I haven't fallen out with Peter, not if he's got any guts. I just told him what I thought of his taking Charlie in for questioning in the state he was in. For goodness' sake, Charlie's no murderer. As you said, Mr Stevens, Georgio – oh, it's so annoying that the man had two names. Anyway, he more than likely fell and hit his head. Why can't they just let the poor man rest in peace?"

"Hmph," Marjorie sniffed.

Fenella glanced at the clock. It was a quarter past eleven. "Anyway, Mum," she said firmly, "it wasn't to talk about me that I came. It was to talk about you. What were you doing that night? Why are you so uneasy about Charlie getting charged? How do you know for certain that Charlie is innocent?"

Marjorie's hands were in her lap. They tightened involuntarily. "I don't know whether I should… say." She swallowed and raised her eyes anxiously. "You see… I hoped that perhaps… Oh, Fen. I'd planned that perhaps if you could get Peter to visit – off the record, you understand – I'd maybe tell him what happened that night."

Fenella gasped. "Tell him what? Mum, you've got me frightened now. What have you done? Oh, Mum, you're not going to end up in prison, are you?"

Marjorie began to cry, large tears running down her cheeks. "I don't know," she sobbed. "I don't know, but I'm scared…" She buried her head in her hands while Fenella stood, horrified.

Next day the bells of the churches across the town were ringing as Fenella wakened. Surprised and alarmed to have slept so long, she sat bolt upright and felt horribly confused. Surely she should be cooking breakfast by now? Then, as the bright sunshine beaming through the curtains told her it was well past breakfast time, she realised had no need to make any guest breakfasts ever again. Momentarily she felt happy, then memories of Marjorie's admissions came flooding back, as well as the realisation of how she had offended Pete; she slumped back and groaned.

Moments later, prefaced by a loud rapping and a verbal, "Ta-ra!", the door burst open and Tom stepped in, a loaded tray in his arms.

Fenella rubbed her eyes. "Good gracious, is it a mirage? Who is this stranger bearing gifts?"

"OK, I know I've never pampered you as I should, but better late than never, eh?" Tom waited for her to sit up and plumped the tray on her lap. "Doesn't it look nice? Em even got me to fetch a rose for you."

A single white bloom was stuck in a wine glass.

"Oh, Tom, how nice. Where did it come from? We've not got roses left in our tubs, have we?"

"M'm… I took a jog in the park and it sort of slipped into my hand in passing."

Fenella laughed. "Someone could have seen you."

"Rubbish. Oh, and we've given Great-Gran breakfast. She was up early."

"Was she?" Fenella looked stricken.

"Don't worry, Emily coped. She didn't mind, she said."

Fenella sipped the hot tea. "M'm, lovely." She shook a finger reprovingly. "You've got a gem of a girl there, Thomas Brian Kelly, and I hope you appreciate her."

Tom stood with his arms folded. "I do." He looked from the window, then turned back and smiled persuasively. "You don't mind if we clear off early, Mum? We've got a lot to do at the flat and I need to get my shirts and stuff ready for next week."

Fenella's spoon hovered over the speckled brown shell of a boiled egg. "Of course I don't mind. You get off whenever. Gran and I will be busy today."

"Great! I'll tell Em. You'll be down before we go?"

"Of course." Fenella smiled, lifting the top of the egg to reveal a liquid golden yolk. She lifted a finger of buttered toast and was surprised at how hungry she felt. It was nice to be waited on.

"Goodbyes are always tricky, aren't they?" Emily smiled, as they stood in the hall. She held out her hand. "Thanks for putting me up, Mrs Kelly."

"Thank you for all your help, Emily, and good luck with your dig, and the rest of your studies."

"Come on, Mum, you'll see Em before she goes back. You must come for a meal with us at the weekend."

"That'd be lovely." Fenella gave Tom a hug. "Good luck, love, for school, on Monday."

"My God," Norah croaked. "It's like the bloomin' Waltons. Goodbye, Tom boy, and all that."

"Cheers, Great-Gran," Tom said, giving Norah a smacking kiss.

Emily shook hands with Norah and gave her a kiss on her withered cheek. "Goodbye, Mrs Tooms. See you again, perhaps, before I go."

"Yes, yes," Norah said, leaning forward in her wheelchair. "They might be puttin' me into a home, but I get parole now and then."

Tom looked over Norah's head to his mother and raised his eyes. "Bye, Mum," he said, taking Emily's hand and hurrying her out. Fenella pushed Norah's chair onto the front step so that they could wave them off together. The Mini accelerated and turned the corner. Fenella felt a pang, such as all parents feel when their chickens flee the nest. She and Norah turned back into the silent house.

"It's the end for us, girl," Norah said, shrewdly echoing Fenella's thoughts. "You might as well help me pack as well. Let's get it over with early on. There's a Western I want to watch later. It'll be the last time I'll be able to see a film in peace."

Fenella grinned. "You'll have Mum's portable TV in your room, Gran, there's no need for self-pity. You'll be fine."

"Says you," Norah said doubtfully. Fenella, wisely, didn't rise to the bait.

Charlie was dozing, his feet up on the settee. He'd spent a restless night. Evie couldn't visit that day. She had to go to a family do. He felt weak and sorry for himself. What had he done to deserve all this bad luck? He'd grafted hard for years. If he'd done one or two bad turns, to get on, like, well, that was the way of the world. If you didn't fight for a share the rest of the bunch would grab the lot.

He sighed deeply and realised his throat was dry. A cup of tea would be good, but he didn't want to move, even if the ache in in his shoulder suggested he was due another painkiller. After a few minutes as his discomfort increased, he heaved himself upright. An unexpected rustle from his pocket made him reach inside it. With a frown he pulled out a crumpled envelope, puzzling to recall where it had come from.

The events of the previous day, disturbing and painful, still rankled. It had been the suddenness of the police swoop that had shocked him. Without a word the bastards had carted him off, like a common criminal. No matter that he'd just been discharged from hospital. No wonder he felt bad; he must be still in shock. He'd never forget that moment, being frog-marched down his drive with a copper on either side. Though it had made him think, when they hustled him into the police car. It made him reflect that maybe always cutting corners and trying to dodge the law was not a good plan. It had been made worse because Fenella Kelly turned up to witness his humiliation. Fenella bloomin' Kelly, lording it over him all her life.

The envelope suddenly felt hot in his fingers. Cripes, it had been Fenella who'd given it him, *and* she'd snapped at that stuck-up Quilliam copper. He'd thought that was weird at the time, but he promptly forgot the episode because by then he was being driven off in a police car.

With shaky fingers Charlie ripped open the envelope and pulled out a flimsy sheet of notepaper. He read the message, frowned, reread it again and once more until he'd properly digested its meaning.

An unaccustomed expression spread across Charlie Peak's patched-up face, like a dawn of bright sunshine after a rumbustious winter storm.

"Bloody hell," he exclaimed. "Who'd ha' thought it? Me luck's changed. Fenella Kelly's wantin' to sell ter me, after all."

His aches forgotten, Charlie tossed the letter into the air and hobbled across the carpet to his expensive cut-glass whisky decanter. "To hell with a cup of tea and a painkiller," he muttered, pouring a generous tot. "Who'd ha' thought it?" he crowed again, gulping at a fiery mouthful of best Scottish malt whisky.

Then his smiled faded as a feeling of disquiet poked a cold finger. Why had she changed her mind? Was it something her mother had told her? If it was… "Hell," Charlie Peake muttered. "She could have me over a barrel."

EIGHTEEN

Fenella reluctantly picked up the phone. After her talk with Marjorie and two sleepless nights she felt impelled to contact Peter. It was high time she apologised. She was a grown woman, what she had done was silly and he hadn't deserved to be embarrassed in front of his colleagues. Also, and more importantly, she hoped he would agree to call on Marjorie. Fenella was more than anxious about what her mother might be hiding. After her outburst, of which she was by now horribly ashamed, she knew he might just cut her dead. Unhappily Marjorie was unaware of the seriousness of their tiff.

As the operator at Ramsey Police Station put her through Fenella's heart bumped frantically. She would not blame Peter if he was conveniently 'out'. Shouting at him in the street had been unforgivable.

He did answer, however, though his tone was brusque. "Fenella, good morning."

Her heart sank. "Erm, good morning, Peter, I'm very sorry to disturb you at work. I'm ringing on behalf of my mother. But first I would like to apologise unreservedly for my utterly atrocious behaviour last week." There was a soft intake of breath and then a gusty sigh. Fenella hoped this was a promising sign. "It was unforgivable; I don't know what got into me."

Peter coughed, or chuckled, then spoke: "Well, yes, I was annoyed at the time, but... well, let's forget it, shall we?"

"Thank you, Peter, that is very forgiving of you. Now, is it possible that we could still meet this evening?"

There was a longer pause, while Fenella held her breath.

Peter sighed. "Possibly."

He's still furious, she thought, her heart sinking. "Um, you see, Mum would like to see you, about, um, the night Georgio, um... died." She hurried on. "Not that she knows anything about how it happened – it's more to do with Mr Peake, she told me."

"Will she be at home this morning?"

"She will, but Peter, could I ask a favour?"

There was a longer pause. "You can ask," he said at last.

"We're taking Gran for lunch to the Grand Island, and then we will be delivering her to the nursing home. Remember? I told you she was going into care."

Peter's voice altered. "Yes, of course I remember, Fenella."

"If you could leave talking to Mum this evening it would be a relief for us both."

"If Marjorie has any relevant information I should hear it as soon as possible, Fenella."

Her grip on the receiver felt clammy. "I know, but I bet you've got paperwork and stuff that needs attention... today will be traumatic, for all of us. I think Mum would appreciate it greatly if you could leave this chat until Gran's dealt with. Today's been hanging over us for, well, years."

Peter did not respond, but Fenella could hear his quiet breathing.

"And I'd appreciate it ever so much, Peter," she whispered.

"Very well," Peter sighed at last. "I'll be round about seven. OK? We'll call on your mum then."

"Thank you. I'll be ready, and we can walk to Mum's place. She won't come here. I did ask her to, especially as Gran will be gone, but she's adamant that she won't set foot in Bayview again."

"Did she?" Now Peter's voice had an interested inflection.

"Thanks a lot, Peter. Bye." Fenella put the phone down hastily, her eyes suddenly filling with silly tears.

"Made up, have you?" Norah enquired gleefully, having wheeled silently behind her. "You've had a face like a wet weekend lately."

"Oh, Gran," Fenella protested, sniffing, "I haven't."

"You did too," Norah snapped. "And I don't want tears today. I may be going to an old gits' home but it's no cause for cryin', so remember that, my girl, and tell your blinking mother as well."

Fenella wiped her eyes. "You're incorrigible, Gran," she said, bending to give the old lady a hug. "I'll miss you and if I want to cry I will."

"Bloomin' heck." Norah wriggled. "Let me go. I want to watch *Good Morning*. See what that yappy TV couple are getting up to."

Fenella grinned, backing off. She followed Norah into the lounge and flicked on the electric fire. The days were cooling.

Once Norah was settled Fenella hurried upstairs to change, her insides bubbling with relief. Peter had relented, thank God. She had tossed and turned overnight, worrying that she'd messed things up for good between them – yet again. And this time to protect Charlie Peake! How ridiculous. She'd upset Charlie Peake enough over the years, so why did she feel this sudden concern for him? Peter was only carrying out his duty that day. She was lucky that he hadn't slammed the phone down on her.

Staring into her dressing-table mirror Fenella blushed. "But he didn't." She grinned, her heart thumping. It was really odd. She'd not bothered about men for years; she'd not met any that she'd particularly fancied. Brian had remained in her heart, and still was, but Peter... Her heart thumped. She wanted him. She wanted to get hold of him, this time, and not let him go. She pulled her hair back, staring accusingly at her reflection, though seeing Peter in her mind's eye. She didn't look too bad for her age, she hoped. He hadn't changed much, looked more mature, which excited her. It was odd, happenstance. As soon as she heard that he was returning she'd been thrilled. She'd hardly dare hope that her presence might have a bearing on his decision to be posted to Ramsey. Meeting him had been almost scary, the immediate connection between them. Unlike years ago he was now sure, mature and direct.

That had taken her aback. It still did.

Her insides tensed. This might be for real. Peter wasn't just any man; he was the only man she knew, or had known, save Brian, that she could truthfully imagine growing old with. How often could any woman say that? Her gaze blurred. What if she messed it up again? *No, don't think that.* Surely it was not too much to ask at her age, to achieve a settled life and a man she truly desired? She'd lived a self-indulgent life too long, clinging to a belief that because she was an artist as well as a guesthouse proprietor, she needed freedom and her own space to be creative. Yet if she'd taken a finance sector job in Douglas she would have earned far more and by now could have been living a very different life, probably at senior management level, as several of her school contemporaries were.

Fifteen years before she'd been happy to take over Bayview from Norah. She'd got tired of the constant hard work of doing the same thing in Douglas. Ramsey life proceeded at a gentler pace and the guests mostly were of a kind, easy-going variety.

Fenella straightened, scrubbing her face with a tissue. *What would have happened to Norah if I'd not been able to take over? And Marjorie? She didn't want to be a landlady again; she'd loved her civil service job. No, I was right to bring Tom here to grow up and I've given hundreds of folk good memories of Bayview and the Isle of Man.*

She grimaced and reached for her usual inexpensive tinted foundation.

"And now," she beamed, dabbing a touch of powder and blusher onto her cheeks, "my future is in the lap of the gods and I'm more excited than I have been for years." She giggled and reached for the pretty bottle of scent that Peter had given her.

She sprayed it lavishly. After applying a slick of crimson lipstick she flung up the window, leaning out, like she used to do when she was a teenager and had come to stay here in her school holidays.

Tonight they would meet and she would tread carefully. The chance of a relationship was precious. She must take care.

"To us." Fenella raised her glass. "To all our futures?"

Norah grimaced and looked as if she was going to say something sarcastic but was quelled by Fenella's warning look.

"Aye. To us." Norah smiled grudgingly, while Marjorie added, "And to our continued good health."

It was a typical Marjorie add-on. Marjorie did not have the happy-go-lucky nature of her mother, who gave her a look as if to say, "Just for once, girl, lighten up."

They sipped the sparkling wine with enjoyment; the meal had passed without incident and even Marjorie seemed relaxed. She'd been as tense as a drum when they were led to the table. But chat and pleasant reminiscences had eased any tension and soon they were laughing at Norah's evident cheerfulness at being treated to such a good lunch. Prior to the meal Fenella had asked for a half bottle of champagne to be served with their dessert. She was determined that this should be a festive occasion, and both Norah and Marjorie had been pleased as the waiter served their celebratory tipple with a flourish.

"I thought a half bottle was wise." Fenella beamed, chinking her glass with Norah's and then Marjorie's. "Any more and we might not be able to walk straight into the nursing home."

"I'd forgotten how good champagne is," Norah cried, running her tongue round her false teeth and savouring the taste. "It's worth a touch of heartburn."

"Oh, Gran, I'm sorry, I forgot."

"I've got you a box of your usual indigestion remedies," Marjorie put in quickly. "Along with a few new bits and pieces for your bathroom." She sipped her champagne and looked indulgently at her mother. This meal had been so peaceful: no tantrums, no playing up.

Norah looked pleased. "Oh? Pressies? I'll be wishin' I'd moved long ago. My, that was a nice meal, Nell. You'll be havin' a job gettin' my chair back into your car, I'll be that heavy."

"We're having a taxi," Fenella said, nodding to the waiter as he arrived with a pot of coffee and a plate of petit fours. "Yes, thank you. That's fine." She turned to Norah. "I thought you'd like to arrive in style, and I didn't want to be done for drink driving."

"Blimey." Norah took one of the petit fours. "I'm the queen of the May today."

Marjorie nodded as Fenella held the coffee pot aloft. "Black, or not?"

"Not likely," Norah said, munching. "Loads o' cream, please."

"Thanks, love, I'll take it black." Once her cup was filled Marjorie stirred a sugar lump into her drink with a hand that trembled slightly, Fenella noticed. Marjorie glanced up, catching Fenella's eye. "Mother, as you're in a good mood and this is the parting of the ways, in some respects, I want to ask you a special favour."

Norah looked wary. "Oh, what?"

"I think it's time that any... secrets in the family were let out into the open. I'd like Fenella to know at least."

"About what?" Norah abruptly adopted her 'helpless old lady' look.

"Mother, stop it. Your bodily functions may not be all they were, but your mind is razor-sharp when you want it to be. You know perfectly well what I'm talking about. The war years."

"I don't think I want to know if it's going to upset Gran," Fenella said hastily. "Let sleeping dogs lie, Mum?" Especially today, she wanted to add. "We've had a really nice meal and now—"

"Because they can't," Marjorie said firmly. "Not after what's happened. For goodness' sake, Fenella, you must be curious about George Stevens and why he was intent on paying for Bayview? No, Nell, you should know, and once you do then the matter can be laid to rest. Don't you think that's right, Mother?"

Norah's lips were pursed tightly so that the deep creases around her mouth were emphasised. Fenella wondered if Marjorie would look like that in a few years – and, worse, would she?

"I don't mind not knowing, Gran," Fenella repeated firmly, laying her hand over Norah's. "And I don't want you to get upset, today of all days."

Norah's eyes looked bleary. *She's had too much wine*, Fenella thought guiltily. *They'll think we're unfit carers at the nursing home, bringing her in sozzled.*

"I dun't know," Norah said. "I dun't know at all." She banged her empty glass on the table. She looked doubtfully at her daughter and granddaughter. "Let's go," she snapped. "Let's get one thing over with, at least."

As Norah backed her wheelchair away from the table a waiter hurried to assist, but she shook him off and wheeled herself through the open double doors to the conservatory annex.

"Oh, Mum," Fenella sighed. "You shouldn't have brought the subject up now. It's only upset her and she was in such a good mood."

"I had to," Marjorie said stubbornly. "We've got to get this out in the open, Fenella." She got up and pushed her chair tidily beneath the table. "I've asked her enough times over the years. This is the first time she's not bitten my head off. Leave me with her for a few moments before we leave. I can't be doing with this secrecy any longer. The truth has to come out, and now's the time." Marjorie opened her bag. "You get her into her coat. I'll settle up."

Fenella did as she was told. That was the thing with mothers. You did as they told you, until they became old, and then you told them what to do. Though some, like Norah, were very old indeed before they gave up the reins.

Fenella stepped out into the cool conservatory area, set with low tables and comfortable settees. Norah had wheeled herself to a window and was staring out at the sea. She looked up warily at Fenella's approach.

Poor Gran, Fenella thought, *helpless and old*.

Fenella would have been surprised, and alarmed, if she knew exactly what was passing through Norah's vindictive mind.

Peter Quilliam drew up outside Bayview. Before he could get out of the car Fenella appeared at the front door, slammed it behind her and came skipping down the steps to meet him.

"Thanks for coming," she said, "and before you say a word, I'm really sorry for flaring up at you that day. I was quite out of order and it was unforgivable. I know I shouldn't have done it. I've always been too quick-tempered, haven't I?"

Peter had come prepared for a certain amount of strife. This apology disarmed him.

He put his hands gently on her shoulders and kissed her cheek so that he smelled the perfume from her and his insides melted. "Apology accepted," he said huskily. "It's good to see you."

Fenella could have wept with relief. Involuntarily she hugged him. "Oh, Pete," she murmured, "you're such a nice guy."

"I am, aren't I?" Peter agreed, and after tucking her arm under his, they set off amiably. "So, you're all on your tod? Gran's settled in? You don't mind walking, do you? I've been cooped up all day."

"No, of course not." She squeezed his arm and heaved a happy sigh. "Um, I wouldn't exactly say that Gran is settled. If I hear a bang in the night I'll know she's done a runner. But yes, she's moved in." Fenella smiled. "Whether they'll keep her, only time will tell."

"Don't worry, she'll be fine. You must be excited, Fen. Once you've sold up you'll be a woman of independence. What are you going to do?" Peter put his arm around her shoulders as they turned into the breeze blowing along North Shore Road.

"I don't know," she murmured, the feel of his arm around her a comfort. "There's only so much independence a woman can take."

"Indeed," Peter said lightly. "But you've had lots of experience. You like being on your own, don't you?"

Fenella punched him lightly in the ribs. "People can change, Peter Quilliam. And it's not just a woman's prerogative. Don't tell me you haven't changed in the past twenty years because I won't believe you."

"M'm, I have," Peter sighed.

They walked in companionable silence. They were passing the wall beside the Mooragh Park when Peter suddenly stopped and swung her round. "So, what you're trying to tell me is that you're now open to offers, is that right?"

Fenella's eyes met his. Peter had nice eyes: brown, with creases at the edge that spoke of humour as well as a pleasant maturity. "I'm open to some offers." She smiled and reached up so that her open lips reached his before he'd even inclined his head.

They exchanged a lingering kiss before a car roaring past, hooting derisively, brought them back to reality. "Unhand me, sir." Fenella laughed. "What behaviour, and you a respectable member of the Isle of Man Constabulary."

Peter ran his hands down her back. "Forward woman," he growled. "Have I got lipstick on?"

"No. Not much, anyway." Fenella gently wiped his lips with her fingers.

Peter gripped her hand and kissed it. "Oh, Fen," he gasped, "must we go to your mum's?"

Fenella took back her hand and tucked it into his. "Yes," she said. "This must be settled." She pulled him along. "Hurry, do.

Then afterwards," she flashed him a look full of meaning, "if you like, we can go back to my place?"

Peter's heart seemed to get stuck in his throat. "Right, then," he said, gripping her hand and starting to run. "You said you wanted to hurry. Let's get this thing settled."

Marjorie, watching from the window, saw them fooling about and laughing. She was glad for Fenella; it looked as if the two of them were finally going to get together. She'd long wished they'd made up after that silly tiff they'd had years before.

She's stubborn, of course, just like her father, Marjorie thought ruefully, her eyes fastening on the framed photograph of Donald on the television. It wasn't a good photo. Didn't do him justice, but it was all she had. Don had fought shy of cameras and had always played silly beggers if she tried to photograph him, even when Fenella was little, which was a pity. Fenella had no photos of herself with her dad, and consequently Tom hardly knew what his grandad had looked like.

The bell rang and Marjorie pressed the switch to open the front door. She heard Fenella and Peter's laughing approach. She doubted they'd be as cheerful shortly.

For an instant before they reached the door Marjorie wondered whether to hold back, to tell Peter just enough and no more. What would it matter?

Then she caught sight of her reflection in the mirror and knew that if she didn't come clean now she never would. And what good would that do? She'd bottled it all up for too many years. The knowledge lying inside her had contributed to what she was now: a nervous, neurotic woman. No, she owed it to herself, as much as to Fenella, to tell the truth.

"Mum? There you are. Here's Peter." Fenella came in, her cheeks glowing, Peter following behind. He held out his hand.

"Hello, Mrs Quayle, good to see you."

"Call me Marjorie, please." She smiled. "Now, sit down, do, both of you." Her eyes flitted from one to the other. "Before we start," she smiled, "I'd like to say how pleased I am that you two have come to your senses, after all the years you've known each other."

"Mum!" Fenella exclaimed.

Peter grinned. "So am I," he said, and took Fenella's hand. He leaned back in the chair. "Right, fire away, Marjorie, what have you got to tell me?"

Marjorie settled herself and folded her hands. "This bit won't take long. I'll make us a coffee when I've got it off my chest, so to speak." She paused and heaved a sigh. "The rest will take a while, so I thought we'd go through that later."

Fenella sat up. "Gran's secret? She gave you permission to tell me?"

"Norah's secret." Marjorie nodded. "Not a very nice one, but…" She shook herself. "Well, here I go. Right, Peter. The night that Georgio died I was feeling quite upset. I'd walked out on Fenella; you don't need to know about that. It was just the final straw when I heard about Georgio's offer to buy Bayview." Marjorie paused, tugging at her cardigan sleeve. "You see, although the various anxieties I had at that time are not exactly connected there is a link to all of them, which you'll understand, later. The igniting spark, which just made me see red, was the proposal to hold an exhibition in the town hall commemorating the war years in Ramsey. I read a piece in the newspaper about it, in which it said that Charlie Peake was the brains – if the word can apply to Charlie – behind the scheme. There was mention of getting people to bring in photographs, memorabilia and all that. Well, because of what had happened in those war years I felt that I just could not bear any celebration of that dreadful time. It would be too much."

Marjorie looked up, gave a half smile. "I'm not trying to excuse my behaviour, but I am trying to explain my 'end-of-tether' feeling that night." She gave a warning look towards Peter, who was listening calmly. Marjorie wondered how calm he was going to be when she'd finished.

"I'd already spoken to Charlie about the exhibition. I met him one day in town and had a word. Not that a word with Charlie has much effect. Like water off a duck's back." Marjorie's lips tightened. "I was his Sunday-school teacher once, you know. I used to help at the Methodist church on Waterloo Road."

"I remember," Fenella said.

"Yes, you'd only have been about five. So was Charlie."

Peter was looking confused. He couldn't quite see how Sunday-school reminiscences were anything to do with Charlie Peake being under suspicion of murder.

"Sorry, I'm veering off the track. Anyway, that night, I was sitting here, doing my embroidery – well, trying to do it, but staring out of the window mostly – when I saw Charlie coming along the river road. He was lurching about and clearly drunk. A bit ahead of him I saw another man, I didn't realise it was Mr Stephani because I hadn't noticed him. It was Charlie who was on my mind."

"So Charlie was following Stephani?"

"I don't know about following him. Maybe it was just coincidence. There were a few other folks about. It was not late – about ten, I suppose. There were some youngsters, jeans, loud music, you know, shouting a bit. But, as I said, it was Charlie I was looking at. He came over the road here and suddenly I decided that I'd had enough of Charlie Peake and I'd go and tell him so."

Marjorie paused, pulled out a tissue and blew her nose. "So I did."

"You went out and confronted him."

"I did. I followed him into the park and steered him into the shelter near the rose garden. I asked him what he thought he was doing, raking up things that good, honest people didn't want raking up again."

"And what did he say?" Fenella was leaning forward in her seat.

"He told me to – well, to go to hell, to be quite blunt, and that was when I got really cross." Marjorie's face twisted with embarrassment and disgust. "I'd been his Sunday-school teacher, and he was telling me to 'go to hell'. Of course, he was very drunk."

"So what did you do?"

"I gave him a good punch and I'm afraid he moved and instead of it landing on his nose, it sort of grazed his cheek and I gave him a black eye."

"Mother!"

"I know. Your father taught me how to stick up for myself when we met. He'd done a bit of amateur boxing. He thought I should know how to protect myself."

"So then what happened?" Peter edged forward. At last Charlie's black eye had been explained, but the next bit was the serious bit. "What did Charlie do then? And what did you do?"

"Charlie ran off."

"He didn't."

"He lumbered away, as though seven devils were after him. I don't know why. I turned to go home. My knuckles were sore. I hadn't meant to hit him so hard. But then I felt guilty that perhaps in his drunkenness he might fall into the lake. So I followed him."

"Go on," Peter murmured.

"I kept well back, and I know he couldn't hear me. He was puffing and blowing and cursing under his breath. He continued along the side of the lake and I expected him to turn off and take the path up to Grove Mount, as his house is that way, after all. Anyway, instead he stopped suddenly then he turned towards the other side of the lake." Marjorie's breath came in a little gasp.

"I'd been so busy watching him and it was getting dark by then. I'd not been looking at any other part of the park, though I think there may have been someone on the far side. Well, I hurried on. I was past the bandstand area and I was looking across the lake, and when I could focus on Charlie – there was light from a streetlight above the hedge – he seemed to be picking himself up. I think he must have tripped."

"But you couldn't see what he'd tripped over or see anyone else?"

"No."

"So you'd not actually seen where Georgio Stephani had gone since you came into the park?"

Marjorie shrugged. "I'd forgotten about him till I thought about it later. As I said, I was a good way away. I might have noticed someone if they'd been in light clothing, but Georgio was wearing a dark coat and the edge of the lake sort of merged into the path. It was quite dusky by then."

"So what happened after Charlie got up?"

"He dusted himself off and blundered back along the foot of the lake then headed through the gate to go up Grove Mount way. Once he'd disappeared I turned back. I guessed he'd soon be indoors."

"So there was no way he could have done anything to the old man in the time between when he ran off from you and tripped at the edge of the lake."

Marjorie shook her head. "No. He might have collided with Georgio, I suppose, but I would have heard a shout or some noise if they'd had a confrontation. There was nothing but a slight thud as Charlie fell, and then he got up, grumbling, and reeled back the way he'd come, heading for home. I could hear him as he climbed the path, gasping and no doubt swearing; he was clearly intent on getting away from anyone else who might be about." Marjorie stopped speaking and smiled wryly. "It's not a creditable tale, is it? Hitting a man when he's drunk and frightening the life out of him."

"I doubt you did him any lasting harm, Marjorie." Peter smiled. "I should stop worrying. I daresay Charlie's pride took more of a knock than his skull."

"Yes," Marjorie said, with satisfaction. "And if he had summoned me I'd have been quite prepared to stand up in court and admit it. He's ridden roughshod over people for years, and I hope he's learned a lesson." Marjorie got up and walked briskly to the kitchen. "I'll fetch the tray," she said. "I shan't be long."

Fenella turned to Peter. "It would be almost funny if it wasn't so serious."

Peter touched her hand comfortingly. "I don't think you need to worry. Your mother's unlikely to get taken to court."

"Oh, I wasn't thinking about that. It still doesn't help in explaining what happened to the old man."

"Well, it does, in a way. Remember Charlie has admitted to finding him there? He didn't say he actually tripped over him. But he did say the man was dead when he came across him."

"Oh."

"It was still bad of Charlie not to call an ambulance."

Marjorie came back. She served coffee and told them to help themselves to biscuits. "Now, refresh yourselves, for the next bit is not so savoury." Marjorie took a gulp of her drink, settled a cushion behind her back and drew a deep breath. "I don't know what you've found out about Georgio Stephani's early life, Peter, but I'm now going to tell you the immense impact that once-handsome young man had on our family."

Fenella reached for Peter's hand. Peter sat up. "Marjorie," he said quickly, "I know most of what happened. I've seen the newspaper reports. My DS read them on microfiche at the library of the Manx Museum."

Marjorie went white – Fenella thought she was going to faint. She stared at Peter.

"What are you talking about? Oh, Mum, sit down, please, you've gone ashen."

"I'm sorry, Marjorie," Peter said hastily. "I should have been more tactful. It must have been a terrible time for you and your mum."

Fenella looked baleful. "For heaven's sake – will one of you tell me what you've found out, and what you've known all this time, Mum?" She glared from Marjorie to Peter and back again. "Come on, please. It can't be that awful, surely?"

NINETEEN

Fenella felt her insides tighten. Unconsciously she reached for Peter's hand. No doubt he was used to hearing people confess. Her insides knotted yet more. Why was she assuming a confession? Whatever had been hidden from her was probably nothing more than a scurrilous episode that would barely shock nowadays.

"I see, m'm, well." Marjorie cleared her throat. "I suppose I should be grateful – as you may appreciate, I don't want to dwell on these memories. They're not pleasant."

Peter stirred. "You were only a child yourself, Marjorie. Tell Fenella the gist, I'm sure that will suffice." He turned to Fenella. "Won't it?"

Fenella shrugged. "Of course. I mean, I know the old man must have been interned here, only I can't understand what might have happened that was so personal concerning Bayview."

Marjorie took a breath, trying to psych herself to feel back at work again. She had often had to orally deliver analyses on tricky social issues. Deep inside she willed herself to slip into the same role. *Be clear, calm and concise*, she told herself. *Don't resort to emotion, just give the facts of this unsavoury family history.* Otherwise she might break down.

"I remember the internee's arrival quite clearly, in June 1941. Four hundred men were transported on a ship. The *Victoria*, I remember it was called. Yes, it was berthed at the end of the pier and the men disembarked in, to my childish eyes, a seemingly never-ending stream." She paused, clearing her throat. "Some of the locals had known that this shipment was coming, though the actual arrival date and the number of men was kept secret until the day itself. Anyway, lots of local gathered to view these strangers who were to live in our houses. We were eager to see them, until they were brought ashore, then a sort of uneasy atmosphere settled over everyone. These men were different, swarthy, most of them, with dark, piercing eyes."

Fenella looked startled.

Marjorie shrugged. "I'm not exaggerating, love. Those men were different from any of our Manxmen. They seemed, well, scary as far as I was concerned. I was nine at the time. I stood on the prom holding Mum's hand and lots of my friends were doing the same, just watching as these strangers were herded from the prom to the quay and then to the swing bridge. We had trailed the procession but once they'd crossed the bridge we were stopped. The guards got the bridge opened so we couldn't follow. Of course we'd seen the encampment being set up. High fences of barbed wire enclosing all the houses where so many of us used to live."

Marjorie paused, took a sip of her cooling tea. "I'd not known much about this influx, nor had my friends. We'd been told at school that foreigners were our enemy, and yet hundreds of men were taking over our homes. Dad was away – he'd joined up a while before. I missed his comforting presence. I remember saying to Mum that I wished Daddy would come home and chase the men away, but she laughed and patted my head. It was then that I realised that the war was a horribly big event, bigger than anything I had known, and that made me unhappy. When I talked to my friends they felt the same. We didn't get much reassurance from our teachers, either." Marjorie sighed. "Without Dad at home Mum was perpetually fretful, easily annoyed. I suppose she was anxious too." Marjorie paused, took a sip of her cooling tea. "Oh, where was I? Oh yes, well, as we walked back home that day Norah seemed oddly excited, I remember her grinning and chuckling to herself. When I asked why she was pleased, she told me to shut up. She was missing Dad badly, of course." Her voice tailed off. She paused, sighed. "Anyway, life settled down – the internees didn't make much difference actually. Then it was the summer holidays, weeks off school. We couldn't play on the beach, but we filled our time messing about. Dad came home on a weekend furlough at the end of that summer. "That was nice. It was so lovely to see him…" Marjorie's voice trailed away.

"Oh, Mum…" Fenella began.

"It's all right, Fen. Yes, anyway, as you do know, it was when he and his two mates returned on the boat to Liverpool that he and two mates were killed as they left the docks. I was at Albert Road School when the news came." She moistened her lips. "The headmaster took me into his office to tell me. One of the cleaners took me home." Marjorie paused. "That is, to where we were living, with Aunt Winnie. I was heartbroken, of course, but I didn't get much sympathy or attention. Norah took centre-stage. She was a mess, howling for days… She didn't seem aware that I was upset too. It was a horrible few weeks. Other kids in my class had lost their dads. No one else's mum went loopy." Marjorie sighed. "Oh dear. This is taking it out of me," she admitted, with a sad smile.

"Mum, you don't have to tell us."

Marjorie sighed. "I do, I must. Anyway, as I said, we were lodging with Winnie Quayle in Waterloo Road; you remember Winnie, Fenella?"

Fenella frowned. "Sort of, I think."

"Good. Well, Winnie kept an eye on Mum – I didn't realise at the time, of course, but she told me later that Mum hated her 'spying', and when she got a chance Norah nipped off to the Mooragh prom, hung about near to Bayview. Whether because she felt nearer to Dad there or whether she was just hungry for male company," Marjorie shrugged, "I don't know. Anyway, apparently she would stand and stare at the men – through the barbed wire. The guards moved her on if she hung around too long. I only heard this later, of course. If that had been all she got up to, well... She couldn't get up to much mischief through a tangle of barbed wire."

Fenella slipped out to the kitchen and put the kettle on for more hot tea. Marjorie smiled and waited until she got back. "Shortly before Christmas that year the authorities allowed groups of internees, under guard, to visit the cinema once a week. This wasn't a popular move with the locals, nor with some of the internees, who frequently spat and jeered at local women if they got too close. Anyway, as luck would have it – bad luck, really – Norah got herself an evening job in the cinema pay desk and, don't ask me how, but she got to know Georgio." Marjorie paused, staring fixedly at nothing.

Fenella wriggled. "Mum, are you all right?"

"Oh, yes. Let me finish, love. So, she met Georgio, and things, umm, sort of, developed."

Peter frowned. "Surely the men were under guard to and from the internment area?"

"Yes, they were, and I daresay the whole business might have died a death if that was all the contact she and he ever got. But later that summer he was allotted a farm job at Hibernia, just outside Ramsey." Marjorie looked up. "The farmers were eager to take on internees as replacements for all the farm men who'd joined up."

Peter nodded. Fenella shifted uncomfortably. This all sounded so unlikely and rather disturbing. She didn't need this.

Marjorie continued. "Work parties were transported to and from the farms. Well, Hibernia isn't far from here. It didn't take much ingenuity for Norah to meet Georgio. The internees had an hour for a midday meal; it was a condition of their employment. While the other men were eating a hot dinner provided by the farmer's wife, Norah and Georgio were having hot sex in one of the fields or a barn."

"Mum!" Fenella exclaimed, shocked and embarrassed.

"There's no point in mincing words, love. They had sex, and often. Of course, again, I didn't know this at the time. Winnie told me, later. To excuse her I suppose Mum wasn't herself. She'd been hit hard by Dad's death, but also..." Marjorie sighed, "and this probably set everything off. She had had a miscarriage – a seven-month-old boy – just before war was declared. Dad was called up when she'd barely recovered from this and when Walter was killed. Well, I suppose she couldn't handle any more grief. Her way of coping was to have sex. Next thing, of course, she was pregnant."

Fenella gasped. Peter looked uneasy.

"It wasn't like today, when no one gives a toss if babies aren't born in wedlock. In the forties it was something to be hidden. If you fell pregnant outside marriage then you had to do something, and fast. Everyone knew that Walter could not be the father."

"What did she do?" Fenella whispered.

"Nothing at all. She acted as if she was proud of her condition. I wasn't aware of what was going on. I noticed that Mum was getting fatter and I wondered why people avoided us in the streets, but I never asked. I suppose I was used to keeping quiet. Kids did in those days. Well, next thing, I was shunted off to stay with Dad's auntie in Sulby. I didn't see Norah for a month. When I got back to Winnie's a baby was sitting in a pram. I thought he was Winnie's. 'He's your little brother,' Mum said, and I'll never forget the look on her face. It was as if Dad and my first little brother had come back."

"Oh, Mum, that is so sad."

"Yes, and oddly the baby seemed to do Norah good. She had something to love, to replace Walter. She'd never taken to me the way she did my little brother. I'm afraid Norah has always valued men more than women."

Fenella frowned. "But I don't understand. How and when did her dislike of Italians occur? And what happened to the baby?"

Marjorie shifted uneasily. Peter glanced at Fenella and grasped her arm. "I think I know the rest, Marjorie. You don't have to put yourself through this, you know."

"It must be done, and now," Marjorie said crossly. "I want Fenella to hear the truth. She must have wondered over the years why my mother and I are so abrasive with one another. Until now I've always felt it best to let sleeping dogs lie, but they can't and won't until I get this off my chest." Marjorie glared at him.

Peter nodded, smiled. "Carry on."

"Thank you. Anyway, Norah was convinced that Georgio would marry her. Apparently he'd spun her tall tales about his rich family. Norah, ever-gullible, went to the authorities, through the local alien board. She said that the child was Georgio's and that he should make an honest woman of her. She believed that one day he would take her back to Italy." Marjorie swallowed. "I don't exactly know what she intended to do with me."

Fenella bit her lip. "Oh, Mum, this sounds unbelievable."

"It was an unbelievable time, a time when the norms of life were turned upside down. People weren't themselves. Certainly my mother wasn't. From the high over having Georgio's baby she suddenly went into an all-time low. Post-natal depression, I suppose they'd call it nowadays, though they didn't admit to such conditions then. Anyway, she got more and more down as it soon became clear that Georgio was shunning her. She chased him, of course. The poor man, I wonder if he ever got any work done at that farm. Then she caught an infection and was laid up. Somehow she'd caught mumps, which was rife in those days. Then I caught it and poor Winnie had the nursing of both of us, and the baby. A letter arrived from the Internment Committee. This was the last straw as far as Norah was concerned. Georgio had stated under oath that he had never had a liaison with Norah and that her child was not his. Furthermore, by the time Norah received the letter Georgio Stephani had already left the island. As a useful agricultural worker he had been sent to work in England."

Fenella heaved a sigh. "Goodness, and how did Gran react?"

"Quite well, for a few days, then one morning she wasn't in her bed. I remember Winnie dressing me in a hurry and telling me to run round the streets to look for her." Marjorie heaved a sigh. She leaned sideways and picked up her embroidery tambour, flicking at a loose thread and tucking the needle into it more firmly. "She was found late the next day in a barn on the farm where Georgio had worked. The baby lay beside her, dead."

Fenella covered her mouth. "Oh no."

"Yes, the poor little chap had suffocated." Marjorie cast her eyes down. "Norah was taken into Ballamona Mental Hospital."

"Oh, Mum." Fenella leapt up and hugged her mother, tears trickling. "What about you?"

Marjorie smiled, pushed her away. "I was fine. I stayed with Winnie – she was very good to me." She patted Fenella's head. "Don't fret, it's years ago. I've lived with these memories so long they don't bother me now. Yes, it was sad, but it was for the best. The little fellow would have had a difficult life. He had olive skin and huge brown eyes, a real Italian bambino."

Fenella perched on the edge of her chair. "I still don't understand why Georgio felt he had to make amends after all these years, especially after the way he left."

"Nor do I." Marjorie shrugged. "It was a small, sordid tragedy, but hardly one for a man to dwell on for years after."

Peter stirred. "I think I may be able to offer an explanation."

Marjorie looked startled. "Really?"

"I said we'd been in touch with the family, and what you've related fills a gap. Apparently Georgio contracted mumps almost as soon as he landed in England. He was quite ill – hospitalised, in fact – and this illness left him impotent."

"Did it indeed?" Marjorie smiled grimly.

"Now, this is only surmise, but Italians are intensely family-oriented. From your account we can assume that the only child Georgio fathered was Norah's. Not only did he never acknowledge his child, but imagine his remorse when he heard that the child had died. If he had been honest and acknowledged the child as his, the baby might have lived. His deceit had virtually condemned his only son to death."

Fenella sniffed. Marjorie handed her a tissue.

"Maybe this explains why he disinherited himself from his Italian connections and anglicised his name. Luigi, his nephew, said that for years Georgio cut off all contact with his family. All his energy went into amassing money. Only recently, with ill health dogging him, had he rekindled the family connections."

"And he must have mulled over what happened," Fenella suggested. "But I still don't understand how he would hear about Bayview and the mortgage."

"More to the point," Peter mused, "how would he have heard about the baby's death?"

"I think Norah probably let him know," Marjorie said. "In the summer of '43, when she was better, she used to take me to the farm where Georgio had worked. The farmer and his wife were a nice couple and two Italians still worked for them. Norah often talked to the pair. I daresay she might have got Georgio's address."

"Or she could have written to the Alien Advisory Bureau," Peter said. "They would have passed a letter on."

Fenella frowned. "But she didn't ever—"

Marjorie smiled. "No. Percy befriended her during her time in the mental hospital and when she came out he moved here and she relied on him from then on."

Fenella asked, "Did he want to marry her?"

"Yes, he asked her a few times and then accepted that it would never be."

A silence fell, into which a sudden babble of children's voices could be heard. Marjorie peered from the window. "Look at that lot cycling through the park. They only do it at dusk."

Peter stretched. "Well, I'm off-duty. I'm not going to chase them."

"Good." Marjorie smiled. "Well, thank you, Peter, and you, Fenella, for listening to that sordid family history. I felt you should know, the way things have turned out."

"Yes," Fenella said slowly. "Yet I can't understand why Gran stayed at Bayview after the war. She must have hated the place."

Marjorie sniffed. "Maybe, but what else could we do? We couldn't sell it; everyone was broke. Our only means of income was to build the business back up. And we did."

"Yes, of course." Fenella smiled, though inside she was feeling hollow. She'd had no idea of what her poor mum had gone through.

"The thing is," Peter said slowly, "am I any further forward with Georgio's death? Was it an accident or not?"

Marjorie gazed at him. "I think you are. He was an old man, and that night he was probably tipsy with memories, with regret and with good Italian wine. He tripped, bumped his head and fell. What is unlikely in that?"

"Nothing." Peter smiled and held out his hand. "Thank you, Marjorie, for your time."

"You're welcome," she said, rising and taking his hand in a firm grip. "And now I think you two should leave. I'm exhausted."

Peter looked at Fenella. "Ready, Fen?"

Fenella smiled. "Yes." She hugged her mother and said goodnight.

Marjorie watched from the window as they strolled away. She felt drained and anxious. Peter was no fool. Had she put things over so that he didn't see the gap? She prayed that the drama of the revelation had blurred any pernickety time calculations on the evening in question.

Peter and Fenella strolled along North Shore Road. Sitting-room lights illumined family scenes in many of the houses they passed. Overblown roses gleamed in the dusky gardens. A chill breeze made Fenella shiver and lean into Peter's encircling arm. He felt her warmth and a surge of desire gripped him, though he felt solicitously tender towards her. How must she feel after that disclosure?

"So what do you think now?" she sighed, as if reading his mind, as they waited at the crossing at the foot of Bowring Road.

"I think it's time to forget the past," Peter murmured, pulling her close.

Fenella felt stirred by his touch. Her mouth dried. "Are you still coming back, after?" she said diffidently as they entered the lounge bar of the Bridge Inn.

"If you're offering," Peter said, looking steadily at her as they waited for the barman to appear.

"Do you really want a drink?" she said huskily, putting her hand on his and pressing his fingers.

"No," Peter said promptly. "I want you."

"Well, why are we wasting time?" Fenella brushed the back of his hand with her lips and looked up, her eyes sparkling. "I've got a bottle of wine at home."

Peter had unzipped his jacket. He fastened it again, twirled her round and they exited, laughing. The barman, who'd just walked through, stared after them, shrugged his shoulders and returned to the noisy public bar.

TWENTY

Next morning Peter left Fenella just after six. As he dropped a kiss on her forehead she stirred but didn't wake. He crept down the creaking stairs feeling euphoric, though he expected pangs of conscience would soon kick in. He had never intended things to happen so fast. He'd intended, when the moment was right, to show a suitable maturity – so much for good intentions. All propriety had utterly dissolved, so clear had the signals been; he had succumbed eagerly, and eventually it was she who had urged him on when he was exhausted and only wanted sleep. God, had he really begged her lovingly to leave him be? He smiled ruefully as he reached the foot of the stairs, his weary loins stirring at the recollection. He was still smiling as he quietly pulled the heavy front door shut. Abruptly he felt the chill air strike through his clothes. It was colder than the day before and a gusty wind cooled any lingering passion. His first reaction was the awareness of a severe lack of sleep. He shivered, pulled his jacket tightly about him, and stepped briskly away. Sniffing the cold air he sensed an intimation of winter in its keen edge. He looked reluctantly at his car as he passed it but knew there was alcohol enough in his body still to slow his reactions. He'd be a fool to take that risk.

He turned towards the town, gasping as the wind pummelled and cut through some of his grogginess. He was within sight of the swing bridge when, prompted by a remorseful pang, he turned, battling the wind to cross the wide promenade to the beach. The tide was high and grey breakers pounded up the sands, sending sprays of spume almost as far as the retaining wall. With half-closed eyes against the flying sand he made for the nearest beach entry, where he'd walked only two days before. His conscience had pricked him since. He needed to look over those burnt remains more closely. Head down, the gusting wind blowing sand into his face, he shielded his eyes and paced fifty yards or so to where the remains lay. He reached the place, gazed around, puzzled. Yes, he had been here, he could tell by the buildings across the road, yet that morning nothing was the same: stones, shingle, crushed weeds and rubble lay in a semi-organised array. Looking keenly around he could not spot any burned debris nor any area where a fire had been attempted. Assaulted by the wind, tears coursed down his cheeks. He fisted them crossly away and once more paced around, scrutinising the stones, weeds and marram grass distributed at his feet. Though it was similar to his earlier visit, something was different. Standing uneasily, buffeted like a clump of weeds himself, he knew he was standing in the right place by means of certain distinctive patches of algae on the promenade wall. He felt unnerved. What had happened? This muddle looked the same, yet it was different.

His mind raced. He recalled an unacknowledged peripheral section of his mind, having been aware of a mechanical crusher recently drawn up on the quay.

His insides plummeted. This area had changed all right. Everything underfoot had been redistributed; that crusher had swept the area. His heart bumped. Gall rose in his throat. Any evidence that might have been lying here had gone. He knew the local authorities implemented annual beach cleans. He clapped a hand over his mouth. Yes, he'd passed that blasted crusher on the day of his run. The implication of it had not even registered, so wrapped up he'd been in his internal meanderings about Charlie, the dead man in the Mooragh, yes, but most of all, Fenella's verbal attack.

He stood, battered by the wind, shocked by his failure of duty. *God, how could I have been so careless?*

Despite the cold he felt his face redden. "Sloppy bloody policing," he cursed. "So self-centred I didn't even think to get some photos. God damn it, what sort of a copper have I become?"

He swallowed uneasily, his heart pounding. He could not recall any time when he'd felt so sick by his lack of diligence. Grimly he paced across the shingle, though there was little point, until a glance at his watch had him hurrying back across the promenade towards the town. Regretting duty undone could not relieve him of duty to come. He had to be at the station in less than an hour.

If only he'd contacted scenes of crime after his run that day. If they had been turned up zilch, OK. Now he wouldn't dare mention what… or hint at what he believed he might have found. He gritted his teeth and jogged fast towards the bridge, the shortest route back home. So much for his unlikely theory. But maybe it would have led nowhere. He could hardly call it a suspicion: that remembered smell. A whiff of déjà vu, more likely? Yet it had rung alarm bells, damn it!

He ran along the narrow tarmac pavement crossing the bridge. It was even more blustery, the painted arches giving scant protection from the wind blowing downriver. Swirls of sand rose from the tidal banks below. His eyes watered. The chill of his body and the knowledge of his carelessness made him nauseous.

Yet if he had investigated further, how in God's name could he have faced Fenella?

He swore beneath his breath. He hadn't wilfully hidden possible evidence. No, true, though the line between carelessness and deliberate obstructiveness might be slight. "Oh God, oh God, what have I done, or not done?"

"Morning!"

Startled, he sidestepped and almost tripped. He'd not noticed a man approaching.

The scent of frying bacon rose from the galley of a burgundy and rust-coated smack as he passed. Two men were busy mopping the deck. As he passed a gust of raucous laughter erupted. Peter grimaced; he recognised one of the men. He'd been in his class at Douglas High School, umpteen years before. Hurriedly he crossed the road. A tired-looking man was sweeping the pavement before a pub.

"Aye, aye." He nodded, dust and cigarette stubs rising with the breeze. Peter gave a curt, "Morning," and hurried on, trying not to imagine what the man might be thinking. He reached one a narrow cut leading to Parliament Street, dodged along it and then it was only a few steps to his street door.

No cars were drawn up outside the front of the courthouse and police station. Peter felt relieved, though that didn't mean he'd not been spotted. If sniggers started as he entered the station he'd know. They'd assume he'd been up to no good. Unless he could say convincingly that he'd taken an early run. Well, he could say it; whether they'd believe him was another matter.

He entered his flat and strode to the windows to pull the curtains open, throwing his keys onto the shelf above the gas fire.

"Anyway, do I care? M'm, maybe?"

Apart from the beach fiasco he felt great; sexually he'd not felt as good for years.

"Fenella Kelly, God, what have I done to deserve you?"

Yet still? He tore his clothes off. Was this situation any different from other occasions in his career when he'd avoided… complications?

He gaped at his reflection in the mirror. "Oh, cripes, too right it's different." Though he was not even going to mentally formulate the differences, because then he would have to justify his actions – and that would be tricky.

He stared from the window, at the fading leaves on the cherry tree across the road and the steely sky above, while not seeing any of it. Hadn't he, not long ago, decided he wanted a simpler life? Was that not why he'd returned home?

All the times across, when he'd been stressed out of his mind and there'd been so much to think about that his head had got so full and he'd felt bogged down by crimes, felons and police procedure. The island, then, had seemed a safe haven. The dogged, repetitious process of dealing with constantly unrepentant ne'er-do-wells had been life-sapping. He'd known that not one in a hundred would change their habits, no matter what probation officers might say. He'd been on a hiding to nothing, and for what...? A good pension and a short retirement before he popped his clogs?

He blinked. He'd been a law keeper since he was a lad. Had it all been a waste of time?

The clock tinged the half hour. He swore, dropped his clothes and loped to the bathroom as though his thoughts were chasing him. Under the shower he shuddered; lathering himself he was vividly aware of the sensual remembrance of Fenella's hands on his body.

All at once he grinned; sex, whew, he had near forgotten how good it could be. The euphoria, the elation, the sheer... Words failed him, though a few remained, making him grin. He wanted her, much more of her. For too long he'd stayed celibate as a matter of pride, or stubbornness. He didn't approve of one-night stands, and so for a long time he'd missed out on making love, in every glorious sense of the word. He grinned, permitted the water to cascade over him; the sensation was cathartic, as he was though washing away his past, preparing him for something else, something better. A simpler way of life? Maybe?

He reached for shampoo. The notion of stepping from constant duty to another existence excited him. That it was being considered after a single night of passion was probably ridiculous. Yet wasn't it time? Long past time, in fact. The lovemaking of the last few hours, and how he felt now, had cracked something inside him, some formerly impenetrable barrier to a better life. Today he could appreciate that there were possibilities of pleasure which he'd not dared consider before.

Returning to his roots had been right. Yet still he felt stifled by routine. Though life here did run at a slower pace, it was not different enough from what he'd done before, and he longed for something other.

Now, through a combination of circumstances, was change not only possible but his for the taking?

He switched the shower off, stepped out. Yeah, yeah, it was all right getting philosophical, but doing so would not get him at the station early enough. Clutching a towel, he padded to the sitting room.

"Ee, it's grand to be alive," he cried, just like his grandpa used to shout. One particular time his grandad had shouted it so loudly the seagulls in Peel Harbour all rose into the air with fright. He, a mere six-year-old, was being led across the wood and rope bridge in Peel Harbour at the time and he had been thrilled. Grandad was his favourite relation when he was little. Grandad took him exploring, taught him about his island home. Walking with him across the flimsy bridge on wheels was just one of the regular summer excitements with Grandad. It was a quick route to Peel Castle at low tide, locals and tourists alike using it as a matter of course. Peter, naked now, smiled at this precious memory as he strolled to his bedroom to dress.

Diagonally opposite, above an estate agent's office, a young woman in a pink dressing gown clutching a mug of tea laughed aloud, having glimpsed Peter's manly body. Cup in hand, she danced between the cluttered furniture, imagining herself naked and desirous, until a fractious wailing brought her crashing down to earth. She picked up the nearby pack of nappies and headed to stem the wailing. Single motherhood was not much fun.

Norah was bracing herself too as she surveyed her breakfast companions. Two were old men, neither of which she had taken to at first glance, and the other an old woman with very little hair but the biggest teeth Norah had ever seen. She looked friendly, though, and smiled a lot, which put her ahead of the men in the manners department. Steered by one of the women in lilac overalls who seemed to run the nursing home, Norah had been placed at this table after being helped with her washing and dressing. Norah had found this process, much to her surprise, quite relaxing. It was good not to have a relationship with one's carer, she decided. Besides, a comforting scent of bacon and eggs had encouraged her to be agreeable. This mouth-watering scent was even stronger in this sunshine-bright room with its picture windows, though another aroma vied, somewhat negatively, of air freshener, disinfectant and a hint of urine. Norah had been prepared for this and it didn't upset her; indeed, somehow this scent felt homely.

"You're new, aren't you, Norah?" Not waiting for a reply, the toothy woman continued. "We wus at the Bethel Sunday School together once, d'ye remember?"

Norah was delighted. She didn't think there'd be many Manx folk in the place. She'd always thought that locals would be cared for by their families. To discover an old playmate was a surprise.

"Blimey," she said, "are you Margaret Throstle?"

Margaret beamed and nodded. "Margaret Cringle, I've been, for sixty years. We lived Port Erin way but once Eddie copped it I came back. The winds down that way'd blow a body from their grave if they wasn't careful."

Norah cackled. Maybe this place wouldn't be so bad. Margaret seemed on her wavelength.

"What about you fellas?" she asked bluntly. "Are you Manx, or from the blighted isle across?"

The smiling one grinned. "I like a good breakfast," he confided.

The glum one sneered. "You and Percy Corlett were the talk of the town jus' after the war."

Margaret and Norah exchanged glances. Cards had been laid on the table. One friend, one idiot, one awkward bugger; it was all right to be going on with.

"I don't intend to die, just yet." Norah grinned. "Oh good, brekkie." A plate of porridge was laid before her and she reached for a spoon. Percy's face flashed into her mind – Percy had loved his porridge. Poor Percy. It was a shame he went so suddenly, but there, life and death were not far apart.

Peter and Fenella met that evening in Ballure Glen, a wooded defile leading to a shingle beach. The glen entrance lay beside the Manx electric tramway bridge on the outskirts of Ramsey. Peter, still a tad disconcerted by how he felt, all things considered, walked to the meeting. Fenella drove and parked in a nearby side road.

"Am I late?" she cried, running towards him, breasts jiggling beneath a striped sweater, a heartening sight for any man.

Peter shook his head, knowing that at that moment, ridiculously, he felt like a love-struck teenager. He kissed her lightly. "No, Fen, you're spot on time." He took her hand. "Are you all right?" His eyes were soft; Fenella's insides quivered. She smiled and squeezed his fingers. They walked to a rickety gate and Peter pushed it open. "Had a good day?"

"M'm, busy. I've heard from Charles." She flushed. "Last week, when I made a fool of myself, I'd delivered him a letter."

Peter smiled. He was not about to criticise. The weight of the guilt inside him hadn't lessened any.

"Anyway, he rang this morning and he was quite civil, and for once I responded likewise."

"Surely you're always civil?"

Fenella grinned. "Not to Charlie, but I've decided grow up, finally. His offer's fair and he's going to contact some clearance people for me. Doing so probably benefits him, but I don't care." She looked up defensively. "I've not been nice to Charles, ever. I'm determined to act differently from now on…"

Peter chuckled. "Well done, it's business, after all, and Charles has done a fair bit of good for the town, all things considered."

"Yes." Fenella nodded. "I mustn't begrudge him his wealth. He didn't have an easy start."

"Good on you." Peter smiled.

She sighed. "I thought of what Mum and Gran had to put up with, and…" She looked up at him anxiously. "You don't think I'm getting soft, do you?"

"Why, because you're selling Bayview to Charles Peake? Or because you're making an effort to treat him nicely? No, of course not. Besides, it's hardly my business to judge. You're your own woman." He put his arms around her. "Oh God, Fen, last night… words fail me… but you've made a middle-aged bloke very, very happy."

Fenella laughed and hugged him back. "You're not middle-aged – well, yes, I suppose you are, but so am I, and for years I've wasted my life painting pictures instead of… having sex with desirable men. It's time I branched out."

He laughed and tucked her hand beneath his arm. "I see. Were you fighting off many admirers, when you were wielding your paintbrush?"

"Actually no, but I rarely went out to meet any."

Peter hesitated. "I am trying to think of a tactful comment, but I can't. If I say that at least you got paid for your art… um… whereas with sex, well, er, you wouldn't have been paid – in the ordinary way of things. Oh, hell, that's come out all wrong, sorry."

Fenella laughed. "You're right, I got paid – that is, I sold a reasonable amount of pictures – but the total was negligible, really. Yet I love to paint… so… there's the nub. What is important in life? It's mostly people, isn't it, not things? All that family history Mum spilled. It was so sad. Gran was clearly mad about Georgio, yet he deserted her, and because of that…" She shrugged helplessly. "She's been a cranky old biddy."

Peter nodded. "And that affected your mum."

"Suppose unwittingly I emulated her, what with Brian dying so young…" She heaved a sigh. "He was a lovely guy."

Peter pulled her close. "He was, and you deserved each other."

She looked up at him. "That's a kind thing to say."

"I'm a kind man," he whispered. "At least I try to be… oh hell, life's a so-and-so, isn't it? I often wish I'd made a better go of it with Susan; she deserved more than I could offer."

Now Fenella squeezed his hand. "We're all fallible."

Peter said nothing. Inside he was agreeing, strongly.

They stepped out into a clearing set with benches and a roughly fashioned swing hanging from a sycamore bough. Peter headed to a bench with a view of the sea set prettily in a frame of foliage. He swallowed hard. He wanted desperately to talk about his recent find, but… "You could paint this view," he said instead, gesturing vaguely.

"I could," Fenella agreed, easing herself with an attractive wriggle onto the swing. "But at present I feel painted out. Oh, I've arranged to see a flat tomorrow."

"What, already?" Peter grinned.

"No point in hanging about. There's a six-month lease on a second-floor place in Queen's Court. If I take it will give me breathing space…" She urged the swing to move faster. "Through to spring anyway. I've decided I need some time off, some pleasure…" She swung higher and her words were lost.

Peter watched and felt his insides contract. How could he possibly burst her bubble of happiness?

He waited till she slowed, caught at the rope of the swing. "You deserve a change of scene, certainly. I feel the same."

"What?" Fenella's feet lowered to bring the swing to a halt. "You've just come home. You don't want to give up your job, do you?"

He shrugged. "Not just yet, I suppose."

"You're disillusioned with the force?" Fenella jumped to the ground.

He shrugged. "I've known for ages that I've lost my direction. I still feel at odds. Policed-out, maybe, to mis-quote you."

Fenella came up to him. "Peter, no! What would you do if you left the force?"

"Fix up my tumbledown cottage at Agneash Live, the life of a hermit, or a 'when I'?"

She laughed. "You can't, you're local, it's only people who come from the colonies who can be 'when I's." She frowned. "What's this about a cottage? I don't recall ever hearing about you having property."

"You don't know everything about me, Fenella Kelly." He smiled, patting her nose. "I wasn't born with a helmet on my head, you know. I have got a family and roots." He paused, put his arm around her. "Auntie Jan, Mum's sister, you won't know her?"

Fenella shook her head.

"She was older than Mum and she left the island when I was still a kid. She settled in Australia. When she made her will she decided that I should have her cottage. She never had kids. She had the place rented out for years, just in case she decided to return." Peter held out his hand and they walked to a bench.

"Goodness, what's the cottage like?" she asked, plumping beside him. "No, sorry, it's none of my business. But, Peter, would you really leave the police?"

He chuckled. "Would you not like it if I didn't wear a uniform?"

She giggled. "Possibly."

"Budge up, that's better. When I decided to come back I was dead set on resigning. I was fed up of drug issues and break-ins and vandalism and, oh, all the sordid stuff. Anyhow I thought things over and decided that if I could get a transfer I would take it, so's to have some employment, and like you said, it would give me a respite to think things over. I didn't know what opportunities were still here. I still don't, I suppose. I allowed myself to be trolleyed into the old groove because it was easy. Now I wish I hadn't. My spark has definitely gone. It's a daily trudge instead of an interesting challenge. I don't want advancement either. I don't want to end up chained to a desk."

Fenella was shocked. "I had no idea." She looked at him keenly. "Have I made a difference?"

He glanced at her. "What do you think?" He smiled, kissing her cheek.

The sound of an approaching barking dog made them giggle and pull apart. A collie and a young couple entered the clearing. They gave them a polite nod before taking the path leading to the beach.

Once their voices had died away Fenella inched closer. "We're both at a turning point, aren't we?"

Peter sighed. "M'mm. Re the cottage – my sister was furious when she found out that I'd inherited when Auntie Jan died."

"Where is Denise now?"

"Staffordshire. She's been gone years. I couldn't see her settling here anyway. She'd probably flog the place."

"So why did you get it?"

"I could say that it was because I was a charming little boy and Denise was a hoyden, but honestly, I don't know."

"M'mm. Does Denise visit much?"

"Occasionally, my parents don't travel a lot now."

"Still in Castletown?"

"M'mn." He squeezed her gently. "I think we should get moving or my bottom will be ridged. This bench is not comfortable."

Fenella jumped up. "Come on then, Grandpa, before you get too maudlin."

"Less of the 'Grandpa', woman. We're a similar age, aren't we?"

Fenella laughed. "Yes, but women wear better than men." She put her arm through his and they headed for the downhill path. Wisely Peter did not contradict her belief.

The tree canopy hanging over the path made it a gloomy descent to the riverside, which had plunged and leapt from the sides of North Barrule many miles distant. The path lay close to this rushing water, which wended its busy way through the stone arch framing the beach and the sea.

"Race you," Fenella cried, jogging ahead.

Peter chased her. It felt good to act lightheartedly, if only temporarily. Whatever happened now he was not about to let go of this glorious woman, literally or figuratively. Though as he laughingly chased her the image of the half-burned embers leapt to the front of his mind along with a remembered distinctive smell.

He swore beneath his breath. All of what he'd seen was conjecture. In no way could conjecture be evidence, especially if he didn't share his suspicions.

TWENTY-ONE

Peter pulled the police car to a halt. Should he? Shouldn't he? He needed to get this off his chest, but was it fair to burden someone else? He swung the door open, got out and locked the car. *Just do it*, he decided. *I need an impartial viewpoint – good or bad, so be it.* He swung the gate of the comfortable-looking semi wide and hurried up the path. He rang the bell before he could change his mind. It opened almost immediately.

"Hi, Dave," he said, trying not to look too serious.

Dave Colvin gazed at him blankly. "What are you doing here…" he said, frowning. "I am on a day off, aren't I? I haven't got my roster mixed up?"

"No, you are off duty, sorry."

"Right, um, come in." Dave Colvin pulled the glazed door wide and ushered him into the narrow hall. Clad in well-worn T-shirt and grubby shorts, Dave was clearly unsettled by this unexpected visit. He ushered Peter into an untidy sitting room. "'Scuse the mess. It's the housekeeper's day off."

Peter frowned. "Do you have a housekeeper?"

Dave grinned. "Yeah, you're looking at him; the wife has started working longer hours and I've been appointed to keep this place under control." He bent to gather up an assortment of small clothing. "The kids got dressed in here this morning. God knows why, they've got good-enough bedrooms." He tossed the clothes into a heap and gestured to a chair. "Coffee?"

"M'm, please – if it's no trouble."

Dave sniffed and sighed. "That's the burden of being a housekeeper, it's work, work, work…" He looked at Peter to share the joke, but Peter seemed not to be in a humorous mood.

"I suppose it is," he said, moving to the window and looking out. "Nice view from here, isn't it? You can see the bay and the tower."

"M'm, I suppose you can." Dave had never been one for views. Maxine had decided on the property. He did as he was bidden; she was a better organiser than he.

"Shan't be a mo. Coffee on the way."

Dave went into the kitchen and pulled the door half closed. He filled the kettle with a crease of anxiety marring his good-natured face. Whatever could be bugging Peter? He looked grim, and that was not good. "Urgh!" Water from the fierce tap, which he'd hated from the day they'd moved in, splashed his T-shirt. One day he'd get a plumber to sort it. He kept meaning to.

"Did you say something?" Peter called.

"Yes, no, um, I'll be in in a minute." Dave grabbed mugs, sugar and milk.

The kettle hadn't quite come to the boil as Peter sauntered in to join him, frowning. "Sorry about this, Dave, I shouldn't have intruded into your day off."

"No probs." Dave shrugged. "I've got nothing pressing apart from housework, I'm glad of the company."

Peter sighed, eased his collar and heaved a sigh. "I've got a problem…"

Dave grunted. "I knew something was up. You've been as twitchy as a ferret for the past few days."

"Have I? Oh…"

The kettle boiled. Dave swiftly made two mugs of strong coffee. He deposited them on a low table that had a small space free of model cars. "Well, sit, Peter, for God's sake, you're making me twitchy. Or shall we go to my office upstairs and I'll interview you properly?"

Peter grinned, heaved a sigh and sat, as directed, though not before moving a Lego construction from the settee.

"The joys of children, eh?" He grinned and then felt sad, for it seemed a long time since his kids had been small, and he could barely remember those days.

Dave swigged his coffee, winced and marched out for a milk carton, which he brought back and topped his cup up with. He offered it to Peter, who shook his head. "Best thing is, spit it out, mate," he said cheerfully. "It can't be anything that bad..." He looked questioningly and Peter winced.

Dave grimaced. "God, Peter, and now you've got me worried, for Pete's sake – oh, sorry, unmeant pun..." He shook his head and stared fixedly at Peter, who had the grace to blush.

"Yeah, OK, I need to ask you something and—"

"Right then, ask me... *now.*"

The roar did the trick: Peter grinned. "You remember when we found Percy dead?"

"What? Oh, m'm, yeah, he was well and truly gone, poor old chap, and there was nothing fishy about his dying, was there?"

"You don't recall anything unusual about the occasion?"

Dave frowned, thought a while. "No... oh wait, wasn't there a slight burnt smell?"

Peter gulped his coffee. "Good, yes, you did note it then? Well, when I say good, it's good that you remember, but not quite so good that it was there to be noticed, not if what I suspect is, erm..." He tailed off, fiddling with his tunic buttons.

Dave leaned back, then wriggled and removed a cuddly rabbit from his chair. "Spit it out, lad, it's something to do with Italian guy's death, is it?"

Peter nodded slowly. He raised his head, his grey eyes looking bleak. "I have an inkling that Percy, and therefore Norah, probably conspired to finish him off."

Dave gaped. "No, you can't be right there, surely? Norah was, and still is, using a wheelchair, and Percy was a timid sort. I know he was a nice guy, but he was a bit, you know, wasn't he? Wouldn't say boo to a goose, in my opinion."

"I agree, theoretically."

"And the inquest was straightforward, a misadventure verdict after weighing up the pros and cons. I mean, honestly, Peter, the old fella, Georgio, he was half canned, wasn't he? He probably fell over his feet and that was that. You can't deny it sounds likely." He gulped his coffee and gaped. "You're not planning on dragging everything up again?"

Peter shrugged. "I don't want to…"

"Besides – cripes, Peter? What about your new lady love? I thought you were cock a hoop that you'd finally got into Fenella's bed." Dave blushed. "Hell, that came out more bluntly than I meant, but you know what I mean."

"I know exactly what you mean," Peter muttered, "but a few days ago… I'd had a run on the beach and by accident I found some remains, half burned. You remember the oar that went missing from the lake that day?"

"What? Oh yeah, it never turned up, did it?"

"No. Anyway, yeah, I'd had a run and was mooching back along the top of the shore – you know, where all the weeds and marram grass grow in a sort of plateau?"

Dave nodded.

"Well, I found some bonfire spots – three, in fact!"

"Nothing odd about that," Dave said. "Kids have always lit fires there."

"M'm, maybe." Peter looked glum. "Yes, but I found what I'm sure were fragments of an oar. The bits were definitely the right colour. I suppose they're painted that colour to stand out and to put people off from nicking them."

Dave didn't look convinced. "And?"

"The smell of that fire was the same as the scent in Percy's room."

"I see." Dave leaned back and stretched uneasily. "So... you collected the bits and took them to SOCO?"

Peter shook his head. "No."

Dave looked surprised, then confused. "Oh? Well, I can understand that. More than likely there'd be nothing to find and—"

"Oh, come on, Dave, I didn't want there to be anything, did I? I certainly didn't want to face the possibility of having found the murder weapon. No, I did nothing, and I've just discovered that any evidence has now gone."

"Sorry? How?"

"You know that digger thing they use to scrape up the excess seaweed and stuff each year?"

Dave gaped. "Yeah, I do, they do it twice a year. So, what you mean is that any evidence, if it was evidence, is not there anymore?"

Peter nodded. "And I feel awful about it."

Dave took a swig of his coffee. He gazed at Peter thoughtfully. "So, you've told me because you want me to collude with you in hiding the truth?"

"God, Dave, no, well, I didn't, but now... oh hell, I don't know. I feel guilty because I think I found something, yet as the evidence has now been obliterated due to my slackness I feel in a real quandary. If I raise this matter it's going to blacken Percy's reputation, so say nothing of Norah's, because she must have been with him when he lit the fire. He probably parked her chair near the sea wall while he did the deed. So I'll destroy both their reputations and at the same time destroy any chance I've got with Fenella too."

Dave grinned. "You're stymied right enough. Would you shack up with a person who accused your gran of being complicit in a murder?"

Peter shook his head.

"Well then, forget it."

Peter grunted. "I'm considering jacking in the job anyhow. When I came back I wasn't sure if I was doing the right thing, staying in the force."

Dave looked shocked. "Oh, come on, it's not the end of the world. And the super would be livid, you've barely been here five minutes."

"It's my life," Peter said curtly, then grinned. "Sorry, Dave, I'm just antsy." He sighed heavily. "Yeah, OK, I may stay on for another couple of years, but I've decided I'm definitely not going to die with my PC boots on."

Dave said nothing; he fiddled with the ears of the toy rabbit he'd picked up. "I'll miss you if you go, but as you say, it's your life." He got up and tossed the rabbit into a piled toy box. "Well, much as it's been good to have this chat, sir, I need to get a wash in the machine if my housekeeping timetable isn't to hit the dust." He smiled broadly. "Not that I'm kicking you out, you understand… well, actually I am, I've got to hoover in here as well, or I'll not be coming up to husbandly scratch for my, um, rumpy-pumpy treats."

Peter laughed and batted Dave on the back. "Thanks for listening, mate. You're a pal."

Dave held the door open. "See you," and he shut it smartly as Peter hurried down the path. Dave felt shocked, both by what Peter had said and how little the man seemed to feel guilty for wavering off the straight and narrow. Yet also he wondered if Peter was seeing things that were not there. How could Norah Tooms, in her wheelchair, have possibly had anything to do with killing that old man? And the idea of the two pensioners lighting a bonfire on the beach; it was plain ridiculous.

Four weeks later Norah was blowing out the lighted candles on a large square celebration cake as everyone cheered her on.

"It's about all I can do." She grimaced cheerfully. "Eighty-five – bloomin' heck! I should be dead by now."

Her words were bold, but there was moisture in her eyes that told Marjorie her mother was thoroughly enjoying the attention of her birthday tea. Fenella and Peter were there, Tom and Emily, Eloise Green, Margaret Throstle, Maisie Colvin, Sarah Davies, as well as a trio of elderly men from the nursing home. As Marjorie had suspected Norah had soon attracted admirers.

As a waiter began cutting the cake into neat slices Marjorie leaned towards Norah. "What about some fresh air, Mum? You're looking very flushed."

"Flushed? I'm bloomin' boilin'. I said this suit'd be too warm, but you would have me wear it."

Marjorie adjusted the cardigan of the coral knitted suit around her mother's shoulders and wheeled her away. "We won't be long, everyone." She smiled. "Mother needs a spot of air."

"I don't," Norah began. Then catching the glint in Marjorie's eye, she amended her comment to a meek, "Aye, a breath of air might be nice."

Norah suspected she'd been yakking too much ever since they got to the hotel, but she'd not been able to shut herself up somehow, overwhelmed as she'd been by all the attention and the novelty of being back in what she thought of as 'the real world'. What with lots of nice gifts, unexpected bunches of flowers and all the flattering things people were saying she'd felt quite dizzy. The couple of sherries she'd drunk had maybe loosened her tongue and helped her keep up with the chat, maybe too much, judging by a few shocked looks, and not just from Marjorie.

Norah wondered had she let something slip that might have been better kept under wraps; she'd talked and been talked to by so many folk. It had been exciting at the time but now she felt a growing unease, for by the way Marjorie was pushing her chair something must be seriously bugging her.

"Slow down, Marje. I'm not a sack, y'know, I do have feelings."

Marjorie took no notice. She pushed her briskly to the French windows, bumped her through the threshold and whizzed her along the paved terrace until she was satisfied that they were both out of earshot of anyone and everyone who might be about.

"Right," she snapped, pushing the wheelchair brake on with a kick that made Norah gasp.

"Crikey." Norah flinched, waited for the storm to burst.

Her daughter glared balefully. As Norah winced Marjorie continued to glare, her chest heaving and a pulse in her neck throbbing fit to burst.

"What've I done?" Norah moaned at last. The fresh air had made her feel suddenly very tired. She'd had a busy morning and a long afternoon; she was almost looking forward to getting back to the nursing home. Still Marjorie stayed silent, her lips pursed like a closed letter box. As the silence lengthened Norah slumped; it was nice here in the quiet of the open air, peaceful, she could easily... Her eyelids drooped...

And still Marjorie stared, as though she was stuffed, too pent up to speak, while her kind blue eyes were laden with sorrow.

The day was mild for early November and there had been spells of fitful sunshine on and off since dawn; there was only a faint breeze. Now as the sun slipped towards the horizon and fingers of shadows stretched across the bay, Marjorie too began to relax. Her fingers loosened their tight hold on the wheelchair handles. The rampant fury that had coursed through for long, long horrible moments was lessening. What was the point in getting upset with Norah? What was done was done. It was too late, much too late for recriminations.

She found, to her surprise, that she was able to smile and suddenly feel soothed by the surroundings.

"I've always loved this place," she murmured at last, gazing around as though nothing was amiss. Norah perked up.

Marjorie beamed in retrospect. "Do you remember Fenella's wedding reception, Mum? It was a day just like this and the photos were lovely, though Don, bless him, dodged them all, as always."

Norah grunted. She did remember, in a sort of blurred focus, that long-ago day – Fenella, very slim, in a long white dress, while she was dolled up in a peculiarly horrible lime two-piece suit. Gawd… it was yonks ago, not, of course, as long ago as when he was about… Feeling suddenly anxious, she peered across the bay. Her eyesight wasn't good now, but she could just about make out the block where Bayview had once stood, where she'd lived for most of her life, near Percy. She missed Percy. It had been a shame that he went so suddenly… just like Bayview, flattened already, by Charlie Peake's men. The foundations of an apartment block were already rising in its place.

Funny, really, that Bayview and all its memories had been whisked away, just like Percy and that other old man…

"You don't talk much about your Don, Marje," Norah remarked huskily. "He was a nice fella."

Marjorie stiffened.

"You've not had much of a life, have you, girl? What with me to put up with, an' all that… occurred." Norah's voice tailed off.

"My life's my business, Mother," Marjorie said tartly. She glanced back towards the hotel to check that there was still no one about, then she calmly wheeled Norah's chair towards the steep slope above the lower garden. They were hidden from view by a thick escallonia hedge.

Marjorie stepped forwards, bending towards her mother. "Just confirm one thing for me, Mum. It was no accident, was it? You and Percy did for Georgio, didn't you?" Despite her outward calm Marjorie's heart was hammering.

Norah clamped her lips together.

"Well?" Marjorie shook the wheelchair irritably. "For heaven's sake, for once in your life – be honest."

Norah shrugged. "Mebbe," she murmured at last.

Marjorie exhaled. She'd suspected for a while – no, she'd known, right from the moment she'd heard of the old man's death. The only person vindictive enough to want him dead was Norah.

"How, for God's sake? He wasn't that feeble. Didn't he struggle? How did you do it?"

Norah didn't answer for a moment. Then after a sniff she said, "I suppose I was ramblin' in there, was I? I said somethin' about the war, did'n I?"

"You said lots of things about lots of times, but yes, one minute you were gabbing about blackouts and the things you used to get up to in the Mooragh when you were a girl, the next, after Sarah made some remark about internment, you chipped in about seeing me and Charlie Peake when we were courting. I couldn't believe it. Luckily there was such a babble I doubt if anyone else took notice. The waiter was nearest, thank goodness; even when you put your hand over your mouth and turned red he didn't look up. That was when I realised you had been there that night."

Norah looked up warily. "Oh, crumbs."

"Yes, Mother, crumbs indeed. If you were there that night it must have been you and Percy I spotted on the far side of the lake. Was it?"

Norah shrugged.

Marjorie put her head close to Norah's ear. "Was it you or Percy who finished that poor old man off?" she said, clearly rattling the wheelchair. "Come on, tell me. I want to know."

A tic twitched at the corner of Norah's left eye. "Poor old man," she spat. "Aye, we finished him, but he was near gone anyhow. Percy fetched an oar from a rowboat and we used it to push his head down after he fell."

"Oh, Mother."

"We hadn't planned it, not really…" Norah's lips tightened and she shot Marjorie an anxious glance.

"Are you saying it was an accident that you waylaid Georgio? Hmph, tell me another."

Norah shrugged. "No, honest, it was... We saw him coming along the river road and guessed he might go to the park, so Percy climbed across the boats to get an oar, jus' in case, like. It wasn't planned, though. We waited, behind a bush, and—"

Marjorie gaped. "What were you thinking of, Mother? Why, for God's sake, after all these years, did you want to harm him?"

"What do you mean, what was I thinking? You know very well what I was thinking. It might've been a lot of years, but I still can't picture the li'l one without it hurtin' here." She pounded her chest. "His li'l han's, his eyes," her voice wobbled, "clear as if it was yesterday." Norah's sentimentality shocked Marjorie.

"Good God, it was over fifty years ago!" Marjorie found herself trembling, picturing the scene beside the lake of Norah and poor harried Percy coshing that feeble old man. She shuddered.

"Rum thing was, what with that an' the fire an' all, it finished Percy off." Norah flashed Marjorie a look. "That wasn't meant to happen."

Marjorie's head buzzed. She barely heard Norah's words. She stared dazedly at the slope before them. One push would be enough. At the very least Norah would be badly injured; more than likely she would die. It would be justice... of a sort.

Marjorie pushed the chair imperceptibly closer to the edge. Norah gasped.

How many times, Marjorie thought, *have I felt this unresolvable anger against this awful, yet occasionally funny and loveable character that is my mother?* To excuse her because of what she'd borne was not the point. Norah was not nice: she was shallow, fickle and cunning. Marjorie's wrists tensed more tightly on the handles.

Norah glanced up fearfully; she muttered words that Marjorie did not hear, for her ears were roaring and her heart pounding. This was it, then; this was what she'd been working up to all her life?

Yes, yes, yes, she should have done it years ago. As soon as she'd been old enough to understand Norah's ego she'd resented it. Now, finally, her mother's life was hers to do with as she pleased. She took a final shuddering breath... and...

"There you are." From close behind a grating voice snapped crossly and a pair of strong arms pushed her away. "I couldn't think where you'd got to." The hands swept the wheelchair from her grasp.

"Christ," Norah mumbled under her breath, "it's the iron bloody maiden." She twisted, her neck sinews straining, "Quick, Marje, do it, for God's sake!"

But it was too late. Nurse Franklin was already manhandling the heavy chair with sharp jerks that made Norah whimper.

Marjorie stepped back, her heart thudding so loudly that she was amazed the nurse could not hear. She gazed helplessly after Norah.

"Say goodbye to your daughter, Mrs Tooms. It's time we got you back to base."

"G'bye," Norah muttered.

"Cheerio, Mum," Marjorie managed.

Norah's hand shot out. "Next time, do it, girl, don't think."

"There, there," Nurse Franklin trilled. Norah released her grip and was wheeled away.

"I'll call on Sunday," Marjorie called, relief flooding through her. What had she been thinking? How could she possibly have wished to kill her mother?"

"I'll prob'ly be dead by then," Norah shouted over her shoulder, then flinched as Nurse Franklin rebuked her.

Marjorie stood still until her heart regained its usual beat. She felt limp as she stared across the bay where lights were flickering here and there, like fireflies. The sight was beautiful, familiar and heart-rending. *This is my home*, she reminded herself. *This is the place where I grew up and dreamed dreams, none of which came true.* Her eyes misted. *And this is the place where I will die.* She wiped her eyes and felt herself shiver. She must go in; it was chilly and she felt so sad. She turned towards the lighted hotel, determined from now on to concentrate on herself, Fenella and Peter, and of course, dear Tom and Emily. *Yes, think of them, hope for the future – perhaps great-grandchildren in time.* Marjorie walked swiftly towards the welcoming warmth of the hotel, looking neither right nor left.

Hidden behind the hedge only on the other side stood Peter, with Fenella in his encircling arm. They stepped from the shadows, their faces grave. He'd been right. A fire on the beach had been started by Percy in an effort to burn the evidence of the broken oar. The next morning the scent of burned wood had clung to Percy's discarded clothes.

Fenella clung to him, shocked and upset. "Oh, Peter, will you tell?" she whispered.

"It must have been a joint deed." Peter sighed. "That he went too is so sad."

"But will you tell, Peter?"

He hugged her. "What good will it do? As far as police records are concerned the case is closed. Accidental death has been recorded. Can you imagine the fuss if I tried to reopen it?"

Fenella clung to him. "But is that fair?"

He kissed her hair. "No, but… oh, look, Marjorie is coming out again. Marjorie, we came out to look for you." He smiled. "We were just thinking of getting some hot tea, weren't we, Fen?"

Marjorie, looking pale, managed a smile. "Were you? I see. Yes, it's chilly out here, but it was good for Mum to get a breath of fresh air before going… back."

Her gaze was questioning. Peter smiled innocently and led both women into the warmth of the hotel lounge.

Fenella put her arm around Marjorie. "You look tired, Mum. Let's plan a holiday together. I can afford it and you deserve one."

"What about Peter?" Marjorie said, surprised and pleased.

Fenella beamed. "We'll allow him to tag along if he wishes."

Peter grinned. "Try and stop me." He laughed.

For writing and publishing news, or
recommendations of new titles to read,
sign up to the Book Guild newsletter: